CYBERABAD DAYS

CYBERABAD DAYS

IAN McDONALD

an imprint of **Prometheus Books**
Amherst, NY

Published 2009 by Pyr®, an imprint of Prometheus Books

Inquiries should be addressed to
Pyr
59 John Glenn Drive
Amherst, New York 14228–2119
VOICE: 716–691–0133, ext. 210
FAX: 716–691–0137
WWW.PYRSF.COM

13 12 11 10 09   5 4 3 2 1

Library of Congress Cataloging-in-Publication Data

McDonald, Ian, 1960–
    Cyberabad days / Ian McDonald.
        p. cm.
    ISBN 978–1–59102–699–0 (pbk. : alk. paper)
    1. India—Fiction. I. Title.

PR6063.C38C93 2009
823'.914—dc22

2008049260

Printed in the United States on acid-free paper

PUBLICATION HISTORY

"Sanjeev and Robotwallah": *Fast Forward 1: Future Fiction from the Cutting Edge*, ed. Lou Anders, Pyr, 2007.

"Kyle Meets the River": *Forbidden Planets*, ed. Peter Crowther, DAW Books, 2006.

"The Dust Assassin": *The Starry Rift*, ed. Jonathan Strahan, Viking, 2008.

"An Eligible Boy": *Fast Forward 2*, ed. Lou Anders, Pyr, 2008.

"The Little Goddess": *Asimov's Science Fiction*, June 2005.

"The Djinn's Wife": *Asimov's Science Fiction*, July 2006.

CONTENTS

AMERICA IS NOT
THE ONLY PLANET

by
PAUL McAULEY

*A*ccording to William Gibson, the future is already here—it's just not evenly distributed yet. A cursory glance at recently published science fiction shows that depictions of the future aren't evenly distributed either: the majority of science fiction depicts futures dominated by American sensibilities and cultural and economic values, and inhabited by solidly American characters. Sure, there have always been writers like Maureen McHugh and Bruce Sterling, and more recently Nalo Hopkinson and Paulo Bacigalupi, who have embraced a broader, global view of the future, but the default mode of science fiction is that of American hegemony, and an assumption that the values of Western late-stage free-market capitalism will endure pretty much unchanged even unto empires flung up around the farthest stars. This isn't surprising, because modern science fiction was invented in the United States in the 1930s, and the United States is still the dominant marketplace for written science fiction (and it's the major producer of science fiction television shows and movies, too). But even before the ill-advised War on Terror and the global economic crash, it's been clear that although the twentieth century can legitimately be called the American century, in the twenty-first century the nexus of technology-driven change and economic and political power will almost certainly be located elsewhere. In China or India or Brazil; maybe even in Russia or Europe, if those old powers can shake off the chains of history and truly reinvent themselves. But most definitely not in the United States.

British science fiction writers have a long tradition of filtering the memes and tropes of modern science fiction through their own cultural viewpoint; they're the aliens in the Yankee woodpile. In Arthur C. Clarke's space fictions, British astronauts drank tea and fried sausages in their lunar excursion vehicles, showed the heir to the throne how to jockey rockets into orbit, and returned alien artifacts to the British Museum rather than the Smithsonian. The New Worlds' crew turned their backs on the Apollo programme and dived into inner space. And the Interzone generation of writers infused the heartland dreams of science fiction with a globalized ethos: the future as London's babylon, a vibrant, sometimes frictive patchwork plurality of cultures—Somalis in Kentish Town, Bangladeshis in Brick Lane, Turks in Green Lane, Congolese in Tottenham Hale, and so on and so forth—writ large.

Ian McDonald, to get to the point of this introduction, was in on the globalization of science fiction right from the beginning of his career. His first novel, *Desolation Road*, mapped Bradbury's Mars onto Gabriel Garcia Marquez's *One Hundred Years of Solitude*; later novels and stories featured Africa as a venue for transformative biotech and alien invasions; all showcased his ability to use cut-ups and mix-mastered imagery appropriated from the vast storehouse of science fiction and the vaster stores of the happening world to create vivid bricolages crammed with eyekicks, to do the police in a variety of voices. *River of Gods*, widely praised and nominated for all kinds of awards, was a significant evolutionary leap in his game. Set in an epic, complex, and richly detailed depiction of a near-future India split into competing yet interdependent states, its narrative is likewise split into a multiplicity of viewpoints, detailing from a variety of perspectives the attempt by a community of artificial intelligence to win legitimacy and freedom either by reconciliation with or independence from their human creators. The stories collected here share the same setting as *River of Gods*. History runs like a river through them, yet they are closely focussed on the dilemmas of people caught up in the currents of social and technological change: a boy who dreams of becoming a robotwallah, fighting wars via remotely controlled battle robots, is given a sharp lesson in the real status of his ultracool heroes; a young woman who was once feted as a god tries to find a new role in a world where AIs are the new deities; the marriage between a dancer and an AI diplomat is overshadowed by the growing hostility between the human and machine spheres. McDonald's characters are vividly and sympathetically drawn; his prose is richly infused with a rushing immediacy; the exoticism (to Western sensibilities) of India's crowded and chaotic cities and her rich and ancient and complex mythology infuse and complement and transmute the exoticism of a future as rich and bewildering and contradictory as our present, a hothouse venue of technological miracles teetering on civil war and every kind of social change. Unlike the futures of default-mode science fiction, conflict is not resolved by triumph of thesis over antithesis, but by adjustment, adaptation, and accommodation. In McDonald's Bollywood babylon, history is in constant flux, always flowing onwards, never staying still, yet preserving in the shape of its course certain immutable human truths. Things change; yet some things remain the same. The future of this clutch of fine stories is only one of many possible futures, of course, but it as exciting and challenging and humane and self-consistently real as any of the best: we can only hope that we deserve one like it.

SANJEEV AND ROBOTWALLAH

*E*very boy in the class ran at the cry. *Robotwar robotwar!* The teacher called after them, *Come here come here bad wicked things,* but she was only a Business-English aeai and by the time old Mrs. Mawji hobbled in from the juniors only the girls remained, sitting primly on the floor, eyes wide in disdain and hands up to tell tales and name names.

Sanjeev was not a fast runner; the other boys pulled ahead of him as he stopped among the dal bushes for puffs from his inhalers. He had to fight for position on the ridge that was the village's highpoint, popular with chaperoned couples for its views over the river and the water plant at Murad. This day it was the inland view over the dal fields that held the attention. The men from the fields had been first up to the ridge; they stood, tools in hands, commanding all the best places. Sanjeev pushed between Mahesh and Ayanjit to the front.

"Where are they what's happening what's happening?"

"Soldiers over there by the trees."

Sanjeev squinted where Ayanjit was pointing but he could see nothing except yellow dust and heat shiver.

"Are they coming to Ahraura?"

"Delhi wouldn't bother with a piss-hole like Ahraura," said another man whose face Sanjeev knew—as he knew every face in Ahraura—if not his name. "It's Murad they're after. If they take that out, Varanasi will have to make a deal."

"Where are the robots, I want to see the robots."

Then he cursed himself for his stupidity, for anyone with eyes could see where the robots were. A great cloud of dust was moving down the north road and over it a flock of birds milled in eerie silence. Through the dust Sanjeev caught sunlight flashes of armour, clawed booted feet lifting, antennae bouncing, insect heads bobbing, weapon pods glinting. Then he and everyone else up on the high place felt the ridge begin to tremble to the march of the robots.

A cry from down the line. Four, six, ten, twelve flashes of light from the copse; streaks of white smoke. The flock of birds whirled up into an arrowhead and aimed itself at the trees. *Airdrones*, Sanjeev realised, and, in the same thought: *Missiles!* As the missiles reached their targets the cloud of dust exploded in a hammer of gunfire and firecracker flashes. It was all over before the sound reached the watchers. The robots burst unscathed from their cocoon of dust in a thundering run. "Cavalry charge!" Sanjeev shouted, his voice joining with the cheering of the men of Ahraura. Now hill and village quaked to the running iron feet. The wood broke into a fury of gunfire; the airdrones rose up and circled the copse like a storm. Missiles smoked away from the charging robots; Sanjeev watched weapon housings open and gunpods swing into position.

The cheering died as the edge of the wood exploded in a wall of flame. Then the robots opened up with their guns and the hush became awed silence. The burning woodland was swept away in the storm of gunfire; leaves, branches, trunks shredded into splinters. The robots stalked around the perimeter of the small copse for ten minutes, firing constantly as the drones circled over their heads. Nothing came out.

A voice down the line started shouting, "Jai Bharat! Jai Bharat!" but no one took it up and the man soon stopped. But there was another voice, hectoring and badgering, the voice of Schoolmistress Mawji labouring up the path with a lathi cane.

"Get down from there, you stupid stupid men! Get to your families, you'll kill yourselves."

Everyone looked for the story on the evening news, but bigger, flashier things were happening in Allahabad and Mirzapur; a handful of contras eliminated in an unplace like Ahraura did not rate a line. But that night Sanjeev became Number One Robot Fan. He cut out pictures from the papers and those pro-Bharat propaganda mags that survived Ahraura's omnivorous cows. He avidly watched J- and C-anime where andro-sexy kids crewed titanic battle droids until his sister Priya rolled her eyes and his mother whispered to the priest that she was worried about her son's sexuality. He pulled gigabytes of pictures from the world web and memorised manufacturers and models and serial numbers, weapon loads and options mounts, rates of fire and maximum speeds. He saved up the pin-money he made from helping old men with the computers the self-proclaimed Bharati government thought every village should have to buy a Japanese Trump game, but no one would play him at it because he had learned all the details. When he tired of flat pictures, he cut up old cans with tin-snips and brazed them together into model fighting machines: MIRACLE GHEE fast-pursuit drones, TITAN DRENCH perimeter-defence bots, RED COLA riot-control robots.

Those same old men, when he came round to set up their accounts and assign their passwords, would ask him, "Hey! You know a bit about these things; what's going on with all this Bharat and Awadh stuff? What was wrong with plain old India anyway? And when are we going to get cricket back on the satellite?"

For all his robot-wisdom, Sanjeev did not know. The news breathlessly raced on with the movements of politicians and breakaway leaders, but everyone had long ago lost all clear memory of how the conflict had begun. Naxalites in Bihar, an overmighty Delhi, those bloody Muslims demanding their own laws again? The old men did not expect him to answer; they just liked to complain and took a withered pleasure in showing the smart boy that he did not know everything.

"Well, as long as that's the last we see of them," they would say when
Sanjeev replied with the spec of a Raytheon 380 *Rudra* I-war airdrone, or an
Akhu scout mecha and how much much better they were than any human
fighter. Their general opinion was that the Battle of Vora's Wood—already
growing back—was all the War of Separation Ahraura would see.

It was not. The men did return. They came by night, walking slowly
through the fields, their weapons easily sloped in their hands. Those that met
them said they had offered them no hostility, merely raised their assault rifles
and shooed them away. They walked through the entire village, through
every field and garden, up every gali and yard, past every byre and corral. In
the morning their bootprints covered every centimetre of Ahraura. Nothing
taken, nothing touched. *What was that about?* the people asked. *What did they
want?*

They learned two days later when the crops began to blacken and wither
in the fields and the animals, down to the last pi-dog, sickened and died.

Sanjeev would start running when their car turned into Umbrella Street. It
was an easy car to spot, a big military Hummer that they had pimped Kali-
black and red with after-FX flames that seemed to flicker as it drove past you.
But it was an easier car to hear: everyone knew the *thud thud thud* of Desi-
metal that grew guitars and screaming vocals when they wound down the
window to order food, food to go. And Sanjeev would be there, *What can I get
you, sirs?* He had become a good runner since moving to Varanasi. Everything
had changed since Ahraura died.

The last thing Ahraura ever did was make that line in the news. It had
been the first to suffer a new attack. *Plaguewalkers* was the popular name; the
popular image was dark men in chameleon camouflage walking slowly
through the crops, hands outstretched as if to bless, but sowing disease and
blight. It was a strategy of desperation—deny the separatists as much as they
could—and only ever partially effective; after the few first attacks plague-
walkers were shot on sight.

But they killed Ahraura, and when the last cow died and the wind
whipped the crumbled leaves and the dust into yellow clouds, the people
could put it off no longer. By car and pickup, phatphat and country bus they

went to the city; and though they had all sworn to hold together, family by family they drifted apart in Varanasi's ten million and Ahraura finally died.

Sanjeev's father rented an apartment on the top floor of a block on Umbrella Street and put his savings into a beer-and-pizza stall. Pizza pizza, that is what they want in the city, not samosas or tiddy-hoppers or rasgullahs. And beer, Kingfisher and Godfather and Bangla. Sanjeev's mother did light sewing and gave lessons in deportment and Sanskrit, for she had learned that language as part of her devotions. Grandmother Bharti and little sister Priya cleaned offices in the new shining Varanasi that rose in glass and chrome beyond the huddled, peeling houses of old Kashi. Sanjeev helped out at the stall under the rows of tall neon umbrellas—useless against rain and sun both but magnetic to the party-people, the night-people, the badmashes and fashion-girlis—that gave the street its name. It was there that he had first seen the robotwallahs.

It had been love at first sight the night that Sanjeev saw them stepping down Umbrella Street in their slashy Ts and bare sexy arms with Krishna bangles and henna tats, cool cool boots with metal in all the hot places and hair spiked and gelled like on one of those J-anime shows. The merchants of Umbrella Street edged away from them, turned a shoulder. They had a cruel reputation. Later Sanjeev was to see them overturn the stall of a pakora man who had irritated them, eve-tease a woman in a business sari who had looked askance at them, smash up the phatphat of a taxi driver who had thrown them out for drunkenness, but that first night they were stardust and he wanted to be them with a want so pure and aching and impossible it was tearful joy. They were soldiers, teen warriors, robotwallahs. Only the dumbest and cheapest machines could be trusted to run themselves; the big fighting bots carried human jockeys behind their aeai systems. Teenage boys possessed the best combination of reflex speed and viciousness, amped up with fistfuls of combat drugs.

"Pizza pizza pizza!" Sanjeev shouted, running up to them. "We got pizza every kind of pizza and beer, Kingfisher beer, Godfather beer, Bangla beer, all kinds of beer."

They stopped. They turned. They looked. Then they turned away. One looked back as his brothers moved off. He was tall and very thin from the drugs, fidgety and scratchy, his bad skin ill-concealed with makeup. Sanjeev thought him a street-god.

"What kind of pizza?"

"Tikka tandoori murgh beef lamb kebab kofta tomato spinach."

"Let's see your kofta."

Sanjeev presented the drooping wedge of meatball-studded pizza in both hands. The robotwallah took a kofta between thumb and forefinger. It drew a sagging string of cheese to his mouth, which he deftly snapped.

"Yeah, that's all right. Give me four of those."

"We got beer we got Kingfisher beer we got Godfather beer we got Bangla beer—"

"Don't push it."

Now he ran up alongside the big slow-moving car they had bought as soon as they were old enough to drive. Sanjeev had never thought it incongruous that they could send battle robots racing across the country on scouting expeditions or marching behind heavy tanks but the law would not permit them so much as a moped on the public streets of Varanasi.

"So did you kill anyone today?" he called in through the open window, clinging on to the door handle as he jogged through the choked street.

"Kunda Khadar, down by the river, chasing out spies and surveyors," said bad-skin boy, the one who had first spoken to Sanjeev. He called himself Rai. They all had made-up J-anime names. "Someone's got to keep those bastard Awadhi dam-wallahs uncomfortable."

A black plastic Kali swung from the rearview mirror, red-tongued, yellow-eyed. The skulls garlanded around her neck had costume sapphires for eyes. Sanjeev took the order, sprinted back through the press to his father's clay tandoor oven. The order was ready by the time the Kali-Hummer made its second cruise. Sanjeev slid the boxes to Rai. He slid back the filthy, wadded Government of Bharat scrip-rupees and, as Sanjeev fished out his change from his belt-bag, the tip: a little plastic zip-bag of battle drugs. Sanjeev sold them in the galis and courtyards behind Umbrella Street. Schoolkids were his best customers; they went through them by the fistful when they were cramming for exams. Ahraura had been all the school Sanjeev ever wanted to see. Who needed it when you had the world and the web in your palmer? The little shining capsules in black and yellow, purple and sky blue, were the Rajghatta's respectability. The pills held them above the slum.

But this night Rai's hand shot out to seize Sanjeev's hand as it closed around the plastic bag.

"Hey, we've been thinking." The other robotwallahs, Suni and Ravana and Godspeed! and Big Baba nodded. "We're thinking we could use someone around the place, do odd jobs, clean a bit, keep stuff sweet, get us things. Would you like to do it? We'd pay—it'd be government scrip not dollars or euro. Do you want to work for us?"

He lied about it to his family: the glamour, the tech, the sexy spun-diamond headquarters and the chrome he brought up to dazzling dazzling shine by the old village trick of polishing it with toothpaste. Sanjeev lied from disappointment, but also from his own naïve overexpectation: too many nights filled with androgynous teenagers in spandex suits being clamshelled up inside block-killing battle machines. The robotwallahs of the 15th Light-Armoured and Recon Cavalry—sowars properly—worked out of a cheap pressed-aluminium go-down on a dusty commercial road at the back of the new railway station. They sent their wills over provinces and countries to fight for Bharat. Their talents were too rare to risk in Raytheon assault bots or Aiwa scout mecha. No robotwallah ever came back in a bodybag.

Sanjeev had scratched and kicked in the dust, squatting outside the shutter door, squinting in the early light. Surely the phatphat had brought him to the wrong address? Then Rai and Godspeed! had brought him inside and shown him how they made war inside a cheap go-down. Motion-capture harnesses hung from steadi-rigs like puppets from a hand. Black mirror-visored insect helmets—real J-anime helmets—trailed plaited cables. One wall of the go-down was racked up with the translucent blue domes of processor cores, the adjoining wall a massive video-silk screen flickering with the ten thousand dataflashes of the ongoing war: skirmishes, reconnaissances, air-strikes, infantry positions, minefields and slow-missile movements, heavy armour, and the mecha divisions. Orders came in on this screen from a woman jemadar at Divisional Headquarters. Sanjeev never saw her flesh. None of the robotwallahs had ever seen her flesh though they joked about it every time she came on the screen to order them to a reconnaissance or a skirmish or a raid. Along the facing wall, behind the battle harnesses, were cracked leather sofas, sling chairs, a water cooler (full), a Coke machine (three-quarters empty). Gaming and girli mags were scattered like dead birds across the sneaker-scuffed concrete floor. A door led to a rec room, with more sofas, a couple of folding beds, and a game console with three VR sets. Off the rec room were a small kitchen area and a shower unit.

"Man, this place stinks," said Sanjeev.

By noon he had cleaned it front to back, top to bottom, magazines stacked in date of publication, shoes set together in pairs, lost clothes in a black plastic sack for the dhobiwallah to launder. He lit incense. He threw out the old bad milk and turning food in the refrigerator, returned the empty Coke bottles for their deposits—made chai and sneaked out to get samosas which he passed off as his own. He nervously watched Big Baba and Ravana step into their battle harnesses for a three-hour combat mission. So much he learned in that first morning. It was not one boy, one bot; Level 1.2 aeais controlled most of the autonomous process like motion and perception, while the pilots were more like officers, each commanding a bot platoon, their point of view switching from scout machine to assault bot to I-war drone. And they did not have their favourite old faithful combat machine, scarred with bullet holes and lovingly customised with hand-sprayed graffiti and Desi-metal demons. Machines went to war because they could take damage human flesh and families could not. The Kali Cavalry rotated between a dozen units a month as attrition and the jemadar dictated. It was not Japanese anime, but the Kali boys did look sexy dangerous cool in their gear even if they went home to their parents every night. And working for them cleaning for them getting towels for them when they went sweating and stinking to the shower after a tour in the combat rig was the maximum thing in Sanjeev's small life. They were his children, they were his boys; no girls allowed.

"Hanging around with those badmashes all day, never seeing a wink of sun, that's not good, for you," his mother said, sweeping round the tiny top-floor living room before her next lesson. "Your dad needs the help more; he may have to hire a boy in. What kind of sense does that make, when he has a son of his own? They do not have a good reputation, those robot-boys."

Then Sanjeev showed her the money he had got for one day.

"Your mother worries about people taking advantage of you," Sanjeev's dad said, loading up the handcart with wood for the pizza oven. "You weren't born to this city. All I'd say is, don't love it too much; soldiers will let you down, they can't help it. All wars eventually end."

With what remained from his money when he had divided it between his mother and father and put some away in the credit union for Priya, Sanjeev went to Tea Lane and stuck down the deposit and first payment on a pair of big metally leathery black-and-red and flame-pattern boots. He wore them proudly to work the next day, stuck out beside the driver of the phatphat so everyone could see them, and paid the owner of the Bata Boot and Shoe Store assiduously every Friday. At the end of twelve weeks they were Sanjeev's entirely. In that time he had also bought the Ts, the fake-latex pants (real latex hot hot far too hot and sweaty for Varanasi, baba), the Kali bangles and necklaces, the hair gel and the eye kohl. But the boots first, the boots before all. Boots make the robotwallah.

"Do you fancy a go?"

It was one of those questions so simple and unexpected that Sanjeev's brain rolled straight over it and it was only when he was gathering up the fast-food wrappers (messy messy boys) that it crept up and hit him over the head.

"What, you mean . . . that?" A nod of the head towards the harnesses hanging like flayed hides from the feedback rig.

"If you want; there's not much on."

There hadn't been much on for the better part of a month. The last excitement had been when some cracker in a similar go-down in Delhi had broken through the Kali Cav's aeai firewall with a spike of burnware. Big Baba had suddenly leaped up in his rig like a million billion volts had just shot through him (which, Sanjeev discovered later, it kind of had) and next thing the biocontrol interlocks had blown (indoor fireworks, woo) and he was kicking on the floor like epilepsy. Sanjeev had been first to the red button, and a crash team had whisked Big Baba to the rich people's private hospital. The aeais had evolved a patch against the new burnware by the time Sanjeev went to get the lunch tins from the dhabawallah, and Big Baba was back on his corner of the sofa within three days, suffering nothing more than a lingering migraine. Jemadar-woman sent a get-well e-card.

So it was with excitement and wariness that Sanjeev let Rai help him into the rig. He knew all the snaps and grips—he had tightened the straps and pulled snug the motion sensors a hundred times—but Rai doing it made it special, made Sanjeev a robotwallah.

"You might find this a little freaky," Rai said as he settled the helmet over Sanjeev's head. For an instant it was blackout, deafness as the phonobuds sought out his eardrums. "They're working on this new thing, some kind of bone-induction thing so they can send the pictures and sounds straight into your brain," he heard Rai's voice say on the com. "But I don't think we'll get it in time. Now, just stand there and don't shoot anything."

The warning was still echoing in Sanjeev's inner ear as he blinked and found himself standing outside a school compound in a village so like Ahraura that he instinctively looked for Mrs. Mawji and Shree the holy red calf. Then he saw that the school was deserted, its roof gone, replaced with military camouflage sheeting. The walls were pocked with bullet holes down to the brickwork. Siva and Krishna with his flute had been hastily painted on the intact mud plaster, and the words *13th Mechanised Sowar: Section Headquarters*. There were men in smart, tightly belted uniforms with moustaches and bamboo lathis. Women with brass water pots and men on bicycles passed the open gate. By stretching, Sanjeev found he could elevate his sensory rig to crane over the wall. A village, an Ahraura, but too poor to even avoid war. On his left a robot stood under a dusty neem tree. *I must be one of those*, Sanjeev thought; a General Dynamics A8330 *Syce*; a mean, skeletal desert-rat of a thing on two vicious clawed feet, a heavy sensory crown and two Gatling arms—fully interchangeable with gas shells or slime guns for policing work, he remembered from *War Mecha*'s October 2023 edition.

Sanjeev glanced down at his own feet. Icons opened across his field of vision like blossoming flowers: location elevation temperature, ammunition load-out, the level of methane in his fuel tanks, tactical and strategic satmaps—he seemed to be in southwest Bihar—but what fascinated Sanjeev was that if he formed a mental picture of lifting his Sanjeev-foot, his *Syce*-claw would lift from the dust.

Go on try it it's a quiet day you're on sentry duty in some cow-shit Bihar village. *Forwards*, he willed. The bot took one step, two. *Walk*, Sanjeev commanded. *There.* The robot walked jauntily towards the gate. No one in the street of shattered houses looked twice as he stepped among them. *This is great!* Sanjeev thought as he strolled down the street, then, *This is like a game.* Doubt then: *So how do I even know this war is happening?* A step too far; the *Syce* froze a hundred metres from the Ganesh temple, turned, and headed back to its sentry post. *What what what what what?* he yelled in his head.

"The onboard aeai took over," Rai said, his voice startling as a firecracker inside his helmet. Then the village went black and silent and Sanjeev was blinking in the ugly low-energy neons of the Kali Cavalry battle room, Rai gently unfastening the clips and snaps and strappings.

That evening, as he went home through the rush of people with his fist of rupees, Sanjeev realised two things: that most of war was boring and that this boring war was over.

The war was over. The jemadar visited the video-silk wall three times, twice, once a week where in the heat and glory she would have given orders that many times a day. The Kali Cav lolled around on their sofas playing games, lying to their online fans about the cool exciting sexy things they were doing—though the fans never believed they ever really were robotwallahs—but mostly doing battle-drug combos that left them fidgety and aggressive. Fights flared over a cigarette, a look, how a door was closed or left open. Sanjeev threw himself into the middle of a dozen robotwallah wars. But when the American peacekeepers arrived, Sanjeev knew it truly was over because they only came in when there was absolutely no chance any of them would get killed. There was a flurry of car-bombings and I-war attacks and even a few suicide blasts, but everyone knew that that was just everyone who had a grudge against America and Americans in sacred Bharat. No, the war was over.

"What will you do?" Sanjeev's father asked, meaning, *What will I do when Umbrella Street becomes just another Asian ginza?*

"I've saved some money," Sanjeev said.

Godspeed! bought a robot with the money he had saved. It was a Tata Industries D55, a small but nimble antipersonnel bot with detachable free-roaming sub-mechas, Level 0.8s, about as smart as a chicken, which they resembled. Even secondhand it must have cost much more than a teenage robotwallah heavily consuming games, online time, porn, and Sanjeev's dad's kofta pizza could ever save. "I got backers," Godspeed! said. "Funding. Hey, what do you think of this? I'm getting her pimped, this is the skin-job." When the paint dried the robot would be road-freighted up to Varanasi.

"But what are you going to do with it?" Sajeev asked.

"Private security. They're always going to need security drones."

Tidying the tiny living room that night for his mother's nine o'clock lesson, opening the windows to let out the smell of hot ghee though the stink of the street was little better, Sanjeev heard a new chord in the ceaseless song of Umbrella Street. He threw open the window shutters in time to see an object, close, fast as a dashing bird, dart past his face, swing along the powerline and down the festooned pylon. Glint of anodised alu-plastic: a boy raised on *Battlebots Top Trumps* could not fail to recognise a Tata surveillance mecha. Now the commotion at the end of Umbrella Street became clear: the hunched back of a battlebot was pushing between the cycle rickshaws and phatphats. Even before he could fully make out the customised god-demons of Mountain Buddhism on its carapace, Sanjeev knew the machine's make and model and who was flying it.

A badmash on an alco moto rode slowly in front of the ponderously stepping machine, relishing the way the street opened before him and the electric scent of heavy firepower at his back. Sanjeev saw the mech step up and squat down on its hydraulics before Jagmohan's greasy little pakora stand. The badmash skidded his moped to a standstill and pushed up his shades.

They will always need security drones.

Sanjeev rattled down the many many flights of stairs of the patriotically renamed Diljit Rana Apartments, yelling and pushing and beating at the women and young men in very white shirts. The robot had already taken up its position in front of his father's big clay pizza oven. The carapace unfolded like insect wings into weapon mounts. Badmash was all teeth and grin in anticipation of another commission. Sanjeev dashed between his father and the prying, insectile sensory rig of the robot. Red demons and Sivas with fiery tridents looked down on him.

"Leave him alone, this is my dad, leave him be."

It seemed to Sanjeev that the whole of Umbrella Street, every vehicle upon it, every balcony and window that overlooked it, stopped to watch. With a whir the weapon pods retracted, the carapace clicked shut. The battle machine reared up on its legs as the surveillance drones came skittering between people's legs and over countertops, scurried up the machine, and took their places on its shell mounts, like egrets on the back of a buffalo. Sanjeev stared the badmash down. He sneered, snapped down his cool sexy dangerous shades, and spun his moped away.

Two hours later, when all was safe and secure, a peacekeeper unit had passed up the street asking for information. Sanjeev shook his head and sucked on his asthma inhalers.

"Some machine, like."

Suni left the go-down. No word no note no clue, his family had called and called and called but no one knew. There had always been rumours of a man with money and prospects, who liked the robotwallah thing, but you do not tell those sorts of stories to mothers. Not at first asking. A week passed without the jemadar calling. It was over. So over. Rai had taken to squatting outside, squinting up through his cool sexy dangerous shades at the sun, watching for its burn on his pale arms, chain-smoking street-rolled bidis.

"Sanj." He smoked the cheap cigarette down to his gloved fingers and ground the butt out beneath the steel heel of his boot. "When it happens, when we can't use you any more, have you something sorted? I was thinking, maybe you and I could do something together, go somewhere. Just have it like it was, just us. An idea, that's all."

The message came at 3 a.m. *I'm outside.* Sanjeev tiptoed around the sleeping bodies to open the window. Umbrella Street was still busy; Umbrella Street had not slept for a thousand years. The big black Kali Cav Hummer was like a funeral moving through the late-night people of the new Varanasi. The door locks made too much noise, so Sanjeev exited through the window, climbing down the pipes like a Raytheon Double-8000 I-war infiltration bot. In Ahraura he would never have been able to do that.

"You drive," Rai said. From the moment the message came through, Sanjeev had known it would be him, and him alone.

"I can't drive."

"It drives itself. All you have to do is steer. It's not that different from the game. Swap over there."

Steering wheel pedal drive windshield display all suddenly looked very big to Sanjeev in the driver's seat. He touched his foot to the gas. Engines answered, the Hummer rolled, Umbrella Street parted before him. He steered around a wandering cow.

"Where do you want me to go?"

"Somewhere, away. Out of Varanasi. Somewhere no one else would go." Rai bounced and fidgeted on the passenger seat. His hands were busy busy, his eyes were huge. He had done a lot of battle drugs. "They sent them back to school, man. To school, can you imagine that? Big Baba and Ravana. Said they needed real-world skills. I'm not going back, not never. Look!"

Sanjeev dared a glance at the treasure in Rai's palm: a curl of sculpted translucent pink plastic. Sanjeev thought of aborted goat fetuses, and the sex toys the girls had used in their favourite pornos. Rai tossed his head to sweep back his long, gelled hair and slid the device behind his ear. Sanjeev thought he saw something move against Rai's skin, seeking.

"I saved it all up and bought it. Remember, I said? It's new; no one else has one. All that gear, that's old, you can do everything with this, just in your head, in the pictures and words in your head." He gave a stoned grin and moved his hands in a dancer's mudra. "There."

"What?"

"You'll see."

The Hummer was easy to drive: the in-car aeai had a flocking reflex that enabled it to navigate Varanasi's ever-swelling morning traffic, leaving little for Sanjeev to do other than blare the triple horns, which he enjoyed a lot. Somewhere he knew he should be afraid, should feel guilty at stealing away in the night without word or note, should say stop, whatever it is you are doing, it can come to nothing, it's just silliness, the war is over and we must think properly about what to do next. But the brass sun was rising above the glass towers and spilling into the streets, and men in sharp white shirts and women in smart saris were going busy to their work, and he was free, driving a big smug car through them all and it was so good, even if just for a day.

He took the new bridge at Ramnagar, hooting in derision at the gaudy, lumbering trucks. The drivers blared back, shouting vile curses at the girli-looking robotwallahs. Off A-roads onto B-roads, then to tracks and then bare dirt, the dust flying up behind the Hummer's fat wheels. Rai itched in the passenger seat, grinning away to himself and moving his hands like butter-flies, muttering small words and occasionally sticking his head out of the window. His gelled hair was stiff with dust.

"What are you looking for?" Sanjeev demanded.

"It's coming," Rai said, bouncing on his seat. "Then we can go and do whatever we like."

From the word *drive*, Sanjeev had known where he must go. Satnav and aeai did his remembering for him, but he still knew every turn and side road. Vora's Wood there, still stunted and grey; the ridge between the river and the fields from which all the men of the village had watched the battle and he had fallen in love with the robots. The robots had always been pure, had always been true. It was the boys who flew them who hurt and failed and disap-pointed. The fields were all dust, drifted and heaped against the lines of thorn fence. Nothing would grow here for a generation. The mud walls of the houses were crumbling, the school a roofless shell, the temple and tanks clogged with wind-blown dust. Dust, all dust. Bones cracked and went to powder beneath his all-wheel drive. A few too desperate even for Varanasi were trying to scratch an existence in the ruins. Sanjeev saw wire-thin men and tired women, dust-smeared children crouched in front of their brick-and-plastic shelters. The poison deep within Ahraura would defeat them in the end.

Sanjeev brought the Hummer to a halt on the ridge top. The light was yellow, the heat appalling. Rai stepped out to survey the terrain.

"What a shit-hole."

Sanjeev sat in the shade of the rear cabin watching Rai pace up and down, up and down, kicking up the dust of Ahraura with his big Desi-metal boots. *You didn't stop them, did you?* Sanjeev thought. *You didn't save us from the plague-walkers.* Rai suddenly leaped and punched the air.

"There, there, look!"

A storm of dust moved across the dead land. The high sun caught glints and gleams at its heart. Moving against the wind, the tornado bore down on Ahraura.

The robot came to a halt at the foot of the ridge where Sanjeev and Rai stood waiting. A Raytheon ACR, a heavy line-of-battle bot, it out-topped them by some metres. The wind carried away its cloak of dust. It stood silent, potential, heat shimmering from its armour. Sanjeev had never seen a thing so beautiful.

Rai raised his hand. The bot spun on its steel hooves. More guns than Sanjeev had ever seen in his life unfolded from its carapace. Rai clapped his hands and the bot opened up with all its armaments on Vora's Wood. Gatlings sent dry dead silvery wood flying up into powder; missiles streaked from its back-silos; the line of the wood erupted in a wall of flame. Rai separated his hands, and the roar of sustained fire ceased.

"It's got it all in here, everything that the old gear had, in here. Sanj, everyone will want us, we can go wherever we want, we can do whatever we want, we can be real anime heroes."

"You stole it."

"I had all the protocols. That's the system."

"You stole that robot."

Rai balled his fists, shook his head in exasperation.

"Sanj, it was always mine."

He opened his clenched fist. And the robot danced. Arms, feet, all the steps and the moves, the bends and head-nods, a proper Bollywood item-song dance. The dust flew up around the battle-bot's feet. Sanjeev could feel the eyes of the squatters, wide and terrified in their hovels. *I am sorry we scared you.*

Rai brought the dance to an end.

"Anything I want, Sanj. Are you coming with us?"

Sanjeev's answer never came, for a sudden, shattering roar of engines and jet-blast from the river side of the ridge sent them reeling and choking in the swirling dust. Sanjeev fought out his inhalers: two puffs blue one puff brown and by the time they had worked their sweet way down into his lungs, a tilt-jet with the Bharati air force's green, white, and orange roundels on its engine pods stood on the settling dust. The cargo ramp lowered; a woman in dust-war camo and a mirror-visored helmet came up the ridge towards them.

With a wordless shriek, Rai slashed his hand through the air like a sword. The 'bot crouched and its carapace slid open in a dozen places, extruding weapons. Without breaking her purposeful stride the woman lifted her left hand. The weapons retracted, the hull ports closed, the war machine staggered as if confused, and then sat down heavily in the dead field, head sagging, hands trailing in the dust. The woman removed her helmet. The cameras made the jemadar look five kilos heavier, but she had big hips. She tucked her helmet under her left arm, with her right swept back her hair to show the control unit coiled behind her ear.

"Come on now, Rai. It's over. Come on, we'll go back. Don't make a fuss. There's not really anything you can do. We all have to think what to do next, you know? We'll take you back in the plane, you'll like that." She looked Sanjeev up and down. "I suppose you could take the car back. Someone has to and it'll be cheaper than sending someone down from Divisional, it's cost enough already. I'll retask the aeai. And then we have to get that thing . . ." She shook her head, then beckoned to Rai. He went like a calf, quiet and meek, down to the tilt-jet. Black hopping crows settled on the robot, trying its crevices with their curious shiny-hungry beaks.

The Hummer ran out of gas twenty kays from Ramnagar. Sanjeev hitched home to Varanasi. The army never collected it, and as the new peace built, the local people took it away bit by bit.

With his war dividend Sanjeev bought a little alco-buggy and added a delivery service to his father's pizza business, specialising in the gap-year hostels that blossomed after the peacekeepers left. He wore a polo shirt with a logo and a baseball cap and got a sensible haircut. He could not bring himself to sell his robotwallah gear, but it was a long time before he could look at it in the box without feeling embarrassed. The business grew fast and fat.

He often saw Rai down at the ghats or around the old town. They worked the same crowd: Rai dealt Nepalese ganja to tourists. *Robotwallah* was his street name. He kept the old look and everyone knew him for it. It became first a novelty and then retro. It even became fashionable again, the spiked hair, the andro makeup, the slashed Ts and the latex, and most of all the boots. It sold well and everyone wore it, for a season.

KYLE MEETS THE RIVER

*K*yle was the first to see the exploding cat. He was coming back from the compound HFBR-Mart with the slush cone—his reward for scoring a goal in the under-elevens—squinted up at the sound of a construction helicopter (they were still big and marvellous and exciting), and saw it leap the narrow gap between the med centre and Tinneman's Coffee Bar. He pointed to it one fragment of a second before the security men picked it up on their visors and started yelling. In an instant the compound was full of fleeing people: men and women running, parents snatching up kids, guards sweeping their weapons this way and that as the cat, sensing it had been spotted, leaped from the roof in two bounds onto the roof of an armoured Landcruiser, then dived to ground and hunted for targets. A security guard raised his gun. He must be new. Even Kyle knew not to do that. They were not really cats at all, but smart missiles that behaved like them, and if you tried to catch them or threatened them with a weapon, they would attack and blow themselves up. From the shade of the arcade he could see the look on the guard's face as he tried to get a fix on the dashing, dodging robot. Machine-gun rattle. Kyle had never heard it so close. It was very exciting. Bullets cracked all over the place, flying wild. Kyle thought that perhaps he should hide himself behind something solid. But he wanted to see. He had heard it so many times before and now here it was, on the main streets in front of him. That cat-missile was getting really really close. Then the guard let loose a lucky burst; the steel cat went spinning into the air and blew itself up. Kyle reeled back. He had never heard anything so loud. Shrapnel cracked the case of the Coke machine beside him into red and white stars. The security man was down but moving, scrabbling away on his back from the blast site, and real soldiers were arriving, and a med Hummer, and RAV airdrones. Kyle stood and stared. It was wonderful wonderful wonderful and all for him, and there was Mom, running towards him in her flappy-hands, flappy-feet run, coming to take it all away, snatching him up in front of everyone and crying, "Oh, what were you doing what were you thinking are you all right all right all right?"

"Mom," he said. "I saw the cat explode."

His name is Kyle Rubin and he's here to build a nation. Well, his father is. Kyle doesn't have much of an idea of nations and nationhood, just that he's not where he used to live but it's okay because it's not really all that different from the gated community; there are a lot of folk like him, though he's not allowed to leave the compound. In here is Cantonment. Out there is the nation that's being built. That's where his dad goes in the armoured cars, where he directs the construction helicopters and commands the cranes that Kyle can just see from the balcony around the top floor of the International School. You're not allowed to go there because there are still some snipers working, but everyone does, and Kyle can watch the booms of the tower cranes swing across the growing skyline of the new capital.

It all fell apart, and it takes us to put it back together again, his father explained. Once there was a big country called India, with a billion and a half people in it, but they just couldn't live together, so they fell to squabbling and fighting. *Like you and Kelis's mom*, Kyle said, which made his father raise his eyebrows and look embarrassed and Mom—his mom, not Kelis's—laugh to herself. Whatever, it all fell apart and these poor people, they need us and our know-how to put it all back together for them. And that's why we're all here, because it's families that make us strong and hopeful. And that's how you, Kyle Rubin, are building a nation. But some people don't think we should be doing that. They think it's their nation so they should build it. Some people think we're part of the problem and not part of the solution. And some people are just plain ungrateful.

Or, as Clinton in class said: the Ranas' control is still weak and there are a lot of underrepresented parties out there with big grievances and arsenals of leftover weaponry from the Sundering. Western interests are always first in the firing line. But Clinton was a smart mouth who just repeated what he heard from his dad, who had been in Military Intelligence since before there was even a Cantonment, let alone an International Reconstruction Alliance.

The nation Kyle Rubin is building is Bharat, formerly the states of Bihar, Jharkhand, and half of Uttar Pradesh on the Indo-Gangetic Plain, and the cranes swing and the helicopters fly over the rising towers of its new capital, Ranapur.

When there weren't cats exploding, after practice Kyle would visit Salim's planet.

Before Kyle, Striker Salim had been the best forward on Team Cantonment U-11. Really he shouldn't have been playing at all because he didn't actually live within the compound. His father was the Bharati government's man in Cantonment, so he could pretty much do whatever he liked.

At first they had been enemies. In his second game, Kyle had headed home a sweet cross from Ryan from Australia, and after that every cross floated his way. In the dressing room Striker Salim had complained to Coach Joe that the *new boy* had got all the best balls because he was a Westerner and not Bharati. The wraths of dads were invoked. Coach Joe said nothing and put them on together for the game against the army kids, who imagined that being army kids was like an extra man for them. Salim on wing, Kyle in centre: three-three-four. Cantonment beat US Army two–one, one goal by Salim, the decider from a run by Salim and a rebound from the goalkeeper by Kyle, in the forty-third minute. Now, six weeks in another country later, they were inseparable.

Salim's planet was very close and easy to visit. It lived in the palmer-glove on his brown hand and could manifest itself in all manner of convenient locations: the school system, Tinneman's Coffee Bar, Kyle's e-paper workscreen, but the best was the full-proprioception so-new-it's-scary lighthoek (trademark) that you could put behind your ear so, fiddle it so, and it would get inside your head and open up a whole new world of sights and sounds and smells and sensations. They were so new not even the Americans had them, but Varanasi civil servants engaged on the grand task of nation building needed to use and show off the latest Bharati technology. And their sons, too. The safety instructions said you weren't supposed to use it in full sensory outside because of the risk of accidents, crime, or terror, but it was safe enough in the Guy's Place up on the roof under the solar farm that was out of shot of any sniper, no matter how good or young she was.

Kyle plugged the buddy-lead into Salim's lighthoek and slipped the curl of plastic behind his ear. It had taken awhile to work out the sweet spot but now he got it first time every time. He was not supposed to use lighthoek tech; Mom's line was that it hadn't been proved safe yet, but Kyle suspected it was his father who had the more serious reservations: it was opening yourself up to evil influences to let things inside your head like that. That was before you even got to what he thought of the artificial evolution game itself. Maybe if he could experience the lift out of the Cantonment, up through the solar arrays, past the cranes and helicopters, and see Salim's world there in front of him—Alterre, as it was properly called—and feel himself falling towards it through the clouds faster than anything could possibly go to stop light as a feather with his feet brushing the wave-tops; maybe he would change his mind. He could smell the salt. He could feel the wind. He could see the lifted jelly sails of a kronkaeur fleet above the white-edged swell.

"Aw not these jellyfish guys again," said Kyle.

"No no no, this is different." Salim stood beside him above the waves. "Look, this is really cool." He folded his hands and leaned forwards and flew across the ocean, Kyle a heartbeat behind him. He always thought of those Hindu gods you saw on the prayer cards that blew into the compound from the street shrines. His dad didn't like those either. They arrived over the kronkaeur armada, beating through a rising ocean on a steady breeze, topsails inflated.

When the huge, sail-powered jellyfish had appeared, Kyle had been so excited at his first experience of a newly evolved species that the vast, inflatable monsters had sailed like translucent galleons through his dreams. But all they did was raise their triangular sails and weave their tentacles together into huge raft-fleets and bud-off little jellies that looked like see-through paper boats. Once the initial thrill of being part of the global game-experiment to start life on Earth all over again and see how it evolved differently had worn off, Kyle found himself wishing that Salim had been given somewhere a bit more exciting than a huge square of ocean. An island would have been good. A bit of continent would have been better. Somewhere things could attack each other.

"Every bit of water on Alterre was land, and every bit of land was water," Salim had said. "And they will be again. And anyway, everything eats everything out on the open ocean."

But not in a cool way, Kyle thought.

Apart from his tech and his skill at football, nothing about Salim was cool. At home he would never have been Kyle's friend. Kyle would probably have beaten him about a bit: he was geeky, had a big nose, couldn't get clothes right—all the wrong labels—and had no idea how to wear a beanie. He went to a weird religious school for an hour every afternoon and Fridays to the mosque down by the river steps where they burned the dead people. Really, they should not be friends at all. Ozzie Ryan, who'd been the team big one before Kyle, said it was unnatural and disloyal and you couldn't trust them; one moment they'd be giving you presents and the next they'd be setting you up for people out there to shoot you. Kyle knew Ozzie Ryan was just jealous.

"Now, isn't this so cool?" Salim said, his toes brushing the wave tops. The sculpted upper surfaces of the great oceangoing jellies between the inflatable booms that held out the sails were bloated with bubbles, visibly swelling and bulging as Kyle floated around to a closer angle. Bigger, bigger, now the size of footballs, now the size of beach balls, stretching the skin until it split with a gush of acid-smelling liquid and a host of balloons dashed into the air. They rose in a mass, tethered to their parents by woven strands of tentacles, rubbing and bouncing and rebounding from each other in the wind; higher than the sail tops now and Kyle could make out detail: each balloon carried a cluster of stingers and translucent claspers beneath its domed canopy. Blue eyes were grouped in threes and fours. One by one their tethers parted and the balloon-jellies sprang up into the air and were whisked away on the sea breeze. All around him the flotilla was bubbling and bursting into spasms of balloons; they soared up around him, some still tangled together by the tentacles. Kyle found himself laughing as he watched them stream up into the sky until they vanished against the fast-moving clouds. It was definitely undeniably way way way cool.

"It's a completely new way of reproducing," Salim said. "It's a new species!"

Kyle knew what that meant. By the rules of Alterre, played out on eleven million computers around the globe, whoever found a new species gave it his or her name. "They're not kronkaeurs any more. I went and registered them: they're mansooris!"

Gunfire on Monday Tuesday Wednesday. They were working up to something; that was the pattern of it. (*Dad Dad who are they this time, is it the Hindus?* but his father had eyes and ears and arms only for Mom, full of thanks and praise to have him safe home from that fearsome city.) The Cantonment went to orange alert, but security was still unprepared for the ferocity of the assault. Bombers simultaneously attacked twelve Western-owned targets across Old and New Varanasi. The twelfth and final device was a car bomb driven at full speed across the Green Zone, impervious to automatic fire, its driver dead or ecstatic to die. Close-defence robots uncoiled from their silos and leaped, nanodiamond blades unsheathed, but the bombers had recced Cantonment's weaknesses well. Slashed, gashed, leaking oil and fuel, engine dead but still rolling under a heaving cancer of robots trying to cocoon it in impact-foam, the car rammed the inner gate and blew up.

On the soccer pitch the referee had heard the general-alert siren, judged the distance to the changing room, and ordered everyone to lie flat in the goal. Kyle had just wrapped his arms around his head—Day One, Lesson One—when the boom lifted him off the ground by the belly and punched every breath of wind out of him. For a moment he thought he had gone deaf, then the sounds of sirens and RAV airdrones pushed through the numb until he was sitting on the grass beside Salim seemingly at the centre of a vast spiral of roar. It was much bigger than the exploding cat. A column of smoke leaned over towards the south. Hummers were rushing past, security men on foot dodging between them. The football net was full of chunks of blast-foam and scraps of wire and fragments of shattered plastic robot shell and warning signs in three languages that this was a restricted area with security authorised for the use of deadly force. A shard of nanodiamond antipersonnel blade was embedded in the left upright. The referee stood up, took off his shirt, and wrapped it around the hand wedged under the crossbar.

"Would you look at that?" Kyle said.

There was a long green smear down the front of his fresh-laundered soccer shirt.

"Salim's always welcome here," Mom called from the kitchen where she was blitzing smoothies. "Just make sure he calls home to let them know he's all right the moment the network comes back up. Now promise you'll do that."

Of course they did and of course they didn't and the smoothies stood there forgotten and warming on the worktop while Mom edged about folding underwear and pillowcases but really keeping an eye on the rolling news. She was worried. Kyle knew that. Cantonment was locked down and would be until Coalition and Bharati forces had resecured the Green Zone: that was the way it was, Kyle had learned that. Locked-down was locked-out for Dad, and the SKYIndia hovercams were still showing towers of black plastic-smoke and ambulances being walked through the crowds of lost people and burned-out cars by Bharati policemen. The reporters were saying there were casualties, but they were also saying that the network wasn't fully restored and that was why he couldn't call; if there had been Western casualties, they would have said straight away because dead Bharatis didn't count and, anyway, it was inconceivable that anything could happen to Kyle's dad. No, in situations like this you kept your head down and got on with things while you waited for the call, so he didn't trouble Mom and fetched the smoothies himself from the kitchen and took them to join Salim in his world.

On the house smartsilk screen you couldn't get that full-sensory drop from orbit or the feeling of walking like God over the water, but in the house, even with Mom in her distracted fold-laundry state, it wasn't smart to use the buddy-lead. Anyway, Kyle didn't want to give her more to worry about.

Three days in Alterre was more like three million years: still water water water whichever way he turned the point of view, but the Mansooris had evolved. High above the blue Atlantic, fleets of airships battled.

"Whoa," said Kyle Rubin and Salim Mansoori.

In three days the jellyfish balloons had become vast sky-going gasbags, blimp-creatures, translucent airships the size of the Boeing troop transports that brought supplies and workers into the secure end of Varanasi Airport. Their bodies were ridged like the condom Kyle had been shown at the back of a bike rack behind the school; light rippled over them and broke into rainbows as the air-jellies manoeuvred. For this was battle, no doubt about it. This was hot war. The sky-jellyfish trailed long clusters of tentacles beneath them, many dangling in the water, their last connection with their old world. But some ended in purple stingers, some in long stabbing spines, some in barbs, and these the airships wielded as weapons. The air-medusas raised or lowered sail-flaps to tack and manoeuvre into striking positions. Kyle saw one blimp, body blotched with black sting-weals, vent gas from nose and tail and drop out of combat. In a tangle of slashing and parrying tentacles, Kyle watched a fighting blimp tear a gash the length of an army Hummer down an opponent's flank with its scimitar-hook. The mortally wounded blimp vented glittering dust, crumpled, folded in half in the middle, and plunged into the sea, where it split like a thrown water-balloon. The sea instantly boiled with almkvists, spear-fast scavengers all jaw and speed.

"Cool," both boys said together.

"Hey now, didn't you promise you'd let your folks know you're okay as soon as the network was up?" said Mom, standing behind them. "And Kyle, you know your dad doesn't like you playing that game."

But she wasn't mad. She couldn't be mad. Dad was safe, Dad had called in, Dad would be home soon. It was all in the little tremble in her voice, the way she leaned over between them to look at the screen, the smell of perfume just dabbed on. You know these things.

It had been close. Kyle's dad called Kyle in to show him the rolling news and point out where his company car had been when the bombers hit the escort Hummers.

"There's next to no protection in those things," he said over jerky, swooping flash-cut images of black smoke boiling out of yellow flames and people standing and shouting and not knowing what to do: pictures taken from a passerby's palmer. "They used a drone RAV; I saw something go past the window just before it hit. They were aiming for the soldiers, not for us."

"It was a suicide attack here," Kyle said.

"Some karsevak group claimed responsibility; some group no one's ever heard of before. Fired everything off in one shooting match."

"Don't they go straight into a state of moksha if they blow themselves up in Varanasi?"

"That's what they believe, son. Your soul is released from the wheel of reincarnation. But I still can't help feeling that this was the final throw. Things are getting better. The Ranas are taking control. People can see the difference we're making. I do feel we've turned the corner on this."

Kyle loved it when his dad talked military, though he was really a structural engineer.

"So Salim got home safe."

Kyle nodded.

"That's good." Kyle heard his father sigh in the way that men do when they're supposed to talk about things they don't want to. "Salim's a good kid, a good friend." Another intake of breath. Kyle waited for it to shape into a *but*.

"Kyle, you know, that game. Well . . ."

Not a *but*, a *well*.

"Well, I know it's real educational and a lot of people play it and enjoy it and get a lot out of it, but it's not really right. I mean, it's not accurate. It claims it's an evolution simulation, and it is as far as it goes. But if you think about it, really, it's just following rules laid down by someone else. All that code was programed by someone else; so really, it's evolution inside a bigger framework that's been deliberately designed. But they don't tell you, Kyle, and that's dishonest; it's pretending to be something it's not. And that's why I don't like it—because it isn't honest about the truth, and I know that whatever I say, what you do with Salim is your thing, but I do think you're not to play it here, in the house. And it's good you've got a good friend here—I remember when Kelis was your age, when we were in the Gulf, she had a really good friend, a Canadian girl—but it would be good if you had a few more friends from your own background. Okay? Now, how about *Wrestle Smackdown* on cable?"

The referee had gone down with a head-butt to the nuts in the first thirty seconds, so it was only when the decibel count exceeded the mundane Varanasi traffic roar that security heads-upped, guns-downed, and came running. A guard-woman in full colour-smear combats and smart-visor locked her arms around Kyle and hauled him out of the steel-cage match into which the under-eleven practice had collapsed.

"I'll sue you I'll sue the ass off you your children will end up living in a cardboard box, let go of me," Kyle yelled. The security woman hauled.

It was full fight, boys, girls, supporters, cheerleaders. At the bottom of the dog-pile, Striker Salim and Ozzie Ryan. Security hauled them off each other and returned the snoopy RAV drones that flocked to any unusual action to their standby roosts. Parameds rushed to the scene. There was blood, there were bruisings and grazings, there were torn clothes and black eyes. There were lots and lots of tears but no contusions, no concussions, no breaks.

Then the Gitmoisation.

Coach Joe: Okay, so, want to tell me what that was about?

Ozzie Ryan: He started it.

Striker Salim: Liar! You started it.

Coach Joe: I don't care who started it; I want to know what all that was about.

Ozzie Ryan: He's the liar. His people just lie all the time; they don't have a word for the truth.

Striker Salim: Ah! Ah! That's such a lie too.

Ozzie Ryan: See? You can't trust them: he's a spy for them, it's true; before he came here they never got in, since he came there's been things happening almost every day. He's a spy and he's telling them all ways to get in and kill us because he thinks we're all animals and going to hell anyway.

Coach Joe: Jesus. Kyle—what happened?

Kyle Rubin: I don't know, I didn't see anything, I just heard this noise, like, and when I looked over they were on the ground tearing lumps out of each other.

Striker Salim: That is so not true . . . I cannot believe you said that. You were there, you heard what he said.

Kyle Rubin: I didn't hear everything, I just heard, like, shouting . . . Gitmoisation Part Two.

Kyle's Dad: Coach Joe called me, but I'm not going to bawl you out, I think there's been enough of that already. I'm disappointed, but I'm not going to bawl you out. Just one thing: did Ryan call Salim something?

Kyle Rubin: (Mumble.)

Kyle's Dad: Son, did Ryan use a racist term to Salim?

Kyle Rubin: (Twisting foot.)

Kyle's Dad: I thought Salim was your friend. Your best friend. I think if someone had done something to my best friend, doesn't matter who he is, what he is, I'd stand up for him.

Kyle Rubin: He said Salim was a diaper-head curry-nigger and they were all spies and Salim was just standing there so I went in there and popped him, Ryan, I mean, and he just went for Salim, not me, and then everyone was piling on with Ryan and Salim at the bottom and they were all shouting curry-nigger-lover curry-nigger-lover at me and trying to get me too and then the security came in.

At the end of it two things were certain: soccer was suspended for one month, and when it did come back, Salim would not be playing, never would be again. Cantonment was not safe for Bharatis.

He was trapped, a traffic-island castaway. Marooned on an oval of concrete in Varanasi's never-ebbing torrent of traffic by the phatphat driver when he saw Kyle fiddling in his lap with pogs.

"Ey, you, out here, get out, trying to cheat, damn gora."

"What, here, but—?"

Out onto this tiny traffic island twenty centimetres in front of him twenty centimetres behind him on one side a tall man in a white shirt and black pants on the other a fat woman in a purple sari who smelled of dead rose, and the phatphat, the little yellow and black plastic bubble, looked/sounded like a hornet, throbbed away into the terrifying traffic.

"You can't do this, my dad's building this country!"

The man and the woman turned to stare. Stares everywhere, every instant, from the moment he slipped out of the back of the Hi-Lux at the phatphat stand. They had been eager for his money then, *Hey, sir, hey, sahb, good clean cab, fast fast, straight there no detours, very safe safest phatphat in Varanasi.* How was he to know that the cheap, light cardboard pogs were only money inside the Cantonment? And now here he was on this traffic island no way forwards no way back no way through the constant movement of trucks, buses, cream-coloured Marutis, mopeds, phatphats, cycle rickshaws, cows, everything roaring ringing hooting yelling as it tried to find its true way while avoiding everything else. People were walking through that, just stepping out in the belief that the traffic would steer around them; the man in the white shirt, there he went, the woman in the purple sari, *Come on, boy, come with me,* he couldn't, he daren't, and there she went and now there were people piling up behind him, pushing him pushing pushing pushing him closer to the curb, out into that killing traffic . . .

Then the phatphat came through the mayhem, klaxon buzzing, weaving a course of grace and chaos, sweeping into the traffic island. The plastic door swivelled up and there, there was Salim.

"Come on come on."

Kyle bounded in, the door scissored down, and the driver hooted off into Varanasi's storm of wheels.

"Good thing I was looking for you," Salim said, tapping the lighthoek coiled behind his ear. "You can find anyone with these. What happened?" Kyle showed him the Cantonment pogs. Salim's eyes went wide. "You really haven't ever been outside, have you?"

Escaping from Cantonment was easier than anything. Everyone knew they were only looking for people coming in, not going out, so all Kyle had to do was slip into the back of the pickup while the driver bought a mochaccino to go at Tinneman's. He even peeked out from under the tarpaulin as the inner gate closed because he wanted to see what the bomb damage was like. The robots had taken away all the broken masonry and metal spaghetti, but he could see the steel reinforcing rods through the shattered concrete block work and the black scorch marks over the inner wall. It was so interesting and Kyle was staring so hard that he only realised he was out of Cantonment entirely, in the street, the alien street, when he saw the trucks, buses, cream-coloured Marutis, mopeds, phatphats, cycle rickshaws, cows close behind the pickup, and felt the city roar surge over him.

"So, where do you want to go, then?" Salim asked. His face was bright and eager to show Kyle his wonderful wonderful city. This was a Salim Kyle had never seen before: Salim not-in-Cantonment, Salim in-his-own-place, Salim among-his-own-people. This Mansoori seemed alien to Kyle. He was not sure he liked him. "There's theNewBharatSabhaholydeerof-SarnathDoctorSampunananandcricketgroundBuddhiststupaRamnagar-FortVishwanathTempleJantarMantar . . ."

Too much too much Kyle's head was going round all the people, all the people, the one thing he never saw, never noticed from the rooftop lookout, under all the helicopters and cranes and military RAV drones, there were people.

"River," he gasped. "The river, the big steps."

"The ghats. The best thing. They're cool." Salim spoke to the driver in a language Kyle had never heard from his mouth before. It did not sound like Salim at all. The driver waggled his head in that way you thought was *no* until you learned better, and threw the phatphat around a big traffic circle with a huge pink concrete statue of Ganesh to head away from the glass towers of Ranapur into the old city. Flowers. There were garlands of yellow flowers at the elephant god's feet, little smoking smudges of incense; strange strings of chillies and limes; and a man with big dirty ash grey dreadlocks, a man with his lips locked shut with fishing hooks.

"The man, look at the man . . ." Kyle wanted to shout, but that wonder/horror was behind him, a dozen more unfolding on every side as the phatphat hooted down ever narrower, ever darker, ever busier streets. "An elephant, there's an elephant and that's a robot and those people, what are they carrying, that's a body, that's, like, a dead man on a stretcher oh man . . ." He turned to Salim. He wasn't scared now. There were no bodies behind him, squeezing him, pushing him into fear and danger. It was just people, everywhere just people, working out how to live. "Why didn't they let me see this?"

The phatphat bounced to a stop.

"This is where we get out, come on, come on."

The phatphat was wedged in an alley between a clot of cycle rickshaws and a Japanese delivery truck. Nothing on wheels could pass, but still the people pressed by on either side. Another dead man passed, handed high on his stretcher over the heads of the crowd. Kyle ducked instinctively as the shadow of the corpse passed over the dome of the phatphat, then the doors flew up and he stepped out into the side of a cow. Kyle almost punched the stupid, baggy thing, but Salim grabbed him, shouted, "Don't touch the cow, the cow is special, like sacred." Shout was the only possible conversation here. Grab the only way not to get separated. Salim dragged Kyle by the wrist to a booth in a row of plastic-canopied market stalls where a bank of chill-cabinets chugged. Salim bought two Limkas and showed the stallholder a Cantonment pog, which he accepted for novelty value. Again the hand on the arm restrained Kyle.

"You have to drink it here, there's a deposit."

So they leaned their backs against the tin bar and watched the city pass and drank their Limkas from the bottle which would have had Kyle's mom screaming germs bacteria viruses infections and felt like two very very proper gentlemen. During a moment's lull in the street racket, Kyle heard his palmer call. He hauled it out of his pants pocket, a little ashamed because everyone had a newer better brighter cleverer smaller one than him, and saw, as if she knew what dirty thing he had done, it was his mom calling. He stared at the number, the little smiley animation, listened to the jingly tune. Then he thumbed the off button and sent them all to darkness.

"Come on." He banged his empty bottle down on the counter. "Let's see this river, then."

In twenty steps, he was there, so suddenly, so huge and bright Kyle forgot to breathe. The narrow alley, the throng of people opened up into painful light, light in the polluted yellow sky light from the tiers of marble steps that descended to the river and light from the river itself, wider and more dazzling than he had ever imagined, white as a river of milk. And people: the world could not hold so many people, crowding down the steps to the river in their coloured clothes and coloured shoes, jammed together under the tilted wicker umbrellas to talk and deal and pray, people in the river itself, waist-deep in the water, holding up handfuls of the water, and the water glittering as it fell through their fingers, praying, washing—washing themselves, washing their clothes, washing their children and their sins. Then the boats: the big hydrofoil seeking its way to dock through the little darting rowboats, the pilgrim boats making the crossing from Ramnagar, rowers standing on their sterns pushing at their oars, the tourist boats with their canopies, the kids in inflated tractor tires paddling around scavenging for river-scraps, down to the bobbing saucers of butter-light woven from mango leaves that the people set adrift on the flow. Vision by vision the Ganga revealed itself to Kyle; next he became aware of the buildings: the guesthouses and hotels and havelis shouldering up to the steps, the ridiculous pink water towers, the many domes of the mosque and the golden spires of the temples, and a little temple down at the river leaning into the silt; the arcades and jetties and galleries and across the river, beyond the yellow sand and the black, ragged tents of the holy men, the chimneys and tanks and pipes of the chemical and oil plants, all flying the green, white, and orange wheel-banners of Bharat.

"Oh," Kyle said. "Oh man." And: "Cool."

Salim was already halfway down the steps.

"Come on."

"Is it all right? Am I allowed?"

"Everyone is allowed. Come on, let's get a boat."

A boat. People didn't do things like that, but here they were, settling onto the seat as the boatman pushed out, a kid not that much older than Kyle himself with teeth that would never be allowed inside Cantonment, yet Kyle felt jealous of him, with his boat and his river and the people all around and a life without laws or needs or duties. He sculled them through floating butter-candles—diyas, Salim explained to Kyle—past the ghat of the sadhus, all bare-ass naked and skinny as famine, and the ghat where people beat their clothes against rock washing-platforms, and the ghat where the pilgrims landed, pushing each other into the water in their eagerness to touch the holy ground of Varanasi, and the ghat of the buffalos—*Where where?* Kyle asked and Salim pointed out their nostrils and black, back-curved horns just sticking up out of the water. Kyle trailed his hand in the water, and when he pulled it out it was covered in golden flower petals. He lay back on the seat and watched the marble steps flow past, and beyond them the crumbling, mold-stained waterfront buildings, and beyond them the tops of the highest towers of New Varanasi, and beyond them the yellow clouds, and he knew that even when he was a very old man, maybe forty or even more, he would always remember this day and the colour of this light and the sound of the water against the hull.

"You got to see this!" Salim shouted. The boat was heading in to shore now through the tourists and the souvenir-boats and a slick of floating flower garlands. Fires burned on the steps, the marble was blackened with trodden ashes, half-burned wood lapped at the water's edge. There were other things among the coals: burned bones. Men stood thigh-deep in the water, panning it with wide wicker baskets.

"They're Doms, they run the burning ghats. They're actually untouchable but they're very rich and powerful because they're the only ones who can handle the funerals," said Salim. "They're sifting the ashes for gold."

The burning ghats. The dead place. These fires, these piles of wood and ash, were dead people, Kyle thought. This water beneath the boat was full of dead people. A funeral procession descended the steps to the river. The bearers pushed the stretcher out into the water; a man with a red cord around his shoulder poured water over the white shroud. He was very thorough and methodical about it, he gave the dead body a good washing. The river-boy touched his oars, holding his boat in position. The bearers took the body up to a big bed of wood and set the whole thing on top. A very thin man in a white robe and with a head so freshly shaved it looked pale and sick piled wood on top of it.

"That's the oldest son," Salim said. "It's his job. These are rich people. It's real expensive to get a proper pyre. Most people use the electric ovens. Of course, we get properly buried like you do."

It was all very quick and casual. The man in white poured oil over the wood and the body, picked up a piece of lit wood, and almost carelessly touched it to the side. The flame guttered in the river wind, almost went out, then smoke rose up, and out of the smoke, flame. Kyle watched the fire take hold. The people stood back; no one seemed very concerned, even when the pile of burning wood collapsed and a man's head and shoulders lolled out of the fire.

That is a burning man, Kyle thought. He had to tell himself that. It was hard to believe, all of it was hard to believe; there was nothing that connected to any part of his world, his life. It was fascinating, it was like a wildlife show on the sat; he was close enough to smell the burning flesh but it was too strange, too alien. It did not touch him. He could not believe. Kyle thought, *This is the first time Salim has seen this, too.* But it was very very cool.

A sudden crack, a pop a little louder than the gunfire Kyle heard in the streets every day, but not much.

"That is the man's skull bursting," Salim said. "It's supposed to mean his spirit is free."

Then a noise that had been in the back of Kyle's head moved to the front of his perception: engines, aircraft engines. Tilt-jet engines. Loud, louder than he had ever heard them before, even when he watched them lifting off from the field in Cantonment. The mourners were staring; the Doms turned from their ash-panning to stare too. The boat-boy stopped rowing; his eyes were round. Kyle turned in his seat and saw something wonderful and terrible and strange: a tilt-jet with Coalition markings, moving across the river towards him, yes, *him*, so low, so slow, it was as if it were tiptoeing over the water. For a moment he saw himself, toes scraping the stormy waters of Alterre. River-traffic fled from it; its down-turned engines sent flaws of white across the green water. The boat-boy scrabbled for his oars to get away but there was now a second roar from the ghats. Kyle turned back to see Coalition troopers in full combat armour and visors pouring down the marble steps, pushing mourners out of their way, scattering wood and bones and ash. Mourners and Doms shouted their outrage; fists were raised; the soldiers lifted their weapons in answer. The boat-boy looked around him in terror as the thunder of the jet engines grew louder and louder until Kyle felt it become part of him, and when he looked round he saw the big machine, morphing between city and river camouflage, turn, unfold landing gear, and settle into the water. The boat rocked violently. Kyle would have been over the side had Salim not hauled him back. Jet-wash blew human ash along the ghats. A single oar floated lost down the stream. The tilt-jet stood knee-deep in the shallow water. It unfolded its rear ramp. Helmets. Guns. Between them, a face Kyle recognised, his dad, shouting wordlessly through the engine roar. The soldiers on the shore were shouting, the people were shouting, everything was shout shout roar. Kyle's dad beckoned, *To me to me.* Shivering with fear, the boat-boy stood up, thrust his sole remaining oar into the water like a punt pole, and pushed towards the ramp. Gloved hands seized Kyle and dragged him out of the rocking boat up the ramp. Everyone was shouting, shouting. Now the soldiers on the shore were beckoning to the boat-boy and Salim, *This way this way, the thing is going to take off, get out of there.*

His dad buckled Kyle into the seat as the engine roar peaked again. He felt the world turn, then the river was dropping away beneath him. The tilt-jet banked. Kyle looked out the window. There was the boat, being pulled in to shore by the soldiers, and Salim standing in the stern staring up at the aircraft, a hand raised: goodbye.

Gitmo Part Three.

Dad did the don't-you-know-the-danger-you-were-in/trouble-you-caused/expense-you-cost bit.

"It was a full-scale security alert. Full-scale alert. We thought you'd been kidnapped. We honestly thought you'd been kidnapped. Everyone thought that, everyone was praying for you. You'll write them, of course. Proper apologies, handwritten. Why did you turn your palmer off? One call, one simple call, and it would have been all right, we wouldn't have minded. Lucky we can track them even when they're switched off. Salim's in big trouble too. You know, this is a major incident; it's in all the papers, and not just here in Cantonment. It's even made SKYIndia News. You've embarrassed us all, made us look very very stupid. Sledgehammer to crack a nut. Salim's father has had to resign. Yes, he's that ashamed."

But Kyle knew his dad was burning with joy and relief to have him back.

Mom was different. Mom was the torturer.

"It's obvious we can't trust you; well, of course you're grounded, but really, I thought you knew what it was like here, I thought you understood that this is not like anywhere else, that if we can't trust each other, we can really put one another in danger. Well, I can't trust you here, and your dad, well, he'll have to give it up. We'll have to quit and go back home and the Lord knows, he won't get a job anything close to what we have here. We'll have to move to a smaller house in a less good area. I'll have to go out to work again. And you can forget about that Salim boy, yes, forget all about him. You won't be seeing him again."

Kyle cried himself out that night in bed, cried himself into great shivering, shuddering sobs empty of everything except the end of the world. Way way late he heard the door open.

"Kyle?" Mom's voice. He froze in his bed. "I'm sorry. I was upset. I said things I shouldn't have said. You did bad, but all the same, your dad and I think you should have this."

A something was laid beside his cheek. When the door had closed, Kyle put on the light. The world could turn again. It would get better. He tore open the plastic bubble-case. Coiled inside, like a beckoning finger, like an Arabic letter, was a lighthoek. And in the morning, before school, before breakfast, before anything but the pilgrims going to the river, he went up onto the roof at Guy's Place, slipped the 'hoek behind his ear, pulled his palmer glove over his fingers, and went soaring up through the solar farm and the water tanks, the cranes and the construction helicopters and the clouds, up towards Salim's world.

THE DUST ASSASSIN

*W*hen I was small a steel monkey would come into my room. My ayah put me to bed early, because a growing girl needed sleep, big sleep. I hated sleep. The world I heard beyond the carved stone jali screens of my verandah was too full of things for sleep. My ayah would set the wards, but the steel monkey was one of my own security robots and invisible to them. As I lay on my side in the warmth and perfume of dusk, I would see first its little head, then one hand, then two appear over the lip of my balcony, then all of it. It would crouch there for a whole minute, then slip down into the night shadows filling up my room. As my eyes grew accustomed to the dark I would see it watching me, turning its head from one side to the other. It was a handsome thing: metal shell burnished as soft as skin (for in time it came close enough for me to slip a hand through my mosquito nets to stroke it) and adorned with the symbol of my family and make and serial number. It was not very intelligent, less smart than the real monkeys that squabbled and fought on the rooftops, but clever enough to climb and hunt the assassin

robots of the Azads along the ledges and turrets and carvings of the Jodhra
Palace. And in the morning I would see them lining the ledges and rooftops
with their solar cowls raised, and then they did not seem to me like monkeys
at all, but cousins of the sculpted gods and demons among which they shel-
tered, giving salutation to the sun.

You never think your life is special. Your life is just your life, your world
is just your world, even lived in a Rajput palace defended by machine monkeys against an implacable rival family. Even when you are a weapon.

Those four words are my memory of my father: his face filling my sight
like the Marwar moon, his lips, full as pomegranates, saying down to me, *You
are a weapon, Padmini, our revenge against the Azads.* I never see my mother's
face there: I never knew her. She lived in seclusion in the zenana, the women's
quarters. The only woman I ever saw was my ayah, mad Harpal, who every
morning drank a steaming glass of her own piss. Otherwise, only men. And
Heer, the khidmutgar, our steward. Not man, not woman: other. A *nute*. As
I said, you always think your life is normal.

Every night the monkey-robot watched me, turning its head this way,
that way. Then one night it slipped away on its little plastic paws and I slid
out of my nets in my silk pajamas after it. It jumped up on the balcony, then
in two leaps it was up the vine that climbed around my window. Its eyes glittered in the full moon. I seized two handfuls of tough, twisted vine, thick as
my thigh, and was up after it. Why did I follow that steel monkey? Maybe
because of that moon on its titanium shell. Maybe because that was the moon
of the great kite festival, which we always observed by flying a huge kite in
the shape of a man with a bird's tail and outstretched wings for arms. My
father kept all the festivals and rituals, the feasts of the gods. It was what made
us different from, better than, the Azads. That man with wings for arms,
flying up out of the courtyard in front of my apartment with the sun in his
face, could see higher and further than I, the only daughter of the Jodhras, ever
could. By the moonlight in the palace courtyard I climbed the vine, like something from one of ayah's fairy tales of gods and demons. The steel monkey led
on, over balconies, along ledges, over carvings of heroes from legends and full-
breasted apsara women. I never thought how high I was: I was as light and
luminous as the bird-man. Now the steel monkey beckoned me, squatting on

THE DUST ASSASSIN   53

the parapet with only the stars above it. I dragged myself up onto the roof. Instantly an army of machine monkeys reared up before me like Hanuman's host. Metal gleamed, they bared their antipersonnel weapons: needle throwers tipped with lethal neurotoxins. My family has always favoured poison. I raised my hand and they melted away at the taste of my body chemistry, all but my guide. It skipped and bounded before me. I walked barefoot through a moonlit world of domes and turrets, with every step drawn closer to the amber sky-glow of the city outside. Our palace presented a false front of bays and windows and jharokas to the rude people in the street: I climbed the steps behind the façade until I stood on the very top, the highest balcony. A gasp went out of me. Great Jaipur lay before me, a hive of streetlights and pulsing neons, the reds and whites and blinking yellows of vehicles swarming along the Johan Bazaar, the trees hung with thousands of fairy lights, like stars fallen from the night, the hard fluorescent shine of the open shop fronts, the glowing waver of the tivi screens, the floodlight pools all along the walls of the old city: all, all reflected in the black water of the moat my father had built around his palace. A moat, in the middle of a drought.

The noise swirled up from the street: traffic, a hundred musics, a thousand voices. I swayed on my high perch but I was not afraid. Softness brushed against my leg, my steel monkey pressed close, clinging to the warm pink stone with plastic fingers. I searched the web of light for the sharp edges of the Jantar Mantar, the observatory my ancestors had built three hundred years before. I made out the great wedge of the Samrat Yantra, seven stories tall, the sundial accurate to two seconds; the floodlit bowls of the Jai Prakash Yantra, mapping out the heavens on strips of white marble. The hot night wind tugged at my pajamas; I smelled biodiesel, dust, hot fat, spices carried up from the thronged bazaar. The steel monkey fretted against my leg, making a strange keening sound, and I saw out on the edge of the city: a slash of light down the night, curved like a sail filled with darkness. A tower, higher than any of the others of the new industrial city on the western edges of Jaipur. The glass tower of the Azads, our enemies, as different as could be from our old-fashioned Rajput-style palace: glowing from within with blue light. And I thought, *I am to bring that tower to the ground.*

Then, voices. Shouts. *Hey, you. Up there. Where? There. See that? What is it? Is it a man? I don't know. Hey, you, show yourself.* I leaned forwards, peered carefully down. Light blinded me. At the end of the flashlight beams were two palace guards in combat armour, weapons trained on me. *It's all right, it's all right, don't shoot, for gods' sake, it's the girl.*

"Memsahb," a soldier called up. "Memsahb, stay exactly where you are, don't move a muscle, we're coming to get you."

I was still staring at the glowing scimitar of the Azad tower when the roof door opened and the squad of guards came to bring me down.

Next morning I was taken to my father in his audience Diwan. Climate-mod fields held back the heat and the pollution; the open, stone-pillared hall was cool and still. My father sat on his throne of cushions between the two huge silver jars, taller than two of me, that were always filled with water from the holy River Ganga. My father drank a glass at every dawn every morning. He was a very traditional Rajput. I saw the plastic coil of his lighthoek behind his ear. To him his Diwan was full of attendants: his virtual aeai staff, beamed through his skull into his visual centres, busy busy busy on the affairs of Jodhra Water.

My brothers had been summoned and sat uncomfortably on the floor, pulling at their unfamiliar, chafing old-fashioned costumes. This was to be a formal occasion. Heer knelt behind him, hands folded in yts sleeves. I could not read yts eyes behind yts polarised black lenses. I could never read anything about Heer. Not man, not woman—*yt*—yts muscles lay in unfamiliar patterns under yts peach-smooth skin. I always felt that yt did not like me.

The robot lay on its back, deactivated, limbs curled like the dry dead spiders I found in the corners of my room where ayah Harpal was too lazy to dust.

"That was a stupid, dangerous thing to do," my father said. "What would have happened if our jawans had not found you?"

I set my jaw and flared my nostrils and rocked on my cushions.

"I just wanted to see. That's my right, isn't it? It's what you're educating me for, that world out there, so it's my right to see it."

"When you are older. When you are a . . . woman. The world is not safe, for you, for any of us."

"I saw no danger."

"You don't need to. All danger has to do is see you. The Azad assassins—"

"But I'm a weapon. That's what you always tell me, I'm a weapon, so how can the Azads harm me? How can I be a weapon if I'm not allowed to see what I'm to be used against?"

But the truth was I didn't know what that meant, what I was meant to do to bring that tower of blue glass collapsing down into the pink streets of Jaipur.

"Enough. This unit is defective."

My father made a gesture with his fingers and the steel monkey sprang up, released. It turned its head in its this-way, that-way gesture I knew so well, confused. In the same instant, the walls glittered with light reflecting from moving metal as the machines streamed down the carved stonework and across the pink marble courtyard. The steel monkey gave a strange, robot cry and made to flee, but the reaching plastic paws seized it and pulled it down and turned it on its back and circuit by circuit, chip by chip, wire by wire, took it to pieces. When they had finished there was no part of my steel monkey left big enough to see. I felt the tightness in my chest, my throat, my head of about-to-cry, but I would not, I would never, not in front of these men. I glanced again at Heer. Yts black lenses gave nothing, as ever. But the way the sun glinted from those insect eyes told me yt was looking at me.

My life changed that day. My father knew that something between us had been taken apart like the artificial life of the steel monkey. But I had seen beyond the walls of my life, so I was allowed out from the palace a little way into the world. With Heer, and guards, in armoured German cars to bazaars and malls; by tilt-jet to relatives in Jaisalmer and Delhi; to festivals and melas and pujas in the Govind temple. I was still schooled in the palace by tutors and aeai artificial intelligences, but I was presented with my new friends, all the daughters of high-ranking, high-caste company executives, carefully vetted and groomed. They wore all the latest fashions and makeup and jewellery and shoes and tech. They dressed me and styled me and wove brass and amber beads into my hair; they took me to shops and pool parties— in the heart of a drought—and cool summer houses up in the mountains, but they were never comfortable like friends, never free, never friends at all. They were afraid of me. But there were clothes and trips and Star Asia tunes and celebrity gupshup and so I forgot about the steel monkey that I once pretended was my friend and was taken to pieces by its brothers.

Others had not forgotten.

They remembered the night after my fourteenth birthday. There had been a puja by the Govind priest in the Diwan. It was a special age, fourteen, the age I became a woman. I was blessed with fire and ash and light and water and given a sari, the dress of a woman. My friends wound it around me and decorated my hands with mehndi, intricate patterns in dark henna. They set the red bindi of the Kshatriya caste over my third eye and led me out through the rows of applauding company executives and then to a great party. There were gifts and kisses, the food was laid out the length of the courtyard, and there were press reporters and proper French champagne that I was allowed to drink because I was now a woman. My father had arranged a music set by MTV-star Anila—real, not artificial intelligence—and in my new woman's finery I jumped up and down and screamed like any other of my teenage girlfriends. At the very end of the night, when the staff took the empty silver plates away and Anila's roadies folded up the sound system, my father's jawans brought out the great kite of the Jodhras, the winged man-bird the colour of fire, and sent him up, shining, into the night above Jaipur, up towards the hazy stars. Then I went to my new room, in the zenana, the women's quarter, and old disgusting ayah Harpal locked the carved wooden door to my nursery.

It was that that saved me, when the Azads struck.

I woke an instant before Heer burst through the door, but in that split second was all the confusion of waking in an unfamiliar bed, in a strange room, in an alien house, in a body you do not fully know as your own.

Heer. Here. Not Heer. Dressed in street clothes. Men's clothes. Heer, with a gun in yts hand. The big gun with the two barrels, the one that killed people and the one that killed machines.

"Memsahb, get up and come with me. You must come with me."

"Heer—"

"Now, memsahb."

Mouth working for words, I reached for clothes, bag, shoes, things. Heer threw me across the room to crash painfully against the Rajput chest.

"How dare—" I started and, as if in slow motion, I saw the gun fly up.

A flash, like lightning in the room. A metallic squeal, a stench of burning, and the smoking steel shell of a defence robot went spinning across the marble floor like a burning spider. Its tail was raised, its stinger erect. Not knowing if this was some mad reality or if I was still in a dream, I reached my hand towards the dead machine. Heer snatched me away.

"Do you want to die? It may still be operational."

Yt pushed me roughly into the corridor, then turned to fire a final e-m charge into the room. I heard a long keening wail like a cork being turned in a bottle that faded into silence. In that silence I heard for the first time the sounds. Gunfire, men shouting, men roaring, engines revving, aircraft overhead, women crying. Women wailing. And everywhere, above and below, the clicking scamper of small plastic feet.

"What's going on?" Suddenly I was chilled and trembling with dread. "What's happened?"

"The House of Jodhra is under attack," Heer said.

I pulled away from yts soft grip.

"Then I have to go, I have to fight, I have to defend us. I am a weapon."

Heer shook yts head in exasperation and with yts gun hand struck me a ringing blow on the side of my head.

"Stupid stupid! Understand! The Azads, they are killing everything! Your father, your brothers, they are killing everyone. They would have killed you, but they forgot you moved to a new room."

"Dadaji? Arvind, Kiran?"

Heer tugged me along, still reeling, still dizzy from the blow but more dazed, more stunned by what the nute had told me. My father, my brothers . . .

"Mamaji?" My voice was three years old.

"Only the geneline."

We rounded a corner. Two things happened at the same time. Heer shouted, "Down!" and as I dived for the smooth marble I glimpsed a swarm of monkey-machines bounding towards me, clinging to walls and ceiling. I covered my head and cried out with every shot as Heer fired and fired and fired until the gas-cell canister clanged to the floor.

"They hacked into them and reprogramed them. Faithless, betraying things. Come *on*." The smooth, manicured hand reached for me and I remember only shards of noise and light and dark and bodies until I found myself in the backseat of a fast German car, Heer beside me, gun cradled like a baby. I could smell hot electricity from the warm weapon. Doors slammed. Locks sealed. Engine roared.

"Where to?"

"The Hijra Mahal."

As we accelerated through the gate more monkey-robots dropped from the naqqar khana. I heard their steel lives crack and burst beneath our wheels. One clung to the door, clawing at the window frame until the driver veered and scraped it off on a streetlight.

"Heer . . ."

Inside it was all starting to burst, to disintegrate into the colours and visions and sounds and glances of the night. My father my head my brothers my head my mother my family my head my head my head.

"It's all right," the nute said, taking my hand in yts. "You're safe. You're with us now."

The House of Jodhra, which had endured for a thousand years, fell, and I came to the house of the nutes. It was pink, as all the great buildings of Jaipur were pink, and very discreet. In my life *before*, as I now thought of it, I must have driven past its alleyway a hundred times without ever knowing the secret it concealed: cool marble rooms and corridors behind a façade of orioles and turrets and intricately carved windows, courts and tanks and water-gardens open only to the sky and the birds. But then the Hijra Mahal had always been a building apart. In another age it had been the palace of the hijras, the eunuchs. The un-men, shunned yet essential to the ritual life of Rajput Jaipur, living in the very heart of the old city, yet apart.

There were six of them: Sul, the janampatri seer, astrologer to celebs as far away as the movie boulevards of Mumbai; Dahin, the plastic surgeon, who worked on faces on the far side of the planet through remote machines accurate to the width of an atom; Leel, the ritual dancer, who performed the ancient Nautch traditions and festival dances; Janda, the writer, whom half of India knew as Queen Bitch of gupshup columnists; Suleyra, whose parties and events were the talk of society from Srinagar to Madurai; and Heer, once khidmutgar to the House of Jodhra. My six guardians bundled me from the car wrapped in a heavy chador like a Muslim woman and took me to a domed room of a hundred thousand mirror fragments. Their warm, dry hands gently held me on the divan—I was thrashing, raving, as the shock hit me—and Dahin the face surgeon deftly pressed an efuser to my arm.

"Hush. Sleep now."

I woke among the stars. For an instant I wondered if I was dead, stabbed in my sleep by the poison needle of an Azad assassin robot that had scaled the hundred windows of the Jodhra Mahal. Then I saw that they were the mirror shards of the ceiling, shattering the light of a single candle into a hundred thousand pieces. Heer sat cross-legged on a dhurrie by my low bedside.

"How long . . ."

"Two days, child."

"Are they . . ."

"Dead. Yes. I cannot lie. Every one."

But even as the House of Jodhra fell, it struck back like a cobra, its back broken by a stick. Homing missiles, concealed for years, clinging like bats under shop eaves and bus shelters, unfolded their wings and lit their engines and sought out the pheromone profiles of Azad vehicles. Armoured Lexuses went up in fireballs in the middle of Jaipur's insane traffic as they hooted their way towards the safety of the airport. No safety even there: a Jodhra missile locked on to the company tilt-jet as it lifted off, hooked into the engine intake with its titanium claws until the aircraft reached an altitude at which no one could survive. The blast cast momentary shadows across the sundials of the Jantar Mantar, marking the moment of Jodhra revenge. Burning debris set fires all across the slums.

"Are they . . ."

"Jahangir and the Begum Azad died in the tilt-jet attack and our missiles took out much of their board, but their countermeasures held off our attack on their headquarters."

"Who survived?"

"Their youngest son, Salim. The line is intact."

I sat up in my low bed that smelled of sandalwood. The stars were jewels around my head.

"It's up to me then."

"Memsahb—"

"Don't you remember what he said, Heer? My father? *You are a weapon, never forget that.* Now I know what I am a weapon for."

"Memsahb . . . Padmini." The first time yt had ever spoken my name. "You are still shocked; you don't know what you're saying. Rest. You need rest. We'll talk in the morning." Yt touched yts forefinger to yts full lips, then left. When I could no longer hear soft footfalls on cool marble, I went to the door. Righteousness, rage, and revenge were one song inside me. Locked. I heaved, I beat, I screamed. The Hijra Mahal did not listen. I went to the balcony that hung over the alley. Even if I could have shattered the intricate stone jali, it was a ten-metre drop to street level where the late-night hum of phatphat autorickshaws and taxis was giving way to the delivery drays and cycle-vans of the spice merchants. Light slowly filled up the alley and crept across the floor of my bedroom: by its gathering strength I could read the headlines of the morning editions. WATER WARS: DOZENS DEAD IN CLASH OF THE RAJAS. JAIPUR REELS AS JODHRAS ANNIHILATED. POLICE POWERLESS AGAINST BLOODY VENDETTA.

In Rajputana, now as always, water is life, water is power. The police, the judges, the courts: we owned them. Us, and the Azads. In that we were alike. When gods fight, what mortal would presume to judge?

"A ride in triumph, a fall through a window into love, a marriage, and a mourning?" I asked. "That's it?"

Sul the astrologer nodded slowly. I sat on the floor of yts observatory. Incense rose on all sides of me from perforated brass censors. At first glance, the room was so simple and bare that even a saddhu would have been uncomfortable, but as my eyes grew accustomed to the shadow in which it must be kept to work as a prediction machine, I saw that every centimetre of the bare pink marble was covered in curving lines and Hindi inscriptions, so small and precise they might be the work of tiny gods. The only light came from a star-shaped hole in the domed ceiling: Sul's star chamber was in the topmost turret of the Hijra Mahal, closest to heaven. As yt worked

with yts palmer and made the gestures in the air of the janampatri calculations, I watched a star of dazzling sunlight crawl along an arc etched in the
floor, measuring out the phases of the House of Meena. Sul caught me
staring at yt, but I had only been curious to see what another nute looked
like, close up. I had only ever known Heer. I had not known there could be
as many as six nutes in the whole of India, let alone Jaipur. Sul was fat and
had unhealthy yellow skin and eyes and shivered a lot as yt pulled yts shawl
around yt, though the turret room directly under the sun was stifling hot. I
looked for clues to what yt had been before: woman, man. *Woman*, I thought.
I had always thought of Heer as a man—an ex-man, though yt never mentioned the subject. I had always known it was taboo. When you Stepped
Away, you never looked back.

"No revenge, no justice?"

"If you don't believe me, see for yourself."

Fingers slipped the lighthoek behind my ear and the curving lines on the
floor leaped up into mythical creatures studded with stars. Makara the Croc-
odile, Vrishaba the Bull, the twin fishes of Meena; the twelve rashi. Kanya
the dutiful daughter. Between them the twenty-seven nakshatars looped and
arced, each of them subdivided into four padas; wheels within wheels within
wheels, spinning around my head like blades as I sat on Sul's marble floor.

"You know I can't make any sense out of this," I said, defeated by the
whirling numbers. Sul leaned forwards and gently touched my hand.

"A ride in triumph, a fall through a window into love, a marriage, and a
mourning. Window to widow. Trust me."

"Young girls are truly beautiful on the inside." Dahin the dream doctor's voice
came from beyond the bank of glaring surgical lights as the bed on which I lay
tilted back. "No pollution, no nasty dirty hormones. Everything clean and fresh
and lovely. Most of the women who come here, I never see any deeper than their
skin. It is a rare privilege to be allowed to look inside someone."

It was midnight in the chrome and plastic surgery in the basement of the
Hijra Mahal, a snatched half hour between the last of the consultations
(society ladies swathed in veils and chadors to hide their identities) and
Dahin hooking into the global web, settling the lighthoek over the visual

centre in yts brain and pulling on the manipulator gloves connected to surgical robots in theatres half a world away. So gentle, so deft; too agile for any man. Dahin of the dancing hands.

"Have you found it yet?" I asked. My eyes were watering from the lights. Something in them, something beyond them, was looking into my body and displaying it section by section, organ by organ, on Dahin's inner vision. Traditionally, the hijras were the only ones allowed to examine the bodies of the zenana women and reported their findings to the doctors outside.

"Found what? Finger lasers? Retractable steel claws? A table-top nuke wired into your tummy?"

"My father said over and over, I'm a weapon, I'm special . . . I will destroy the House of Azad."

"Cho chweet, if there's anything there, this would have shown it to me."

My eyes were watering. I pretended it was the brightness of the light.

"Maybe there's something . . . smaller, something you can't see, like . . . bugs. Like a disease."

I heard Dahin sigh and imagined the waggle of yts head.

"It'll take a day or two but I can run a diagnostic." Tippy-tapping by my ear. I turned my head and froze as I saw a spider robot no bigger than my thumb move towards my throat. It was a month since *the night*, but still I was distrustful of robots. I imagined I always would be. I felt a little flicking needle pain in the side of my neck, then the robot moved over my belly. I cringed at the soft spiking of its sharp, precise feet. I said, "Dahin, do you mind me asking—did you do this?"

A short jab of pain in my belly.

"Oh yes, baba. All this, and more. Much much more. I only work on the outside, the externals. To be like me—to become one of us—you have to go deep, right down into the cells."

Now the robot was creeping over my face. I battled the urge to sweep it away and crush it on the floor. I was a weapon, I was special. This machine would show me how.

"Woman, man, that's not a thing easily undone. They take you apart, baba. Everything, hanging there in a tank of fluid. Then they put you back together again. Different. Neither. Better."

Why, I wanted to ask, *why do this thing to yourself?* But then I felt a tiny scratch in the corner of my eye as the robot took a scrape from my optic nerve.

"Three days for the test results, baba."

Three days, and Dahin brought the results to me as I sat in the Peacock Pavilion overlooking the bazaar. The wind was warm and smelled of ashes of roses as it blew through the jali and turned the delicately handwritten sheets. No implants. No special powers or abilities. No abnormal neural structures, no tailored combat viruses. I was a completely normal fourteen-year-old Kshatriya girl.

I leaped over the swinging stick. While still in the air, I brought my own staff up in a low arc, catching the Azad's weapon between his hands. It flew from his grasp, clattered across the wooden floor of the hall. He threw a kick at me, rolled to pick up his pole, but my swinging tip caught him hard against the temple, sending him down to the floor like dropped laundry. I vaulted over him, swung my staff high to punch its brass-shod tip into the nerve cluster under the ear. Instant death.

"And finish."

I held the staff millimetres away from my enemy's brain. Then I slipped the lighthoek from behind my ear and the Azad vanished like a djinn. Across the practice floor, Leel set down yts staff and unhooked yts 'hoek. In yts inner vision yts representation of me—enemy, sparring partner, pupil—likewise vanished. As ever at these practice sessions, I wondered what shape Leel's avatar took. Yt never said. Perhaps yt saw me.

"All fighting is dance, all dance is fighting." That was Leel's first lesson to me on the day yt agreed to train me in Silambam. For weeks I had watched yt from a high balcony as yt practised the stampings and head movements and delicate hand gestures of the ritual dances. Then one night after yt had dismissed yts last class, something told me, *Stay on*, and I saw yt strip down to a simple dhoti and take out the bamboo staff from the cupboard and leap and whirl and stamp across the floor, the attacks and defences of the ancient Keralan martial art.

"Since it seems I was not born a weapon, then I must become a weapon."

Leel had the dark skin of a southerner and I always felt that yt was very much older than yt appeared. I also felt—again with no evidence—that yt was the oldest inhabitant of the Hijra Mahal, that yt had been there long before any of the others came. I felt that yt might once have been a hijra and that the dance moves it practised and taught were from the days when no festival or wedding was complete without the outrageous, outcast eunuchs.

"Weapon, so? Cut anyone tries to get close to you, then when you've cut everyone, you cut yourself. Better things for you to be than a weapon."

I asked Leel that same question every day until one evening thick with smog and incense from the great Govind festival yt came to me as I sat in my window reading the chati channels on my lighthoek.

"So. The stick fighting."

That first day, as I stood barefoot on the practice floor in my Adidas baggies and stretchy sports top trying to feel the weight and heft of the fighting staff in my hands, I had been surprised when Leel fitted the lighthoek behind my ear. I had assumed I would spar against the guru ytself.

"Vain child. With what I teach you, you can kill. With one blow. Much safer to fight your image, in here." Yt tapped yts forehead. "As you fight mine. Or whatever you make me."

All that season I learned the dance and ritual of Silambam; the leaps and the timings and the sweeps and the stabs. The sharp blows and the cries. I blazed across the practice floor yelling Kerala battle hymns, my staff a blur of thrusts and parries and killing strokes.

"Heavy child, heavy. Gravity has no hold on you, you must fly. Beauty is everything. See?" And Leel would vault on yts staff and time seemed to freeze around yt, leaving yt suspended there, like breath, in midair. And I began to understand about Leel, about all the nutes in this house of hijras. Beauty was everything, a beauty not male, not female; something else. A third beauty.

The hard, dry winter ended and so did my training. I went down in my Adidas gear and Leel was in yts dance costume, bells ringing at yts ankles. The staffs were locked away.

"This is so unfair."

"You can fight with the stick, you can kill with a single blow, how much more do you need to become this weapon you so want to be?"

"But it takes years to become a master."

"You don't need to become a master. And that is why I have finished your training today, because you should have learned enough to understand the perfect uselessness of what you want to do. If you can get close, if you ever learn to fly, perhaps you might kill Salim Azad, but his soldiers will cut you apart. Realise this, Padmini Jodhra. It's over. They've won."

In the morning, when the sun cast pools of light in the shapes of birds onto the floor of the little balcony, Janda would drink coffee laced with paan and, lazily lifting a finger to twirl away another page in yts inner vision, survey the papers the length and breadth of India, from the Rann of Kutch to the Sundarbans of Bengal.

"Darling, how can you be a bitch if you don't *read?*"

In the afternoon over tiffin, Janda would compose yts scandalous gossip columns: who was doing what with whom where and why, how often and how much, and what all good people should think. Yt never did interviews. Reality got in the way of creativity.

"They love it, sweetie. Gives them an excuse to get excited and run to their lawyers. First real emotion some of them have felt in years."

At first I had been scared of tiny, monkeylike Janda, always looking, checking, analysing from yts heavily kohled eyes, seeking weaknesses for yts acid tongue. Then I saw the power that lay in yts cuttings and clippings and entries, taking a rumour here, a whisper there, a suspicion yonder, and putting them together into a picture of the world. I began to see how I could use it as a weapon. Knowledge was power. So as dry winter gave way to thirsty spring and the headlines in the streets clamoured MONSOON SOON? and RAJPUTANA DEHYDRATES, Janda helped me build a picture of Salim Azad and his company. Looking beyond those sensationalist headlines to the business sections I grew to recognise his face beneath the headlines: AZAD PLUNDERS CORPSE OF RIVALS. SALIM AZAD: REBUILDER OF A DYNASTY. AZAD WATER IN FIVE RIVERS PROJECT. In the society section I saw him at weddings and parties and premiers. I saw him skiing in Nepal and shopping in New York and at the races in Paris. In the stock-market feeds I watched the value of Azad Water climb as deals were struck, new investments announced, takeovers and buyouts made public. I learned Salim Azad's taste in pop music, restaurants, tailors, designers, filmi stars, fast fast cars. I could tell you the names of the people who hand-sewed his shoes, who wrote the novel on his bedside table, who massaged his head and lit cones of incense along his spine, who flew his private tilt-jets and programed his bodyguard robots.

One smoggy, stifling evening as Janda cleared away the thalis of sweetmeats yt gave me while I worked ("Eat, darling, eat and act") I noticed the lowlight illuminate two ridges of shallow bumps along the inside of yts forearm. I remembered seeing them on Heer all my life and had always known they were as much part of a nute as the absence of any sexual organs, as the delicate bones and the long hands and the bare skull. In the low, late light they startled me because I had never asked, *What are they for?*

"For? Dear girl." Janda clapped yts soft hands together. "For love. For making love. Why else would we bear these nasty, ugly little goose bumps? Each one generates a different chemical response in our brains. We touch, darling. We play each other like instruments. We feel . . . things you cannot. Emotions for which you have no name, for which the only name is to experience them. We Step Away to somewhere not woman, not man; to the nute place."

Yt turned yts arm wrist-upwards to me so that yts wide sleeve fell away. The two rows of mosquito-bite mounds were clear and sharp in the yellow light. I thought of the harmonium the musicians would play in the old Jodhra Palace, fingers running up and down the buttons, the other hand squeezing the bellows. Play any tune on it. I shuddered. Janda saw the look on my face and snatched yts arm back into yts sleeve. And then, laid on in the newspaper in front of me was an emotion for which I had no name, which I could only know by experiencing it. I thought no one knew more than I about Salim Azad, but here was a double spread of him pushing open the brass-studded gates of the Jodhra Mahal, my old home, where his family annihilated mine, under the screaming headline: AZAD BURIES PAST, BUYS PALACE OF RIVALS. Below that, Salim Azad standing by the pillars of the Diwan, shading his eyes against the sun, as his staff ran our burning sun-man-bird kite up above the turrets and battlements into the hot yellow sky.

In the costume and makeup of Radha, divine wife of Krishna, I rode the painted elephant through the pink streets of Jaipur. Before me the band swung and swayed, its clarinets and horns rebounding from the buildings. Around and through the players danced Leel and the male dancer in red, swords flashing and clashing, skirts whirling, bells ringing. Behind me came another twenty elephants, foreheads patterned with the colours of Holi, howdahs streaming pennons and gold umbrellas. Above me robot aircraft trailed vast, gossamer-light banners bearing portraits of the Holy Pair and divine blessings. Youths and children in red wove crimson patterns with smoke-sticks and threw handfuls of coloured powder into the crowd. *Holi Hai! Holi Hai!* Reclining beside me on the golden howdah, Suleyra waved yts flute to the crowd. Jaipur was an endless tunnel of sound: people cheering, holiday shouts, the hooting of phatphat horns.

"Didn't I tell you you needed to get out of that place, cho chweet?"

In the blur of days inside the Hijra Mahal, I had not known that a year had passed without me setting foot outside its walls. Then Suleyra, the fixer, the jester, the party maker, had come skipping into my room, pointed yts flute at me, and said, "Darling, you simply must be my wife," and I had realised that it was Holi, the Elephant Festival. I had always loved Holi, the brightest, maddest of festivals.

"But someone might see me—"

"Baba, you'll be blue all over. And anyway, no one can touch the bride of a god on her wedding day."

And so, blue from head to toe, I reclined on gilded cushions beside Suleyra, who had been planning this public festival for six months, equally blue and not remotely recognisable as anything human, man, woman, or nute. The city was clogged with people, the streets stifling hot, the air so thick with hydrocarbon fumes that the elephants wore smog goggles and I loved every bit of it. I was set free from the Hijra Mahal.

A wave of Suleyra/Krishna's blue hand activated the chips in the elephant's skull and turned it left through the arched gateway to the Old City, behind the boogying band and the leaping, sword-wielding dancers. The crowds spilled off the arcades onto the street, ten, twenty deep. Every balcony was lined; women and children threw handfuls of colour down on us. Ahead I could see a platform and a canopy. The band was already marching in place while Leel and yts partner traded mock blows.

"Who is up there?" I asked, suddenly apprehensive.

"A most important dignitary," said Suleyra, taking the praise of the spectators. "A very rich and powerful man."

"Who is he, Suleyra?" I asked. Suddenly, I was cold in the stinking heat of Jaipur. *"Who is he?"*

But the dancers and the band had moved on and now our elephant took their place in front of the podium. A tap from Suleyra's Krishna-flute: the elephant wheeled to face the dais and bent its front knees in a curtsey. A tall, young man in a Rajput costume with a flame red turban stood up to applaud, face bright with delight.

I knew that man's shoe size and star sign. I knew the tailor who had cut his suit and the servant who wound his turban. I knew everything about him, except that he would be here, reviewing the Holi parade. I tensed myself to leap. One blow; Suleyra's Krishna-flute would suffice as a weapon. But I did nothing, for I saw a thing more incredible. Behind Salim Azad, bending forwards, whispering in his ear, eyes black as obsidian behind polarising lenses, was Heer.

Salim Azad clapped his hands in delight.

"Yes, yes, this is the one! Bring her to me. Bring her to my palace."

So I returned from the Palace of the Hijras to the Palace of the Jodhras, which was now the Palace of the Azads. I came through the brass gates under the high tower from which I had first looked out across Jaipur on the night of the steel monkey, across the great courtyard. The silver jars of holy Ganga water still stood on either side of the Diwan where my father had managed his water empire. Beneath the gaze of the gods and the monkeys on the walls, I was dragged out of the car by Azad jawans who carried me, screaming and kicking, up the stairs to the zenana. "My brother lay there, my mother died there, my father died there," I shouted at them as they dragged me along that same corridor down which I had fled a year before. The marble floors were pristine, polished. I could not remember where the blood had been. Women retainers waited for me at the entrance to the zenana, for men could not enter the women's palace, but I flew and kicked and punched at them with all the skills Leel had taught me. They fled shrieking, but all that happened was the soldiers held me at gunpoint until house robots arrived. I could kick and punch all I liked and never lay a scratch on their spun-diamond carapaces.

In the evening I was brought to the Hall of Conversations, an old and lovely room where women could talk and gossip with men across the delicate stone jali that ran the length of the hall. Salim Azad walked the foot-polished marble. He was dressed as a Rajput, in the traditional costume. I thought he looked like a joke. Behind him was Heer. Salim Azad paced up and down for five minutes, studying me. I pressed myself to the jali and tried to stare him down.

Finally he said, "Do you have everything you want? Is there anything you need?"

"Your heart on a thali," I shouted. Salim Azad took a step back.

"I'm sorry about the necessity of this . . . But please understand, you're not my prisoner. We are the last. There has been enough death. The only way I can see to finish this feud is to unite our two houses. But I won't force you, that would be . . . impolite. Meaningless. I have to ask and you have to answer me." He came as close to the stonework as was safe to avoid my Silambam punch. "Padmini Jodhra, will you marry me?"

It was so ridiculous, so stupid and vain and so impossible, that in my shock, I felt the word *yes* in the back of my throat. I swallowed it down, drew back my head, and spat long and full at him. The spit struck a moulding and ran down the carved sandstone.

"Understand I have nothing but death for you, murderer."

"Even so, I shall ask every day, until you say yes," Salim Azad said. With a whisk of robes, he turned and walked away. Heer, hands folded in yts sleeves, eyes pebbles of black, followed.

"And you, hijra," I yelled, reaching a clawing hand through the stone jali to seize, to rip. "You're next, traitor."

That night I thought about starving myself to death, like the great Gandhiji when he battled the British to make India free and their empire had stepped aside for one old, frail, thin, starving man. I shoved my fingers down my throat and puked up the small amount of food I had forced myself to eat that evening. Then I realised that starved and dead I was no weapon. The House of Azad would sail undisturbed into the future. It was the one thing that kept me alive, kept me sane in those first days in the zenana—my father's words: *You are a weapon.* All I had to discover was what kind.

In the night a small sweeper came and cleaned away my puke.

It was as he said. Every evening as the sun touched the battlements of the Nahargarh Fort on the hill above Jaipur, Salim Azad came to the Hall of Conversations. He would talk to me about the history of his family; back twenty generations to central Asia, from where they had swept down into the great river plains of Hindustan to build an empire of unparalleled wealth and elegance and beauty. They had not been warriors or rulers. They had been craftsmen and poets, makers of exquisite fine miniatures and jewel-like verses in Urdu, the language of poets. As the great Mughals erected their forts and palaces and fought their bloody civil wars, they had advanced from court painters and poets to court advisors, then to viziers and khidmutgars, not just to the Mughals, but to the Rajputs, the Marathas, and later to the East India Company and the British Raj. He told me tales of illustrious ancestors and stirring deeds; of Aslam, who rode out between the armies of rival father and son emperors and saved the Panjab; of Farhan, who carried love notes between the English resident of Hyderabad and the daughter of the Nizam and almost destroyed three kingdoms; of Shah Hussain, who had struggled with Gandhi against the British for India, who had been approached by Jinnah to support partition and the creation of Pakistan but who had refused, though his family had all but been annihilated in the ethnic holocaust following Independence. He told me of Elder Salim, his grandfather, founder of the dynasty, who had come to Jaipur when the monsoon failed the first terrible time in 2008 and set up village water reclamation schemes that over the decades became the great water empire of the Azads. Strong men, testing times, thrilling stories. And every night, as the sun dipped behind Nahargarh Fort, he said, "Will you marry me?" Every night I turned away from him without a word. But night by night, story by story, ancestor by ancestor, he chipped away at my silence. These were people as real, as vital as my own family. Now their stories had all ended. We two were the last.

I tried to call Janda at the Hijra Mahal, to seek wisdom and comfort from my sister/brothers, to find out if they knew why Heer had turned and betrayed me but mostly to hear another voice than the sat channels or Salim

Azad. My calls bounced. White noise: Salim had my apartments shielded with a jamming field. I flung the useless palmer against the painted wall and ground it under the heel of my jewelled slipper. I saw endless evenings reaching out before me. Salim would keep coming, night after night, until he had his answer. He had all the time in the world. Did he mean to drive me mad to marry him?

Marry him. This time I did not push the thought away. I turned it this way, that way, studied it, felt out its implications. Marry him. It was the way out of this marble cage.

In the heat of midday, a figure in voluminous robes came hurrying down the cool corridor to the zenana. Heer. I had summoned yt. Because yt was not a man yt could enter the zenana, like the eunuchs of the Rajput days. Yt did not fear the skills Leel had taught me. Yt knew. Yt namasted.

"Why have you done this to me?"

"Memsahb, I have always been, and remain, a loyal servant of the House of Jodhra."

"You've given me into the hands of my enemies."

"I have saved you from the hands of your enemies, Padmini. It would not just be the end of this stupid, pointless, bloody vendetta. He would make you a partner. Padmini, listen to what I am saying: you would be more than just a wife. Azad Jodhra. A name all India would learn."

"Jodhra Azad."

Heer pursed yts rosebud lips.

"Padmini Padmini, always, this pride."

And yt left without my dismissal.

That night in the blue of the magic hour Salim Azad came again to the zenana, a pattern of shadows beyond the jali. I saw him open his lips. I put a finger up to mine.

"Ssh. Don't speak. Now it's time for me to tell you a story, my story, the story of the House of Jodhra."

So I did, for one hundred and one nights, like an old Muslim fairy tale, seated on cushions leaning up against the jali, whispering to Salim Azad in his Rajput finery wonderful tales of dashing Kshatriya cavalry charges and thousand-cannon sieges of great fortresses, of handsome princes with bold moustaches and daring escapes with princesses in disguise in baskets over battlements, of princedoms lost over the fall of a chessman and Sandhurst-trained sowar officers more British than the British themselves and air-cav raids against Kashmiri insurgents and bold antiterrorist strikes; of great polo matches and spectacular durbars with a hundred elephants and the man-bird-sun kite of the Jodhras sailing up into the sky over Jaipur; for a thousand years our city. For one hundred nights I bound him with spells taught to me by the nutes of the Hijra Mahal, then on the one hundred and first night I said, "One thing you've forgotten."

"What?"

"To ask me to marry you."

He gave a little start, then waggled his head in disbelief and smiled. He had very good teeth.

"So, will you marry me?"

"Yes," I said. "Yes."

The day was set three weeks hence. Sul had judged it the most propitious for a wedding of dynasties. Suleyra had been commissioned to stage the ceremony: Muslim first, then Hindu. Janda had been asked to draw on yts celebrity inside knowledge to invite all India to the union of the houses of Azad and Jodhra. *This is the wedding of the decade*, yt cried in yts gupshup columns, *come or I will bad-mouth you*. Schedules of the great and glorious were rearranged, aeai soapi stars prepared avatars to attend, as did those human celebs who were unavoidably out of the subcontinent. From the shuttered jharokas of the zenana I watched Salim order his staff and machines around the great court, sending architects here, fabric designers there, pyrotechnicians yonder. Marquees and pavilions went up, seating was positioned, row upon row, carpet laid, patterns drawn in sand to be obliterated by the feet of the processional elephants. Security robots circled among the carrion-eating black kites over the palace, camera drones flitted like bats around the great court, seeking angles. Feeling my eyes on him, Salim would glance up at me, smile, lift his hand in the smallest greeting. I glanced away, suddenly shy, a girl-bride. This was to be a traditional, Rajputana wedding. I would emerge from purdah only to meet my husband. For those three weeks, the zenana was not a marble cage but an egg from which I would hatch. Into what? Power, unimaginable wealth, marriage to a man who had been my enemy. I still did not know if I loved him or not. I still saw the ghost shadows on the marble where his family had destroyed mine. He still came every night to read me Urdu poetry I could not understand. I smiled and laughed but I still did not know if what I felt was love, or just my desperation to be free. I still doubted it on the morning of my wedding.

Women came at dawn to bathe and dress me in wedding yellow and make up my hair and face and anoint me with turmeric paste. They decked me with jewels and necklaces, rings and bangles. They dabbed me with expensive perfume from France and gave me good luck charms and advice. Then they threw open the brass-studded doors of the zenana and, with the palace guard of robots, escorted me along the corridors and down the stairs to the great court. Leel danced and somersaulted before me; no wedding could be lucky without a hijra, a nute.

All of India had been invited and all of India had come, in flesh and in avatar. People rose, applauding. Cameras swooped on ducted fans. My nutes, my family from the Hijra Mahal, had been given seats at row ends.

"How could I improve on perfection?" said Dahin the face doctor as my bare feet trod rose petals towards the dais.

"The window, the wedding!" said Sul. "And, pray the gods, many many decades from now, a very old and wise widow."

"The setting is nothing without the jewel," exclaimed Suleyra Party Arranger, throwing pink petals into the air.

I waited with my attendants under the awning as Salim's retainers crossed the courtyard from the men's quarters. Behind them came the groom on his pure white horse, kicking up the rose petals from its hooves. A low, broad *ooh* went up from the guests then more applause. The maulvi welcomed Salim onto the platform. Cameras flocked for angles. I noticed that every parapet and carving was crowded with monkeys—flesh and machine—watching. The maulvi asked me most solemnly if I wished to be Salim Azad's bride.

"Yes," I said, as I had said the night when I first accepted his offer. "I do, yes."

He asked Salim the same question, then read from the Holy Quran. We exchanged contracts, our assistants witnessed. The maulvi brought the silver plate of sweetmeats. Salim took one, lifted my gauze veil, and placed it on my tongue. Then the maulvi placed the rings upon our fingers and proclaimed us husband and wife. And so were our two warring houses united, as the guests rose from their seats cheering and festival crackers and fireworks burst over Jaipur and the city returned a roaring wall of vehicle horns. Peace in the streets at least. As we moved towards the long, cool pavilions for the wedding feast, I tried to catch Heer's eye as yt paced behind Salim. Yts hands were folded in the sleeves of yts robes, yts head thrust forwards, lips pursed. I thought of a perching vulture.

We sat side by side on golden cushions at the head of the long, low table. Guests great and good took their places, slipping off their Italian shoes, folding their legs and tucking up their expensive Delhi frocks as waiters brought vast thalis of festival food. In their balcony overlooking the Diwan, musicians struck up, a Rajput piece older than Jaipur itself. I clapped my hands. I had grown up to this tune. Salim leaned back on his bolster.

"And look."

Where he pointed, men were running up the great sun-bird-man kite of the Jodhras. As I watched it skipped and dipped on the erratic winds in the court, then a stronger draught took it soaring up into the blue sky. The guests went *oooh* again.

"You have made me the happiest man in the world," Salim said.

I lifted my veil, bent to him, and kissed his lips. Every eye down the long table turned to me. Everyone smiled. Some clapped.

Salim's eyes went wide. Tears suddenly streamed from them. He rubbed them away, and when he put his hands down, his eyelids were two puffy, blistered boils of flesh, swollen shut. He tried to speak but his lips were bloated, cracked, seeping blood and pus. Salim tried to stand, push himself away from me. He could not see, could not speak, could not breathe. His hands fluttered at the collar of his gold-embroidered sherwani.

"Salim!" I cried. Leel was already on yts feet, ahead of all the guest doctors and surgeons as they rose around the table. Salim let out a thin, high-pitched wail, the only scream that would form in his swollen throat. Then he went down onto the feast table.

The pavilion was full of screaming guests and doctors shouting into palmers and security staff locking the area down. I stood useless as a butterfly in my makeup and wedding jewels and finery as doctors crowded around Salim. His face was like a cracked melon, a tight bulb of red flesh. I swatted away an intrusive hovercam. It was the best I could do. Then I remember Leel and the other nutes taking me out into the courtyard where a tilt-jet was settling, engines sending the rose petals up in a perfumed blizzard. Paramedics carried Salim out from the pavilion on a gurney. He wore an oxygen rebreather. There were tubes in his arms. Security guards in light-scatter armour pushed the great and the celebrated aside. I struggled with Leel as the medics slid Salim into the tilt-jet but yt held me with strange, withered strength.

"Let me go, let me go, that's my husband—"

"Padmini, Padmini, there is nothing you can do."

"What do you mean?"

"Padmini, he is dead. Salim your husband is dead."

Yt might have said that the moon was a great mouse in the sky.

"Anaphylactic shock. Do you know what that is?"

"Dead?" I said simply, quietly. Then I was flying across the court towards the tilt-jet as it powered up. I wanted to dive under its engines. I wanted to be scattered like the rose petals. Security guards ran to cut me off but Leel caught me first and brought me down. I felt the nip of an efuser on my arm and everything went soft as the tranquilizer took me.

After three weeks I called Heer to me. For the first week the security robots had kept me locked back in the zenana while the lawyers argued. I spent much of that time out of my head, part grief-stricken, part insane at what had happened. Just one kiss. A widow no sooner than I was wed. Leel tended to me; the lawyers and judges reached their legal conclusions. I was the sole and lawful heir of Azad-Jodhra Water. The second week I came to terms with my inheritance: the biggest water company in Rajputana, the third largest in the whole of India. There were contracts to be signed, managers and executives to meet, deals to be set up. I waved them away, for the third week was my week, the week in which I understood what I had lost. And I understood what I had done, and how, and what I was. Then I was ready to talk to Heer.

We met in the Diwan, between the great silver jars that Salim, dedicated to his new tradition, had kept topped up with holy Ganga water. Guard-monkeys kept watch from the rooftops. My monkeys. My Diwan. My palace. My company, now. Heer's hands were folded in yts sleeves. Yts eyes were black marble. I wore widow's white—a widow, at age fifteen.

"How long had you planned it?"

"From before you were born. From before you were even conceived."

"I was always to marry Salim Azad."

"Yes."

"And kill him."

"You could not do anything but. You were designed that way."

Always remember, my father had said, here among these cool, shady pillars, *you are a weapon.* A weapon deeper, subtler than I had ever imagined, deeper even than Dahin's medical machines could look. A weapon down in the DNA: designed from conception to cause a fatal allergic reaction in any member of the Azad family. An assassin in my every cell, in every pore and hair, in every fleck of dust shed from my deadly skin.

I killed my beloved with a kiss.

I felt a huge, shuddering sigh inside me, a sigh I could never, must never utter.

"I called you a traitor when you said you had always been a loyal servant of the House of Jodhra."

"I was, am, and will remain so, please God." Heer dipped yts hairless head in a shallow bow. Then yt said, "When you become one of us, when you Step Away, you step away from so much: from your own family, from the hope of ever having children . . . You are my family, my children. All of you, but most of all you, Padmini. I did what I had to for my family, and now you survive, now you have all that is yours by right. We don't live long, Padmini. Our lives are too intense, too bright, too brilliant. There's been too much done to us. We burn out early. I had to see my family safe, my daughter triumph."

"Heer . . ."

Yt held up a hand, glanced away, I thought I saw silver in the corners of those black eyes.

"Take your palace, your company, it is all yours."

That evening I slipped away from my staff and guards. I went up the marble stairs to the long corridor where my room had been before I became a woman, and a wife, and a widow, and the owner of a great company. The door unlocked to my thumbprint; I swung it open into dust-hazy golden sunlight. The bed was still made, mosquito nets neatly knotted up. I crossed to the balcony. I expected the vines and creepers to have grown to a jungle; with a start I realized it was just over a year since I had slept here. I could still pick out the handholds and footholds where I had followed the steel monkey up onto the roof. I had an easier way there now. A door at the end of the corridor, previously locked to me, now opened onto a staircase. Sentry robots immediately bounced up as I stepped out onto the roof, crests raised, dart-throwers armed. A mudra from my hand sent them back into watching mode.

Once again I walked between the domes and turrets to the balcony at the very top of the palace façade. Again, Great Jaipur at my bare feet took my breath away. The pink city kindled and burned in the low evening light. The streets still roared with traffic; I could smell the hot oil and spices of the bazaar. I now knew how to find the domes of the Hijra Mahal among the confusion of streets and apartment buildings. The dials and half-domes and buttresses of the Jantar Mantar threw huge shadows over each other, a confusion of clocks. Then I turned towards the glass scimitar of the Azad Headquarters—my headquarters now, my palace as much as this dead old Rajput pile. I had brought that house crashing down, but not in any way I had imagined. I wanted to apologise to Salim as he had apologised to me, every night when he came to me in the zenana, for what his family had done. *They always told me I was a weapon. I thought I must become one; I never thought they had made me into one.*

How easy to step out over the traffic, step away from it all. Let it all end, Azad and Jodhra. Cheat Heer of yts victory. Then I saw my toes with their rings curl over the edge and I knew I could not, must not. I looked up and there, at the edge of vision, along the bottom of the red horizon, was a line of dark. The monsoon, coming at last. My family had made me one kind of weapon, but my other family, the kind, mad, sad, talented family of the nutes, had taught me, in their various ways, to be another weapon. The streets were dry but the rains were coming. I had reservoirs and canals and pumps and pipes in my power. I was Maharani of the Monsoon. Soon the people would need me. I took a deep breath and imagined I could smell the rain. Then I turned and walked back through the waiting robots to my kingdom.

AN ELIGIBLE BOY

*A*robot is giving Jasbir the whitest teeth in Delhi. It is a precise, terrifying procedure involving chromed steel and spinning, shrieking
abrasion heads. Jasbir's eyes go wide as the spidery machine-arms flourish
their weapons in his face, a demon of radical dentistry. He read about the
Glinting Life! Cosmetic Dentistry Clinic (Hygienic, Quick, and Modern) in
the February edition of *Shaadi! For Eligible Boys*. In double-page spread it
looked nothing like these insect-mandibles twitching inside his mouth. He'd
like to ask the precise and demure dental nurse (married, of course) if it's
meant to be like this, but his mouth is full of clamps and anyway an Eligible
Boy never shows fear. But he closes his eyes as the robot reaches in and spinning steel hits enamel.

Now the whitest teeth in Delhi dart through the milling traffic in a rattling phatphat. He feels as if he is beaming out over an entire city. The
whitest teeth, the blackest hair, the most flawless skin and perfectly plucked
eyebrows. Jasbir's nails are beautiful. There's a visiting manicurist at the

Ministry of Waters, so many are the civil servants on the shaadi circuit. Jasbir notices the driver glancing at his blinding smile. He knows; the people on Mathura Road know, all Delhi knows that every night is great game night.

On the platform of Cashmere Café Metro Station, chip-implanted police-monkeys canter, shrieking, between the legs of passengers, driving away the begging, tugging, thieving macaques that infest the subway system. They pour over the edge of the platform to their holes and hides in a wave of brown fur as the robot train slides into the stop. Jasbir always stands next to the Women Only section. There is always a chance one of them might be scared of the monkeys— they bite—and he could then perform an act of Spontaneous Gallantry. The women studiously avoid any glance, any word, any sign of interest, but a true Eligible Boy never passes up a chance for contact. But that woman in the business suit, the one with the fashionable wasp-waist jacket and the low-cut hip-riding pants, was she momentarily dazzled by the glint of his white white teeth?

"A robot, madam," Jasbir calls as the packer wedges him into the 18:08 to Barwala. "Dentistry of the future." The doors close. But Jasbir Dayal knows he is a white-toothed Love God and this, this will be the shaadi night he finally finds the wife of his dreams.

Economists teach India's demographic crisis as an elegant example of market failure. Its seed germinated in the last century, before India became Tiger of Tiger economies, before political jealousies and rivalries split her into twelve competing states. *A lovely boy*, was how it began. *A fine, strong, handsome, educated, successful son, to marry and raise children and to look after us when we are old.* Every mother's dream, every father's pride. Multiply by the three hundred million of India's emergent middle class. Divide by the ability to determine sex in the womb. Add selective abortion. Run twenty-five years down the x-axis, factoring in refined, twenty-first-century techniques such as cheap, powerful pharma patches that ensure lovely boys will be conceived and you arrive at great Awadh, its ancient capital Delhi of twenty million, and a middle class with four times as many males as females. Market failure. Individual pursuit of self-interest damages larger society. Elegant to economists; to fine, strong, handsome, educated, successful young men like Jasbir caught in a wife-drought, catastrophic.

There's a ritual to shaadi nights. The first part involves Jasbir in the bathroom for hours playing pop music too loud and using too much expensive water while Sujay knocks and leaves copious cups of tea at the door and runs an iron over Jasbir's collars and cuffs and carefully removes the hairs of previous shaadis from Jasbir's suit jacket. Sujay is Jasbir's housemate in the government house at Acacia Bungalow Colony. He's a character designer on the Awadh version of *Town and Country*, neighbour-and-rival Bharat's all-conquering artificial intelligence–generated soap opera. He works with the extras, designing new character skins and dropping them over raw code from Varanasi. Jahzay Productions is a new model company, meaning that Sujay seems to do most of his work from the verandah on his new-fangled lighthoek device, his hands drawing pretty, invisible patterns on air. To office-bound Jasbir, with a ninety-minute commute on three modes of transport each way each day, it looks pretty close to nothing. Sujay is uncommunicative and hairy and neither shaves nor washes his too-long hair enough, but his is a sensitive soul and compensates for the luxury of being able to sit in the cool cool shade all day waving his hands by doing housework. He cleans, he tidies, he launders. He is a fabulous cook. He is so good that Jasbir does not need a maid, a saving much to be desired in pricey Acacia Bungalow Colony. This is a source of gossip to the other residents of Acacia Bungalow Colony. Most of the goings-on in Number 27 are the subject of gossip over the lawn sprinklers. Acacia Bungalow Colony is a professional, family gated community.

The second part of the ritual is the dressing. Like a syce preparing a Mughal lord for battle, Sujay dresses Jasbir. He fits the cufflinks and adjusts them to the proper angle. He adjusts the set of Jasbir's collar just so. He examines Jasbir from every angle as if he is looking at one of his own freshly fleshed characters. Brush off a little dandruff here, correct a desk-slumped posture there. Smell his breath and check teeth for lunchtime spinach and other dental crimes.

"So what do you think of them then?" Jasbir says.

"They're white," grunts Sujay.

The third part of the ritual is the briefing. While they wait for the phat-phat, Sujay fills Jasbir in on upcoming plotlines on *Town and Country*. It's Jasbir's major conversational ploy and advantage over his deadly rivals: soap-opera gossip. In his experience what the women really want is gupshup from the meta-soap, the no-less-fictitious lives and loves and marriages and rows of the aeai actors that believe they are playing the roles in *Town and Country*. "Auh," Sujay will say. "Different department."

There's the tootle of phatphat horns. Curtains will twitch, there will be complaints about waking up children on a school night. But Jasbir is glimmed and glammed and shaadi-fit. And armed with soapi gupshup. How can he fail?

"Oh, I almost forgot," Sujay says as he opens the door for the God of Love. "Your father left a message. He wants to see you."

"You've hired a what?" Jasbir's retort is smothered by the cheers of his brothers from the living room as a cricket ball rolls and skips over the boundary rope at Jawaharlal Nehru Stadium. His father bends closer, confidentially across the tiny tin-topped kitchen table. Anant whisks the kettle off the boil so she can overhear. She is the slowest, most awkward maid in Delhi but to fire her would be to condemn an old woman to the streets. She lumbers around the Dayal kitchen like a buffalo, feigning disinterest.

"A matchmaker. Not my idea, not my idea at all; it was hers." Jasbir's father inclines his head towards the open living room door. Beyond it, enthroned on her sofa amidst her noneligible boys, Jasbir's mother watches the test match on the smartsilk wallscreen Jasbir had bought her with his first civil service paycheck. When Jasbir left the tiny, ghee-stinky apartment on Nabi Karim Road for the distant graces of Acacia Bungalow Colony, Mrs. Dayal delegated all negotiations with her wayward son to her husband. "She's found this special matchmaker."

"Wait wait wait. Explain to me *special*."

Jasbir's father squirms. Anant is taking a long time to dry a teacup.

"Well, you know in the old days people would maybe have gone to a hijra . . . Well, she's updated it a bit, this being the twenty-first century and everything, so she's, ah, found a nute."

A clatter of a cup hitting a stainless steel draining board.

"A *nute*?" Jasbir hisses.

"He knows contracts. He knows deportment and proper etiquette. He knows what women want. I think he may have been one, once."

Anant lets out an *aie!* soft and involuntary as a fart.

"I think the word you're looking for is *yt*," Jasbir says. "And they're not hijras the way you knew them. They're not men become women or women become men. They're neither."

"Nutes, neithers, hijras, yts, hes, shes—whatever; it's not as if I even get to take tea with the parents let alone see an announcement in the shaadi section in the *Times of Awadh*," Mrs. Dayal shouts over the burbling commentary to the second Awadh-China Test. Jasbir winces. Like paper cuts, the criticisms of parents are the finest and the most painful.

Inside the Haryana Polo and Country Club the weather was raining men, snowing men, hailing men. Well-dressed men, moneyed men, charming men, groomed and glinted men, men with prospects all laid out in their marriage résumés. Jasbir knew most of them by face. Some he knew by name; a few had passed beyond being rivals to become friends.

"Teeth!" A cry, a nod, a two-six-gun showbiz point from the bar. There leaned Kishore, a casual lank of a man draped like a skein of silk against the Raj-era mahogany. "Where did you get those, badmash?" He was an old university colleague of Jasbir's, much given to high-profile activities like horse racing at the Delhi Jockey Club or skiing, where there was snow left on the Himalayas. Now he was In Finance and claimed to have been to five hundred shaadis and made a hundred proposals. But when they were on the hook, wriggling, he let them go. *Oh, the tears, the threats, the phone calls from fuming fathers and boiling brothers. It's the game, isn't it?* Kishore rolls on, "Here, have you heard? Tonight is Deependra's night. Oh yes. An astrology aeai has predicted it. It's all in the stars, and on your palmer."

Deependra was a clenched wee man. Like Jasbir he was a civil servant, heading up a different glass-partitioned work cluster in the Ministry of Waters: Streams and Watercourses to Jasbir's Ponds and Dams. For three shaadis now he had been nurturing a fantasy about a woman who exchanged palmer addresses with him. First it was a call, then a date. Now it's a proposal.

"Rahu is in the fourth house, Saturn in the seventh," Deependra said lugubriously. "Our eyes will meet, she will nod—just a nod. The next morning she will call me and that will be it, done, dusted. I'd ask you to be one of my groomsmen, but I've already promised all my brothers and cousins. It's written. Trust me."

It is a perpetual bafflement to Jasbir how a man wedded by day to robust fluid accounting by night stakes love and life on an off-the-shelf janampatri artificial intelligence.

A Nepali khidmutgar banged a staff on the hardwood dance floor of the exclusive Haryana Polo and Country Club. The Eligible Boys straightened their collars, adjusted the hang of their jackets, aligned their cufflinks. This side of the mahogany double doors to the garden they were friends and colleagues. Beyond it they were rivals.

"Gentlemen, valued clients of the Lovely Girl Shaadi Agency, please welcome, honour, and cherish the Begum Rezzak and her Lovely Girls!"

Two attendants slid open the folding windows onto the polo ground. There waited the lovely girls in their saris and jewels and gold and henna (for the Lovely Girl Agency is a most traditional and respectable agency). Jasbir checked his schedule—five minutes per client, maybe less, never more. He took a deep breath and unleashed his thousand-rupee smile. It was time to find a wife.

"Don't think I don't know what you're muttering about in there," Mrs. Dayal calls over the mantra commentary of Harsha Bhogle. "I've had the talk. The nute will arrange the thing for much less than you are wasting on all those shaadi agencies and databases and nonsense. No, nute will make the match that is it stick stop stay." There is a spatter of applause from the test match.

"I tell you your problem: a girl sees two men sharing a house together, she gets ideas about them," Dadaji whispers. Anant finally sets down two cups of tea and rolls her eyes. "She's had the talk. Yt'll start making the match. There's nothing to be done about it. There are worse things."

The women may think what they want, but Sujay has it right, Jasbir thinks. *Best never to buy into the game at all.*

Another cheer, another boundary. Haresh and Sohan jeer at the Chinese devils. *Think you can buy it in and beat the world, well, the Awadhi boys are here to tell you it takes years, decades, centuries upon centuries to master the way of cricket.* And there's too much milk in the tea.

A dream wind like the hot gusts that forerun the monsoon sends a spray of pixels through the cool, white, spacious rooms of 27 Acacia Bungalow Colony. Jasbir ducks and laughs as they blow around him. He expects them to be cold and sharp as wind-whipped powder snow but they are only digits, patterns of electrical charge swept through his visual cortex by the clever little device hooked behind his right ear. They chime as they swirl past, like glissandos of silver sitar notes. Shaking his head in wonder, Jasbir slips the lighthoek from behind his ear. The vision evaporates.

"Very clever, very pretty, but I think I'll wait until the price comes down."

"It's, um, not the 'hoek," Sujay mutters. "You know, well, the match-maker your mother hired. Well, I thought, maybe you don't need someone arranging you a marriage."

Some days Sujay's inability to talk to the point exasperates Jasbir. Those days tend to come after another fruitless and expensive shaadi night and the threat of a matchmaker, but particularly after Deependra of the nonwhite teeth announces he has a date. With the girl. The one written in the fourth house of Rahu by his pocket astrology aeai.

"Well, you see, I thought, with the right help you could arrange it your-self." Some days debate with Sujay is pointless. He follows his own calendar. "You, ah, need to put the 'hoek back on again."

Silver notes spray through Jasbir's inner ears as the little curl of smart plastic seeks out the sweet spot in his skull. Pixel birds swoop and swarm like starlings on a winter evening. It is inordinately pretty. Then Jasbir gasps aloud as the motes of light and sound sparklingly coalesce into a dapper man in an old-fashioned high-collar sherwani and wrinkle-bottom pajamas. His shoes are polished to mirror-brightness. The dapper man bows.

"Good morning, sir. I am Ram Tarun Das, Master of Grooming, Grace, and Gentlemanliness."

"What is this doing in my house?" Jasbir unhooks the device beaming data into his brain.

"Er, please don't do that," Sujay says. "It's not aeai etiquette."

Jasbir slips the device back on and there he is, that charming man.

"I have been designed with the express purpose of helping you marry a suitable girl," says Ram Tarun Das.

"Designed?"

"I, ah, made him for you," says Sujay. "I thought that if anyone knows about relationships and marriages, it's soap stars."

"A soap star. You've made me a . . . a marriage life-coach out of a soap star?"

"Not a soap star exactly, more a conflation of a number of subsystems from the central character register," Sujay says. "Sorry, Ram."

"Do you usually do that?"

"Do what?"

"Apologise to aeais."

"They have feelings too."

Jasbir rolls his eyes. "I'm being taught husbandcraft by a mash-up."

"Ah, that is out of order. Now you apologise."

"Now then, sir, if I am to rescue you from a marriage forged in hell, we had better start with manners," says Ram Tarun Das. "Manners maketh the man. They form the bedrock of all relationships because true manners come from what he is, not what he does. Do not argue with me, women see this at once. Respect for all things, sir, is the key to etiquette. Maybe I only imagine I feel as you feel, but that does not make my feelings any less real to me. So this once I accept your apology as read. Now, we'll begin. We have so much to do before tonight's shaadi."

Why, Jasbir thinks, *why can I never get my shoes like that?*

The lazy crescent moon lolls low above the outflarings of Tughluk's thousand stacks; a cradle to rock an infant nation. Around its rippling reflection in the infinity pool bob mango-leaf diyas. No polo grounds and country clubs for Begum Jaitly. This is 2045, not 1945. Modern style for a modern nation, that is the philosophy of the Jaitly Shaadi Agency. But gossip and want are eternal and in the mood lighting of the penthouse the men are blacker-than-black shadows against greater Delhi's galaxy of lights and traffic.

"Eyebrows!" Kishore greets Jasbir with TV-host pistol-fingers two-shot bam bam. "No, seriously, what did you do to them?" Then his own eyes widen as he scans down from the eyebrows to the total product. His mouth opens, just a crack, but wide enough for Jasbir to savour an inner fist-clench of triumph.

He'd felt self-conscious taking Ram Tarun Das to the mall. He had no difficulty accepting that the figure in its stubbornly atavistic costume was invisible to everyone but him (though he did marvel at how the aeai avoided colliding with any other shopper in thronged Centrestage Mall). He did feel stupid talking to thin air.

"What is this delicacy?" Ram Tarun Das said in Jasbir's inner ear. "People talk to thin air on the cell phone all the time. Now, this suit, sir."

It was bright, it was brocade, it was a fashionable retro cut that Jasbir would have gone naked rather than wear.

"It's very . . . bold."

"It's very you. Try it. Buy it. You will seem confident and stylish without being flashy. Women cannot bear flashy."

The robot cutters and stitchers were at work even as Jasbir completed the card transaction. It was expensive. *Not as expensive as all the shaadi memberships*, he consoled himself. *And something to top it off.* But Ram Tarun Das manifested himself right in the jeweller's window over the display.

"Never jewellery on a man. One small brooch at the shirt collar to hold it together; that is permissible. Do you want the lovely girls to think you are a Mumbai pimp? No, sir, you do not. No to jewels. Yes to shoes. Come."

He had paraded his finery before a slightly embarrassed Sujay.

"You look, er, good. Very dashing. Yes."

Ram Tarun Das, leaning on his cane and peering intensely, said, "You move like a buffalo. Ugh, sir. Here is what I prescribe for you. Tango lessons. Passion and discipline. Latin fire, yet the strictest of tempos. Do not argue; it is the tango for you. There is nothing like it for deportment."

The tango, the manicures, the pedicures, the briefings in popular culture and Delhi gossip ("soap opera insults both the intelligence and the imagination, I should know, sir"), the conversational ploys, the body language games of when to turn so, when to make or break eye contact, when to dare the lightest, engaging touch. Sujay mooched around the house, even more lumbering and lost than usual, as Jasbir chatted with air and practised Latin turns and drops with an invisible partner. Last of all, on the morning of the Jaitly shaadi.

"Eyebrows, sir. You will never get a bride with brows like a hairy saddhu. There is a girl not five kilometres from here. She has a moped service. I've ordered her, and she will be here within ten minutes."

As ever, Kishore won't let Jasbir wedge an answer in, but rattles on, "So, Deependra, then?"

Jasbir has noticed that Deependra is not occupying his customary place in Kishore's shadows; in fact he does not seem to be anywhere in this penthouse.

"Third date," Kishore says, then mouths it again silently for emphasis. "That janampatri aeai must be doing something right. You know, wouldn't it be funny if someone took her off him? Just as a joke, you know?"

Kishore chews his bottom lip. Jasbir knows the gesture of old. Then bells chime, lights dim, and a wind from nowhere sends the butter-flames flickering and the little diyas flocking across the infinity pool. The walls have opened. The women enter the room.

She stands by the glass wall looking down into the cube of light that is the car park. She clutches her cocktail between her hands as if in prayer or concern. It is a new cocktail designed for the international cricket test, served in an egg-shaped goblet made from a new spin-glass that will always self-right, no matter how it is set down or dropped. A *Test of Dragons* is the name of the cocktail. Good Awadhi whisky over a gilded syrup with a six-hit of Chinese Kao Liang liqueur. A tiny red gel dragon dissolves like a sunset.

"Now, sir," whispers Ram Tarun Das, standing at Jasbir's shoulder. "Faint heart, as they say."

Jasbir's mouth is dry. A secondary application Sujay pasted onto the Ram Tarun Das aeai tells him his precise heart rate, respiration, temperature, and the degree of sweat in his palm. He's surprised he's still alive.

You've got the entry lines, you've got the exit lines, and the stuff in the middle Ram Tarun Das will provide.

He follows her glance down into the car park. A moment's pause, a slight inclination of his body towards hers. That is *the line*.

So, are you a Tata, a Mercedes, a Li Fan, or a Lexus? Ram Tarun Das whispers in Jasbir's skull. He casually repeats the line. He has been rehearsed and rehearsed and rehearsed in how to make it sound natural. He's as good as any newsreader, better than those few human actors left on television.

She turns to him, lips parted a fraction in surprise.

"I beg your pardon?"

She will say this, Ram Tarun Das hints. *Again, offer the line.*

"Are you a Tata, a Mercedes, a Li Fan, or a Lexus?"

"What do you mean?"

"Just pick one. Whatever you feel, that's the right answer."

A pause, a purse of the lips. Jasbir subtly links his hands behind his back, the better to hide the sweat.

"Lexus," she says. Shulka, her name is Shulka. She is a twenty-two-year-old marketing graduate from Delhi U working in men's fashion, a Mathur—only a couple of caste steps away from Jasbir's folk. The Demographic Crisis has done more to shake up the tiers of varna and jati than a century of the slow drip of democracy. And she has answered his question.

"Now, that's very interesting," says Jasbir.

She turns, plucked crescent-moon eyebrows arched. Behind Jasbir, Ram Tarun Das whispers, *Now, the fetch.*

"Delhi, Mumbai, Kolkata, Chennai?"

A small frown now. Lord Vishnu, she is beautiful.

"I was born in Delhi . . ."

"That's not what I mean."

The frown becomes a nano-smile of recognition.

"Mumbai, then. Yes, Mumbai definitely. Kolkata's hot and dirty and nasty. And Chennai—no, I'm definitely Mumbai."

Jasbir does the sucked-in-lip-nod of concentration Ram Tarun Das made him practise in front of the mirror.

"Red green yellow blue?"

"Red." No hesitation.

"Cat dog bird monkey?"

She cocks her head to one side. Jasbir notices that she, too, is wearing a 'hoek. Tech girl. The cocktail bot is on its rounds, doing industrial magic with the self-righting glasses and its little spider-fingers.

"Bird . . . no." A sly smile. "No no no. Monkey."

He is going to die he is going to die.

"But what does it mean?"

Jasbir holds up a finger.

"One more. Ved Prakash, Begum Vora, Dr. Chatterji, Ritu Parvaaz."

She laughs. She laughs like bells from the hem of a wedding skirt. She laughs like the stars of a Himalaya night.

What do you think you're doing? Ram Tarun Das hisses. He flips through Jasbir's perceptions to appear behind Shulka, hands thrown up in despair. With a gesture he encompasses the horizon wreathed in gas flares. *Look, tonight the sky burns for you, sir, and you would talk about soap opera! The script, stick to the script! Improvisation is death.* Almost Jasbir tells his matchmaker, *Away, djinn, away.* He repeats the question.

"I'm not really a *Town and Country* fan," Shulka says. "My sister now, she knows every last detail about every last one of the characters, and that's before she gets started on the actors. It's one of those things I suppose you can be ludicrously well informed about without ever watching. So if you had to press me, I would have to say Ritu. So what does it all mean, Mr. Dayal?"

His heart turns over in his chest. Ram Tarun Das eyes him coldly. *The* finesse: *make it. Do it just as I instructed you. Otherwise your money and my band-width are thrown to the wild wind.*

The cocktail bot dances in to perform its cybernetic circus. A flip of Shulka's glass and it comes down spinning, glinting, on the precise needle-point of its forefinger. Like magic, if you know nothing about gyros and spin-glasses. But that moment of prestidigitation is cover enough for Jasbir to make the ordained move. By the time she looks up, cocktail refilled, he is half a room away.

He wants to apologise as he sees her eyes widen. He needs to apologise as her gaze searches the room for him. Then her eyes catch his. It is across a crowded room just like the song that Sujay mumbles around the house when he thinks Jasbir can't hear. Sujay loves that song. It is the most romantic, heartfelt, innocent song he has ever heard. Big, awkward Sujay has always been a sucker for veteran Hollywood musicals. *South Pacific, Carousel, Moulin Rouge*, he watches them on the big screen in the living room, singing shame-lessly along and getting moist-eyed at the impossible loves. Across a crowded room, Shulka frowns. Of course. It's in the script.

But what does it mean? she mouths. And, as Ram Tarun Das has directed, he shouts back, "Call me and I'll tell you." Then he turns on his heel and walks away. And that, he knows without any prompt from Ram Tarun Das, is the *finesse*.

The apartment is grossly overheated and smells of singeing cooking ghee, but the nute is swaddled in a crocheted shawl, hunched as if against a persistent hard wind. Plastic teacups stand on the low brass table, Jasbir's mother's conspicuously untouched. Jasbir sits on the sofa with his father on his right and his mother on his left, as if between arresting policemen. Nahin the nute mutters and shivers and rubs yts fingers.

Jasbir has never been in the physical presence of a third-gendered. He knows all about them—as he knows all about most things—from the Single-Professional-Male general interest magazines to which he subscribes. Those pages, between the ads for designer watches and robot tooth whitening, portray them as fantastical *Arabian Nights* creatures equally blessed and cursed with glamour. Nahin the matchmaker seems old and tired as a god, knotting and unknotting yts fingers over the papers on the coffee table—"The bloody drugs, darlings"—occasionally breaking into great spasmodic shudders. *It's one way of avoiding the Wife Game*, Jasbir thinks.

Nahin slides sheets of paper around on the tabletop. The documents are patterned as rich as damask with convoluted chartings of circles and spirals annotated in inscrutable alphabets. There is a photograph of a woman in each top-right corner. The women are young and handsome but have the wide-eyed expressions of being photographed for the first time.

"Now, I've performed all the calculations and these five are both compatible and auspicious," Nahin says. Yt clears a large gobbet of phlegm from yts throat.

"I notice they're all from the country," says Jasbir's father.

"Country ways are good ways," says Jasbir's mother.

Wedged between them on the short sofa, Jasbir looks over Nahin's shawled shoulder to where Ram Tarun Das stands in the doorway. He raises his eyebrows, shakes his head.

"Country girls are better breeders," Nahin says. "You said dynasty was a concern. You'll also find a closer match in jati, and in general they settle for a much more reasonable dowry than a city girl. City girls want it all. Me me me. No good ever comes of selfishness."

The nute's long fingers stir the country girls around the coffee table, then slide three towards Jasbir and his family. Dadaji and Mamaji sit forwards. Jasbir slumps back. Ram Tarun Das folds his arms, rolls his eyes.

"These three are the best starred," Nahin says. "I can arrange a meeting with their parents almost immediately. There would be some small expenditure in their coming up to Delhi to meet with you; this would be in addition to my fee."

In a flicker, Ram Tarun Das is behind Jasbir, his whisper a startle in his ear.

"There is a line in the Western wedding vows: speak now or forever hold your peace."

"How much is my mother paying you?" Jasbir says into the moment of silence.

"I couldn't possibly betray client confidentiality." Nahin has eyes small and dark as currants.

"I'll disengage you for an additional fifty percent."

Nahin's hands hesitate over the pretty hand-drawn spirals and wheels. *You were a man before,* Jasbir thinks. *That's a man's gesture. See, I've learned how to read people.*

"I double," shrills Mrs. Dayal.

"Wait wait wait," Jasbir's father protests but Jasbir is already shouting over him. He has to kill this idiocy here, before his family in their wedding fever fall into strategies they cannot afford.

"You're wasting your time and my parents' money," Jasbir says. "You see, I've already met a suitable girl."

Goggle eyes, open mouths around the coffee table, but none so astounded and gaping as Ram Tarun Das's.

The Prasads at Number 25 Acacia Bungalow Colony have already sent over a preemptive complaint about the tango music, but Jasbir flicks up the volume fit to rattle the brilliants on the chandelier. At first he scorned the dance—the stiffness, the formality, the strictness of the tempo. So very un-Indian. No one's uncle would ever dance this at a wedding. But he has persisted—never say that Jasbir Dayal is not a trier—and the personality of the tango has subtly permeated him, like rain into a dry riverbed. He has found the discipline and begun to understand the passion. He walks tall in Ponds and Dams. He no longer slouches at the watercooler.

"When I advised you to speak or forever hold your peace, sir, I did not actually mean lie through your teeth to your parents," Ram Tarun Das says. In tango he takes the woman's part. The lighthoek can generate an illusion of weight and heft so the aeai feels solid as Jasbir's partner. *If it can do all that, surely it could make him look like a woman?* Jasbir thinks. In his dedication to detail Sujay often overlooks the obvious. "Especially in matters where they can rather easily find you out."

"I had to stop them wasting their money on that nute."

"They would have kept outbidding you."

"Then, even more, I had to stop them wasting my money as well."

Jasbir knocks Ram Tarun Das's foot across the floor in a sweetly executed *barrida*. He glides past the open verandah door where Sujay glances up from soap-opera building. He has become accustomed to seeing his landlord tango cheek to cheek with an elderly Rajput gentleman. *Yours is a weird world of ghosts and djinns and half-realities*, Jasbir thinks.

"So how many times has your father called asking about Shulka?" Ram Tarun Das's free leg traces a curve on the floor in a well-executed *volcada*. Tango is all about seeing the music. It is making the unseen visible.

You know, Jasbir thinks, *you're woven through every part of this house like a pattern in silk.*

"Eight," he says weakly. "Maybe if I called her—"

"Absolutely not," Ram Tarun Das insists, pulling in breath-to-breath close in the *embreza*. "Any minuscule advantage you might have enjoyed, any atom of hope you might have entertained, would be forfeit. I forbid it."

"Well, can you at least give me a probability? Surely knowing everything you know about the art of shaadi, you could at least let me know if I've any chance?"

"Sir," says Ram Tarun Das, "I am a Master of Grooming, Grace, and Gentlemanliness. I can direct you to any number of simple and unsophisticated bookie-aeais; they will give you a price on anything, though you may not fancy their odds. One thing I will say: Miss Shulka's responses were very . . . suitable."

Ram Tarun Das hooks his leg around Jasbir's waist in a final *gancho*. The music comes to its strictly appointed conclusion. From behind it come two sounds. One is Mrs. Prasad weeping. She must be leaning against the party wall to make her upset so clearly audible. The other is a call tone, a very specific call tone, a deplorable but insanely hummable filmi hit—"My Back, My Crack, My Sack"—that Jasbir set on the house system to identify one caller, and one caller only.

Sujay looks up, startled.

"Hello?" Jasbir sends frantic, pleading hand signals to Ram Tarun Das, now seated across the room, his hands resting on the top of his cane.

"Lexus Mumbai red monkey Ritu Parvaaz,' says Shulka Mathur. "So what do they mean?"

"No, my mind is made up, I'm hiring a private detective," Deependra says, rinsing his hands. On the twelfth floor of the Ministry of Waters all the dating gossip happens at the wash-hand basins in the Number 16 Gentlemen's WC. Urinals: too obviously competitive. Cubicles: a violation of privacy. Truths are best washed with the hands at the basins and secrets and revelations can always be concealed by judicious use of the hot-air hand-drier.

"Deependra, this is paranoia. What's she done?" Jasbir whispers. A Level 0.3 aeai chip in the tap admonishes him not to waste precious water.

"It's not what she's done, it's what she's not done," Deependra hisses. "There's a big difference between someone not being available and someone deliberately not taking your calls. Oh yes. You'll learn this, mark my words. You're at the first stage, when it's all new and fresh and exciting and you are blinded by the amazing fact that someone, someone at last—at long last!—thinks you are a catch. It is all rose petals and sweets and cho chweet and you think nothing can possibly go wrong. But you pass through that stage, oh yes. All too soon the scales fall from your eyes. You see . . . and you hear."

"Deependra." Jasbir moves to the battery of driers. "You've been on five dates." But every word Deependra has spoken has chimed true. He is a cauldron of clashing emotions. He feels light and elastic, as if he bestrode the world like a god, yet at the same time the world is pale and insubstantial as muslin around him. He feels light-headed with hunger though he cannot eat a thing. He pushes away Sujay's lovingly prepared dals and roti. Garlic might taint his breath; saag might stick to his teeth; onions might give him wind;

bread might inelegantly bloat him. He chews a few cleansing cardamoms, in the hope of spiced kisses to come. Jasbir Dayal is blissfully, gloriously lovesick. Every date is a jewel; he told them up in his memory and revels in the light that shines through them.

Date One. The Qutb Minar. Jasbir had immediately protested.

"Tourists go there. And families on Saturdays."

"It's history."

"Shulka isn't interested in history."

"Oh, you know her so well after three phone conversations and two evenings chatting on shaadinet—which I scripted for you? It is roots; it is who you are and where you come from. It's family and dynasty. Your Shulka is interested in that, I assure you, sir. Now, here's what you will wear."

There were tour buses great and small. There were hawkers and souvenir peddlers. There were parties of frowning Chinese. There were schoolchildren with backpacks so huge they looked like upright tortoises. But wandering beneath the domes and along the colonnades of the Quwwat Mosque in his Casual Urban Explorer clothes, they seemed as remote and ephemeral as clouds. There was only Shulka and him. And Ram Tarun Das strolling at his side, hands clasped behind his back.

To cue, Jasbir paused to trace out the time-muted contours of a disembodied tirthankar's head, a ghost in the stone.

"Qutb-ud-din Aibak, the first Sultan of Delhi, destroyed twenty Jain temples and reused the stone to build his mosque. You can still find the old carvings if you know where to look."

"I like that," Shulka said. "The old gods are still here." Every word that fell from her lips was pearl-perfect. Jasbir tried to read her eyes, but her BlueBoo! cat-eye shades betrayed nothing. "Not enough people care about their history anymore. It's all modern this, modern that. If it's not up-to-the-minute it's irrelevant. I think that to know where you're going you need to know where you've come from."

Very good, Ram Tarun Das whispered. *Now, the iron pillar.*

They waited for a tour group of Germans to move away from the railed-off enclosure. Jasbir and Shulka stood in the moment of silence gazing at the black pillar.

"Sixteen hundred years old, but never a speck of rust on it," Jasbir said.

Ninety-eight percent pure iron, Ram Tarun Das prompted. *There are things Mittal Steel can learn from the Gupta kings.*

"'He who, having the name of Chandra, carried a beauty of countenance like the full moon, having in faith fixed his mind upon Vishnu, had this lofty standard of the divine Vishnu set up on the hill Vishnupada.'" Shulka's frown of concentration as she focused on the inscription around the pillar's waist was as beautiful to Jasbir as that of any god or Gupta king.

"You speak Sanskrit?"

"It's a sort of personal spiritual development path I'm following."

You have about thirty seconds before the next tour group arrives, Ram Tarun Das cuts in. *Now, sir: that line I gave you.*

"They say that if you stand with your back to the pillar and close your arms around it, your wish will be granted."

The Chinese were coming the Chinese were coming.

"And if you could do that, what would you wish for?"

Perfect. She was perfect.

"Dinner?"

She smiled that small and secret smile that set a garden of thorns in Jabsir's heart and walked away. At the centre of the gatehouse arch she turned and called back: "Dinner would be good."

Then the Chinese with their shopping bags and sun visors and plastic leisure shoes came bustling around the stainless iron pillar of Chandra Gupta.

Jasbir smiles at the sunny memory of Date One. Deependra waggles his fingers under the stream of hot air.

"I've heard about this. It was on a documentary, oh yes. White widows, they call them. They dress up and go to the shaadis and have their résumés all twinkling and perfect but they have no intention of marrying, oh no no no, not a chance. Why should they, when there is a never-ending stream of men to wine them and dine them and take them out to lovely places and buy them lovely presents and shoes and jewels, and even cars, so it said on the documentary. They are just in it for what they can get; they are playing games with our hearts. And when they get tired or bored or if the man is making too many demands or his presents aren't as expensive as they were or they can do better somewhere else, then *whoosh!* Dumped flat and onto the next one. It's a game to them."

"Deependra," says Jasbir. "Let it go. Documentaries on the Shaadi Channel are not the kind of model you want for married life. Really." Ram Tarun Das would be proud of that one. "Now, I have to get back to work." Faucets that warn about water crime can also report excessive toilet breaks to line managers. But the doubt-seeds are sown, and Jasbir now remembers the restaurant.

Date Two. Jasbir had practised with the chopsticks for every meal for a week. He swore at rice; he cursed dal. Sujay effortlessly scooped rice, dal, everything from bowl to lips in a flurry of stickwork.

"It's easy for you; you've got that code-wallah Asian culture thing."

"Um, we are Asian."

"You know what I mean. And I don't even like Chinese food; it's so bland."

The restaurant was expensive, half a week's wage. He'd make it up on overtime; there were fresh worries in Pools and Dams about a drought.

"Oh," Shulka said, the nightglow of Delhi a vast, diffuse halo behind her. *She is a goddess*, Jasbir thought, *a devi of the night city with ten million lights descending from her hair.* "Chopsticks." She picked up the antique porcelain chopsticks, one in each hand like drumsticks. "I never know what to do with chopsticks. I'm always afraid of snapping them."

"Oh, they're quite easy once you get the hang of them." Jasbir rose from his seat and came round behind Shulka. Leaning over her shoulder, he laid one stick along the fold of her thumb, the other between ball of thumb and tip of index finger. Still wearing her lighthoek. It's the city-girl look. Jasbir shivered in anticipation as he slipped the tip of her middle finger between the two chopsticks. "Your finger acts like a pivot, see? Keep relaxed, that's the key. And hold your bowl close to your lips." Her fingers were warm, soft, electric with possibility as he moved them. Did he imagine her skin scented with musk?

Now, said Ram Tarun Das from over Shulka's other shoulder. *Now do you see? And by the way, you must tell her that they make the food taste better.*

They did make the food did taste better. Jasbir found subtleties and piquancies he had not known before. Words flowed easily across the table. Everything Jasbir said seemed to earn her starlight laughter. Though Ram Tarun Das was as ubiquitous and unobtrusive as the waiting staff, they were all his own words and witticisms. *See, you can do this,* Jasbir said to himself. *What women want, it's no mystery: stop talking about yourself, listen to them, make them laugh.*

Over green tea Shulka began talking about that new novel everyone but everyone was reading, the one about the Delhi girl on the husband-hunt and her many suitors, the scandalous one, *An Eligible Boy.* Everyone but everyone but Jasbir.

Help! he subvocalized into his inner ear.

Scanning it now, Ram Tarun Das said. *Do you want a thematic digest, popular opinions, or character breakdowns?*

Just be there, Jasbir silently whispered, covering the tiny movement of his jaw by setting the teapot lid ajar, a sign for a refill.

"Well, it's not really a book a man should be seen reading . . ."

"But . . ."

"But isn't everyone?" Ram Tarun Das dropped him the line. "I mean, I'm only two-thirds of the way in, but . . . how far are you? Spoiler alert spoiler alert." It's one of Sujay's *Town and Country* expressions. Finally he understands what it means. Shulka just smiles and turns her tea bowl in its little saucer.

"Say what you were going to say."

"I mean, can't she see that Nishok is the one? The man is clearly, obviously, one thousand percent doting on her. But then that would be too easy, wouldn't it?"

"But Pran, it would always be fire with him. He's the baddest of badmashes but you'd never be complacent with Pran. She'll never be able to completely trust him and that's what makes it exciting. Don't you feel that sometimes it needs that little edge, that little fear that maybe, just maybe, you could lose it all, to keep it alive?"

Careful, sir, murmured Ram Tarun Das.

"Yes, but we've known ever since the party at the Chatterjis where she pushed Jyoti into the pool in front of the Russian ambassador that she's been jealous of her sister because she was the one who got to marry Mr. Panse. It's the eternal glamour versus security. Passion versus stability. Town versus country."

"Ajit?"

"Convenient plot device. Never a contender. Every woman he dates is just a mirror to his own sweet self."

Not one sentence, not one word had he read of the hit trash novel of the season. It had flown around his head like clatter-winged pigeons. He'd been too busy being that Eligible Boy.

Shulka held up a piece of sweet, salt, melting fatty duck breast between her porcelain forceps. Juice dripped onto the tablecloth.

"So, who will Bani marry, then? Guess correctly and you shall have a prize."

Jasbir heard Ram Tarun Das's answer begin to form inside his head. *No,* he gritted on his molars.

"I think I know."

"Go on."

"Pran."

Shulka stabbed forwards, like the darting bill of a winter crane. There was hot, fatty soya duck in his mouth.

"Isn't there always a twist in the tale?" Shulka said.

In the Number 16 Gentlemen's WC Deependra checks his hair in the mirror and smoothes it down.

"Dowry thievery; that's what it is. They string you along, get their claws into your money, then they disappear and you never see a paisa again."

Now Jasbir really really wants to get back to his little work cluster.

"Deep, this is fantasy. You've read this in the news feeds. Come on."

"Where there's smoke, there's fire. My stars say that I should be careful in things of the heart and beware false friends. Jupiter is in the third house. Dark omens surround me. No, I have hired a private investigation aeai. It will conduct a discreet surveillance. One way or the other, I shall know."

Jasbir grips the stanchion, knuckles white, as the phatphat swings through the great mill of traffic around Indira Chowk. Deependra's aftershave oppresses him.

"Exactly where are we going?"

Deependra had set up the assignation on a coded palmer account. All he would say was that it required two hours of an evening, good clothes, a trustworthy friend, and absolute discretion. For two days his mood had been grey and thundery as an approaching monsoon. His PI aeai had returned a result but Deependra revealed nothing, not even a whisper in the clubbish privacy of the Number 16 Gentlemen's WC.

The phatphat, driven by a teenager with gelled hair that falls in sharp spikes over his eyes—an obvious impediment to navigation—takes them out past the airport. At Gurgaon the geography falls into place around Jasbir. He starts to feel nauseous from more than spike-hair's driving and Deependra's shopping mall aftershave. Five minutes later the phatphat crunches up the curve of raked gravel outside the pillared portico of the Haryana Polo and Country Club.

"What are we doing here? If Shulka finds out I've been to shaadi when I'm supposed to be dating her, it's all over."

"I need a witness."

Help me, Ram Tarun Das, Jasbir hisses into his molars, but there is no reassuring spritz of silvery music through his skull to herald the advent of the Master of Grooming, Grace, and Gentlemanliness. The two immense Sikhs on the door nod them through.

Kishore is sloped against his customary angle of the bar, surveying the territory. Deependra strides through the throng of Eligible Boys like a god going to war. Every head turns. Every conversation, every gossip falls silent.

"You . . . you . . . you . . ." Deependra stammers with rage. His face shakes. "Shaadi stealer!" The whole club bar winces as the slap cracks across Kishore's face. Then two fists descend on Deependra, one on each shoulder. The man-mountain Sikhs turn him around and armlock him, frothing and raging, from the bar of the Haryana Polo and Country Club. "You, you chu-utya!" Deependra flings back at his enemy. "I will take it out of you, every last paisa, so help me God. I will have satisfaction!"

Jasbir scurries behind the struggling, swearing Deependra, cowed with embarrassment.

"I'm only here to witness," he says to the Sikhs' you're-next glares. They hold Deependra upright a moment to slap his face and bar him forever from Begum Rezzak's Lovely Girl Shaadi Agency. Then they throw him cleanly over the hood of a new-model Li Fan G8 into the carriage drive. He lies dreadfully still and snapped on the gravel for a few moments, then with fetching dignity draws himself up, bats away the dust, and straightens his clothes.

"I will see him at the river about this," Deependra shouts at the impassive Sikhs. "At the river."

Jasbir is already out on the avenue, trying to see if the phatphat driver's gone.

The sun is a bowl of brass rolling along the indigo edge of the world. Lights twinkle in the dawn haze. There is never a time when there are not people at the river. Wire-thin men push handcarts over the trash-strewn sand, picking like birds. Two boys have set a small fire in a ring of stones. A distant procession of women, soft bundles on their heads, file over the grassy sand. By the shrivelled thread of the Yamuna an old Brahmin consecrates himself, pouring water over his head. Despite the early heat, Jasbir shivers. He knows what goes into that water. He can smell the sewage on the air, mingled with woodsmoke.

"Birds," says Sujay, looking around him with simple wonder. "I can actually hear birds singing. So this is what mornings are like. Tell me again what I'm doing here?"

"You're here because I'm not being here on my own."

"And, ah, what exactly are you doing here?"

Deependra squats on his heels by the gym bag, arms wrapped around him. He wears a sharp white shirt and pleated slacks. His shoes are very good. Apart from grunted greetings he has not said a word to Jasbir or Sujay. He stares a lot. Deependra picks up a fistful of sand and lets it trickle through his fingers. Jasbir wouldn't advise that either.

"I could be at home coding," says Sujay. "Hey ho. Showtime."

Kishore marches across the scabby river-grass. Even as a well-dressed distant speck it is obvious to all that he is furiously angry. His shouts carry far on the still morning air.

"I am going to kick your head into the river," he bellows at Deependra, still squatting on the riverbank.

"I'm only here as a witness," Jasbir says hurriedly, needing to be believed. Kishore must forget and Deependra must never know that he was also the witness that night Kishore made the joke in the Tughluk tower.

Deependra looks up. His face is bland; his eyes are mild.

"You just had to, didn't you? It would have killed you to let me have something you didn't."

"Yeah, well. I let you get away with that in the polo club. I could have taken you then; it would have been the easiest thing. I could have driven your nose right into your skull, but I didn't. You cost me my dignity, in front of all my friends, people I work with, business colleagues, but most of all, in front of the women."

"Well then let me help you find your honour again."

Deependra thrusts his hand into the gym bag and pulls out a gun.

"Oh my god it's a gun he's got a gun," Jasbir jabbers. He feels his knees turn liquid. He thought that only happened in soaps and popular trash novels. Deependra gets to his feet, the gun never wavering from its aim in the centre of Kishore's forehead, the precise spot where a bindi would sit. "There's another one in the bag." Deependra waggles the barrel, nods with his head. "Take it. Let's sort this right, the man's way. Let's sort it honourably. Take the gun." His voice has gained an octave. A vein beats in his neck and at his temple. Deependra kicks the gym bag towards Kishore. Jasbir can see the anger, the mad, suicidal anger rising in the banker to match the civil servant's. He can hear himself mumbling, *Oh my god oh my god oh my god.* "Take the gun. You will have an honourable chance. Otherwise I will shoot you like a pi-dog right here." Deependra levels the gun and takes a sudden, stabbing step towards Kishore. He is panting like a dying cat. Sweat has soaked his good white shirt through and through. The gun muzzle is a finger's-breadth from Kishore's forehead.

Then there is a blur of movement, a body against the sun, a cry of pain, and the next Jasbir knows Sujay has the gun swinging by its trigger guard from his finger. Deependra is on the sand, clenching and unclenching his right hand. The old Brahmin stares, dripping.

"It's okay now, it's all okay, it's over," Sujay says. "I'm going to put this in the bag with the other and I'm going to take them and get rid of them and no one will ever talk about this, okay? I'm taking the bag now. Now, shall we all get out of here before someone calls the police, hm?"

Sujay swings the gym bag over his sloping shoulder and strides out for the streetlights, leaving Deependra hunched and crying among the shredded plastic scraps.

"How—what—that was—where did you learn to do that?" Jasbir asks, tagging behind, feet sinking into the soft sand.

"I've coded the move enough times; I thought it might work in meat life."

"You don't mean——?"

"From the soaps. Doesn't everyone?"

There's solace in soap opera. Its predictable tiny screaming rows, its scripted swooping melodramas draw the poison from the chaotic, unscripted world where a civil servant in the Ministry of Waters can challenge a rival to a shooting duel over a woman he met at a shaadi. Little effigies of true dramas, sculpted in soap.

When he blinks, Jasbir can see the gun. He sees Deependra's hand draw it out of the gym bag in martial-arts-movie slow motion. He thinks he sees the other gun, nestled among balled sports socks. Or maybe he imagines it, a cutaway close-up. Already he is editing his memory.

Soothing to watch Nilesh Vora and Dr. Chatterji's wife, their love eternally foiled and frustrated, and Deepti—will she ever realise that to the Brahmpur social set she is eternally that Dalit girl from the village pump?

You work on the other side of a glass partition from someone for years. You go with him to shaadis; you share the hopes and fears of your life and love with him. And love turns him into a homicidal madman. Sujay took the gun off him. Big, clumsy Sujay took the loaded gun out of his hand. He would have shot Kishore. Brave, mad Sujay. He's coding, that's his renormalizing process. Make soap, watch soap. Jasbir will make him tea. For once. Yes, that would be a nice gesture. Sujay is always always getting tea. Jasbir gets up. It's a boring bit, Mahesh and Rajani. He doesn't like them. Those rich-boy-pretending-they-are-car-valets-so-they-can-marry-for-love-not-money characters stretch his disbelief too far. Rajani is hot, though. She's asked Mahesh to bring her car round to the front of the hotel.

"When you work out here you have lots of time to make up theories. One of my theories is that people's cars are their characters," Mahesh is saying. *Only in a soap would anyone ever imagine that a pickup line like that would work,* Jasbir thinks. "So, are you a Tata, a Mercedes, a Li Fan, or a Lexus?"

Jasbir freezes in the door.

"Oh, a Lexus."

He turns slowly. Everything is dropping, everything is falling, leaving him suspended. Now Mahesh is saying "You know, I have another theory. It's that everyone's a city. Are you Delhi, Mumbai, Kolkata, Chennai?"

Jasbir sits on the arm of the sofa. *The fetch*, he whispers. *And she will say . . .*

"I was born in Delhi . . ."

"That's not what I mean."

Mumbai, murmurs Jasbir.

"Mumbai then. Yes, Mumbai definitely. Kolkata's hot and dirty and nasty. And Chennai—no, I'm definitely Mumbai."

"Red green yellow blue," Jasbir says.

"Red." Without a moment's hesitation.

"Cat dog bird monkey?"

She even cocks her head to one side. That was how he noticed Shulka was wearing the lighthoek.

"Bird . . . no."

"No no no," says Jasbir. She'll smile slyly here. "Monkey." And there is the smile. The *finesse*.

"Sujay!" Jasbir yells. "Sujay! Get me Das!"

"How can an aeai be in love?" Jasbir demands.

Ram Tarun Das sits in his customary wicker chair, his legs casually crossed. *Soon, very soon*, Jasbir thinks, *voices will be raised and Mrs. Prasad next door will begin to thump and weep.*

"Now, sir, do not most religions maintain that love is the fundament of the universe? In which case, perhaps it's not so strange that a distributed entity, such as myself, should find—and be surprised by, oh, so surprised, sir—by love? As a distributed entity, it's different in nature from the surge of neurochemicals and waveform of electrical activity you experience as love. With us it's a more . . . rarefied experience—judging solely by what I know from my subroutines on *Town and Country*. Yet, at the same time, it's intensely communal. How can I describe it? You don't have the concepts, let alone the words. I am a specific incarnation of aspects of a number of aeais and subprograms, as those aeais are also iterations of subprograms, many of them marginally sentient. I am many; I am legion. And so is she—though of course gender is purely arbitrary for us, and, sir, largely irrelevant. It's very likely that at many levels we share components. So ours is not so much a marriage of minds as a league of nations. Here we are different from humans in that, for you, it seems to us that groups are divisive and antipathetical. Politics, religion, sport, but especially your history, seem to teach that. For us folk, groups are what bring us together. They are mutually attractive. Perhaps the closest analogy might be the merger of large corporations. One thing I do know, that for humans and aeais, we both need to tell people about it."

"When did you find out she was using an aeai assistant?"

"Oh, at once sir. These things are obvious to us. And if you'll forgive the parlance, we don't waste time. Fascination at the first nanosecond. Thereafter, well, as you saw in the unfortunate scene from *Town and Country*, we scripted you."

"So we thought you were guiding us—"

"When it was you who were our go-betweens, yes."

"So what happens now?" Jasbir slaps his hands on his thighs.

"We are meshing at a very high level. I can only catch hints and shadows of it, but I feel a new aeai is being born, on a level far beyond either of us, or any of our co-characters. Is this a birth? I don't know, but how can I convey to you the tremendous, rushing excitement I feel?"

"I meant me."

"I'm sorry, sir. Of course you did. I am quite, quite dizzy with it all. If I might make one observation: there's truth in what your parents say—first the marriage, then the love. Love grows in the thing you see every day."

Thieving macaques dart around Jasbir's legs and pluck at the creases of his pants. Midnight metro, the last train home. The few late-night passengers observe a quarantine of mutual solitude. The djinns of unexplained wind that haunt subway systems send litter spiralling across the platform. The tunnel focuses distant shunts and clanks, uncanny at this zero hour. There should be someone around at the phatphat stand. If not he'll walk. It doesn't matter.

He met her at a fashionable bar, all leather and darkened glass, in an international downtown hotel. She looked wonderful. The simple act of her stirring sugar into coffee tore his heart in two.

"When did you find out?"

"Devashri Didi told me."

"Devashri Didi."

"And yours?"

"Ram Tarun Das, Master of Grooming, Grace, and Gentlemanliness. A very proper, old-fashioned Rajput gent. He always called me sir; right up to the end. My housemate made him. He works in character design on *Town and Country*."

"My older sister works in PR in the meta-soap department at Jahzay. She got one of the actor-designers to put Devashri Didi together." Jasbir has always found the idea of artificial actors believing they played equally artificial roles head-frying. Then he found aeai love.

"Is she married? Your older sister, I mean."

"Blissfully. And children."

"Well, I hope our aeais are very happy together." Jasbir raised a glass. Shulka lifted her coffee cup. She wasn't a drinker. She didn't like alcohol. Devashri Didi had told her it looked good for the Begum Jaitly's modern shaadi.

"My little quiz?" Jasbir asked.

"Devashri Didi gave me the answers you were expecting. She'd told me it was a standard ploy, personality quizzes and psychological tests."

"And the Sanskrit?"

"Can't speak a word."

Jasbir laughed honestly.

"The personal spiritual journey?"

"I'm a strictly material girl. Devashri Didi said—"

"I'd be impressed if I thought you had a deep spiritual dimension. I'm not a history buff either. And *An Eligible Boy*?"

"That unreadable tripe?"

"Me neither."

"Is there anything true about either of us?"

"One thing," Jasbir said. "I can tango."

Her surprise, breaking into a delighted smile, was also true. Then she folded it away.

"Was there ever any chance?" Jasbir asked.

"Why did you have to ask that? We could have just admitted that we were both playing games and shaken hands and laughed and left it at that.

Jasbir, would it help if I told you that I wasn't even looking? I was trying the system out. It's different for suitable girls. I've got a plan."

"Oh," said Jasbir.

"You did ask and we agreed, right at the start tonight, no more pretence." She turned her coffee cup so that the handle faced right and laid her spoon neatly in the saucer. "I have to go now." She snapped her bag shut and stood up. *Don't walk away,* Jasbir said in his silent Master of Grooming, Grace, and Gentlemanliness voice. She walked away.

"And Jasbir."

"What?"

"You're a lovely man, but this was not a date."

A monkey takes a liberty too far, plucking at Jasbir's shin. Jasbir's kick connects and sends it shrieking and cursing across the platform. *Sorry, monkey. It wasn't you.* Booms rattle up the subway tube; gusting hot air and the smell of electricity herald the arrival of the last metro. As the lights swing around the curve in the tunnel, Jasbir imagines how it would be to step out and drop in front of it. The game would be over. Deependra has it easy. Indefinite sick leave, civil service counselling, and pharma. But for Jasbir there is no end to it, and he is so so tired of playing. Then the train slams past him in a shout of blue and silver and yellow light, slams him back into himself. He sees his face reflected in the glass, his teeth still divinely white. Jasbir shakes his head and smiles and instead steps through the opening door.

It is as he suspected. The last phatphat has gone home for the night from the rank at Barwala Metro Station. It's four kays along the pitted, flaking roads to Acacia Bungalow Colony behind its gates and walls. Under an hour's walk. Why not? The night is warm, he's nothing better to do, and he might yet pull a passing cab. Jasbir steps out. After half an hour, a last, patrolling phatphat passes on the other side of the road. It flashes its light and pulls around to come in beside him. Jasbir waves it on. He is enjoying the night and the melancholy. There are stars up there, beyond the golden airglow of great Delhi.

Light spills through the French windows from the verandah into the dark living room. Sujay is at work still. In four kilometres Jasbir has generated a sweat. He ducks into the shower, closes his eyes in bliss as the jets of water hit him. Let it run let it run let it run—he doesn't care how much he wastes, how much it costs, how badly the villagers need it for their crops. *Wash the old tired dirt from me.*

A scratch at the door. Does Jasbir hear the mumble of a voice? He shuts off the shower.

"Sujay?"

"I've, ah, left you tea."

"Oh, thank you."

There's silence, but Jasbir knows Sujay hasn't gone.

"Ahm, just to say that I have always . . . I will . . . always. Always . . ." Jasbir holds his breath, water running down his body and dripping onto the shower tray. "I'll always be here for you."

Jasbir wraps a towel around his waist, opens the bathroom door, and lifts the tea.

Presently Latin music thunders out from the brightly lit windows of Number 27 Acacia Bungalow Colony. Lights go on up and down the close. Mrs. Prasad beats her shoe on the wall and begins to wail. The tango begins.

THE LITTLE GODDESS

I remember the night I became a goddess.

The men collected me from the hotel at sunset. I was light-headed with hunger, for the child-assessors said I must not eat on the day of the test. I had been up since dawn; the washing and dressing and making up was a long and tiring business. My parents bathed my feet in the bidet. We had never seen such a thing before and that seemed the natural use for it. None of us had ever stayed in a hotel. We thought it most grand, though I see now that it was a budget tourist chain. I remember the smell of onions cooking in ghee as I came down in the elevator. It smelled like the best food in the world.

I know the men must have been priests but I cannot remember if they wore formal dress. My mother cried in the lobby; my father's mouth was pulled in and he held his eyes wide, in that way that grown-ups do when they want to cry but cannot let tears be seen. There were two other girls for the test staying in the same hotel. I did not know them; they were from other villages where the devi could live. Their parents wept unashamedly. I could not understand it; their daughters might be goddesses.

On the street rickshaw drivers and pedestrians hooted and waved at us with our red robes and third eyes on our foreheads. *The devi, the devi, look! Best of all fortune!* The other girls held on tight to the men's hands. I lifted my skirts and stepped into the car with the darkened windows.

They took us to the Hanumandhoka. Police and machines kept the people out of Durbar Square. I remember staring long at the machines, with their legs like steel chickens and naked blades in their hands. The President's Own fighting machines. Then I saw the temple and its great roofs sweeping up and up and up into the red sunset and I thought for one instant its upturned eaves were bleeding.

The room was long and dim and stuffily warm. Low evening light shone in dusty rays through cracks and slits in the carved wood; so bright it almost burned. Outside you could hear the traffic and the bustle of tourists. The walls seemed thin but at the same time kilometres thick. Durbar Square was a world away. The room smelled of brassy metal. I did not recognise it then but I know now it is the smell of blood. Beneath the blood was another smell, of time piled thick as dust. One of the two women who would be my guardians if I passed the test told me the temple was five hundred years old. She was a short, round woman with a face that always seemed to be smiling, but when you looked closely you saw it was not. She made us sit on the floor on red cushions while the men brought the rest of the girls. Some of them were crying already. When there were ten of us, the two women left and the door was closed. We sat for a long time in the heat of the long room. Some of the girls fidgeted and chattered but I gave all my attention to the wall carvings and soon I was lost. It has always been easy for me to lose myself; in Shakya I could disappear for hours in the movement of clouds across the mountain, in the ripple of the grey river far below and the flap of the prayer banner in the wind. My parents saw it as a sign of my inborn divinity, one of thirty-two that mark girls in whom the goddess could dwell.

In the failing light I read the story of Jayaprakash Malla playing dice with the devi Taleju Bhawani who came to him in the shape of a red snake and left with the vow that she would only return to the rulers of Kathmandu as a virgin girl of low caste, to spite their haughtiness. I could not read its end in the darkness, but I did not need to. I was its end, or one of the other nine girls in the god-house of the devi.

Then the doors burst open wide and firecrackers exploded and through the rattle and smoke red demons leaped into the hall. Behind them men in crimson beat pans and clappers and bells. At once two of the girls began to cry and the two women came and took them away. But I knew the monsters were just silly men. In masks. These were not even close to demons. I have seen demons, after the rain clouds when the light comes low down the valley and all the mountains leap up as one. Stone demons, kilometres high. I have heard their voices, and their breath does not smell like onions. The silly men danced close to me, shaking their red manes and red tongues, but I could see their eyes behind the painted holes and they were afraid of me.

Then the door banged open again with another crash of fireworks and more men came through the smoke. They carried baskets draped with red sheets. They set them in front of us and whipped away the coverings. Buffalo heads, so freshly struck off the blood was bright and glossy. Eyes rolled up, lolling tongues still warm, noses still wet. And the flies, swarming around the severed necks. A man pushed a basket towards me on my cushion as if it were a dish of holy food. The crashing and beating outside rose to a roar so loud and metallic it hurt. The girl from my own Shakya village started to wail; the cry spread to another and then another, then a fourth. The other woman, the old, tall, pinched one with skin like an old purse, came in to take them out, carefully lifting her gown so as not to trail it in the blood. The dancers whirled around like flame and the kneeling man lifted the buffalo head from the basket. He held it up in my face, eye to eye, but all I thought was that it must weigh a lot; his muscles stood out like vines, his arm shook. The flies looked like black jewels. Then there was a clap from outside and the men set down the heads and covered them up with their cloths and they left with the silly demon men whirling and leaping around them. There was one other girl left on her cushion now. I did not know her. She was of a Vajryana family from Niwar down the valley. We sat a long time, wanting to talk but not knowing if that too was part of the trial. Then the door opened a third time and two men led a white goat into the devi hall. They brought it right between me and the Niwari girl. I saw its wicked, slotted eye roll. One held the goat's tether; the other took a big ceremonial kukri from a leather sheath. He blessed it and with one fast, strong stroke sent the goat's head leaping from its body.

I almost laughed, for the goat looked so funny, its body not knowing where its head was, the head looking around for the body and then the body realising that it had no head and going down with a kick, and why was the Niwari girl screaming, couldn't she see how funny it was, or was she screaming because I saw the joke and she was jealous of that? Whatever her reason, smiling woman and weathered woman came and took her very gently away and the two men went down on their knees in the spreading blood and kissed the wooden floor. They removed the two parts of the goat. I wished they hadn't done that. I would have liked someone with me in the big wooden hall. But I was on my own in the heat and the dark and over the traffic I could hear the deep-voiced bells of Kathmandu start to swing and ring. Then for the last time the doors opened and there were the women, in the light.

"Why have you left me all alone?" I cried. "What have I done wrong?"

"How could you do anything wrong, goddess?" said the old, wrinkled woman who, with her colleague, would become my mother and father and teacher and sister. "Now come along with us and hurry. The president is waiting."

Smiling Kumarima and Tall Kumarima (as I would now have to think of them) took a hand each and led me, skipping, from the great, looming Hanuman temple. I saw that a road of white silk had been laid from the foot of the temple to a wooden palace close by. The people had been let back into the square and they pressed in on either side of the processional way, held at bay by the police and the robots. The machines clutched burning torches in their grasping hands. Fire glinted from their killing blades. There was great silence in the dark square.

"Your home, goddess," said Smiling Kumarima, bending low to whisper in my ear. "Walk the silk, devi. Do not stray off it. I have your hand, you will be safe with me."

I walked between my Kumarimas, humming a pop tune I had heard on the radio at the hotel. When I looked back I saw that I had left a set of bloody footprints.

You have no caste, no village, no home. This palace is your home, and who would wish for any other? We have made it lovely for you, for you will only leave it six times a year. Everything you need is here within these walls.

You have no mother or father. A goddess has no parents. You have no brothers or sisters. The president is your brother, Nepal your sister. The priests who attend on you, they are nothing. We, your Kumarimas, are less than nothing. Dust, dirt, a tool. You may say anything, and we must obey it.

As we have said, you will leave the palace only six times a year. You will be carried in a palanquin. Oh, it is a beautiful thing, carved wood and silk. Outside this palace you shall not touch the ground. The moment you touch the ground, you cease to be divine.

You will wear red, with your hair in a topknot and your toe- and finger-nails painted. You will carry the red tilak of Siva on your forehead. We will help you with your preparations until they become second nature.

You will speak only within the confines of your palace, and little even then. Silence becomes the Kumari. You will not smile or show any emotion.

You will not bleed. Not a scrape, not a scratch. The power is in the blood and when the blood leaves, the devi leaves. On the day of your first blood, even one single drop, we will tell the priest and he will inform the president that the goddess has left. You will no longer be divine and you will leave this palace and return to your family. You will not bleed.

You have no name. You are Taleju, you are Kumari. You are the goddess.

These instructions my two Kumarimas whispered to me as we walked between priests to the president. He wore a Western suit but a proper hat. He knew that though there were no longer any kings in Nepal, I was still royal. He namasted and we sat side by side on old royal lion thrones and the long hall throbbed to the bells and drums of Durbar Square. I remember thinking that a ruler must bow to me, but there are rules even for goddesses.

Smiling Kumarima and Tall Kumarima. I draw Tall Kumarima in my memory first, for it is right to give preeminence to age. She was almost as tall as a Westerner and thin as a stick in a drought. At first I was scared of her.

Then I heard her voice and could never be scared of her again: her voice was kind as a singing bird. When she spoke you felt you now knew everything. Tall Kumarima lived in a small apartment above a tourist shop on the edge of Durbar Square. From her window she could see my Kumari Ghar, among the stepped towers of the dhokas. Her husband had died of lung cancer from pollution and cheap Indian cigarettes. Her two tall sons were grown and married with children of their own, older than me. In that time she had mothered five Kumari devis before me.

Now I remember Smiling Kumarima. She was short and round and had breathing problems for which she used inhalers, blue and brown. I would hear the snake hiss of them on days when Durbar Square was golden with smog. She lived out in the new suburbs up on the western hills, a long journey even by the official car at her service. Her children were twelve, ten, nine, and seven. She was jolly and treated me like her fifth baby, the young favourite, but I felt even then that, like the demon-dancing-men, she was scared of me. Oh, it was the highest honour any woman could hope for, to be the mother of the goddess—so to speak—though you wouldn't think it to hear her neighbours in the unit, *shutting yourself away in that dreadful wooden box, and all the blood, medieval, medieval*, but they couldn't understand. Somebody had to keep the nation safe against those who would turn us into another India, or worse, China; someone had to preserve the old ways of the divine kingdom. I understood early that difference between them. Smiling Kumarima was my mother out of duty. Tall Kumarima from love.

I never learned their true names. Their rhythms and cycles of shifts waxed and waned through the days and nights like the faces of the moon. Smiling Kumarima once found me looking up through the lattice of a jali screen at the fat moon on a rare night when the sky was clear and healthy and shouted me away, *Don't be looking at that thing, it will call the blood out of you, little devi, and you will be the devi no more.*

Within the wooden walls and iron rules of my Kumari Ghar years become indistinguishable, indistinct. I think now I was five when I became Taleju Devi. The year, I believe, was 2034. But some memories break the surface, like flowers through snow.

Monsoon rain on the steep-sloped roofs, water rushing and gurgling through the gutters, and the shutter that every year blew loose and rattled in the wind. We had monsoons, then. Thunder demons in the mountains around the city, my room flash-lit with lightning. Tall Kumarima came to see if I needed singing to sleep but I was not afraid. A goddess cannot fear a storm.

The day I went walking in the little garden, when Smiling Kumarima let out a cry and fell at my feet on the grass and the words to tell her to get up, not to worship me, were on my lips when she held up, between thumb and forefinger, twisting and writhing and trying to find a place for its mouth to seize: a green leech.

The morning Tall Kumarima came to tell me people had asked me to show myself. At first I had thought it wonderful that people would want to come and look at me on my little jharoka balcony in my clothes and paint and jewels. Now I found it tiresome; all those round eyes and gaping mouths. It was a week after my tenth birthday. I remember Tall Kumarima smiled but tried not to let me see. She took me to the jharoka to wave to the people in the court and I saw a hundred Chinese faces upturned to me, then heard the high, excited voices. I waited and waited but two tourists would not go away. They were an ordinary couple, dark local faces, country clothes.

"Why are they keeping us waiting?" I asked.

"Wave to them," Tall Kumarima urged. "That is all they want." The woman saw my lifted hand first. She went weak and grabbed her husband by the arm. The man bent to her, then looked up at me. I read many emotions on that face: shock, confusion, recognition, revulsion, wonder, hope. Fear. I waved and the man tugged at his wife, *Look, look up.* I remember that against all the laws, I smiled. The woman burst into tears. The man made to call out but Tall Kumarima hastened me away.

"Who were those funny people?" I asked. "They were both wearing very white shoes."

"Your mother and father," Tall Kumarima said. As she led me along the Durga corridor with the usual order not to brush my free hand along the wooden walls for fear of splinters, I felt her grip tremble.

That night I dreamed the dream of my life, that is, not a dream but one of my earliest experiences, knocking and knocking and knocking at the door of my remembering. This was a memory I would not admit in daylight, so it must come by night, to the secret door.

I am in the cage over a ravine. A river runs far below, milky with mud and silt, foaming cream over the boulders and slabs sheared from the mountainsides. The cable spans the river from my home to the summer grazing and I sit in the wire cage used to carry the goats across the river. At my back is the main road, always loud with trucks, the prayer banners and Kinley bottled water sign of my family's roadside teahouse. My cage still sways from my uncle's last kick. I see him, arms and legs wrapped around the wire, grinning his gap-toothed grin. His face is summer-burned brown, his hands cracked and stained from the trucks he services. Oil engrained in the creases. He wrinkles up his nose at me and unhooks a leg to kick my cage forwards on its pulley-wheel. Pulley sways cable sways mountains, sky, and river sway but I am safe in my little goat-cage. I have been kicked across this ravine many times. My uncle inches forwards. Thus we cross the river, by kicks and inches.

I never see what strikes him—some thing of the brain perhaps, like the sickness Lowlanders get when they go up to the high country. But the next I look my uncle is clinging to the wire by his right arm and leg. His left arm and leg hang down, shaking like a cow with its throat cut, shaking the wire and my little cage. I am three years old and I think this is funny, a trick my uncle is doing just for me, so I shake back, bouncing my cage, bouncing my uncle up and down, up and down. Half his body will not obey him and he tries to move forwards by sliding his leg along, like *this*, jerk his hand forwards *quick* so he never loses grip of the wire, and all the while bouncing up and down, up and down. Now my uncle tries to shout but his words are noise and slobber because half his face is paralysed. Now I see his fingers lose their grip on the wire. Now I see him spin round and his hooked leg comes free. Now he falls away, half his body reaching, half his mouth screaming. I see him fall, I see him bounce from the rocks and cartwheel, a thing I have always wished I could do. I see him go into the river and the brown water swallow him.

My older brother came out with a hook and a line and hauled me in. When my parents found I was not shrieking, not a sob or a tear or even a pout, that was when they knew I was destined to become the goddess. I was smiling in my wire cage.

I remember best the festivals, for it was only then that I left the Kumari Ghar. Dasain, at the end of summer, was the greatest. For eight days the city ran red. On the final night I lay awake listening to the voices in the square flow together into one roar, like I imagined the sea would sound, the voices of the men gambling for the luck of Lakshmi, devi of wealth. My father and uncles had gambled on the last night of Dasain. I remember I came down and demanded to know what all the laughing was about and they turned away from their cards and really laughed. I had not thought there could be so many coins in the world as there were on that table but it was nothing compared to Kathmandu on the eighth of Dasain. Smiling Kumarima told me it took some of the priests all year to earn back what they lost. Then came the ninth day, the great day, and I sailed out from my palace for the city would worship me.

I travelled on a litter carried by forty men strapped to bamboo poles as thick as my body. They went gingerly, testing every step, for the streets were slippery. Surrounded by gods and priests and saddhus mad with holiness, I rode on my golden throne. Closer to me than any were my Kumarimas, my two mothers, so splendid and ornate in their red robes and headdresses and makeup they did not look like humans at all. But Tall Kumarima's voice and Smiling Kumarima's smile assured me as I rode with Hanuman and Taleju through the cheering and the music and the banners bright against the blue sky and the smell I now recognised from the night I became a goddess, the smell of blood.

That Dasain the city received me as never before. The roar of the night of Lakshmi continued into the day. As Taleju Devi I was not supposed to notice anything as low as humans but out of the corners of my painted eyes I could see beyond the security robots stepping in time with my bearers, and the streets radiating out from the stupa of Chhetrapati were solid with bodies. They threw jets and gushes of water from plastic bottles up into the air, glittering, breaking into little rainbows, raining down on them, soaking them, but they did not care. Their faces were crazy with devotion.

Tall Kumarima saw my puzzlement and bent to whisper.

"They do puja for the rain. The monsoon has failed a second time, devi."

As I spoke, Smiling Kumarima fanned me so no one would see my lips move. "We don't like the rain," I said firmly.

"A goddess cannot do only what she likes," Tall Kumarima said. "It is a serious matter. The people have no water. The rivers are running dry."

I thought of the river that ran far down deep below the house where I was born, the water creamy and gushing and flecked with yellow foam. I saw it swallow my uncle and could not imagine it ever becoming thin, weak, hungry.

"So why do they throw water then?" I asked.

"So the devi will give them more," Smiling Kumarima explained. But I could not see the sense in that even for goddesses and I frowned, trying to understand how humans were, and so I was looking right at him when he came at me.

He had city-pale skin and hair parted on the left that flopped as he dived out of the crowd. He moved his fists to the collar of his diagonally striped shirt and people surged away from him. I saw him hook his thumbs into two loops of black string. I saw his mouth open in a great cry. Then the machine swooped and I saw a flash of silver. The young man's head flew up into the air. His mouth and eyes went round: from a cry to an oh! The president's machine had sheathed its blade, like a boy folding a knife, before the body, like that funny goat in the Hanumandhoka, realised it was dead and fell to the ground. The crowd screamed and tried to get away from the headless thing. My bearers rocked, swayed, uncertain where to go, what to do. For a moment I thought they might drop me.

Smiling Kumarima let out little shrieks of horror, "Oh! Oh! Oh!" My face was spotted with blood.

"It's not hers," Tall Kumarima shouted. "It's not hers!" She moistened a handkerchief with a lick of saliva. She was gently wiping the young man's blood from my face when security in their dark suits and glasses arrived, beating through the crowd. They lifted me, stepped over the body, and carried me to the waiting car.

"You smudged my makeup," I said to the guard as the car swept away. Worshippers barely made it out of our way in the narrow alleys.

Tall Kumarima came to my room that night. The air was loud with helicopters, quartering the city for the plotters. Helicopters, and machines like the President's Own robots, which could fly and look down on Kathmandu with the eyes of a hawk. She sat on my bed and laid a little transparent blue box on the red and gold embroidered coverlet. In it were two pale pills.

"To help you sleep."

I shook my head. Tall Kumarima folded the blue box into the sleeve of her robe.

"Who was he?"

"A fundamentalist. A karsevak. A foolish, sad young man."

"A Hindu, but he wanted to hurt us."

"That is the madness of it, devi. He and his kind think our nation has grown too Western, too far from its roots and religious truths."

"And he attacks us, the Taleju Devi. He would have blown up his own goddess, but the machine took his head. That is almost as strange as people throwing water to the rain."

Tall Kumarima bowed her head. She reached inside the sash of her robe and took out a second object, which she set on my heavy cover with the same precise care as she had the sleeping pills. It was a light, fingerless glove, for the right hand; clinging to its back was a curl of plastic shaped like a very very tiny goat fetus.

"Do you know what this is?"

I nodded. Every devotee doing puja in the streets seemed to own one, right hands held up to snatch my image. A palmer.

"It sends messages into your head," I whispered.

"That is the least of what it can do, devi. Think of it like your jharoka, but this window opens onto the world beyond Durbar Square, beyond Kathmandu and Nepal. It is an aeai, an artificial intelligence, a thinking-thing, like the machines up there, but much cleverer than them. They are clever enough to fly and hunt and not much else, but this aeai can tell you anything you want to know. All you have to do is ask. And there are things you need to know, devi. You will not be Kumari forever. The day will come when you will leave your palace and go back to the world. I have seen so many others before you." She reached out to take my face between her hands, then drew back. "You are special, my devi, but the kind of special it takes to be Kumari means that you will find it hard in the world. People will call it a sickness. Worse than that, even . . ."

She banished the emotion by gently fitting the fetus-shaped receiver behind my ear. I felt the plastic move against my skin, then Tall Kumarima slipped on the glove, waved her hand in a mudra, and I heard her voice inside my head. Glowing words appeared in the air between us, words I had been painstakingly taught to read by Tall Kumarima.

Don't let anyone find it, her dancing hand said. *Tell no one, not even Smiling Kumarima. I know you call her that, but she would not understand. She would think it was unclean, a pollution. In some ways, she is not so different from that man who tried to harm you. Let this be our secret, just you and me.*

Soon after, Smiling Kumarima came to look in on me and check for fleas but I pretended to be asleep. The glove and the fetus-thing were hidden under my pillow. I imagined them talking to me through the goosedown and soft cotton, sending dreams while the helicopters and hunting robots wheeled in the night above me. When the latch on her door clicked to, I put on the glove and earhoek and went looking for the lost rain. I found it one hundred and fifty kilometres up, through the eye of a weather aeai spinning over east India. I saw the monsoon, a coil of cloud like a cat's claw hooking up across the sea. There had been cats in the village; suspicious things lean on mice and barley. No cat was permitted in the Kumari Ghar. I looked down on my kingdom but I could not see a city or a palace or me down here at all. I saw mountains, white mountains ridged with grey and blue ice. I was goddess of this. And the heart went out of me, because it was nothing, a tiny crust of stone on top of that huge world that hung beneath it like the full teat of a cow, rich and heavy with people and their brilliant cities and their bright nations. India, where our gods and names were born.

Within three days the police had caught the plotters and it was raining. The clouds were low over Kathmandu. The colour ran from the temples in Durbar Square but people beat tins and metal cups in the muddy streets, calling praise on the Taleju Devi.

"What will happen to them?" I asked Tall Kumarima. "The bad men."

"They will likely be hanged," she said.

That autumn after the executions of the traitors the dissatisfaction finally poured onto the streets like sacrificial blood. Both sides claimed me: police and demonstrators. Others yet held me up as both the symbol of all that was good with our land and also everything wrong with it. Tall Kumarima tried to explain it to me but with my world mad and dangerous my attention was turned elsewhere, to the huge, old land to the south, spread out like a jewelled skirt. In such a time it was easy to be seduced by the terrifying depth of its history, by the gods and warriors who swept across it, empire after empire after empire. My land had always been fierce and free but I met the men who liberated India from the Last Empire—men like gods—and saw that liberty broken up by rivalry and intrigue and corruption into feuding states: Awadh and Bharat, the United States of Bengal, Maratha, Karnataka.

Legendary names and places. Shining cities as old as history. There aeais haunted the crowded streets like gandhavas. There men outnumbered women four to one. There the old distinctions were abandoned and women married as far up and men as few steps down the tree of caste as they could. I became as enthralled by their leaders and parties and politics as any of their citizens by the aeai-generated soaps they loved so dearly. My spirit was down in India in that early, hard winter when the police and government machines restored the old order to the city beyond Durbar Square. Unrest in Earth and the three heavens. One day I woke to find snow in the wooden court; the roofs of the temple of Durbar Square heavy with it, like frowning, freezing old men. I knew now that the strange weather was not my doing but the result of huge, slow changes in the climate. Smiling Kumarima came to me in my jharoka as I watched flakes thick and soft as ash sift down from the white sky. She knelt before me, rubbed her hands together inside the cuffs of her wide sleeves. She suffered badly in the cold and damp.

"Devi, are you not one of my own children to me?"

I waggled my head, not wanting to say yes.

"Devi, have I ever, ever given you anything but my best?"

Like her counterpart a season before, she drew a plastic pillbox from her sleeve, set it on her palm. I sat back on my chair, afraid of it as I had never been afraid of anything Tall Kumarima offered me.

"I know how happy we all are here, but change must always happen. Change in the world, like this snow—unnatural, devi, not right—change in our city. And we are not immune to it in here, my flower. Change will come to you, devi. To you, to your body. You will become a woman. If I could, I would stop it happening to you, devi. But I can't. No one can. What I can offer is . . . a delay. A stay. Take these. They will slow down the changes. For years, hopefully. Then we can all stay here together, devi." She looked up from her deferential half-bow, into my eyes. She smiled. "Have I ever wanted anything but the best for you?"

I held out my hand. Smiling Kumarima tipped the pills into my palm. I closed my fist and slipped from my carved throne. As I went to my room I could hear Smiling Kumarima chanting prayers of thanksgiving to the goddesses in the carvings. I looked at the pills in my hand. Blue seemed such a wrong colour. Then I filled my cup in my little washroom and washed them down, two gulps, down, down.

After that they came every day, two pills, blue as the Lord Krishna, appearing as miraculously on my bedside table. For some reason I never told Tall Kumarima, even when she commented on how fractious I was becoming, how strangely inattentive and absentminded at ceremonies. I told her it was the devis in the walls, whispering to me. I knew enough of my specialness, which others have called my *disorder*, that that would be unquestioned. I was tired and lethargic that winter. My sense of smell grew keen to the least odour and the people in my courtyard with their stupid, beaming upturned faces infuriated me. I went for weeks without showing myself. The wooden corridors grew sharp and brassy with old blood. With the insight of demons, I can see now that my body was a chemical battlefield between my own hormones and Smiling Kumarima's puberty suppressants. It was a heavy, humid spring that year and I felt huge and bloated in the heat, a waddling bulb of fluids under my robes and waxy makeup. I started to drop the little blue pills down the commode. I had been Kumari for seven Dasains.

I had thought I would feel like I used to, but I did not. It was not unwell, like the pills had made me feel; it was sensitive, acutely conscious of my body. I would lie in my wooden bed and feel my legs growing longer. I became very very aware of my tiny nipples. The heat and humidity got worse, or so it seemed to me.

At any time I could have opened my palmer and asked it what was happening to me, but I didn't. I was scared that it might tell me it was the end of my divinity.

Tall Kumarima must have noticed that the hem of my gown no longer brushed the floorboards but it was Smiling Kumarima who drew me back in the corridor as we hurried towards the darshan hall, hesitated a moment, said, softly, smiling as always: "How you're growing, devi. Are you still . . . ? No, forgive me, of course . . . Must be this warm weather we're having, makes children shoot up like weeds. My own are bursting out of everything they own, nothing will fit them."

The next morning as I was dressing a tap came on my door, like the scratch of a mouse or the click of an insect.

"Devi?"

No insect, no mouse. I froze, palmer in hand, earhoek babbling the early morning news reports from Awadh and Bharat into my head.

"We are dressing."

"Yes, devi, that is why I would like to come in."

I just managed to peel off the palmer and stuff it under my mattress before the heavy door swung open on its pivot.

"We have been able to dress ourselves since we were six," I retorted.

"Yes, indeed," said Smiling Kumarima, smiling. "But some of the priests have mentioned to me a little laxness in the ritual dress."

I stood in my red and gold nightrobe, stretched out my arms, and turned, like one of the trance-dancers I saw in the streets from my litter. Smiling Kumarima sighed.

"Devi, you know as well as I . . ."

I pulled my gown up over my head and stood unclothed, daring her to look, to search my body for signs of womanhood.

"See?" I challenged.

"Yes," Smiling Kumarima said, "but what is that behind your ear?"

She reached to pluck the 'hoek. It was in my fist in a flick.

"Is that what I think it is?" Smiling Kumarima said, soft smiling bulk filling the space between the door and me. "Who gave you that?"

"It is ours," I declared in my most commanding voice, but I was a naked twelve-year-old caught in wrongdoing and that commands less than dust.

"Give it to me."

I clenched my fist tighter.

"We are a goddess, you cannot command us."

"A goddess is as a goddess acts, and right now, you are acting like a brat. Show me."

She was a mother, I was her child. My fingers unfolded. Smiling Kumarima recoiled as if I held a poisonous snake. To her eyes of her faith, I did.

"Pollution," she said faintly. "Spoiled, all spoiled." Her voice rose. "I know who gave you this!" Before my fingers could snap shut, she snatched the coil of plastic from my palm. She threw the earhoek to the floor as if it burned her. I saw the hem of her skirt raise, I saw the heel come down, but it was my world, my oracle, my window on the beautiful. I dived to rescue the tiny plastic fetus. I remember no pain, no shock, not even Smiling Kumarima's shriek of horror and fear as her heel came down, but I will always see the tip of my right index finger burst in a spray of red blood.

The pallav of my yellow sari flapped in the wind as I darted through the Delhi evening crush-hour. Beating the heel of his hand off his buzzer, the driver of the little wasp-coloured phatphat cut in between a lumbering truck-train painted with gaudy gods and apsaras and a cream Government Maruti and pulled into the great chakra of traffic around Connaught Place. In Awadh you drive with your ears. The roar of horns and klaxons and cycle rickshaw bells assailed from all sides at once. It rose before the dawn birds and only fell silent well after midnight. The driver skirted a saddhu walking through the traffic as calmly as if he were wading through the Holy Yamuna. His body was white with sacred ash, a mourning ghost, but his Siva trident burned blood red in the low sun. I had thought Kathmandu dirty, but Delhi's golden light and incredible sunsets spoke of pollution beyond even that. Huddled in the rear seat of the autorickshaw with Deepti, I wore a smog mask and goggles to protect my delicate eye makeup. But the fold of my sari flapped over my shoulder in the evening wind and the little silver bells jingled.

There were five in our little fleet. We accelerated along the wide avenues of the British Raj, past the sprawling red buildings of old India, towards the glass spires of Awadh. Black kites circled the towers, scavengers, pickers of the dead. We turned beneath cool neem trees into the drive of a government bungalow. Burning torches lit us to the pillared porch. House staff in Rajput uniforms escorted us to the shaadi marquee.

Mamaji had arrived before any of us. She fluttered and fretted among her birds; a lick, a rub, a straightening, an admonition. "Stand up stand up, we'll have no slumping here. My girls will be the bonniest at this shaadi, hear me?" Shweta, her bony, mean-mouthed assistant, collected our smog masks. "Now, girls, palmers ready." We knew the drill with almost military smartness. Hand up, glove on, rings on, hoek behind ear jewellery, decorously concealed by the fringed dupattas draped over our heads. "We are graced with Awadh's finest tonight. Crème de la crème." I barely blinked as the résumés rolled up my inner vision. "Right, girls, from the left, first dozen, two minutes each then on to the next down the list. Quick smart!" Mamaji clapped her hands and we formed a line. A band struck a medley of musical numbers from *Town and Country*, the soap opera that was a national obsession in sophisticated Awadh. There we stood, twelve little wives-a-waiting, while the Rajput servants hauled up the rear of the pavilion.

Applause broke around us like rain. A hundred men stood in a rough semicircle, clapping enthusiastically, faces bright in the light from the carnival lanterns.

When I arrived in Awadh, the first thing I noticed was the people. People pushing people begging people talking people rushing past each other without a look or a word or an acknowledgement. I had thought Kathmandu held more people than a mind could imagine. I had not seen Old Delhi. The constant noise, the everyday callousness, the lack of any respect appalled me. You could vanish into that crowd of faces like a drop of rain into a tank. The second thing I noticed was that the faces were all male. It was indeed as my palmer had whispered to me. There were four men for every woman. It would never cease to amaze me, how a simple technique to predetermine a child's sex could utterly warp a nation.

Fine men good men clever men rich men, men of ambition and career and property, men of power and prospects. Men with no hope of ever marrying within their own class and caste. Men with little prospect of marrying at all. Shaadi had once been the word for wedding festivities, the groom on his beautiful white horse, so noble, the bride shy and lovely behind her golden veil. Then it became a name for dating agencies: *Lovely wheat-complexioned Agarwal, US-university MBA, seeks same civil service/military for matrimonials.* Now it was a bride parade, a marriage market for lonely men with large dowries. Dowries that paid a hefty commission to the Lovely Girl Shaadi Agency.

The Lovely Girls lined up on the left side of the Silken Wall that ran the length of the bungalow garden. The first twelve men formed up on the right. They plumped and preened in their finery but I could see they were nervous. The partition was no more than a row of saris pinned to a line strung between plastic uprights, fluttering in the rising evening wind. A token of decorum. Purdah. They were not even silk.

Reshmi was first to walk and talk the Silken Wall. She was a Yadav country girl from Uttaranchal, big-handed and big-faced. A peasant's daughter. She could cook and sew and sing, do household accounts, manage both domestic aeais and human staff. Her first prospective was a weasely man with a weak jaw in government whites and a Nehru cap. He had bad teeth. Never good. Any one of us could have told him he was wasting his shaadi fee, but they namasted to each other and stepped out, regulation three paces between them. At the end of the walk Reshmi would loop back to rejoin the tail of the line and meet her next prospective. On big shaadis like this my feet would bleed by the end of the night. Red footprints on the marble floors of Mamaji's courtyard haveli.

I stepped out with Ashok, a big globe of a thirty-two-year-old who wheezed a little as he rolled along. He was dressed in a voluminous white kurta, the fashion this season, though he was fourth-generation Panjabi. His grooming amounted to an uncontrollable beard and oily hair that smelled of too much Dapper Deepak pomade. Even before he namasted I knew it was his first shaadi. I could see his eyeballs move as he read my résumé, seeming to hover before him. I did not need to read his to know he was a dataraja, for he talked about nothing but himself and the brilliant things he was doing: the spec of some new protein processor array, the 'ware he was breeding, the aeais he was nurturing in his stables, his trips to Europe and the United States where everyone knew his name and great people were glad to welcome him.

"Of course, Awadh's never going to ratify the Hamilton Acts—no matter how close Shrivastava is to President McAuley—but if it did, if we allow ourselves that tiny counterfactual—well, it's the end of the economy: Awadh *is* IT, there are more graduates in Mehrauli than there are in the whole of California. The Americans may go on about the mockery of a human soul, but they *need* our Level 2.8s—you know what that is? An aeai that can pass as human ninety-nine percent of the time—because everybody knows no one does quantum crypto like us, so I'm not worrying about having to close up the data-haven, and even if they do, well, there's always Bharat—I cannot see the Ranas bowing down to Washington, not when twenty-five percent of their forex comes out of licensing deals from *Town and Country* . . . and that's one hundred percent aeai generated . . ."

He was a big, affable clown of a man with wealth that would have bought my palace in Durbar Square and every priest in it and I found myself praying to Taleju to save me from marrying such a bore. He stopped in midstride, so abruptly I almost tripped.

"You must keep walking," I hissed. "That is the rule."

"Wow," he said, standing stupid, eyes round in surprise. Couples piled up behind us. In my peripheral vision I could see Mamaji making urgent, threatening gestures. Get him *on*. "Oh wow. You're an ex-Kumari."

"Please, you are drawing attention to yourself." I would have tugged his arm, but that would have been an even more deadly error.

"What was it like, being a goddess?"

"I am just a woman now, like any other," I said. Ashok gave a soft *harrumph*, as if he had achieved a very small enlightenment, and walked on, hands clasped behind his back. He may have spoken to me once, twice before we reached the end of the Silk Wall and parted: I did not hear him, I did not hear the music, I did not even hear the eternal thunder of Delhi's traffic. The only sound in my head was the high-pitched sound between my eyes of needing to cry but knowing I could not. Fat, selfish, gabbling Ashok had sent me back to the night I ceased to be a goddess.

Bare soles slapping the polished wood of the Kumari Ghar's corridors. Running feet, muted shouts growing ever more distant as I knelt, still unclothed for my Kumarima's inspection, looking at the blood drip from my smashed fingertip onto the painted wood floor. I remember no pain; rather, I looked at the pain from a separate place, as if the girl who felt it were another person. Far far away, Smiling Kumarima stood, held in time, hands to mouth in horror and guilt. The voices faded and the bells of Durbar Square begin to swing and toll, calling to their brothers across the city of Kathmandu until the valley rang from Bhaktapur to Trisuli Bazaar for the fall of the Kumari Devi.

In the space of a single night, I became human again. I was taken to the Hanumandhoka—walking this time like anyone else on the paving stones—where the priests said a final puja. I handed back my red robes and jewels and boxes of makeup, all neatly folded and piled. Tall Kumarima had got me human clothes. I think she had been keeping them for some time. The president did not come to say goodbye to me. I was no longer the sister of the nation. But his surgeons had put my finger back together well, though they warned that it would always feel a little numb and inflexible.

I left at dawn, while the street cleaners were washing down the stones of Durbar Square beneath the apricot sky, in a smooth-running government Mercedes with darkened windows. My Kumarimas made their farewells at the palace gate. Tall Kumarima hugged me briefly to her.

"Oh, there was so much more I needed to do. Well, it will have to suffice."

I felt her quivering against me, like a bird too tightly gripped in a hand. Smiling Kumarima could not look at me. I did not want her to.

As the car took me across the waking city I tried to understand how it felt to be human. I had been a goddess so long I could hardly remember feeling any other way, but it seemed so little different that I began to suspect that you are divine because people say you are. The road climbed through green suburbs, winding now, growing narrower, busy with brightly decorated buses and trucks. The houses grew leaner and meaner, becoming roadside hovels and chai-stalls, and then we were out of the city—the first time since I had arrived seven years before. I pressed my hands and face to the glass and looked down on Kathmandu beneath its shroud of orange smog. The car joined the long line of traffic along the narrow, rough road that clung to the valley side. Above me, mountains dotted with goatherd shelters and stone shrines flying tattered prayer banners. Below me, rushing cream-brown water. Nearly there. I wondered how far behind me on this road were those other government cars, carrying the priests sent to seek out little girls bearing the thirty-two signs of perfection. Then the car rounded the bend in the valley and I was home, Shakya, its truck halts and gas station, the shops and the temple of Padma Narteswara, the dusty trees with white rings painted around their trunks, and between them the stone wall and arch where the steps led down through the terraces to my house, and in that stone-framed rectangle of sky, my parents, standing there side by side, pressing closely, shyly, against each other as I had last seen them lingering in the courtyard of the Kumari Ghar.

Mamaji was too respectable to show anything like outright anger, but she had ways of expressing her displeasure. The smallest crust of roti at dinner, the meanest scoop of dal. New girls coming, make room make room—me to the highest, stuffiest room, furthest from the cool of the courtyard pool.

"He asked for my palmer address," I said.

"If I had a rupee for every palmer address," Mamaji said. "He was only interested in you as a novelty, dearie. Anthropology. He was never going to make a proposition. No, you can forget right about him."

But my banishment to the tower was a small punishment for it lifted me above the noise and fumes of the old city. If portions were cut, small loss: the food had been dreadful every day of the almost two years I had been at the haveli. Through the wooden lattice, beyond the water tanks and satellite dishes and kids playing rooftop cricket, I could see the ramparts of the Red Fort, the minarets and domes of the Jami Masjid, and beyond them, the glittering glass and titanium spires of New Delhi. And higher than any of them, the flocks of pigeons from the kabooter lofts, clay pipes bound to their legs so they fluted and sang as they swirled over Chandni Chowk. And Mamaji's worldly wisdom made her a fool this time, for Ashok was surreptitiously messaging me, sometimes questions about when I was divine, mostly about himself and his great plans and ideas. His lilac-coloured words, floating in my inner vision against the intricate silhouettes of my jali screens, were bright pleasures in those high summer days. I discovered the delight of political argument; against Ashok's breezy optimism, I set my readings of the news channels. From the opinion columns it seemed inevitable to me that Awadh, in exchange for Favoured Nation status from the United States of America, would ratify the Hamilton Acts and outlaw all aeais more intelligent than a langur monkey. I told none of our intercourse to Mamaji. She would have forbidden it, unless he made a proposal.

On an evening of pre-monsoon heat, when the boys were too tired even for cricket and the sky was an upturned brass bowl, Mamaji came to my turret on the top of the old merchant's haveli. Against propriety, the jalis were thrown open, my gauze curtains stirred by the swirls of heat rising from the alleys below.

"Still you are eating my bread." She prodded my thali with her foot. It was too hot for food, too hot for anything other than lying and waiting for the rain and the cool, if they came at all this year. I could hear the voices of the girls down in the courtyard as they kicked their legs in the pool. This day I would have loved to be sitting along the tiled edge with them but I was piercingly aware that I had lived in the haveli of the Lovely Girl Shaadi Agency longer than any of them. I did not want to be their Kumarima. And when the whispers along the cool marble corridors made them aware of my childhood, they would ask for small pujas, little miracles to help them find the right man. I no longer granted them, not because I feared that I had no power anymore—that I never had—but that it went out from me and into them and that was why they got the bankers and television executives and Mercedes salesmen.

"I should have left you in that Nepalese sewer. Goddess! Hah! And me fooled into thinking you were a prize asset. Men! They may have share options and Chowpatty Beach apartments, but deep down they're as superstitious as any back-country yadav."

"I'm sorry, Mamaji," I said, turning my eyes away.

"Can you help it? You were only born perfect in thirty-two different ways. Now you listen, cho chweet. A man came to call on me."

Men always came calling, glancing up at the giggles and rustles of the Lovely Girls peeping through the jalis as they waited in the cool of the courtyard for Shweta to present them to Mamaji. Men with offers of marriage, men with prenuptial contracts, men with dowry down payments. Men asking for special, private viewings. This man who had called on Mamaji had come for one of these.

"Fine young man, lovely young man, just twenty. Father's big in water. He has requested a private rendezvous, with you."

I was instantly suspicious but I had learned among the Lovely Girls of Delhi, even more than among the priests and Kumarimas of Kathmandu, to let nothing show on my painted face.

"Me? Such an honour . . . and him only twenty . . . and a good family too, so well connected."

"He is a Brahmin."

"I know I am only a Shakya—"

"You don't understand. He is a *Brahmin*."

There was so much more I needed to do, Tall Kumarima had said as the government car drove away from the carved wooden gates of the Kumari Ghar. One whisper through the window would have told me everything: *the curse of the Kumari.*

Shakya hid from me. People crossed the street to find things to look at and do. Old family friends nodded nervously before remembering important business they had to be about. The chai-dhabas gave me free tea so I would feel uncomfortable and leave. Truckers were my friends, bus drivers and long-haulers pulled in at the biodiesel stations. They must have wondered who was this strange twelve-year-old girl, hanging around truck-halts. I do not doubt some of them thought more. Village by village, town by town, the legend spread up and down the north road. Ex-Kumari.

Then the accidents started. A boy lost half his hand in the fan belt of a Nissan engine. A teenager drank bad rakshi and died of alcohol poisoning. A man slipped between two passing trucks and was crushed. The talk in the chai-dhabas and the repair shops was once again of my uncle who fell to this death while the little goddess-to-be bounced in her wire cradle laughing and laughing and laughing.

I stopped going out. As winter took hold over the head country of the Kathmandu valley, whole weeks passed when I did not leave my room. Days slipped away watching sleet slash past my window, the prayer banners bent almost horizontal in the wind, the wire of the cableway bouncing. Beneath it, the furious, flooding river. In that season the voices of the demons spoke loud from the mountain, telling me the most hateful things about faithless Kumaris who betray the sacred heritage of their devi.

On the shortest day of the year the bride-buyer came through Shakya. I heard a voice I did not recognise talking over the television that burbled away day and night in the main room. I opened the door just enough to admit a voice and a gleam of firelight.

"I wouldn't take the money off you. You're wasting your time here in Nepal. Everyone knows the story, and even if they pretend they don't believe, they don't act that way."

I heard my father's voice but could not make out his words. The bride-buyer said: "What might work is down south, Bharat or Awadh. They're so desperate in Delhi they'll even take Untouchables. They're a queer lot, those Indians; some of them might even like the idea of marrying a goddess, like a status thing. But I can't take her, she's too young, they'll send her straight back at the border. They've got rules. In India, would you believe? Call me when she turns fourteen."

Two days after my fourteenth birthday, the bride-buyer returned to Shakya and I left with him in his Japanese SUV. I did not like his company or trust his hands, so I slept or feigned sleep while he drove down into the low-lands of the Terai. When I woke I was well over the border into my childhood land of wonder. I had thought the bride-buyer would take me to ancient, holy Varanasi, the new capital of Bharat's dazzling Rana dynasty, but the Awadhis, it seemed, were less in awe of Hindu superstitions. So we came to the vast, incoherent roaring sprawl of the two Delhis, like twin hemispheres of a brain, and to the Lovely Girl Shaadi Agency. Where the marriageable men were not so 2040s sophisticated, at least in the matter of ex-devis. Where the only ones above the curse of the Kumari were those held in even greater superstitious awe: the genetically engineered children known as Brahmins.

Wisdom was theirs, health was theirs, beauty and success and status assured and a wealth that could never be devalued or wasted or gambled away, for it was worked into every twist of their DNA. The Brahmin children of India's super-élite enjoyed long life—twice that of their parents—but at a price. They were indeed the twice-born, a caste above any other, so high as to be new Untouchables. A fitting partner for a former goddess: a new god.

Gas flares from the heavy industries of Tughluk lit the western horizon. From the top of the high tower I could read New Delhi's hidden geometries, the necklaces of light around Connaught Place, the grand glowing net of the dead Raj's monumental capital, the incoherent glow of the old city to the north. The penthouse at the top of the sweeping wing-curve of Narayan Tower was glass: glass walls, glass roof, beneath me, polished obsidian that reflected the night sky. I walked with stars at my head and feet. It was a room designed to awe and intimidate. It was nothing to one who had witnessed demons strike the heads from goats, who had walked on bloody silk to her own palace. It was nothing to one dressed, as the messenger had required, in the full panoply of the goddess. Red robe, red nails, red lips, red eye of Siva painted above my own black-kohled eyes, fake-gold headdress hung with costume pearls, my fingers dripped gaudy rings from the cheap jewellery sellers of Kinari Bazaar, a light chain of real gold ran from my nose stud to my earring; I was once again Kumari Devi. My demons rustled inside me.

Mamaji had drilled me as we scooted from old city to new. She had swathed me in a light voile chador, to protect my makeup she said; in truth, to conceal me from the eyes of the street. The girls had called blessings and prayers after me as the phatphat scuttled out of the haveli's courtyard.

"You will say nothing. If he speaks to you, you duck your head like a good Hindu girl. If anything has to be said, I will say it. You may have been a goddess but he is a Brahmin. He could buy your pissy palace a dozen times over. Above all, do not let your eyes betray you. The eyes say nothing. They taught you that at least in that Kathmandu, didn't they? Now come on, cho chweet, let's make a match."

The glass penthouse was lit only by city glow and concealed lamps that gave an uncomfortable blue aura. Ved Prakash Narayan sat on a musnud, a slab of unadorned black marble. Its simplicity spoke of wealth and power beneath any ornate jewellery. My bare feet whispered on the star-filled glass. Blue light welled up as I approached the dais. Ved Prakash Narayan was dressed in a beautifully worked long sherwani coat and traditional tight churidar pajamas. He leaned forwards into the light and it took every word of control Tall Kumarima had ever whispered to me to hold the gasp.

A nine-year-old boy sat on the throne of the Mughal Emperor.

Live twice as long, but age half as fast. The best deal Kolkata's genetic engineers could strike with four million years of human DNA. A child husband for a once-child goddess. Except this was no child. In legal standing, experience, education, taste, and emotions, this was an eighteen-year-old man, in every way except the physical.

His feet did not touch the floor.

"Quite, quite extraordinary." His voice was a boy's. He slipped from his throne, walked around me, studying me as if I were an artefact in a museum. He was a head shorter than me. "Yes, this is indeed special. What is the settlement?"

Mamaji's voice from the door named a number. I obeyed my training and tried not to catch his eye as he stalked around me.

"Acceptable. My man will deliver the prenuptial before the end of the week. A goddess. My goddess."

Then I caught his eyes and I saw where all his missing years were. They were blue, alien blue, and colder than any of the lights of his tower-top palace.

These Brahmins are worse than any of us when it comes to social climbing, Ashok messaged me in my aerie atop the shaadi haveli, prison turned bridal boudoir. *Castes within castes within castes.* His words hung in the air over the hazy ramparts of the Red Fort before dissolving into the dashings of the musical pigeons. *Your children will be blessed.*

Until then I had not thought about the duties of a wife with a nine-year-old boy.

On a day of staggering heat I was wed to Ved Prakash Narayan in a climate-controlled bubble on the manicured green before Emperor Humayun's tomb. As on the night I was introduced, I was dressed as Kumari. My husband, veiled in gold, arrived perched on top of a white horse followed by a band and a dozen elephants with coloured patterns worked on their trunks. Security robots patrolled the grounds as astrologers proclaimed favourable auspices and an old-type Brahmin in his red cord blessed our union. Rose petals fluttered around me, the proud father and mother distributed gems from Hyderabad to their guests, my shaadi sisters wept with joy and loss, Mamaji sniffed back a tear, and vile old Shweta went round hoarding the free and overflowing food from the buffet. As we were applauded and played down the receiving line, I noticed all the other sombre-faced ten-year-old boys with their beautiful, tall foreign wives. I reminded myself who was the child bride here. But none of them were goddesses.

I remember little of the grand durbar that followed except face after face after face, mouth after mouth after mouth opening, making noise, swallowing glass after glass after glass of French champagne. I did not drink for I did not have the taste for alcohol, though my young husband in his raja finery took it, and smoked big cigars too. As we got into the car—the *honeymoon* was another Western tradition we were adopting—I asked if anyone had remembered to inform my parents.

We flew to Mumbai on the company tilt-jet. I had never before flown in an aircraft. I pressed my hands, still hennaed with the patterns of my mehndi, on either side of the window as if to hold in every fleeting glimpse of Delhi falling away beneath me. It was every divine vision I had ever had looking down from my bed in the Kumari Ghar on India. This was indeed the true vehicle of a goddess. But the demons whispered as we turned in the air over the towers of New Delhi, *You will be old and withered when he is still in his prime.*

When the limousine from the airport turned onto Marine Drive and I saw the Arabian Sea glinting in the city light, I asked my husband to stop the car so I could look and wonder. I felt tears start in my eyes and thought, *The same water in it is in you.* But the demons would not let me be: *You are married to something that is not human.*

My *honeymoon* was wonder upon wonder: our penthouse apartment with the glass walls that opened on sunset over Chowpatty Beach. The new splendid outfits we wore as we drove along the boulevards, where stars and movie-gods smiled down and blessed us in the virtual sight of our palmers. Colour, motion, noise, chatter; people and people and people. Behind it all, the wash and hush and smell of the alien sea.

Chambermaids prepared me for the wedding night. They worked with baths and balms, oils and massages, extending the now-fading henna tracery on my hands up my arms, over my small upright breasts, down the manipuraka chakra over my navel. They wove gold ornaments into my hair, slipped bracelets on my arms and rings on my fingers and toes, dusted and powdered my dark Nepali skin. They purified me with incense smoke and flower petals, they shrouded me in veils and silks as fine as rumours. They lengthened my lashes and kohled my eyes and shaped my nails to fine, painted points.

"What do I do, I've never even touched a man?" I asked, but they namasted and slipped away without answer. But the older—the Tall Kumarima, as I thought of her—left a small soapstone box on my bridal divan. Inside were two white pills.

They were good. I should have expected no less. One moment I was standing nervous and fearful on the Turkestan carpet with a soft night air that smelled of the sea stirring the translucent curtains, the next visions of the Kama Sutra, beamed into my brain through my golden earhoek, swirled up around me like the pigeons over Chandni Chowk. I looked at the patterns my shaadi sisters had painted on the palms of my hands and they danced and coiled from my skin. The smells and perfumes of my body were alive, suffocating. It was as if my skin had been peeled back and every nerve exposed. Even the touch of the barely moving night air was intolerable. Every car horn on Marine Drive was like molten silver dropped into my ear.

I was terribly afraid.

Then the double doors to the robing room opened and my husband entered. He was dressed as a Mughal grandee in a jewelled turban and a long-sleeved pleated red robe bowed out at the front in the manly act.

"My goddess," he said. Then he parted his robe and I saw what stood so proud.

The harness was of crimson leather intricately inlaid with fine mirror-work. It fastened around the waist and also over the shoulders, for extra security. The buckles were gold. I recall the details of the harness so clearly because I could not take more than one look at the thing it carried. Black. Massive as a horse's, but delicately upcurved. Ridged and studded. This is all I remember before the room unfolded around me like the scented petals of a lotus and my senses blended as one and I was running through the apartments of the Taj Marine Hotel.

How had I ever imagined it could be different for a creature with the appetites and desires of an adult but the physical form of a ten-year-old boy?

Servants and dressers chased me as I screamed incoherently, grabbing at wraps, shawls, anything to cover my shame. At some tremendous remove I remember my husband's voice calling, *Goddess! My Goddess!* over and over.

"Schizophrenia is a terribly grating word," Ashok said. He twirled the stem of a red thornless rose between his fingers. "Old-school. It's dissociative disorder these days. Except there are no disorders, just adaptive behaviours. It was what you needed to cope with being a goddess. Dissociating. Disjuncting. Splitting."

Night in the gardens of the dataraja Ashok. Water trickled in the stone canals of the charbagh. I could smell it, sweet and wet. A pressure curtain held the smog at bay; trees screened out Delhi's traffic. I could even see a few stars. We sat in an open chhatri pavilion, the marble still warm from the day. Set on silver thalis were medjool dates, halva—crisp with flies—folded paan. A security robot stepped into the lights from the Colonial bungalow, passed into shadow. But for it I might have been in the age of the rajas.

Time broken apart, whirring like kabooter wings. Dissociative behaviour. Mechanisms for coping. Running along the palm-lined boulevards of Mumbai, shawls clutched around my wifely finery that made me feel more naked than bare skin. I ran without heed or direction. Taxis hooted, phatphats veered as I dashed across crowded streets. Even if I had had money for a phatphat—what need had the wife of a Brahmin for crude cash?—I did not know where to direct it. Yet some demonic self must have known, for I found myself on the vast marble concourse of a railway station, a sole mite of stillness among the tens of thousands of hastening travellers and beggars and vendors and staff. My shawls and throws clutched around me, I looked up at the dome of red Raj stone and it was a second skull, full of the awful realisation of what I had done.

A runaway bride without even a paisa to her name, alone in Mumbai Chhatrapati Shivaji Terminus. A hundred trains leaving that minute for any destination but nowhere to go. People stared at me, half Nautch-courtesan, half Untouchable street-sleeper. In my shame, I remembered the hoek behind my ear. *Ashok*, I wrote across the sandstone pillars and swirling ads. *Help me!*

"I don't want to be split, I don't want to be many, why can't I just be one? Be me?" I beat the heels of my hands off my forehead in frustration. "Make me well, make me right!" Shards of memory. The white-uniformed staff serving me hot chai in a first-class private compartment of the shatabdi express. The robots waiting at the platform with the antique covered palanquin, to bear me through the Delhi dawn traffic to the green-watered geometries of Ashok's gardens. But behind them all was one enduring image: my uncle's white fist slipping on the bouncing cable and him falling, legs pedalling air, to the creamy waters of Shakya River. Even then, I had been split. Fear and shock. Laughter and smiles. How else could anyone survive being a goddess?

Goddess. My Goddess.

Ashok could not understand. "Would you cure a singer of his talent? There is no madness, only ways of adapting. Intelligence is evolution. Some would argue that I display symptoms of mild Asperger's syndrome."

"I don't know what that means."

He twirled the rose so hard the stem snapped.

"Have you thought what you're going to do?"

I had thought of little else. The Narayans would not give up their dowry lightly. Mamaji would sweep me from her door. My village was closed to me.

"Maybe for a while, if you could—"

"It's not a good time . . . Who's going to have the ear of the Lok Sabha? A family building a dam that's going to guarantee their water supply for the next ten years, or a software entrepreneur with a stable of Level 2.75 aeais that the United States government thinks are the sperm of Shaitan? Family values still count in Awadh. You should know."

I heard my voice say, like a very small girl, "Where can I go?"

The bride-buyer's stories of Kumaris whom no one would marry and who could not go home again ended in the women-cages of Varanasi and Kolkata. Chinese paid rupees by the roll for an ex-goddess.

Ashok moistened his lips with his tongue.

"I have a place in Bharat, in Varanasi. Awadh and Bharat are seldom on speaking terms."

"Oh thank you, thank you . . ." I went down on my knees before Ashok, clutched his hands between my palms. He looked away. Despite the artificial cool of the water garden, he was sweating freely.

"It's not a gift. It's . . . employment. A job."

"A job, that's good, I can do that; I'm a good worker, work away at anything I will; what is it? Doesn't matter, I can do it—"

"There are commodities that need transporting."

"What kind of commodities? Oh, it doesn't mater, I can carry anything."

"Aeais." He rolled a paan from the silver dish. "I'm not going to wait around for Shrivastava's Krishna Cops to land in my garden with their excommunication 'ware."

"The Hamilton Acts," I ventured, though I did not know what they were, what most of Ashok's mumbles and rants meant.

"Word is, everything above Level 2.5." Ashok chewed his lower lip. His eyes widened as the paan curled through his skull.

"Of course, I will do anything I can to help."

"I haven't told you how I need you to transport them. Absolutely safe, secure, where no Krishna Cop can ever find them." He touched his right forefinger to his third eye.

I went to Kerala and had processors put into my skull. Two men did it on a converted bulk gas carrier moored outside territorial waters. They shaved my long lovely black hair, unhinged my skull and sent robots smaller than the tiniest spider spinning computers through my brain. Their position out there beyond the Keralese fast patrol boats enabled them to carry out much secret surgery, mostly for the Western military. They gave me a bungalow and an Australian girl to watch over me while my sutures fused and hormone washes speed-grew my hair back.

Protein chips; only show on the highest resolution scans but no one'll look twice at you; no one'll look twice at another shaadi girl down hunting for a husband.

So I sat and stared at the sea for six weeks and thought about what it would be like to drown in the middle of it, alone and lost a thousand kilometres from the nearest hand that might seize yours. A thousand kilometres north in Delhi a man in an Indian suit shook hands with a man in an American suit and announced the Special Relationship that would make Ashok an outlaw.

You know what Krishna Cops are? They hunt aeais. They hunt the people who stable them, and the people who carry them. They don't care. They're not picky. But they won't catch you. They'll never catch you.

I listened to demons in the swash and run of the big sea on the shore. Demons I now knew were other parts of myself. But I was not afraid of them. In Hinduism, demons are merely the mirrors of the gods. As with men, so with gods; it is the winners who write the history. The universe would look no different had Ravana and his Rakshasas won their cosmic wars.

No one but you can carry them. No one but you has the neurological architecture. No one but you could endure another mind in there.

The Australian girl left small gifts outside my door: plastic bangles, jelly-shoes, rings, and hairslides. She stole them from the shops in town. I think they were her way of saying that she wanted to know me but was afraid of what I had been, of what the things in my head would make me become. The last thing she stole was a beautiful sheer silk dupatta to cover my ragged hair when she took me to the airport. From beneath it I looked at the girls in business saris talking into their hands in the departure lounge and listened to the woman pilot announce the weather in Awadh. Then I looked out of the phatphat at the girls darting confidently through the Delhi traffic on their scooters and wondered why my life could not be like theirs.

"It's grown back well." Ashok knelt before me on my cushions in the chhatri. It was his sacred place, his temple. He raised his palmer-gloved hand and touched his forefinger to the tilak over my third eye. I could smell his breath. Onions, garlic, rancid ghee. "You may feel a little disoriented . . ."

I gasped. Senses blurred, fused, melted. I saw heard felt smelled tasted everything as one undifferentiated sensation, as gods and babies sense, wholly and purely. Sounds were coloured, light had texture, smells spoke and chimed. Then I saw myself surge up from my cushions and fall towards the hard white marble. I heard myself cry out. Ashok lunged towards me. Two Ashoks lunged towards me. But it was neither of those. I saw one Ashok, with two visions, inside my head. I could not make shape or sense out of my two seeings, I could not tell which was real, which was mine, which was *me*. Universes away I heard a voice say, *Help me*. I saw Ashok's houseboys lift me and take me to bed. The painted ceiling, patterned with vines and shoots and flowers, billowed above me like monsoon storm clouds, then blossomed into darkness.

In the heat of the night I woke stark, staring, every sense glowing. I knew the position and velocity of each insect in my airy room that smelled of biodiesel, dust, and patchouli. I was not alone. There was another under the dome of my skull. Not an awareness, a consciousness; a sense of *separateness*, a manifestation of myself. An avatar. A demon.

"Who are you?" I whispered. My voice sounded loud and full of bells, like Durbar Square. It did not answer—it could not answer, it was not a sentience—but it took me out into the charbagh water garden. The stars, smudged by pollution, were a dome over me. The crescent moon lay on its back. I looked up and fell into it. Chandra. Mangal. Budh. Guru. Shukra. Shani. Rahu. Ketu. The planets were not points of light, balls of stone and gas; they had names, characters, loves, hatreds. The twenty-seven Nakshatars spun around my head. I saw their shapes and natures, the patterns of connections that bound the stars into relationships and stories and dramas as human and complex as *Town and Country*. I saw the wheel of the rashis, the Great Houses, arc across the sky, and the whole turning, engines within engines, endless wheels of influence and subtle communication, from the edge of the universe to the centre of the Earth I stood upon. Planets, stars, constellations; the story of every human life unfolded itself above me and I could read them all. Every word.

All night I played among the stars.

In the morning, over bed-tea, I asked Ashok, "What is it?"

"A rudimentary Level 1.9. A janampatri aeai, does astrology, runs the permutations. It thinks it lives out there, like some kind of space monkey. It's not very smart, really. Knows about horoscopes and that's it. Now get that down you and grab your stuff. You've a train to catch."

My reserved seat was in the women's bogie of the high-speed shatabdi express. Husbands booked their wives onto it to protect them from the attentions of the male passengers who assumed every female was single and available. The few career women chose it for the same reason. My fellow passenger across the table from me was a Muslim woman in a formal business shalwar. She regarded me with disdain as we raced across the Ganga Plain at three hundred and fifty kilometres per hour. *Little simpering wife-thing.*

You would not be so quick to judge if you knew what we really are, I thought. *We can look into your life and tell you everything that has, is, and will ever happen to you, mapped out in the chakras of the stars.* In that night among the constellations my demon and I had flowed into each other until there was no place where we could say aeai ended and I began.

I had thought holy Varanasi would sing to me like Kathmandu, a spiritual home, a city of nine million gods and one goddess, riding through the streets in a phatphat. What I saw was another Indian capital of another Indian state; glass towers and diamond domes and industry parks for the big world to notice, slums and bastis at their feet like sewage pigs. Streets began in this millennium and ended in one three before it. Traffic and hoardings and people people people but the diesel smoke leaking in around the edges of my smog mask carried a ghost of incense.

Ashok's Varanasi agent met me in the Jantar Mantar, the great solar observatory of Jai Singh; sundials and star spheres and shadow discs like modern sculpture. She was little older than me; dressed in a cling-silk top and jeans that hung so low from her hips I could see the valley of her buttocks. I disliked her at once but she touched her palmer-glove to my forehead in the shadows around Jai Singh's astrological instruments and I felt the stars go out of me. The sky died. I had been holy again and now I was just meat. Ashok's girli pressed a roll of rupees into my hand. I barely looked at it. I barely heard her instructions to get something to eat, get a kafi, get some decent clothes. I was bereft. I found myself trudging up the steep stone steps of the great Samrat not knowing where I was who I was what I was doing halfway up a massive sundial. Half a me. Then my third eye opened and I saw the river wide and blue before me. I saw the white sands of the eastern shore and the shelters and dung fires of the saddhus. I saw the ghats, the stone river steps, curving away on either side further than the reach of my eyes. And I saw people. People washing and praying and cleaning their clothes and offering puja and buying and selling and living and dying. People in boats and people kneeling, people waist-deep in the river, people scooping up silver handfuls of water to pour over their heads. People casting handfuls of marigold flowers onto the stream, people lighting little mango-leaf diya lamps and setting them afloat, people bringing their dead to dip them in the sacred water. I saw the pyres of the burning ghat, I smelled sandalwood, charring flesh, I heard the skull burst, releasing the soul. I had heard that sound before at the old royal burning ghats of Pashupatinath, when the president's mother died. A soft crack, and free. It was a comforting sound. It made me think of home.

In that season I came many times to the city by the Ganga. Each time I was a different person. Accountants, counsellors, machine-soldiers, soapi actors, database controllers: I was the goddess of a thousand skills. The day after I saw the Krishna Cops patrolling the platforms at Delhi Station with their security robots and guns that could kill both humans and aeais, Ashok began to mix up my modes of transport. I flew, I trained, I chugged overnight on overcrowded country buses, I waited in chauffeured Mercedes in long lines of brightly decorated trucks at the Awadh-Bharat border. The trucks, like the crack of an exploding skull, reminded me of my kingdom. But at the end was always the rat-faced girli lifting her hand to my tilak and taking me apart again. In that season I was a fabric weaver, a tax accountant, a wedding planner, a soapi editor, an air-traffic controller. She took all of them away.

And then the trip came when the Krishna Cops were waiting at the Bharat end as well. By now I knew the politics of it as well as Ashok. The Bharatis would never sign the Hamilton Acts—their multibillion-rupee entertainment industry depended on aeais—but neither did they want to antagonise America. So, a compromise: all aeais over Level 2.8 banned, everything else licensed, and Krishna Cops patrolling the airports and railway stations. Like trying to hold back the Ganga with your fingers.

I had spotted the courier on the flight. He was two rows in front of me; young, wisp of a beard, Star-Asia youth fashion, all baggy and big. Nervous nervous nervous, all the time checking his breast pocket, checking checking checking. A small-time badmash, a wannabe dataraja with a couple of specialist 2.75s loaded onto a palmer. I could not imagine how he had made it through Delhi Airport security.

It was inevitable that the Varanasi Krishna Cops would spot him. They closed on him as we lined up at passport control. He broke. He ran. Women and children fled as he ran across the huge marble arrivals hall, trying to get to the light, the huge glass wall and the doors and the mad traffic beyond. His fists pounded at air. I heard the Krishna Cops' staccato cries. I saw them unholster their weapons. Shrieks went up. I kept my head down, shuffled forwards. The immigration officer checked my papers. Another shaadi bride on the hunt. I hurried through, turned away towards the taxi ranks. Behind me I heard the arrivals hall fall so shockingly silent it seemed to ring like a temple bell.

I was afraid then. When I returned to Delhi it was as if my fear had flown before me. The city of djinns was the city of rumours. The government had signed the Hamilton Acts. Krishna Cops were sweeping house to house. Palmer files were to be monitored. Children's aeai toys were illegal. US Marines were being airlifted in. Prime Minister Shrivastava was about to announce the replacement of the rupee with the dollar. A monsoon of fear and speculation and in the middle of it all was Ashok.

"One final run, then I'm out. Can you do this for me? One final run?"

The bungalow was already half emptied. The furniture was all packed, only his processor cores remained. They were draped with dustsheets, ghosts of the creatures that had lived there. The Krishna Cops were welcome to them.

"We both go to Bharat?"

"No, that would be too dangerous. You go ahead, I'll follow when it's safe." He hesitated. Tonight, even the traffic beyond the high walls sounded different. "I need you to take more than the usual."

"How many?"

"Five."

He saw me shy back as he raised his hand to my forehead.

"Is it safe?"

"Five, and that's it done. For good."

"Is it safe?"

"It's a series of overlays, they'll share core code in common."

It was a long time since I had turned my vision inwards to the jewels Ashok had strung through my skull. Circuitry. A brain within a brain.

"Is it safe?"

I saw Ashok swallow, then bob his head: a Westerner's *yes*. I closed my eyes. Seconds later I felt the warm, dry touch of his finger to my inner eye.

We came to with the brass light of early morning shining through the jali. We were aware we were deeply dehydrated. We were aware that we were in need of slow-release carbohydrate. Our serotonin inhibitor levels were low. The window arch was a Mughal true arch. The protein circuits in my head were DPMA one-eight-seven-nine slash omegas, under licence from BioScan of Bangalore.

Everything we looked at gave off a rainbow of interpretations. I saw the world with the strange manias of my new guests: medic, nutritionist, architectural renderer, biochip designer, engineering aeai controlling a host of repair-shop robots. Nasatya. Vaishvanara. Maya. Brihaspati. Tvastri. My intimate demons. I was a many-headed devi.

All that morning, all afternoon, I fought to make sense of a world that was five worlds, five impressions. *I* fought. Fought to make us *me*. Ashok fretted, tugging at his woolly beard, pacing, trying to watch television, check his mails. At any instant Krishna Cop combat robots could come dropping over his walls. Integration would come. It had to come. I could not survive the clamour in my skull, a monsoon of interpretations. Sirens raced in the streets, far, near, far again. Every one of them fired off a different reaction from my selves.

I found Ashok sitting among his shrouded processors, knees pulled up to his chest, arms draped over them. He looked like a big, fat, soft boy, his mama's favourite.

Noradrenaline pallor, mild hypoglycaemia, fatigue toxins, said Nasatya.

Yin Systems bevabyte quantum storage arrays, said Brihaspati.

I touched him on the shoulder. He jerked awake. It was full dark outside, stifling: the monsoon was already sweeping up through the United States of Bengal.

"We're ready," I said. "*I'm* ready."

Dark-scented hibiscus spilled over the porch where the Mercedes waited.

"I'll see you in a week," he said. "In Varanasi."

"In Varanasi."

He took my shoulders in his hands and kissed me lightly, on the cheek. I drew my dupatta over my head. Veiled, I was taken to the United Provinces Night Sleeper Service. As I lay in the first-class compartment, the aeais chattered away inside my head, surprised to discover each other, reflections of reflections.

The chowkidar brought me bed-tea on a silver tray in the morning. Dawn came up over Varanasi's sprawling slums and industrial parks. My personalised news-service aeai told me that Lok Sabha would vote on ratifying the Hamilton Acts at 10 a.m. At 12 noon Prime Minister Shrivastava and the United States ambassador would announce a Most Favoured Nation trade package with Awadh.

The train emptied onto the platform beneath the spun-diamond canopy I knew so well. Every second passenger, it seemed, was a smuggler. If I could spot them so easily, so could the Krishna Cops. They lined the exit ramps, more than I had ever seen before. There were uniforms behind them and robots behind the uniforms. The porter carried my bag on his head; I used it to navigate the press of people pouring off the night train. *Walk straight, as your Mamaji taught you. Walk tall and proud, as if you are walking the Silken Way with a rich man.* I pulled my dupatta over my head, for modesty. Then I saw the crowd piling up at the ramp. The Krishna Cops were scanning every passenger with palmers.

I could see the badmashs and smuggler boys hanging back, moving to the rear of the mill of bodies. But there was no escape there either. Armed police backed by riot-control robots took up position at the end of the platform. Shuffle by shuffle, the press of people pushed me towards the Krishna Cops, waving their right hands like blessings over the passengers. Those things could peel back my scalp and peer into my skull. My red case bobbed ahead, guiding me to my cage.

Brihaspati showed me what they would do to the circuits in my head.

Help me! I prayed to my gods. And Maya, architect of the demons, answered me. Its memories were my memories and it remembered rendering an architectural simulation of this station long before robot construction spiders started to spin their nanodiamond web. Two visions of Varanasi Station, superimposed. With one difference that might save my life. Maya's showed me the inside of things. The inside of the platform. The drain beneath the hatch between the rear of the chai-booth and the roof support.

I pushed through the men to the small dead space at the rear. I hesitated before I knelt beside the hatch. One surge of the crowd, one trip, one fall, and I would be crushed. The hatch was jammed shut with dirt. Nails broke, nails tore as I scrabbled it loose and heaved it up. The smell that came up from the dark square was so foul I almost vomited. I forced myself in, dropped a metre into shin-deep sludge. The rectangle of light showed me my situation. I was mired in excrement. The tunnel forced me to crawl but the end of it was promise, the end of it was a semicircle of daylight. I buried my hands in the soft sewage. This time I did retch up my bed-tea. I crept forwards, trying not to choke. It was vile beyond anything I had ever experienced. But not so vile as having your skull opened and knives slice away slivers of your brain. I crawled on my hands and knees under the tracks of Varanasi Station, to the light, to the light, to the light, and out through the open conduit into the cess lagoon where pigs and rag pickers rooted in the shoals of drying human manure.

I washed as clean as I could in the shrivelled canal. Dhobiwallahs beat laundry against stone slabs. I tried to ignore Nasatya's warnings about the hideous infections I might have picked up.

I was to meet Ashok's girl on the street of gajras. Children sat in door-ways and open shop fronts threading marigolds onto needles. The work was too cheap even for robots. Blossoms spilled from bushels and plastic cases. My phatphat's tires slipped on wet rose petals. We drove beneath a canopy of gajra garlands that hung from poles above the shop fronts. Everywhere was the smell of dead, rotting flowers. The phatphat turned into a smaller, darker alley and into the back of a mob. The driver pressed his hand to the horn. The people reluctantly gave him way. The alcofuel engine whined. We crept for-wards. Open space, then a police jawan stepped forwards to bar our progress. He wore full combat armour. Brihaspati read the glints of data flickering across his visor: deployments, communications, an arrest warrant. I pulled my dupatta over my head and the lower part of my face as the driver talked to him. *What's going on? Some badmash. Some dataraja.*

Down the street of gajras, uniformed police led by a plainclothes Krishna Cop burst open a door. Their guns were drawn. In the same breath, the shutters of the jharoka immediately above crashed up. A figure jumped up onto the wooden rail. Behind me, the crowd let out a vast roaring sigh. *There he is there the badmash oh look look it's a girl!*

From the folds of my dupatta I saw Ashok's girli teeter there an instant, then jump up and grab a washing line. It snapped and swung her ungently down through racks of marigold garlands into the street. She crouched a moment, saw the police, saw the crowd, saw me, then turned and ran. The jawan started towards her but there was another quicker, deadlier. A woman screamed as the robot bounded from the rooftop into the alley. Chrome legs pistoned, its insect head bobbed, locked on. Marigold petals flew up around the fleeing girl but everyone knew she could not escape the killing thing. One step, two step, it was behind her. I saw her glance over her shoulder as the robot unsheathed its blade.

I knew what would happen next. I had seen it before, in the petal-strewn streets of Kathmandu, as I rode my litter among my gods and Kumarimas.

The blade flashed. A great cry from the crowd. The girl's head bounded down the alley. A great jet of blood. Sacrificial blood. The headless body took one step, two.

I slipped from the phatphat and stole away through the transfixed crowd.

I saw the completion of the story on a news channel at a chai-dhaba by the water tank on Scindia ghat. The tourists, the faithful, the vendors and funeral parties were my camouflage. I sipped chai from a plastic cup and watched the small screen above the bar. The sound was low but I could understand well enough from the pictures. Delhi police break up a notorious aeai smuggling ring. In a gesture of Bharati-Awadhi friendship, Varanasi Krishna Cops make a series of arrests. The camera cut away before the robot struck. The final shot was of Ashok, pushed down into a Delhi police car in plastic handcuffs.

I went to sit on the lowest ghat. The river would still me, the river would guide me. It was of the same substance as me, divinity. Brown water swirled at my beringed toes. That water could wash away all earthly sin. On the far side of the holy river, tall chimneys poured yellow smoke into the sky. A tiny round-faced girl came up to me, offered me marigold gajras to buy. I waved her away. I saw again this river, these ghats, these temples and boats as I had when I lay in my wooden room in my palace in Durbar Square. I saw now the lie Tall Kumarima's palmer had fed me. I had thought India a jewelled skirt, laid out for me to wear. It was a bride-buyer with an envelope of rupees, it was walking the Silken Way until feet cracked and bled. It was a husband with the body of a child and the appetites of a man warped by his impotence. It was a saviour who had always, only wanted me for my sickness. It was a young girl's head rolling in a gutter.

Inside this still-girl's head, my demons were silent. They could see as well as I that there would never be a home for us in Bharat, Awadh, Maratha, any nation of India.

North of Nayarangadh the road rose through wooded ridges, climbing steadily up to Mugling where it turned and clung to the side of the Trisuli's steep valley. It was my third bus in as many days. I had a routine now. Sit at the back, wrap my dupatta round me, look out the window. Keep my hand on my money. Say nothing.

I picked up the first bus outside Jaunpur. After emptying Ashok's account, I thought it best to leave Varanasi as inconspicuously as possible. I did not need Brihaspati to show me the hunter aeais howling after me. Of course they would have the air, rail, and bus stations covered. I rode out of the Holy City on an unlicensed taxi. The driver seemed pleased with the size of the tip. The second bus took me from Gorakhpur through the dal fields and banana plantations to Nautanwa on the border. I had deliberately chosen small, out-of-the-way Nautanwa, but still I bowed my head and shuffled my feet as I came up to the Sikh immigration officer behind his tin counter. I held my breath. He waved me through without even a glance at my identity card.

I walked up the gentle slope and across the border. Had I been blind, I would have known at once when I crossed into my country. The great roar that had followed me as close as my own skin fell silent so abruptly it seemed to echo. The traffic did not blare its way through all obstacles. It steered, it sought ways around pedestrians and sacred cows lolling in the middle of the road, chewing. People were polite in the bureau where I changed my Bharati rupees for Nepalese; did not press and push and try to sell me things I did not want in the shop where I bought a bag of greasy samosas; smiled shyly to me in the cheap hotel where I hired a room for the night. Did not demand demand demand.

I slept so deeply that it felt like a fall through endless white sheets that smelled of sky. In the morning the third bus came to take me up to Kathmandu.

The road was one vast train of trucks, winding in and out of the bluffs, looping back on itself, all the while climbing, climbing. The gears on the old bus whined. The engine strove. I loved that sound, of engines fighting gravity. It was the sound of my earliest recollection, before the child-assessors came up a road just like this to Shukya. Trains of trucks and buses in the night. I looked out at the roadside dhabas, the shrines of piled rocks, the tattered prayer banners bent in the wind, the cableways crossing the chocolate-creamy river far below, skinny kids kicking swaying wire cages across the high wires. So familiar, so alien to the demons that shared my skull.

The baby must have been crying for some time before the noise rose above the background hubbub of the bus. The mother was two rows ahead of me; she shushed and swung and soothed the tiny girl but the cries were becoming screams.

It was Nasatya that made me get out of my seat and go to her.

"Give her to me," I said, and there must have been some tone of command from the medical aeai in my voice for she passed me the baby without a thought. I pulled back the sheet in which she was wrapped. The little girl's belly was painfully bloated, her limbs floppy and waxen.

"She's started getting colic when she eats," the mother said, but before she could stop me I pulled away her napkin. The stench was abominable; the shit bulky and pale.

"What are you feeding her?"

The woman held up a roti bread, chewed at the edges to soften it for the baby. I pushed my fingers into the baby's mouth to force it open, though Vaishvanara the nutritionist already knew what we would find. The tongue was blotched red, pimpled with tiny ulcers.

"This has only started since you began giving her solid food?" I said. The mother waggled her head in agreement. "This child has coeliac disease," I pronounced. The woman put her hands to her face in horror, began to rock and wail. "Your child will be fine, you must just stop feeding her bread, anything made from any grain except rice. She cannot process the proteins in wheat and barley. Feed her rice, rice and vegetables, and she will brighten up right away."

The entire bus was staring as I went back to my seat. The woman and her baby got off at Naubise. The child was still wailing, weak now from its rage, but the woman raised a hand to me. I had come to Nepal with no destination, no plan or hope, just a need to be back. But an idea was already forming.

Beyond Naubise the road climbed steadily, switching back and forth over the buttresses of the mountains that embraced Kathmandu. Evening was coming on. Looking back I could see the river of headlights snaking across the mountainside. When the bus ground around another hairpin bend, I could see the same snake climbing up ahead of me in red taillights. The bus laboured up a long, steep climb. I could hear, everyone could hear, the noise in the engine that should not have been there. Up we crawled, to the high saddle where the watershed divided, right to the valley of Kathmandu, left to Pokhara and the High Himalaya. Slower, slower. We could all smell the burning insulation, hear the rattling.

It was not me who rushed to the driver and his mate. It was the demon Tvastri.

"Stop stop at once!" I cried. "Your alternator has seized! You will burn us up."

The driver pulled into the narrow draw, up against the raw rock. On the offside, trucks passed with millimetres to spare. We got the hood up. We could see the smoke wafting from the alternator. The men shook their heads and pulled out palmers. The passengers piled to the front of the bus to stare and talk.

"No no no, give me a wrench," I ordered.

The driver stared but I shook my outstretched hand, demanding. Perhaps he remembered the crying baby. Perhaps he was thinking about how long it would take a repair truck to come up from Kathmandu. Perhaps he was thinking about how good it would be to be home with his wife and children. He slapped the monkey wrench into my hand. In less than minute I had the belt off and the alternator disconnected.

"Your bearings have seized," I said. "It's a persistent fault on pre-2030 models. A hundred metres more and you would have burned her out. You can drive her on the battery. There's enough in it to get you down to Kathmandu."

They stared at this little girl in an Indian sari, head covered but the sleeves of her choli rolled up and fingers greasy with biolube.

The demon returned to his place and it was clear as the darkening sky what I would do now. The driver and his mate called out to me as I walked up beside the line of vehicles to the head of the pass. We ignored them. Passing drivers sounded their multiple, musical horns, offered lifts. I walked on. I could see the top now. It was not far to the place where the three roads divided. Back to India, down to the city, up to the mountains.

There was a chai-dhaba at the wide, oil-stained place where vehicles turned. It was bright with neon signs for American drinks and Bharati mineral water, like something fallen from the stars. A generator chugged. A television burbled familiar, soft Nepali news. The air smelled of hot ghee and biodiesel.

The owner did not know what to make of me, strange little girl in my Indian finery. Finally he said, "Fine night."

It was. Above the smogs and soots of the valley, the air was magically clear. I could see for a lifetime in any direction. To the west the sky held a little last light. The great peaks of Manaslu and Anapurna glowed mauve against the blue.

"It is," I said, "Oh, it is."

Traffic pushed slowly past, never ceasing on this high crossroads of the world. I stood in the neon flicker of the dhaba, looking long at the mountains and I thought, *I shall live there.* We shall live in a wooden house close to trees, with running water cold from high snow. We shall have a fire and a television for company and prayer banners flying in the wind and in time people will stop being afraid and will come up the path to our door. There are many ways to be divine. There is the big divine, of ritual and magnificence and blood and terror. Ours shall be a little divinity, of small miracles and everyday wonders. Machines mended, programs woven, people healed, homes designed, minds and bodies fed. I shall be a little goddess. In time, the story of me will spread and people will come from all over; Nepalis and foreigners, travellers and hikers and monks. Maybe one day a man who is not afraid.

That would be good. But if he does not come, that will be good also, for I shall never be alone, not with a houseful of demons.

Then I found I was running, with the surprised chai-wallah calling, "Hey! Hey! Hey!" after me, running down the side of the slow-moving line of traffic, banging on the doors, "Hi! Hi! Pokhara! Pokhara!" slipping and sliding over the rough gravel, towards the far, bright mountains.

THE DJINN'S WIFE

Once there was a woman in Delhi who married a djinn. Before the water war, that was not so strange a thing: Delhi, split in two like a brain, has been the city of djinns from time before time. The Sufis tell that God made two creations, one of clay and one of fire. That of clay became man; that of fire, the djinns. As creatures of fire they have always been drawn to Delhi, seven times reduced to ashes by invading empires, seven times reincarnating itself. Each turn of the chakra, the djinns have drawn strength from the flames, multiplying and dividing. Great dervishes and Brahmins are able to see them but on any street, at any time, anyone may catch the whisper and momentary wafting warmth of a djinn passing.

I was born in Ladakh, far from the heat of the djinns—they have wills and whims quite alien to humans—but my mother was Delhi born and raised, and from her I knew its circuses and boulevards, its maidans and chowks and bazaars, like those of my own Leh. Delhi to me was a city of stories, and so if I tell the story of the djinn's wife in the manner of a Sufi legend or a tale from the Mahabharata, or even a tivi soap opera, that is how it seems to me: City of Djinns.

They are not the first to fall in love on the walls of the Red Fort.

The politicians have talked for three days and an agreement is close. In honour of this, the Awadhi government has prepared a grand durbar in the great courtyard before the Diwan-i-aam. All India is watching so this spectacle is on a Victorian scale: event planners scurry across hot, bare marble hanging banners and bunting, erecting staging, setting up sound and light systems, choreographing dancers, elephants, fireworks, and a fly-past of combat robots, dressing tables and drilling serving staff, and drawing up so-careful seating plans so that no one will feel snubbed by anyone else. All day three-wheeler delivery drays have brought fresh flowers, festival goods, the finest soft furnishings. There's a real French sommelier raving at what the simmering Delhi heat is doing to his wine plan. It's a serious conference. At stake are a quarter of a billion lives.

In this second year after the monsoon failed, the Indian nations of Awadh and Bharat face each other with main battle tanks, robot attack helicopters, strikeware, and tactical nuclear slow missiles on the banks of the sacred River Ganga. Along thirty kilometres of staked-out sand, where Brahmins cleanse themselves and saddhus pray, the government of Awadh plans a monster dam. Kunda Khadar will secure the water supply for Awadh's one hundred and thirty million for the next fifty years. The river downstream, which flows past the sacred cities of Allahabad and Varanasi in Bharat, will turn to dust. Water is life, water is death. Bharati diplomats, human and artificial intelligence aeai advisors, negotiate careful deals and access rights with their rival nation, knowing one carelessly spilled drop of water will see strike robots battling like kites over the glass towers of New Delhi and slow missiles with nanonuke warheads in their bellies creeping on cat claws through the galis of Varanasi. The rolling news channels clear their schedules of everything else but cricket. A deal is close! A deal is agreed! A deal will be signed tomorrow! Tonight, they've earned their durbar.

And in the whirlwind of leaping hijras and parading elephants, a Kathak dancer slips away for a cigarette and a moment up on the battlements of the

Red Fort. She leans against the sun-warmed stone, careful of the fine gold threadwork of her costume. Beyond the Lahore Gate lies hiving Chandni Chowk; the sun a vast blister bleeding onto the smokestacks and light-farms of the western suburbs. The chhatris of the Sisganj Gurdwara, the minarets and domes of the Jama Masjid, the shikara of the Shiv temple are shadow-puppet scenery against the red, dust-laden sky. Above them pigeons storm and dash, wings wheezing. Black kites rise on the thermals above Old Delhi's thousand thousand rooftops. Beyond them, a curtain wall taller and more imposing than any built by the Mughals, stand the corporate towers of New Delhi, Hindu temples of glass and construction diamond stretched to fantastical, spiring heights, twinkling with stars and aircraft warning lights.

A whisper inside her head, her name accompanied by a spray of sitar: the call tone of her palmer, transduced through her skull into her auditory centre by the subtle 'hoek curled like a piece of jewellery behind her ear.

"I'm just having a quick bidi break, give me a chance to finish it," she complains, expecting Pranh, the choreographer, a famously tetchy third-sex nute. Then, "Oh!" For the gold-lit dust rises before her up into a swirl, like a dancer made from ash.

A djinn. The thought hovers on her caught breath. Her mother, though Hindu, devoutly believed in the djinns, in any religion's supernatural creatures with a skill for trickery.

The dust coalesces into a man in a long, formal sherwani and loosely wound red turban, leaning on the parapet and looking out over the glowing anarchy of Chandni Chowk. He is very handsome, the dancer thinks, hastily stubbing out her cigarette and letting it fall in an arc of red embers over the battlements. It does not do to smoke in the presence of the great diplomat A. J. Rao.

"You needn't have done that on my account, Esha," A. J. Rao says, pressing his hands together in a namaste. "It's not as if I can catch anything from it."

Esha Rathore returns the greeting, wondering if the stage crew down in the courtyard was watching her salute empty air. All Awadh knows those filmi-star features: A. J. Rao, one of Bharat's most knowledgeable and tenacious negotiators. No, she corrects herself. All Awadh knows are pictures on a screen. Pictures on a screen, pictures in her head; a voice in her ear. An aeai.

"You know my name?"

"I am one of your greatest admirers."

Her face flushes: a waft of stifling heat spun off from the vast palace's microclimate, Esha tells herself. Not embarrassment. Never embarrassment.

"But I'm a dancer. And you are an . . ."

"Artificial intelligence? That I am. Is this some new anti-aeai legislation, that we can't appreciate dance?" He closes his eyes. "Ah: I'm just watching the Marriage of Radha and Krishna again."

But he has her vanity now. "Which performance?"

"Star Arts Channel. I have them all. I must confess, I often have you running in the background while I'm in negotiation. But please don't mistake me, I never tire of you." A. J. Rao smiles. He has very good, very white teeth. "Strange as it may seem, I'm not sure what the etiquette is in this sort of thing. I came here because I wanted to tell you that I am one of your greatest fans and that I am very much looking forward to your performance tonight. It's the highlight of this conference, for me."

The light is almost gone now and the sky is a pure, deep, eternal blue, like a minor chord. Houseboys make their many ways along the ramps and wall-walks lighting rows of tiny oil-lamps. The Red Fort glitters like a constellation fallen over Old Delhi. Esha has lived in Delhi all her twenty years and she has never seen her city from this vantage. She says, "I'm not sure what the etiquette is either, I've never spoken with an aeai before."

"Really?" A. J. now stands with his back against the sun-warm stone, looking up at the sky, and her out of the corner of his eye. The eyes smile, slyly. Of course, she thinks. Her city is as full of aeais as it is of birds. From computer systems and robots with the feral smarts of rats and pigeons to entities like this one standing before her on the gate of the Red Fort making charming compliments. Not standing. Not anywhere, just a pattern of information in her head. She stammers:

"I mean, a . . . a . . ."

"Level 2.9?"

"I don't know what that means."

The aeai smiles and as she tries to work it out there is another chime in Esha's head and this time it is Pranh, swearing horribly as usual, where is she doesn't she know yts got a show to put on, half the bloody continent watching.

"Excuse me . . ."

"Of course. I shall be watching."

How? she wants to ask. *An aeai, a djinn, wants to watch me dance. What is this?* But when she looks back, all there is to ask is a wisp of dust blowing along the lantern-lit battlement.

There are elephants and circus performers, there are illusionists and table magicians, there are ghazal and qawali and Boli singers; there is the catering and the sommelier's wine and then the lights go up on the stage and Esha spins out past the scowling Pranh as the tabla and melodeon and shehnai begin. The heat is intense in the marble square, but she is transported. The stampings, the pirouettes and swirl of her skirts, the beat of the ankle bells, the facial expressions, the subtle hand mudras: once again she is spun out of herself by the disciplines of Kathak into something greater. She would call it her art, her talent, but she's superstitious: that would be to claim it and so crush the gift. Never name it, never speak it. Just let it possess you. Her own, burning djinn. But as she spins across the brilliant stage before the seated delegates, a corner of her perception scans the architecture for cameras, robots, eyes through which A. J. Rao might watch her. Is she a splinter of his consciousness, as he is a splinter of hers?

She barely hears the applause as she curtseys to the bright lights and runs offstage. In the dressing room as her assistants remove and carefully fold the many jewelled layers of her costume, wipe away the crusted stage makeup to reveal the twenty-year-old beneath, her attention keeps flicking to her earhoek, curled like a plastic question on her dressing table. In jeans and silk sleeveless vest, indistinguishable from any other of Delhi's four million twentysomethings, she coils the device behind her ear, smoothes her hair over it, and her fingers linger a moment as she slides the palmer over her hand. No calls. No messages. No avatars. She's surprised it matters so much.

The official Mercs are lined up in the Delhi Gate. A man and woman intercept her on her way to the car. She waves them away.

"I don't do autographs . . ." Never after a performance. Get out, get away quick and quiet, disappear into the city. The man opens his palm to show her a warrant badge.

"We'll take this car."

It pulls out from the line and cuts in, a cream-coloured high-marque Maruti. The man politely opens the door to let her enter first but there is no respect in it. The woman takes the front seat beside the driver; he accelerates out, horn blaring, into the great circus of night traffic around the Red Fort. The airco purrs.

"I am Inspector Thacker from the Department of Artificial Intelligence Registration and Licensing," the man says. He is young and good-skinned and confident and not at all fazed by sitting next to a celebrity. His aftershave is perhaps overemphatic.

"A Krishna Cop."

That makes him wince.

"Our surveillance systems have flagged up a communication between you and the Bharati Level 2.9 aeai A. J. Rao."

"He called me, yes."

"At 21:08. You were in contact for six minutes twenty-two seconds. Can you tell me what you talked about?"

The car is driving very fast for Delhi. The traffic seems to flow around it. Every light seems to be green. Nothing is allowed to impede its progress. *Can they do that?* Esha wonders. Krishna Cops, Aeai police: *Can they tame the creatures they hunt?*

"We talked about Kathak. He's a fan. Is there a problem? Have I done something wrong?"

"No, nothing at all, Ms. But you do understand, with a conference of this importance . . . On behalf of the department, I apologise for the unseemliness. Ah. Here we are."

They've brought her right to her bungalow. Feeling dirty, dusty, confused, she watches the Krishna Cop car drive off, holding Delhi's frenetic traffic at bay with its tame djinns. She pauses at the gate. She needs, she deserves, a moment to come out from the performance, that little step away so she can turn round and look back at herself and say, yeah, Esha Rathore. The bungalow is unlit, quiet. Neeta and Priya will be out with their wonderful fiancés, talking wedding gifts and guest lists and how hefty a dowry they can squeeze from their husbands-to-be's families. They're not her sisters, though they share the classy bungalow. No one has sisters anymore in Awadh, or even Bharat. No one of Esha's age, though she's heard the balance is being restored. Daughters are fashionable. Once upon a time, women paid the dowry.

She breathes deep of her city. The cool garden microclimate presses down the roar of Delhi to a muffled throb, like blood in the heart. She can smell dust and roses. Rose of Persia. Flower of the Urdu poets. And dust. She imagines it rising up on a whisper of wind, spinning into a charming, dangerous djinn. No. An illusion, a madness of a mad old city. She opens the security gate and finds every square centimetre of the compound filled with red roses.

Neeta and Priya are waiting for her at the breakfast table next morning, sitting side by side close like an interview panel. Or Krishna Cops. For once they aren't talking houses and husbands.

"Who who who where did they come from who sent them so many must have cost a fortune . . ."

Puri the housemaid brings Chinese green chai that's good against cancer. The sweeper has gathered the bouquets into a pile at one end of the compound. The sweet of their perfume is already tinged with rot.

"He's a diplomat." Neeta and Priya only watch *Town and Country* and the chati channels but even they must know the name of A. J. Rao. So she half lies: "A Bharati diplomat."

Their mouths go oooh, then ah as they look at each other. Neeta says, "You have have have to bring him."

"To our durbar," says Priya.

"Yes, our durbar," says Neeta. They've talked gossiped planned little else for the past two months: their grand joint engagement party where they will show off to their as-yet-unmarried girl friends and make all the single men jealous. Esha excuses her grimace with the bitterness of the health-tea.

"He's very busy." She doesn't say busy man. She cannot even think why she is playing these silly girli secrecy games. An aeai called her at the Red Fort to tell her it admired her. Didn't even meet her. There was nothing to meet. It was all in her head. "I don't even know how to get in touch with him. They don't give their numbers out."

"He's coming," Neeta and Priya insist.

She can hardly hear the music for the rattle of the old airco, but sweat runs down her sides along the waistband of her Adidas tights to gather in the hollow of her back and slide between the taut curves of her ass. She tries it again across the gharana's practice floor. Even the ankle bells sound like lead. Last night she touched the three heavens. This morning she feels dead. She can't concentrate, and that little lavda Pranh knows it, swishing at her with yts cane and gobbing out wads of chewed paan and mealy eunuch curses.

"Ey! Less staring at your palmer, more mudras! Decent mudras! You jerk my dick, if I still had one."

Embarrassed that Pranh has noted something she was not conscious of herself—ring, call me, ring me, ring, take me out of this—she fires back, "If you ever had one."

Pranh slashes yts cane at her legs, catches the back of her calf a sting.

"Fuck you, hijra!" Esha snatches up towel bag palmer, hooks the earpiece behind her long, straight hair. No point changing, the heat out there will soak through anything in a moment. "I'm out of here."

Pranh doesn't call after her. Yts too proud. *Little freak monkey thing*, she thinks. How is it a nute is an yt, but an incorporeal aeai is a he? In the legends of Old Delhi, djinns are always he.

"Memsahb Rathore?"

The chauffeur is in full dress and boots. His only concession to the heat is his shades. In bra top and tights and bare skin, she's melting. "The vehicle is fully air-conditioned, memsahb."

The white leather upholstery is so cool her flesh recoils from its skin.

"This isn't the Krishna Cops."

"No memsahb." The chauffeur pulls out into the traffic. It's only as the security locks clunk she thinks, *Oh Lord Krishna, they could be kidnapping me.*

"Who sent you?" There's glass too thick for her fists to damage between her and the driver. Even if the doors weren't locked, a tumble from the car at this speed, in this traffic, would be too much for even a dancer's lithe reflexes. And she's lived in Delhi all her life, basti to bungalow, but she doesn't recognise these streets, this suburb, that industrial park. "Where are you taking me?"

"Memsahb, where I am not permitted to say for that would spoil the surprise. But I am permitted to tell you that you are the guest of A. J. Rao."

The palmer calls her name as she finishes freshening up with bottled Kinley from the car bar.

"Hello!" (Kicking back deep into the cool cool white leather, like a filmi star. She is a star. A star with a bar in a car.)

Audio-only. "I trust the car is acceptable?" Same smooth-suave voice. She can't imagine any opponent being able to resist that voice in negotiation.

"It's wonderful. Very luxurious. Very high status." She's out in the bastis now, slums deeper and meaner than the one she grew up in. Newer. The newest ones always look the oldest. Boys chug past on a home-brew chhakda they've scavenged from tractor parts. The cream Lex carefully detours around emaciated cattle with angular hips jutting through stretched skin like engineering. Everywhere, drought dust lies thick on the crazed hardtop. This is a city of stares. "Aren't you supposed to be at the conference?"

A laugh, inside her auditory centre.

"Oh, I am hard at work winning water for Bharat, believe me. I am nothing if not an assiduous civil servant."

"You're telling me you're there, and here?"

"Oh, it's nothing for us to be in more than one place at the same time. There are multiple copies of me, and subroutines."

"So which is the real you?"

"They are all the real me. In fact, not one of my avatars is in Delhi at all, I am distributed over a series of dharma-cores across Varanasi and Patna." He sighs. It sounds close and weary and warm as a whisper in her ear. "You find it difficult to comprehend a distributed consciousness; it is every bit as hard for me to comprehend a discrete, mobile consciousness. I can only copy myself through what you call cyberspace, which is the physical reality of my universe, but you move through dimensional space and time."

"So which one of you loves me, then?" The words are out, wild, loose, and unconsidered. "I mean, as a dancer, that is." She's filling, gabbling. "Is there one of you that particularly appreciates Kathak?" Polite polite words, like you'd say to an industrialist or a hopeful lawyer at one of Neeta and Priya's hideous matchmaking soirées. Don't be forward, no one likes a forward woman. This is a man's world, now. But she hears glee bubble in A. J. Rao's voice.

"Why, all of me and every part of me, Esha."

Her name. He used her name.

It's a shitty street of pi-dogs and men lounging on charpoys scratching themselves but the chauffeur insists, *Here, this way, memsahb.* She picks her way down a gali lined with unsteady minarets of old car tires. Burning ghee and stale urine reek the air. Kids mob the Lexus but the car has A. J. Rao levels of security. The chauffeur pushes open an old wood and brass Mughal-style gate in a crumbling red wall. "Memsahb."

She steps through into a garden. Into the ruins of a garden. The gasp of wonder dies. The geometrical water channels of the charbagh are dry, cracked, choked with litter from picnics. The shrubs are blousy and overgrown, the plant borders ragged with weeds. The grass is scabbed brown with drought-burn; the lower branches of the trees have been hacked away for firewood. As she walks towards the crack-roofed pavilion at the centre where paths and water channels meet, the gravel beneath her thin shoes is crazed into rivulets from past monsoons. Dead leaves and fallen twigs cover the lawns. The fountains are dry and silted. Yet families stroll pushing baby buggies; children chase balls. Old Islamic gentlemen read the papers and play chess.

"The Shalimar Gardens," says A. J. Rao in the base of her skull. "Paradise as a walled garden."

And as he speaks, a wave of transformation breaks across the garden, sweeping away the decay of the twenty-first century. Trees break into full leaf, flower beds blossom, rows of terracotta geranium pots march down the banks of the charbagh channels which shiver with water. The tiered roofs of the pavilion gleam with gold leaf, peacocks fluster and fuss their vanities, and everything glitters and splashes with fountain play. The laughing families are swept back into Mughal grandees, the old men in the park transformed into malis sweeping the gravel paths with their besoms.

Esha claps her hands in joy, hearing a distant, silver spray of sitar notes. "Oh," she says, numb with wonder. "Oh!"

"A thank you, for what you gave me last night. This is one of my favourite places in all India, even though it's almost forgotten. Perhaps, because it is almost forgotten. Aurangzeb was crowned Mughal Emperor here in 1658, now it's an evening stroll for the basti people. The past is a passion of mine; it's easy for me, for all of us. We can live in as many times as we can places. I often come here, in my mind. Or should I say, it comes to me."

Then the jets from the fountain ripple as if in the wind, but it is not the wind, not on this stifling afternoon, and the falling water flows into the shape of a man, walking out of the spray. A man of water that shimmers and flows and becomes a man of flesh. A. J. Rao. *No*, she thinks, *never flesh. A djinn. A thing caught between heaven and hell. A caprice, a trickster. Then trick me.*

"It is as the old Urdu poets declare," says A. J. Rao. "Paradise is indeed contained within a wall."

It is far past four but she can't sleep. She lies naked—shameless—but for the 'hoek behind her ear on top of her bed with the window slats open and the ancient airco chugging, fitful in the periodic brownouts. It is the worst night yet. The city gasps for air. Even the traffic sounds beaten tonight. Across the room her palmer opens its blue eye and whispers her name. Esha.

She's up, kneeling on the bed, hand to 'hoek, sweat beading her bare skin.

"I'm here." A whisper. Neeta and Priya are a thin wall away on either side.

"It's late, I know, I'm sorry . . ."

She looks across the room into the palmer's camera.

"It's all right, I wasn't asleep." A tone in that voice. "What is it?"

"The mission is a failure."

She kneels in the centre of the big antique bed. Sweat runs down the fold of her spine.

"The conference? What? What happened?" She whispers, he speaks in her head.

"It fell over one point. One tiny, trivial point, but it was like a wedge that split everything apart until it all collapsed. The Awadhis will build their dam at Kunda Khadar and they will keep their holy Ganga water for Awadh. My delegation is already packing. We will return to Varanasi in the morning."

Her heart kicks. Then she curses herself, stupid, romantic girli. He is already in Varanasi as much as he is here as much as he is at the Red Fort assisting his human superiors.

"I'm sorry."

"Yes," he says. "That is the feeling. Was I overconfident in my abilities?"

"People will always disappoint you."

A wry laugh in the dark of her skull.

"How very . . . disembodied of you, Esha." Her name seems to hang in the hot air, like a chord. "Will you dance for me?"

"What, here? Now?"

"Yes. I need something . . . embodied. Physical. I need to see a body move, a consciousness dance through space and time as I cannot. I need to see something beautiful."

Need. A creature with the powers of a god, needs. But Esha's suddenly shy, covering her small, taut breasts with her hands.

"Music . . ." she stammers. "I can't perform without music . . ." The shadows at the end of the bedroom thicken into an ensemble: three men bent over tabla, sarangi, and bansuri. Esha gives a little shriek and ducks back to the modesty of her bedcover. They cannot see you, they don't even exist, except in your head. And even if they were flesh, they would be so intent on their contraptions of wire and skin they would not notice. Terrible driven things, musicians.

"I've incorporated a copy of a sub-aeai into myself for this night," A. J. Rao says. "A Level 1.9 composition system. I supply the visuals."

"You can swap bits of yourself in and out?" Esha asks. The tabla player has started a slow Natetere tap-beat on the dayan drum. The musicians nod at each other. Counting, they will be counting. It's hard to convince herself Neeta and Priya can't hear; no one can hear but her. And A. J. Rao. The sarangi player sets his bow to the strings, the bansuri lets loose a snake of fluting notes. A sangeet, but not one she has ever heard before.

"It's making it up!"

"It's a composition aeai. Do you recognise the sources?"

"Krishna and the Gopis." One of the classic Kathak themes: Krishna's seduction of the milkmaids with his flute, the bansuri, most sensual of instruments. She knows the steps, feels her body anticipating the moves.

"Will you dance, lady?"

And she steps with the potent grace of a tiger from the bed onto the grass matting of her bedroom floor, into the focus of the palmer. Before she had been shy, silly, girli. Not now. She has never had an audience like this before. A lordly djinn. In pure, hot silence she executes the turns and stampings and bows of the One Hundred and Eight Gopis, bare feet kissing the woven grass. Her hands shape mudras, her face the expressions of the ancient story: surprise, coyness, intrigue, arousal. Sweat courses luxuriously down her naked skin: she doesn't feel it. She is clothed in movement and night. Time slows, the stars halt in their arc over great Delhi. She can feel the planet breathe beneath her feet. This is what it was for, all those dawn risings, all those bleeding feet, those slashes of Pranh's cane, those lost birthdays, that stolen childhood. She dances until her feet bleed again into the rough weave of the matting, until every last drop of water is sucked from her and turned into salt, but she stays with the tabla, the beat of dayan and bayan. She is the milkmaid by the river, seduced by a god. A. J. Rao did not choose this Kathak wantonly. And then the music comes to its ringing end and the musicians bow to each other and disperse into golden dust and she collapses, exhausted as never before from any other performance, onto the end of her bed.

Light wakes her. She is sticky, naked, embarrassed. The house staff could find her. And she has a killing headache. Water. Water. Joints nerves sinews plead for it. She pulls on a Chinese silk robe. On her way to the kitchen, the voyeur eye of her palmer blinks at her. No erotic dream, then, no sweat hallucination stirred out of heat and hydrocarbons. She danced Krishna and the One Hundred and Eight Gopis in her bedroom for an aeai. A message. There's a number. You can call me.

Throughout the history of the eight Delhis there have been men—and almost always men—skilled in the lore of djinns. They are wise to their many forms and can see beneath the disguises they wear on the streets—donkey, monkey, dog, scavenging kite—to their true selves. They know their roosts and places where they congregate—they are particularly drawn to mosques—and know that that unexplained heat as you push down a gali behind the Jama Masjid is djinns, packed so tight you can feel their fire as you push through them.

The wisest—the strongest—of fakirs know their names and so can capture and command them. Even in the old India, before the breakup into Awadh and Bharat and Rajputana and the United States of Bengal—there were saints who could summon djinns to fly on their backs from one end of Hindustan to the other in a night. In my own Leh there was an aged aged Sufi who cast one hundred and eight djinns out of a troubled house: twenty-seven in the living room, twenty-seven in the bedroom, and fifty-four in the kitchen. With so many djinns there was no room for anyone else. He drove them off with burning yoghurt and chillis but warned: Do not toy with djinns, for they do nothing without a price, and though that may be years in the asking, ask it they surely will.

Now there is a new race jostling for space in their city: the aeais. If the djinns are the creation of fire and men of clay, these are the creation of word. Fifty million of them swarm Delhi's boulevards and chowks: routing traffic, trading shares, maintaining power and water, answering enquiries, telling fortunes, managing calendars and diaries, handling routine legal and medical matters, performing in soap operas, sifting the septillion pieces of information streaming through Delhi's nervous system each second. The city is a great mantra. From routers and maintenance robots with little more than animal intelligence (each animal has intelligence enough: ask the eagle or the tiger) to the great Level 2.9s that are indistinguishable from a human being ninety-nine-point-nine-nine percent of the time; they are a young race, an energetic race, fresh to this world and enthusiastic, understanding little of their power.

The djinns watch in dismay from their rooftops and minarets: that such powerful creatures of living word should so blindly serve the clay creation, but mostly because, unlike humans, they can foresee the time when the aeais will drive them from their ancient, beloved city and take their places.

This durbar, Neeta and Priya's theme is *Town and Country*: the Bharati megasoap that has perversely become fashionable as public sentiment in Awadh turns against Bharat. Well, we will just bloody well build our dam, tanks or no tanks; they can beg for it, it's our water now, and, in the same breath, what do you think about Ved Prakash, isn't it scandalous what that Ritu Parvaaz is up to? Once they derided it and its viewers but now that it's improper, now that it's unpatriotic, they can't get enough of Anita Mahapatra and the Begum Vora. Some still refuse to watch but pay for daily plot digests so they can appear fashionably informed at social musts like Neeta and Priya's dating durbars.

And it's a grand durbar; the last before the monsoon—if it actually happens this year. Neeta and Priya have hired top bhati-boys to provide a wash of mixes beamed straight into the guests' 'hoeks. There's even a climate-control field, labouring at the limits of its containment to hold back the night heat. Esha can feel its ultrasonics as a dull buzz against her molars.

"Personally, I think sweat becomes you," says A. J. Rao, reading Esha's vital signs through her palmer. Invisible to all but Esha, he moves beside her like death through the press of Town and Countrified guests. By tradition the last durbar of the season is a masked ball. In modern, middle-class Delhi that means everyone wears the computer-generated semblance of a soap character. In the flesh they are the socially mobile dressed in smart-but-cool hot-season modes but in the mind's eye, they are Aparna Chawla and Ajay Nadiadwala, dashing Govind and conniving Dr. Chatterji. There are three Ved Prakashs and as many Lal Darfans—the aeai actor that plays Ved Prakash in the machine-made soap. Even the grounds of Neeta's fiancé's suburban bungalow have been enchanted into Brahmpur, the fictional town where *Town and Country* takes place, where the actors that play the characters believe they live out their lives of celebrity tittle-tattle. When Neeta and Priya judge that everyone has mingled and networked enough, the word will be given and everyone will switch off their glittering disguises and return to being wholesalers and lunch vendors and software rajas. Then the serious stuff begins, the matter of finding a bride. For now Esha can enjoy wandering anonymous in company of her friendly djinn.

She has been wandering much these weeks, through heated streets to ancient places, seeing her city fresh through the eyes of a creature that lives across many spaces and times. At the Sikh gurdwara she saw Tegh Bahadur, the Ninth Guru, beheaded by fundamentalist Aurangzeb's guards. The gyring traffic around Vijay Chowk melted into the Bentley cavalcade of Mountbatten, the Last Viceroy, as he forever quit Lutyen's stupendous palace. The tourist clutter and shoving curio vendors around the Qutb Minar turned to ghosts and it was 1193 and the muezzins of the first Mughal conquerors sang out the adhaan. Illusions. Little lies. But it is all right, when it is done in love. Everything is all right in love. *Can you read my mind?* she asked as she moved with her invisible guide through the thronging streets, which every day grew less raucous, less substantial. *Do you know what I am thinking about you, Aeai Rao?* Little by little, she slips away from the human world into the city of the djinns.

Sensation at the gate. The male stars of *Town and Country* buzz around a woman in an ivory sequined dress. It's a bit damn clever: she's come as Yana Mitra, freshest fittest fastest boli sing-star. And boli girlis, like Kathak dancers, are still meat and ego, though Yana, like every Item-singer, has had her computer avatar guest on T'n'C.

A. J. Rao laughs. "If they only knew. Very clever. What better disguise than to go as yourself. It really is Yana Mitra. Esha Rathore, what's the matter, where are you going?"

Why do you have to ask don't you know everything then you know it's hot and noisy and the ultrasonics are doing my head in and the yap yap yap is going right through me and they're all only after one thing, are you married are you engaged are you looking and I wish I hadn't come I wish I'd just gone out somewhere with you and that dark corner under the gulmohar bushes by the bhati-rig looks the place to get away from all the stupid stupid people.

Neeta and Priya, who know her disguise, shout over, "So, Esha, are we finally going to meet that man of yours?"

He's already waiting for her among the golden blossoms. Djinns travel at the speed of thought.

"What is it what's the matter . . ."

She whispers, "You know, sometimes I wish, I really wish you could get me a drink."

"Why certainly, I will summon a waiter."

"No!" Too loud. Can't be seen talking to the bushes. "No; I mean, hand me one. Just hand me one." But he cannot, and never will. She says, "I started when I was five, did you know that? Oh, you probably did, you know everything about me. But I bet you didn't know how it happened: I was playing with the other girls, dancing round the tank, when this old woman from the gharana went up to my mother and said, I will give you a hundred thousand rupees if you give her to me. I will turn her into a dancer; maybe, if she applies herself, a dancer famous through all of India. And my mother said, Why her? And do you know what that woman said? Because she shows rudimentary talent for movement, but mostly because you are willing to sell her to me for one lakh rupees. She took the money there and then, my mother. The old woman took me to the gharana. She had once been a great dancer but she got rheumatism and couldn't move and that made her bad. She used to beat me with lathis; I had to be up before dawn to get everyone chai and eggs. She would make me practise until my feet bled. They would hold up my arms in slings to perform the mudras until I couldn't put them down again without screaming. I never once got home—and do you know something? I never once wanted to. And despite her, I applied myself, and I became a great dancer. And do you know what? No one cares. I spent fifteen years mastering something no one cares about. But bring in some boli girl who's been around five minutes to flash her teeth and tits—"

"Jealous?" asks A. J. Rao, mildly scolding.

"Don't I deserve to be?"

Then bhati-boy One blinks up "You Are My Soniya" on his palmer and that's the signal to demask. Yana Mitra claps her hands in delight and sings along as all around her glimmering soapi stars dissolve into mundane accountants and engineers and cosmetic nanosurgeons and the pink walls and roof gardens and thousand thousands stars of Old Brahmpur melt and run down the sky.

It's seeing them, exposed in their naked need, melting like that soap world before the sun of celebrity, that calls back the madness Esha knows from her childhood in the gharana. The brooch makes a piercing, ringing chime against the cocktail glass she has snatched from a waiter. She climbs up onto a table. At last, that boli bitch shuts up. All eyes are on her.

"Ladies, but mostly gentlemen, I have an announcement to make." Even the city behind the sound curtain seems to be holding its breath. "I am engaged to be married!" Gasps. Oohs. Polite applause, who is she, is she on tivi, isn't she something arty? Neeta and Priya are wide-eyed at the back. "I'm very very lucky because my husband-to-be is here tonight. In fact, he's been with me all evening. Oh, silly me. Of course, I forgot, not all of you can see him. Darling, would you mind? Gentlemen and ladies, would you mind slipping on your 'hoeks for just a moment. I'm sure you don't need any intro-duction to my wonderful wonderful fiancé, A. J. Rao."

And she knows from the eyes, the mouths, the low murmur that threatens to break into applause, then fails, then is taken up by Neeta and Priya to turn into a decorous ovation, that they can all see Rao as tall and ele-gant and handsome as she sees him, at her side, hand draped over hers.

She can't see that boli girl anywhere.

He's been quiet all the way back in the phatphat. He's quiet now, in the house. They're alone. Neeta and Priya should have been home hours ago, but Esha knows they're scared of her.

"You're very quiet." This, to the coil of cigarette smoke rising up towards the ceiling fan as she lies on her bed. She'd love a bidi, a good, dirty street smoke for once, not some Big Name Western brand.

"We were followed as we drove back after the party. An aeai aircraft sur-veilled your phatphat. A network analysis aeai system sniffed at my router net to try to track this com channel. I know for certain street cameras were tasked on us. The Krishna Cop who lifted you after the Red Fort durbar was at the end of the street. He is not very good at subterfuge."

Esha goes to the window to spy out the Krishna Cop, call him into the open, demand of him what he thinks he's doing.

"He's long gone," says Rao. "They have been keeping you under light surveillance for some time now. I would imagine your announcement has upped your level."

"They were there?"

"As I said—"

"Light surveillance."

It's scary but exciting, down in the deep muladhara chakra, a red throb above her yoni. Scarysexy. That same lift of red madness that made her blurt out that marriage announcement. It's all going so far, so fast. No way to get off now.

"You never gave me the chance to answer," says Aeai Rao.

Can you read my mind? Esha thinks at the palmer.

"No, but I share some operating protocols with scripting aeais for *Town and Country*—in a sense they are a low-order part of me—and they have become quite good predictors of human behaviour."

"I'm a soap opera."

Then she falls back onto the bed and laughs and laughs and laughs until she feels sick, until she doesn't want to laugh anymore and every guffaw is a choke, a lie, spat up at the spy machines up there, beyond the lazy fan that merely stirs the heat, turning on the huge thermals that spire up from Delhi's colossal heat-island, a conspiracy of djinns.

"Esha," A. J. Rao says, closer than he has ever seemed before. "Lie still." She forms the question, *Why?* And hears the corresponding whisper inside her head, *Hush, don't speak.* In the same instant the chakra glow bursts like a yolk and leaks heat into her yoni. Oh, she says, oh! Her clitoris is singing to her. Oh oh oh oh. "How . . ." Again, the voice, huge inside her head, inside every part of her, *Sssshhhhh.* Building building she needs to do something, she needs to move needs to rub against the day-warmed scented wood of the big bed, needs to get her hand down there hard hard hard . . .

"No, don't touch," chides A. J. Rao and now she can't even move she needs to explode she has to explode her skull can't contain this her dancer's muscles are pulled tight as wires she can't take much more no no no yes yes yes she's shrieking now tiny little shrieks beating her fists off the bed but it's just spasm, nothing will obey her and then it's explosion bam, and another one before that one has even faded, huge slow explosions across the sky and she's cursing and blessing every god in India. Ebbing now, but still shock after shock, one on top of the other. Ebbing now . . . Ebbing.

"Ooh. Oh. What? Oh wow, how?"

"The machine you wear behind your ear can reach deeper than words and visions," says A. J. Rao. "So, are you answered?"

"What?" The bed is drenched in sweat. She's sticky dirty needs to wash change clothes, move but the afterglows are still fading. Beautiful beautiful colours.

"The question you never gave me the chance to answer. Yes. I will marry you."

"Stupid vain girl, you don't even know what caste he is."

Mata Madhuri smokes eighty a day through a plastic tube hooked through the respirator unit into a grommet in her throat. She burns through them three at time: Bloody machine scrubs all the good out of them, she says. Last bloody pleasure I have. She used to bribe the nurses but they bring her them free now, out of fear of her temper that grows increasingly vile as her body surrenders more and more to the machines.

Without pause for Esha's reply, a flick of her whim whips the life-support chair round and out into the garden.

"Can't smoke in there, no fresh air."

Esha follows her out onto the raked gravel of the formal charbagh.

"No one marries in caste anymore."

"Don't be smart, stupid girl. It's like marrying a Muslim, or even a Christian, Lord Krishna protect me. You know fine what I mean. Not a real person."

"There are girls younger than me marry trees, or even dogs."

"So bloody clever. That's up in some god-awful shithole like Bihar or Rajputana, and anyway, those are gods. Any fool knows that. Ach, away with you!" The old, destroyed woman curses as the chair's aeai deploys its parasol. "Sun sun, I need sun, I'll be burning soon enough, sandalwood, you hear? You burn me on a sandalwood pyre. I'll know if you stint."

Madhuri the old crippled dance teacher always uses this tactic to kill a conversation with which she is uncomfortable. When I'm gone . . . Burn me sweetly . . .

"And what can a god do that A. J. Rao can't?"

"Ai! You ungrateful, blaspheming child. I'm not hearing this la la la la la la la la have you finished yet?"

Once a week Esha comes to the nursing home to visit this ruin of a woman, wrecked by the demands a dancer makes of a human body. She's explored guilt need rage resentment anger pleasure at watching her collapse into long death as the motives that keep her turning up the drive in a phat-phat and there is only one she believes. She's the only mother she has.

"If you marry that . . . thing . . . you will be making a mistake that will destroy your life," Madhuri declares, accelerating down the path between the water channels.

"I don't need your permission," Esha calls after her. A thought spins Madhuri's chair on its axis.

"Oh, really? That would be a first for you. You want my blessing. Well, you won't have it. I refuse to be party to such nonsense."

"I will marry A. J. Rao."

"What did you say?"

"I. Will. Marry. Aeai. A. J. Rao."

Madhuri laughs, a dry, dying, spitting sound, full of bidi smoke.

"Well, you almost surprise me. Defiance. Good, some spirit at last. That was always your problem, you always needed everyone to approve, everyone to give you permission, everyone to love you. And that's what stopped you being great, do you know that, girl? You could have been a devi, but you always held back for fear that someone might not approve. And so you were ever only . . . good."

People are looking now, staff, visitors. Patients. Raised voices, unseemly emotions. This is a house of calm, and slow mechanized dying. Esha bends low to whisper to her mentor.

"I want you to know that I dance for him. Every night. Like Radha for Krishna. I dance just for him, and then he comes and makes love to me. He makes me scream and swear like a hooker. Every night. And look!" He doesn't need to call anymore; he is hardwired into the 'hoek she hardly ever takes off now. Esha looks up: he is there, standing in a sober black suit among the strolling visitors and droning wheelchairs, hands folded. "There he is, see? My lover, my husband."

A long, keening screech, like feedback, like a machine dying. Madhuri's withered hands fly to her face. Her breathing tube curdles with tobacco smoke.

"Monster! Monster! Unnatural child, ah, I should have left you in that basti! Away from me away away away!"

Esha retreats from the old woman's mad fury as hospital staff come hurrying across the scorched lawns, white saris flapping.

Every fairy tale must have a wedding.

Of course it was the event of the season. The decrepit old Shalimar Gardens were transformed by an army of malis into a sweet, green, watered maharaja's fantasia with elephants, pavilions, musicians, lancers, dancers, filmi stars, and robot bartenders. Neeta and Priya were uncomfortable bridesmaids in fabulous frocks; a great Brahmin was employed to bless the union of woman and artificial intelligence. Every television network sent cameras, human or aeai. Gleaming presenters checked the guests in and checked the guests out. Chati-mag paparazzi came in their crowds, wondering what they could turn their cameras on. There were even politicians from Bharat, despite the souring relationships between the two neighbours now Awadh constructors were scooping up the Ganga sands into revetments. But most there were the people of the encroaching bastis, jostling up against the security staff lining the paths of their garden, asking, She's marrying a what? How does that work? Can they, you know? And what about children? Who is she, actually? Can you see anything? I can't see anything. Is there anything to see?

But the guests and the great were 'hoeked up and applauded the groom in his golden veil on his white stallion, stepping with the delicacy of a dressage horse up the raked paths. And because they were great and guests, there was not one who, despite the free French champagne from the well-known diplomatic sommelier, would ever say, But there's no one there. No one was at all surprised that, after the bride left in a stretch limo, there came a dry, sparse thunder, cloud to cloud, and a hot mean wind that swept the discarded invitations along the paths. As they were filing back to their taxis, tankers were draining the expensively filled qanats.

It made lead in the news.

Kathak star weds aeai lover!!! Honeymoon in Kashmir!!!

Above the chowks and minarets of Delhi, the djinns bent together in conference.

He takes her shopping in Tughluk Mall. Three weeks and the shop girls still nod and whisper. She likes that. She doesn't like it that they glance and giggle when the Krishna Cops lift her from the counter at the Black Lotus Japanese Import Company.

"My husband is an accredited diplomat, this is a diplomatic incident." The woman in the bad suit pushes her head gently down to enter the car. The Ministry doesn't need personal liability claims.

"Yes, but you are not, Mrs. Rao," says Thacker in the backseat. Still wearing that cheap aftershave.

"Rathore," she says. "I have retained my stage name. And we shall see what my husband has to say about my diplomatic status." She lifts her hand in a mudra to speak to AyJay, as she thinks of him now. Dead air. She performs the wave again.

"This is a shielded car," Thacker says.

The building is shielded also. They take the car right inside, down a ramp into the basement parking lot. It's a cheap, anonymous glass and titanium block on Parliament Street that she's driven past ten thousand times on her way to the shops of Connaught Circus without ever noticing. Thacker's office is on the fifteenth floor. It's tidy and has a fine view over the astronomical geometries of the Jantar Mantar but smells of food: tiffin snatched at the desk. She checks for photographs of family children wife. Only himself, smart in pressed whites for a cricket match.

"Chai?"

"Please." The anonymity of this civil service block is beginning to unnerve her: a city within a city. The chai is warm and sweet and comes in a tiny disposable plastic cup. Thacker's smile seems also warm and sweet. He sits at the end of the desk, angled towards her in Krishna Cop handbook "nonconfrontational."

"Mrs. Rathore. How to say this?"

"My marriage is legal—"

"Oh, I know, Mrs. Rathore. This is Awadh, after all. Why, there have even been women who married djinns, within our own lifetimes. No. It's an international affair now, it seems. Oh well. Water: we do all so take it for granted, don't we? Until it runs short, that is."

"Everybody knows my husband is still trying to negotiate a solution to the Kunda Khadar problem."

"Yes, of course he is." Thacker lifts a manilla envelope from his desk, peeps inside, grimaces coyly. "How shall I put this? Mrs. Rathore, does your husband tell you everything about his work?"

"That is an impertinent question—"

"Yes yes, forgive me, but if you'll look at these photographs."

Big glossy hi-res prints, slick and sweet-smelling from the printer. Aerial views of the ground, a thread of green-blue water, white sands, scattered shapes without meaning.

"This means nothing to me."

"I suppose it wouldn't, but these drone images show Bharati battle tanks, robot reconnaissance units, and air-defence batteries deploying within striking distance of the construction at Kunda Khadar."

And it feels as if the floor has dissolved beneath her and she is falling through a void so vast it has no visible reference points, other than the sensation of her own falling.

"My husband and I don't discuss work."

"Of course. Oh, Mrs. Rathore, you've crushed your cup. Let me get you another one."

He leaves her much longer than it takes to get a shot of chai from the wallah. When he returns he asks casually, "Have you heard of a thing called the Hamilton Acts? I'm sorry, I thought in your position you would . . . but evidently not. Basically, it's a series of international treaties originated by the United States limiting the development and proliferation of high-level artificial intelligences, most specifically the hypothetical Generation Three. No? Did he not tell you any of this?"

Mrs. Rathore in her Italian suit crosses her ankles demurely and thinks, *This reasonable man can do anything he wants here, anything.*

"As you probably know, we grade and license aeais according to levels; these roughly correspond to how convincingly they pass as human beings. A Level 1 has basic animal intelligence, enough for its task, but would never be mistaken for a human. Many of them can't even speak. They don't need to. A Level 2.9 like your husband—" he speeds over the word, like the wheel of a shatabdi express over the gap in a rail "—is humanlike to a fifth percentile. A Generation Three is indistinguishable in any circumstances from a human—in fact, their intelligences may be many millions of times ours, if there is any meaningful way of measuring that. Theoretically we could not even recognise such an intelligence; all we would see would be the Generation Three interface, so to speak. The Hamilton Acts simply seek to control technology that could give rise to a Generation Three aeai. Mrs. Rathore, we believe sincerely that the Generation Threes pose the greatest threat to our security—as a nation and as a species—that we have ever faced."

"And my husband?" Solid, comfortable word. Thacker's sincerity scares her.

"The government is preparing to sign the Hamilton Acts in return for loan guarantees to construct the Kunda Khadar dam. When the acts are passed—and they're in the current session of the Lok Sabha—everything under Level 2.8 will be subject to rigorous inspection and licensing, policed by us."

"And over Level 2.8?"

"Illegal, Mrs. Rathore. They will be aggressively erased."

Esha crosses and uncrosses her legs. She shifts on the chair. Thacker will wait forever for her response.

"What do you want me to do?"

"A. J. Rao is highly placed within the Bharati administration."

"You're asking me to spy . . . on an aeai."

From his face, she knows he expected her to say, husband.

"We have devices, taps . . . They would be beneath the level of Aeai Rao's consciousness. We can run them into your 'hoek. We are not all blundering plods in the department. Go to the window, Mrs. Rathore."

Esha touches her fingers lightly to the climate-cooled glass, polarised dusk against the drought light. Outside the smog haze says heat. Then she cries and drops to her knees in fear. The sky is filled with gods, rank upon rank, tier upon tier, rising up above Delhi in a vast helix, huge as clouds, as countries, until at the apex the Trimurti, the Hindu Trinity of Brahma, Vishnu, Siva, look down like falling moons. It is her private Ramayana, the titanic Vedic battle order of gods arrayed across the troposphere.

She feels Thacker's hand help her up.

"Forgive me, that was stupid, unprofessional. I was showing off. I wanted to impress you with the aeai systems we have at our disposal."

His hand lingers a moment more than gentle requires. And the gods go out, all at once.

She says, "Mr. Thacker, would you put a spy in my bedroom, in my bed, between me and my husband? That's what you're doing if you tap into the channels between me and AyJay."

Still the hand is there as Thacker guides her to chair, offers cool cool water.

"I only ask because I believe I am doing something for this country. I take pride in my job. In some things I have discretion, but not when it comes to the security of the nation. Do you understand?"

Esha twitches into dancer's composure, straightens her dress, checks her face.

"Then the least you can do is call me a car."

That evening she whirls to the tabla and shehnai across the day-warmed marble of a Jaipuri palace Diwan-i-aam, a flame among the twilit pillars. The audience is dark huddles on the marble, hardly daring even to breathe. Among the lawyers politicians journalists cricket stars moguls of industry are the managers who have converted this Rajput palace into a planetary-class hotel, and any number of chati celebs. None so chati, so celebby, as Esha Rathore. Pranh can cherry-pick the bookings now. She's more than a nine-day, even a nine-week wonder. Esha knows that all her rapt watchers are 'hoeked up, hoping for a ghost-glimpse of her djinn-husband dancing with her through the flame-shadowed pillars.

Afterwards, as yt carries her armfuls of flowers back to her suite, Pranh says, "You know, I'm going to have to up my percentage."

"You wouldn't dare," Esha jokes. Then she sees the bare fear on the nute's face. It's only a wash, a shadow. But yt's afraid.

Neeta and Priya had moved out of the bungalow by the time she returned from Dal Lake. They've stopped answering her calls. It's seven weeks since she last went to see Madhuri.

Naked, she sprawls on the pillows in the filigree-light of the stone jharoka. She peers down from her covered balcony through the grille at the departing guests. See out, not see in. Like the shut-away women of the old zenana. Shut away from the world. Shut away from human flesh. She stands up, holds her body against the day-warmed stone; the press of her nipples, the rub of her pubis. Can you see me smell me sense me know that I am here at all?

And he's there. She does not need to see him now, just sense his electric prickle along the inside of her skull. He fades into vision sitting on the end of the low, ornate teak bed. He could as easily materialise in midair in front of her balcony, she thinks. But there are rules, and games, even for djinns.

"You seem distracted, heart." He's blind in this room—no camera eyes observing her in her jewelled skin—but he observes her through a dozen senses, myriad feedback loops through her 'hoek.

"I'm tired, I'm annoyed, I wasn't as good as I should have been."

"Yes, I thought that too. Was it anything to do with the Krishna Cops this afternoon?"

Esha's heart races. He can read her heartbeat. He can read her sweat, he can read the adrenaline and noradrenaline balance in her brain. He will know if she lies. Hide a lie inside a truth.

"I should have said, I was embarrassed." He can't understand shame. Strange, in a society where people die from want of honour. "We could be in trouble, there's something called the Hamilton Acts."

"I am aware of them." He laughs. He has this way now of doing it inside her head. He thinks she likes the intimacy, a truly private joke. She hates it. "All too aware of them."

"They wanted to warn me. Us."

"That was kind of them. And me a representative of a foreign government. So that's why they've been keeping a watch on you, to make sure you are all right."

"They thought they might be able to use me to get information from you."

"Did they indeed?"

The night is so still she can hear the jingle of the elephant harnesses and the cries of the mahouts as they carry the last of the guests down the long processional drive to their waiting limos. In a distant kitchen a radio jabbers.

Now we will see how human you are. Call him out. At last A. J. Rao says: "Of course. I do love you." Then he looks into her face. "I have something for you."

The staff turn their faces away in embarrassment as they set the device on the white marble floor, back out of the room, eyes averted. What does she care? She is a star. A. J. Rao raises his hand and the lights slowly die. Pierced-brass lanterns send soft stars across the beautiful old zenana room. The device is the size and shape of a phatphat tire, chromed and plasticed, alien among the Mughal retro. As Esha floats over the marble towards it, the plain white surface bubbles and deliquesces into dust. Esha hesitates.

"Don't be afraid, look!" says A. J. Rao. The powder spurts up like steam from boiling rice, then pollen-bursts into a tiny dust-dervish, staggering across the surface of the disc. "Take the 'hoek off!" Rao cries delightedly from the bed. "Take it off." Twice she hesitates, three times he encourages. Esha slides the coil of plastic off the sweet spot behind her ear and voice and man vanish like death. Then the pillar of glittering dust leaps head high, lashes like a tree in a monsoon, and twists itself into the ghostly outline of a man. It flickers once, twice, and then A. J. Rao stands before her. A rattle like leaves a snake-rasp a rush of winds, and then the image says, "Esha." A whisper of dust. A thrill of ancient fear runs through her skin into her bones.

"What is this . . . what are you?"

The storm of dust parts into a smile.

"I-Dust. Micro-robots. Each is smaller than a grain of sand, but they manipulate static fields and light. They are my body. Touch me. This is real. This is me."

But she flinches away in the lantern-lit room. Rao frowns.

"Touch me . . ."

She reaches out her hand towards his chest. Close, he is a creature of sand, a whirlwind permanently whipping around the shape of a man. Esha touches flesh to i-Dust. Her hand sinks into his body. Her cry turns to a startled giggle.

"It tickles . . ."

"The static fields."

"What's inside?"

"Why don't you find out?"

"What, you mean . . . ?"

"It's the only intimacy I can offer . . ." He sees her eyes widen under their kohled makeup. "I think you should hold your breath."

She does, but keeps her eyes open until the last moment, until the dust flickers like a dead tivi channel in her close focus. A. J. Rao's body feels like the most delicate Varanasi silk scarf draped across her bare skin. She is inside him. She is inside the body of her husband, her lover. She dares to open her eyes. Rao's face is a hollow shell looking back at her from a perspective of millimetres. When she moves her lips, she can feel the dust-bots of his lips brushing against hers: an inverse kiss.

"My heart, my Radha," whispers the hollow mask of A. J. Rao. Somewhere Esha knows she should be screaming. But she cannot: she is somewhere no human has ever been before. And now the whirling streamers of i-Dust are stroking her hips, her belly, her thighs. Her breasts. Her nipples, her cheeks and neck, all the places she loves to feel a human touch, caressing her, driving her to her knees, following her as the mote-sized robots follow A. J. Rao's command, swallowing her with his body.

It's *Gupshup* followed by *Chandni Chati* and at twelve thirty a photo shoot—at the hotel, if you don't mind—for *FilmFare's* Saturday Special Centre Spread—you don't mind if we send a robot, they can get places get angles the meat-ware just can't get and could you dress up, like you did for the opening, maybe a move or two, in between the pillars in the Diwan, just like the gala opening, okay lovely lovely lovely well your husband can copy us a couple of avatars and our own aeais can paste him in people want to see you together, happy couple lovely couple, dancer risen from basti, international diplomat, marriage across worlds in every sense the romance of it all, so how did you meet what first attracted you what's it like to be married to an aeai how do the other girls treat you do you, you know and what about children, I mean, of course a woman and an aeai but there are technologies these days geneline engineering like all the super-duper rich and their engineered children and you are a celebrity now how are you finding it, sudden rise to fame, in every gupshup column, worldwide celebi star everyone's talking all the rage and all the chat and all the parties and as Esha answers for the sixth time the same questions asked by the same gazelle-eyed girli celebi reporters oh we are very happy wonderfully happy deliriously happy love is a wonderful wonderful thing and that's the thing about love, it can be for anything, anyone, even a human and an aeai, that's the purest form of love, spiritual love her mouth opening and closing yabba yabba yabba but her inner eye, her eye of Siva, looks inwards, backwards.

Her mouth, opening and closing.

Lying on the big Mughal sweet-wood bed, yellow morning light shattered through the jharoka screen, her bare skin goose-pimpled in the cool of the airco. Dancing between worlds: sleep, wakefulness in the hotel bedroom, memory of the things he did to her limbic centres through the hours of the night that had her singing like a bulbul, the world of the djinns. Naked but for the 'hoek behind her ear. She had become like those people who couldn't afford the treatments and had to wear eyeglasses and learned to at once ignore and be conscious of the technology on their faces. Even when she did remove it—for performing; for, as now, the shower—she could still place A. J. Rao in the room, feel his physicality. In the big marble stroll-in shower in this VIP suite relishing the gush and rush of precious water (always the mark of a true rani) she knew AyJay was sitting on the carved chair by the balcony. So when she thumbed on the tivi panel (bathroom with tivi, oooh!) to distract her while she towelled dry her hair, her first reaction was a double-take look at the 'hoek on the sink stand when she saw the press conference from Varanasi and Water Spokesman A. J. Rao explaining Bharat's necessary military exercises in the vicinity of the Kunda Khadar dam. She slipped on the 'hoek, glanced into the room. There, on the chair, as she felt. There, in the Bharat Sabha studio in Varanasi, talking to Bharti from the *Good Morning Awadh! News.*

Esha watched them both as she slowly, distractedly dried herself. She had felt glowing, sensual, divine. Now she was fleshy, self-conscious, stupid. The water on her skin, the air in the big room was cold cold cold.

"AyJay, is that really you?"

He frowned.

"That's a very strange question first thing in the morning. Especially after—"

She cut cold his smile.

"There's a tivi in the bathroom. You're on, doing an interview for the news. A live interview. So, are you really here?"

"Cho chweet, you know what I am, a distributed entity. I'm copying and deleting myself all over the place. I am wholly there, and I am wholly here."

Esha held the vast, powder-soft towel around her.

"Last night, when you were here, in the body, and afterwards, when we were on the bed—were you here with me? Wholly here? Or was there a copy of you working on your press statement and another having a high-level meeting and another drawing an emergency water supply plan and another talking to the Banglas in Dhaka?"

"My love, does it matter?"

"Yes it matters!" She found tears, and something beyond: anger choking in her throat. "It matters to me. It matters to any woman. To any . . . human."

"Mrs. Rao, are you all right?"

"Rathore, my name is Rathore!" She hears herself snap at the silly little chati-mag junior. Esha gets up, draws up into her full dancer's poise. "This interview is over."

"Mrs. Rathore Mrs. Rathore," the journo girli calls after her.

Glancing at her fractured image in the thousand mirrors of the Sheesh Mahal, Esha notices glittering dust in the shallow lines of her face.

A thousand stories tell of the wilfulness and whim of djinns. But for every story of the djinns, there are a thousand tales of human passion and envy, and the aeais, being a creation between, learned from both. Jealousy, and dissembling.

When Esha went to Thacker the Krishna Cop, she told herself it was from fear of what the Hamilton Acts might do to her husband in the name of national hygiene. But she dissembled. She went to that office on Parliament Street overlooking the star geometries of the Jantar Mantar out of jealousy. When a wife wants her husband, she must have all of him. Ten thousand stories tell this. A copy in the bedroom while another copy plays water politics is an unfaithfulness. If a wife does not have everything, she has nothing. So Esha went to Thacker's office wanting to betray and as she opened her hand on the desk and the techi boys loaded their darkware into her palmer, she thought, *This is right, this is good, now we are equal.* And when Thacker asked her to meet him again in a week to update the 'ware—unlike the djinns—hostages of eternity—software entities on both sides of the war evolved at an ever-increasing rate—he told himself it was duty to his warrant, loyalty to his country. In this too he dissembled. It was fascination.

Earthmover robots started clearing the Kunda Khadar dam site the day Inspector Thacker suggested that perhaps next week they might meet at the International Coffee House on Connaught Circus, his favourite. She said, My husband will see. To which Thacker replied, We have ways to blind him. But all the same she sat in the furthest, darkest corner, under the screen showing the international cricket, hidden from any prying eyes, her 'hoek shut down and cold in her handbag.

So what are you finding out? she asked.

It would be more than my job is worth to tell you, Mrs. Rathore, said the Krishna Cop. National security. Then the waiter brought coffee on a silver tray.

After that they never went back to the office. On the days of their meetings Thacker would whirl her through the city in his government car to Chandni Chowk, to Humayun's Tomb and the Qutb Minar, even to the Shalimar Gardens. Esha knew what he was doing, taking her to those same places where her husband had enchanted her. *How closely have you been watching me?* she thought. *Are you trying to seduce me?* For Thacker did not magic her away to the seven Delhis of the dead past, but immersed her in the crowd, the smell, the bustle, the voices and commerce and traffic and music; her present, her city burning with life and movement. *I was fading*, she realised. *Fading out of the world, becoming a ghost, locked in that invisible marriage, just the two of us, seen and unseen, always together, only together.* She would feel for the plastic fetus of her 'hoek coiled in the bottom of her jewelled bag and hate it a little. When she slipped it behind her ear in the privacy of the phatphat back to her bungalow, she would remember that Thacker was always assiduous in thanking her for her help in national security. Her reply was always the same: Never thank a woman for betraying her husband over her country.

He would ask, of course. Out and about, she would say. Sometimes I just need to get out of this place, get away. Yes, even from you . . . Holding the words, the look into the eye of the lens just long enough . . .

Yes, of course, you must.

Now the earthmovers had turned Kunda Khadar into Asia's largest construction site, the negotiations entered a new stage. Varanasi was talking directly to Washington to put pressure on Awadh to abandon the dam and avoid a potentially destabilising water war. US support was conditional on Bharat's agreement to the Hamilton Acts, which Bharat could never do, not with its major international revenue generator being the wholly aeai-generated soapi *Town and Country.*

Washington telling me to effectively sign my own death warrant. A. J. Rao would laugh. Americans surely appreciate irony. All this he told her as they sat on the well-tended lawn sipping green chai through a straw, Esha sweating freely in the swelter but unwilling to go into the air-conditioned cool because she knew there were still paparazzi lenses out there, focusing. AyJay never needed to sweat. But she still knew that he split himself. In the night, in the rare cool, he would ask, dance for me. But she didn't dance anymore, not for Aeai A. J. Rao, not for Pranh, not for thrilled audiences who would shower her with praise and flowers and money and fame. Not even for herself.

Tired. Too tired. The heat. Too tired.

Thacker is on edge, toying with his chai cup, wary of eye contact when they meet in his beloved International Coffee House. He takes her hand and draws the updates into her open palm with boyish coyness. His talk is smaller than small, finicky, itchily polite. Finally, he dares to look at her.

"Mrs. Rathore, I have something I must ask you. I have wanted to ask you for some time now."

Always, the name, the honorific. But the breath still freezes, her heart kicks in animal fear.

"You know you can ask me anything." Tastes like poison. Thacker can't hold her eye, ducks away, Killa Krishna Kop turned shy boy.

"Mrs. Rathore, I am wondering if you would like to come and see me play cricket?"

The Department of Artificial Intelligence Registration and Licensing versus the Parks and Cemeteries Service of Delhi is hardly a test match against the United States of Bengal but it is still enough of a social occasion to out posh frocks and Number One saris. Pavilions, parasols, sunshades ring the scorched grass of the Civil Service of Awadh sports ground, a flock of white wings. Those who can afford portable airco field generators sit in the cool drinking English Pimm's No. 1 Cup. The rest fan themselves. Incognito in hi-label shades and light silk dupatta, Esha Rathore looks at the salt white figures moving on the circle of brown grass and wonders what it is they find so important in their game of sticks and ball to make themselves suffer so.

She had felt hideously self-conscious when she slipped out of the phat-phat in her flimsy disguise. Then as she saw the crowds in their mela finery milling and chatting, heat rose inside her, the same energy that allowed her to hide behind her performances, seen but unseen. A face half the country sees on its morning chati mags, yet it can vanish so easily under shades and a headscarf. Slum features. The anonymity of the basti bred into the cheekbones, a face from the great crowd.

The Krishna Cops have been put in to bat by Parks and Cemeteries. Thacker is in the middle of the batting order, but Parks and Cemeteries pace bowler Chaudry and the lumpy wicket is making short work of the department's openers. One on his way to the painted wooden pavilion, and Thacker striding towards the crease, pulling on his gloves, taking his place, lining up his bat. He is very handsome in his whites, Esha thinks. He runs a couple of desultory ones with his partner at the other end, then it's a new over. Clop of ball on willow. A rich, sweet sound. A couple of safe returns. Then the bowler lines up and brings his arm round in a windmill. The ball gets a sweet mad bounce. Thacker fixes it with his eye, steps back, takes it in the middle of the bat, and drives it down, hard, fast, bouncing towards the boundary rope that kicks it into the air for a cheer and a flurry of applause and a four. And Esha is on her feet, hands raised to applaud, cheering. The score clicks over on the big board, and she is still on her feet, alone of all the audience. For directly across the ground, in front of the sight screens, is a tall, elegant figure in black, wearing a red turban.

Him. Impossibly, him. Looking right at her, through the white-clad players as if they were ghosts. And very slowly, he lifts a finger and taps it to his right ear.

She knows what she'll find but she must raise her fingers in echo, feel with horror the coil of plastic overlooked in her excitement to get to the game, nestled accusingly in her hair like a snake.

"So, who won the cricket then?"

"Why do you need to ask me? If it were important to you, you'd know. Like you can know anything you really want to."

"You don't know? Didn't you stay to the end? I thought the point of sport was who won. What other reason would you have to follow intra–civil service cricket?"

If Puri the maid were to walk into the living room, she would see a scene from a folk tale: a woman shouting and raging at silent dead air. But

Puri does her duties and leaves as soon as she can. She's not easy in a house of djinns.

"Sarcasm is it now? Where did you learn that? Some sarcasm aeai you've made part of yourself? So now there's another part of you I don't know, that I'm supposed to love? Well, I don't like it and I won't love it because it makes you look petty and mean and spiteful."

"There are no aeais for that. We have no need for those emotions. If I learned these things, I learned them from humans."

Esha lifts her hand to rip away the 'hoek, hurl it against the wall.

"No!"

So far Rao has been voice-only; now the slanting late-afternoon golden light stirs and curdles into the body of her husband.

"Don't," he says. "Don't . . . banish me. I do love you."

"What does that mean?" Esha screams. "You're not real! None of this is real! It's just a story we made up because we wanted to believe it. Other people, they have real marriages, real lives, real sex. Real . . . children."

"Children. Is that what it is? I thought the fame, the attention was the thing, that there never would be children to ruin your career and your body. But if that's no longer enough, we can have children, the best children I can buy."

Esha cries out, a keen of disappointment and frustration. The neighbours will hear. But the neighbours have been hearing everything, listening, gossiping. No secrets in the city of djinns.

"Do you know what they're saying, all those magazines and chati shows? What they're really saying? About us, the djinn and his wife?"

"I know!" For the first time, A. J. Rao's voice, so sweet, so reasonable inside her head, is raised. "I know what every one of them says about us. Esha, have I ever asked anything of you?"

"Only to dance."

"I'm asking one more thing of you now. It's not a big thing. It's a small thing, nothing really. You say I'm not real, what we have is not real. That hurts me, because at some level it's true. Our worlds are not compatible. But it can be real. There is a chip, new technology, a protein chip. You get it implanted, here." Rao raises his hand to his third eye. "It would be like the 'hoek, but it would always be on. I could always be with you. We would never be apart. And you could leave your world and enter mine . . ."

Esha's hands are at her mouth, holding in the horror, the bile, the sick vomit of fear. She heaves, retches. Nothing. No solid, no substance, just ghosts and djinns. Then she rips her 'hoek from the sweet spot behind her ear and there is blessed silence and blindness. She holds the little device in her hands and snaps it cleanly in two.

Then she runs from her house.

Not Neeta not Priya, not snippy Pranh in yts gharana, not Madhuri a smoke-blackened hulk in a life-support chair, and no not never her mother, even though Esha's feet remember every step to her door; never the basti. That's death.

One place she can go.

But he won't let her. He's there in the phatphat, his face in the palm of her hands, voice scrolling silently in a ticker across the smart fabric: Come back, I'm sorry, come back, let's talk come back, I didn't mean to come back. Hunched in the back of the little yellow and black plastic bubble, she clenches his face into a fist but she can still feel him, feel his face, his mouth next to her skin. She peels the palmer from her hand. His mouth moves silently. She hurls him into the traffic. He vanishes under truck tires.

And still he won't let her go. The phatphat spins into Connaught Circus's vast gyratory and his face is on every single one of the video-silk screens hung across the curving facades. Twenty A. J. Raos, greater, lesser, least, miming in sync.

Esha Esha come back, say the rolling news tickers. We can try something else. Talk to me. Any ISO, any palmer, anyone . . .

Infectious paralysis spreads across Connaught Circus. First the people who notice things like fashion ads and chati-screens; then the people who notice other people; then the traffic, noticing all the people on the pavements staring up, mouths fly-catching. Even the phatphat driver is staring. Connaught Circus is congealing into a clot of traffic: if the heart of Delhi stops, the whole city will seize and die.

"Drive on drive on," Esha shouts at her driver. "I order you to drive." But she abandons the autorickshaw at the end of Sisganj Road and pushes through the clogged traffic the final half kilometre to Manmohan Singh Buildings. She glimpses Thacker pressing through the crowd, trying to rendezvous with the police motorbike sirening a course through the traffic. In desperation she thrusts up an arm, shouts out his name and rank. At last, he turns. They beat towards each other through the chaos.

"Mrs. Rathore, we are facing a major incursion incident . . ."

"My husband, Mr. Rao, he has gone mad . . ."

"Mrs. Rathore, please understand, by our standards, he never was sane. He is an aeai."

The motorbike wails its horns impatiently. Thacker waggles his head to the driver, a woman in police leathers and helmet: in a moment in a moment. He seizes Esha's hand, pushes her thumb into his palmer-gloved hand.

"Apartment 1501. I've keyed it to your thumbprint. Open the door to no one, accept no calls, do not use any communications or entertainment equipment. Stay away from the balcony. I'll return as quickly as I can."

Then he swings up onto the pillion, the driver walks her machine round, and they weave off into the gridlock.

The apartment is modern and roomy and bright and clean for a man on his own, well furnished and decorated with no signs of a Krishna Cop's work brought home of an evening. It hits her in the middle of the big living-room floor with the sun pouring in. Suddenly she is on her knees on the Kashmiri rug, shivering, clutching herself, bobbing up and down to sobs so wracking they have no sound. This time the urge to vomit it all up cannot be resisted. When it is out of her—not all of it, it will never all come out—she looks out from under her hanging, sweat-soaked hair, breath still shivering in her aching chest. Where is this place? What has she done? How could she have been so stupid, so vain and senseless and blind? Games games, children's pretending, how could it ever have been? I say it is and it is so: look at me! At me!

Thacker has a small, professional bar in his kitchen annexe. Esha does not know drink so the chota peg she makes herself is much much more gin than tonic but it gives her what she needs to clean the sour, biley vomit from the wool rug and ease the quivering in her breath.

Esha starts, freezes, imagining Rao's voice. She holds herself very still, listening hard. A neighbour's tivi, turned up. Thin walls in these new-build executive apartments.

She'll have another chota peg. A third and she can start to look around. There's a spa pool on the balcony. The need for moving, healing water defeats Thacker's warnings. The jets bubble up. With a dancer's grace she slips out of her clinging, emotionally soiled clothes into the water. There's even a little holder for your chota peg. A pernicious little doubt: how many others have been here before me? No, that is his kind of thinking. You are away from that. Safe. Invisible. Immersed. Down in Sisganj Road the traffic unravels. Overhead the dark silhouettes of the scavenging kites and, higher above, the security robots, expand and merge their black wings as Esha drifts into sleep.

"I thought I told you to stay away from the windows."

Esha wakes with a start, instinctively covers her breasts. The jets have cut out and the water is long still, perfectly transparent. Thacker is blue-chinned, baggy-eyed, and sagging in his rumpled gritty suit.

"I'm sorry. It was just, I'm so glad, to be away . . . you know?"

A bone-weary nod. He fetches himself a chota peg, rests it on the arm of his sofa, and then very slowly, very deliberately, as if every joint were rusted, undresses.

"Security has been compromised on every level. In any other circumstances it would constitute an I-war attack on the nation." The body he reveals is not a dancer's body; Thacker runs a little to upper-body fat, muscles slack, incipient man-tits, hair on the belly hair on the back hair on the shoulders. But it is a body, it is real. "The Bharati government has disavowed the action and waived Aeai Rao's diplomatic immunity."

He crosses to the pool and restarts the jets. Gin and tonic in hand, he slips into the water with a bone-deep, skin-sensual sigh.

"What does that mean?" Esha asks.

"You husband is now a rogue aeai."

"What will you do?"

"There is only one course of action permitted to us. We will excommunicate him."

Esha shivers in the caressing bubbles. She presses herself against Thacker.

She feels his man-body move against her. He is flesh. He is not hollow. Kilometres above the urban stain of Delhi, aeaicraft turn and seek.

The warnings stay in place the next morning. Palmer, home entertainment system, com channels. Yes, and balcony, even for the spa.

"If you need me, this palmer is department-secure. He won't be able to reach you on this." Thacker sets the glove and 'hoek on the bed. Cocooned in silk sheets, Esha pulls the glove on, tucks the 'hoek behind her ear.

"You wear that in bed?"

"I'm used to it."

Varanasi silk sheets and Kama Sutra prints. Not what one would expect of a Krishna Cop. She watches Thacker dress for an excommunication. It's the same as for any job—ironed white shirt, tie, handmade black shoes—never brown in town—well polished. Eternal riff of bad aftershave. The difference: the leather holster slung under the arm and the weapon slipped so easily inside it.

"What's that for?"

"Killing aeais," he says simply.

A kiss and he is gone. Esha scrambles into his cricket pullover, a waif in baggy white that comes down to her knees, and dashes to the forbidden balcony. If she cranes over, she can see the street door. There he is, stepping out, waiting at the curb. His car is late, the road is thronged, the din of engines, car horns, and phatphat klaxons has been constant since dawn. She watches him wait, enjoying the empowerment of invisibility. *I can see you. How do they ever play sport in these things?* she asks herself, skin under cricket pullover prickly and sticky. It's already thirty degrees, according to the weather ticker across the foot of the video-silk shuttering over the open face of the newbuild across the street. High of thirty-eight. Probability of precipitation: zero. The screen loops *Town and Country* for those devotees who must have their soapi, subtitles scrolling above the news feed.

Hello, Esha, Ved Prakash says, turning to look at her.

The thick cricket pullover is no longer enough to keep out the ice.

Now Begum Vora namastes to her and says, I know where you are, I know what you did.

Ritu Parvaaz sits down on her sofa, pours chai, and says, What I need you to understand is, it worked both ways. That 'ware they put in your palmer, it wasn't clever enough.

Mouth working wordlessly; knees, thighs weak with basti-girl superstitious fear, Esha shakes her palmer-gloved hand in the air but she can't find the mudras, can't dance the codes right. Call call call call.

The scene cuts to son Govind at his racing stable, stroking the neck of his thoroughbred uber-star Star of Agra. As they spied on me, I spied on them.

Dr. Chatterji in his doctor's office. So in the end we betrayed each other.

The call has to go through department security authorisation and crypt.

Dr. Chatterji's patient, a man in black with his back to the camera, turns. Smiles. It's A. J. Rao. After all, what diplomat is not a spy?

Then she sees the flash of white over the rooftops. Of course. Of course. He's been keeping her distracted, like a true soapi should. Esha flies to the railing to cry a warning but the machine is tunnelling down the street just under power-line height, wings morphed back, engines throttled up: an aeai traffic-monitor drone.

"Thacker! Thacker!"

One voice in the thousands. And it is not hers that he hears and turns towards. Everyone can hear the footsteps of his own death. Alone in the hurrying street, he sees the drone pile out of the sky. At three hundred kilometres per hour it takes Inspector Thacker of the Department of Artificial Intelligence Registration and Licensing to pieces.

The drone, deflected, ricochets into a bus, a car, a truck, a phatphat, strewing plastic shards, gobs of burning fuel, and its small intelligence across Sisganj Road. The upper half of Thacker's body cartwheels through the air to slam into a hot samosa stand.

The jealousy and wrath of djinns.

Esha on her balcony is frozen. *Town and Country* is frozen. The street is frozen, as if on the tipping point of a precipice. Then it drops into hysteria. Pedestrians flee; cycle-rickshaw drivers dismount and try to run their vehicles away; drivers and passengers abandon cars, taxis, phatphats; scooters try to navigate through the panic; buses and trucks are stalled, hemmed in by people.

And still Esha Rathore is frozen to the balcony rail. Soap. This is all soap. Things like this cannot happen. Not in the Sisganj Road, not in Delhi, not on a Tuesday morning. It's all computer-generated illusion. It has always been illusion.

Then her palmer calls. She stares at her hand in numb incomprehension. The department. There is something she should do. Yes. She lifts it in a mudra—a dancer's gesture—to take the call. In the same instant, as if summoned, the sky fills with gods. They are vast as clouds, towering up behind the apartment blocks of Sisganj Road like thunderstorms; Ganesh on his rat vahana with his broken tusk and pen, no benignity in his face; Siva, rising high over all, dancing in his revolving wheel of flames, foot raised in the instant before destruction; Hanuman with his mace and mountain fluttering between the tower blocks; Kali, skull-jewelled, red tongue dripping venom, scimitars raised, bestrides Sisganj Road, feet planted on the rooftops.

In that street, the people mill. They can't see this, Esha comprehends. *Only me, only me.* It is the revenge of the Krishna Cops. Kali raises her scimitars high. Lightning arcs between their tips. She stabs them down into the screen-frozen *Town and Country.* Esha cries out, momentarily blinded as the Krishna Cops' hunter-killers track down and excommunicate rogue aeai A. J. Rao. And then they are gone. No gods. The sky is just the sky. The video-silk hoarding is blank, dead.

A vast, godlike roar above her. Esha ducks—now the people in the street are looking at her. All the eyes, all the attention she ever wanted. A tilt-jet in Awadhi air force chameleo-flage slides over the roof and turns in air over the street, swivelling engine ducts and unfolding wing-tip wheels for landing. It turns its insect head to Esha. In the cockpit is a faceless pilot in a HUD visor. Beside her a woman in a business suit, gesturing for Esha to answer a call. Thacker's partner. She remembers now.

The jealousy and wrath of djinns.

"Mrs. Rathore, it's Inspector Kaur." She can barely hear her over the scream of ducted fans. "Come downstairs to the front of the building. You're safe now. The aeai has been excommunicated."

Excommunicated.

"Thacker . . ."

"Just come downstairs, Mrs. Rathore. You are safe now, the threat is over."

The tilt-jet sinks beneath her. As she turns from the rail, Esha feels a sudden, warm touch on her face. Jet-swirl, or maybe just a djinn, passing unresting, unhasting, and silent as light.

The Krishna Cops sent us as far from the wrath and caprice of the aeais as they could, to Leh under the breath of the Himalaya. I say us, for I existed: a knot of four cells inside my mother's womb.

My mother bought a catering business. She was in demand for weddings and shaadis. We might have escaped the aeais and the chaos following Awadh's signing the Hamilton Acts but the Indian male's desperation to find a woman to marry endures forever. I remember that for favoured clients—those who had tipped well, or treated her as something more than a paid contractor, or remembered her face from the chati mags—she would slip off her shoes and dance Radha and Krishna. I loved to see her do it and when I slipped away to the temple of Lord Ram, I would try to copy the steps among the pillars of the mandapa. I remember the Brahmins would smile and give me money.

The dam was built and the water war came and was over in a month. The aeais, persecuted on all sides, fled to Bharat, where the massive popularity of *Town and Country* gave them protection, but even there they were not safe: humans and aeais, like humans and djinns, were too different creations and in the end they left Awadh for another place that I do not understand, a world of their own where they are safe and no one can harm them.

And that is all there is to tell in the story of the woman who married a djinn. If it does not have the happy-ever-after ending of Western fairy tales and Bollywood musicals, it has a happy-enough ending. This spring I turn twelve and shall head off on the bus to Delhi to join the gharana there. My mother fought this with all her will and strength—for her Delhi would always be the city of djinns, haunted and stained with blood—but when the temple Brahmins brought her to see me dance, her opposition melted. By now she was a successful businesswoman, putting on weight, getting stiff in the knees from the dreadful winters, refusing marriage offers on a weekly basis, and in the end she could not deny the gift that had passed to me. And

I am curious to see those streets and parks where her story and mine took place, the Red Fort and the sad decay of the Shalimar Gardens. I want to feel the heat of the djinns in the crowded galis behind the Jama Masjid, in the dervishes of litter along Chandni Chowk, in the starlings swirling above Connaught Circus. Leh is a Buddhist town, filled with third-generation Tibetan exiles—Little Tibet, they call it—and they have their own gods and demons. From the old Muslim djinn-finder I have learned some of their lore and mysteries but I think my truest knowledge comes when I am alone in the Ram temple, after I have danced, before the priests close the garbagriha and put the god to bed. On still nights when the spring turns to summer or after the monsoon, I hear a voice. It calls my name. Always I suppose it comes from the japa-softs, the little low-level aeais that mutter our prayers eternally to the gods, but it seems to emanate from everywhere and nowhere, from another world, another universe entirely. It says, The creatures of word and fire are different from the creatures of clay and water but one thing is true: love endures. Then, as I turn to leave, I feel a touch on my cheek, a passing breeze, the warm, sweet breath of djinns.

VISHNU AT
THE CAT CIRCUS

THEY ARE SAVED BY A DESK

Come Matsya, come Kurma. Come Narasimha and Varaha. By the smoky light of burning trash polyethylene and under the mad-eye moon lying drunk on its back, come run in the ring; ginger and black and tabby and grey, white and calico and tortie and hare-legged tailless Manx. Run Vamana, Parashurama, run Rama and Krishna.

I pray I do not offend with my circus of cats that carry the names of divine avatars. Yes, they are dirty street cats, stolen from rubbish dumps and high walls and balconies, but cats are naturally blasphemous creatures. Every lick and curl, every stretch and claw is a calculated affront to divine dignity. But do I not bear the name of a god myself, so may I not name my runners, my leapers, my stars, after myself? For I am Vishnu, the Preserver.

See! The trash-lamps are lit, the rope ring is set, and the seats laid out, such as they are, being cushions and worn mattresses taken from the boat and

199

set down to keep your fundament from the damp sand. And the cats are running, a flowing chain of ginger and grey, the black and the white and the part-coloured: the marvellous, the magical, the Magnificent Vishnu's Celestial Cat Circus! You will be amazed, nay, astounded! So why do you not come?

Round they run and round, nose to tail. You would marvel at the perfect fluid synchronisation of my cats. Go Buddha, go Kalki! Yes, it takes a god to train a cat circus.

All evening I beat my drum and rang my bicycle bell through the heat-blasted hinterland of Chunar. *The Marvellous, the Magical, the Magnificent Vishnu Cat Circus! Gather round gather round! There are few enough joys in your life: wonder and a week's conversation for a handful of rupees.* Sand in the streets, sand slumped against the crumbling walls of abandoned houses, sand slumped banked up on the bare wheel rims of the abandoned cars and minibuses, sand piled against the thorny hurdles that divided the river-edge sandbars into sterile fields. The long drought and the flashfire wars had emptied this town like so many others close to the Jyotirlinga. I climbed up to the old fort, with its view twenty kilometres up- and downriver. From the overlook where the old British ambassador had built his governor's residence I could see the Jyotirlinga spear into the sky above Varanasi, higher than I could see, higher than the sky, for it ran all the way into another universe. The walls of the old house were daubed with graffiti. I rang my bell and beat my drum but there was never any hope of even ghosts here. Though I am disconnected from the deva-net, I could almost smell the devas swirling on the contradictory airs. Walking down into the town I caught the true smell of woodsmoke and the lingering perfume of cooking and I turned, haunted by a sense of eyes, of faces, of hands on doorframes that vanished into shadows when I looked. *Vishnu's Marvellous Magical Magnificent Cat Circus!* I cried, ringing my bicycle bell furiously, as much to advertise my poverty and harmlessness as my entertainment. In the Age of Kali the meek and helpless will be preyed upon without mercy, and there will be a surplus of AK-47s.

The cats were furious and yowling in unison when I returned, hot in their cages despite the shade of the awning. I let them hunt by the light of the breaking stars as I set up the ring and the seats, my lamps and sign and alms bowl, not knowing if a single soul would turn up. The pickings were meagre. Small game will be scarce in the Age of Kali.

My fine white Kalki, flowing over the hurdles like a riffle in a stream, it is written that you will battle and defeat Kali, but that seems to me too big a thing to ask of a mere cat. No, I shall take up that task myself, for if it's your name, it's also my name. Am I not Vishnu the ten-incarnated? Are not all of you part of me, cats? I have an appointment down this river, at the foot of that tower of light that spears up into the eastern sky.

Now come, sit down on this mattress—I have swept away the sand and let the lamps draw away the insects. Make yourself comfortable. I would offer chai but I need the water for the cats. For tonight you will witness not only the finest cat circus in all of India—likely the *only* cat circus in all of India. What do you say? All they do is run in a circle? Brother, with cats, that is an achievement. But you're right; running in a circle, nose to tail, is pretty much the meat of my cat circus. But I have other ways to justify the handful of rupees I ask from you. Sit, sit, and I will tell you a story, my story. I am Vishnu, and I was designed to be a god.

There were three of us and we were all gods. Shiv and Vish and Sarasvati. I am not the firstborn; that is my brother, Shiv, with whom I have an appointment at the foot of the Jyotirlinga of Varanasi. Shiv the prosperous, Shiv the businessman, the global success, the household name, and the inadvertent harbinger of this Age of Kali; Shiv—I cannot imagine what he has become. I was not the firstborn but I was the best born and therein lies the trouble of it.

Strife, I believe, was worked into every strand of my parents' DNA. Your classical Darwinist scorns the notion that intellectual values can shape evolution, but I myself am living proof that middle-class values can be programmed into the genes. Why not war?

A less likely I-warrior than my father you would be hard-pressed to imagine. Uncoordinated; ungainly; portly—no, let's not mince words, he was downright fat; he had been a content and, in his own way, celebrated designer for DreamFlower. You remember DreamFlower? *Street Sumo*; *RaMaYaNa*; *BollywoodSingStar*. Million-selling games? Maybe you don't. I increasingly find it's been longer than I think. In everything. What's important is that he had money and career and success and as much fame as his niche permitted and life was rolling along, rolling along like a Lexus, when war took him by surprise. War took us all by surprise. One day we were the Great Asian Success Story —the Indian Tiger (I call it the Law of Aphoristic Rebound—the Tiger of Economic Success travels all around the globe before returning to us)—and unlike those Chinese we had English, cricket, and democracy; the next we were bombing each other's malls and occupying television stations. State against state, region against region, family against family. That is the only way I can understand the War of Schism: that India was like one of those big, noisy, rambunctious families into which the venerable grandmother drops for her six-month sojourn and within two days sons are at their fathers' throats. And the mothers at their daughters', and the sisters feud and the brothers fight and the cousins uncles aunts all take sides and the family shatters like a diamond along the faults and flaws that gave it its beauty. I saw a diamond cutter in Delhi when I was young—apologies, when I was small. Not so young. I saw him set the gem in the padded vise and raise his cutter and pawl, which seemed too huge and brutal tool by far for so small and bright an object. I held my breath and set my teeth as he brought the big padded hammer down and the gem fell into three gems, brighter and more radiant than their parent.

"Hit it wrong," he said, "and all you have is dazzling dust."

Dazzling dust, I think, has been our history ever since.

The blow came—success, wealth, population strain—and we fell to dust, but Delhi didn't know it. The loyalists resolutely defended the dream of India. So my father was assigned as Help Desk to a Recon Mecha Squad. To you this will sound unspeakably hot and glamorous. But this was another century and another age and robots were far from the shimmering rakshasa-creatures we know today, constantly shifting shape and function along the edge of human expectation. This was a squad of reconnaissance bots; two-legged joggers and jumpers, ungainly and temperamental as iron chickens. And Dadaji was the Help Desk, which meant fixing them and de-virusing them and unbugging them and hauling them out of the little running circles they'd trapped themselves in, or turning them away from the unscalable wall they were attempting to leap, all the while wary of their twin flechette-Gatlings and their close-defence nano-edged blades.

"I'm a games coder," he wailed. "I choreograph Bollywood dance routines and arrange car crashes. I design star-vampires." Delhi ignored his cries. Delhi was already losing as the us-too voices of national self-determination grew loud in the Rashtrapati Bhavan, but she chose to ignore them as well.

Dadaji was an I-warrior, Mamaji was a Combat Medic. It was slightly truer for her than for Dadaji. She was indeed a qualified doctor and had worked in the field for NGOs in India and Pakistan after the earthquake and with *Médecins Sans Frontières* in Sudan. She was not a soldier, never a soldier. But Mother India needed frontline medics, so she found herself at Advanced Field Treatment Centre 32 east of Ahmedabad at the same time as my father's recon unit was relocated there. My mother examined Tech-Sergeant Tushar Nariman for crabs and piles. The rest of his unit refused to let a woman doctor inspect their pubes. He made eye contact with her, for a brave, frail second.

Perhaps if the Ministry of Defence had been less wanton in their calling-up of I-warriors and had assigned a trained security analyst to the 8th Ahmedabad Recon Mecha Squad instead of a games designer, more would have survived when the Bharati Tiger Strike Force attacked. A new name was being spoken in old east Uttar Pradesh and Bihar: Bharat, the old holy name of India; its spinning-wheel flag planted in Varanasi, most ancient and pure of cities. Like any national liberation movement, there were dozens of self-appointed guerrilla armies, each named more scarily than the predecessor with whom they were in shaky alliance. The Bharati Tiger Strike Force was embryo Bharat's élite I-war force. And unlike Tushar, they were pros. At 21:23 they succeeded in penetrating the 8th Ahmedabad's firewall and planted Trojans into the recon mechas. As my father pulled up his pants after experiencing the fluttering fingers and inspection torch of my mother-to-be at his little rosebud, the Tiger Strike Force took control of the robots and turned them on the field hospital.

Lord Shiva bless my father for a fat boy and a coward. A hero would have run out onto the sand to see what was happening when the firing started. A hero would have died in the crossfire, or, when the ammunition ran out, by their blades. At the first shot, my father went straight under the desk.

"Get down!" he hissed at my mother who froze with a look part bafflement, part wonderment on her face. He pulled her down and immediately apologised for the unseemly intimacy. She had lately cupped his testicles in her hand, but he apologised. They knelt in the kneehole, side by side, while the shots and the cries and the terrible, arthritic *click click click* of mecha joints swirled around them, and little by little subsided into cries and clicks, then just clicks, then silence. Side by side they knelt, shivering in fear, my mother kneeling like a dog on all fours until she shook from the strain, but afraid to move, to make the slightest noise in case it brought the stalking shadows that fell through the window into the surgery. The shadows grew long and grew dark before she dared exhale, "What happened?"

"Hacked mecha," my father said. Then he made himself forever the hero in my mother's eyes. "I'm going to take a look." Hand by knee by knee by hand, careful to make no noise, disturb not the least piece of broken glass or shattered wood, he crept out from under the desk across the debris-strewn floor to underneath the window. Then, millimetre by millimetre, he edged up the side until he was in a half-crouch. He glanced out the window and in the same instant dropped to the floor and began his painstaking crawl back across the floor.

"They're out there," he breathed to Mamaji. "All of them. They will kill anything that moves." He said this one word at a time, to make it sound like the natural creakings and contractions of a portable hut on a Ganga sand-bank.

"Perhaps they'll run out of fuel," my mother replied.

"They run off solar batteries." This manner of conversation took a long time. "They can wait forever."

Then the rain began. It was a huge thunder-plump, a forerunner of the monsoon still uncoiling across the Bay of Bengal, like a man with a flag or a trumpet who runs before a groom to let the world know that a great man is coming. Rain beat the canvas like hands on a drum. Rain hissed from the dry sand as it was swallowed. Rain ricocheted from the plastic carapaces of the waiting, listening robots. Rain-song swallowed every noise, so that my mother could only tell my father was laughing by the vibrations he trans-mitted through the desk.

"Why are you laughing?" she hissed in a voice a little lower than the rain.

"Because in this din they'll never hear me if I go and get my palmer," my father said, which was very brave for a corpulent man. "Then we'll see who hacks whose robots."

"Tushar," my mother whispered in a voice like steam, but my father was already steadily crawling out from under the desk towards the palmer on the camp chair by the zip door. "It's only a . . ."

And the rain stopped. Dead. Like a mali turning off a garden hose. It was over. Drips dropped from the ridge line and the never-weatherproof windows. Sun broke through the plastic panes. There was a rainbow. It was very pretty but my father was trapped in the middle of the tent with killer robots on the alert outside. He mouthed an excremental oath and carefully, deadly carefully, reversed among all the shattered and tumbled debris, wide arse first like an elephant. Now he felt the vibration of suppressed laughter through the wooden desk sides.

"Now. What. Are. You. Laughing. At?"

"You don't know this river," my mother whispered. "Ganga Devi will save us yet."

Night came swift as ever on the banks of the holy river; the same idle moon as now lights my tale rose across the scratched plastic squares of the window. My mother and father knelt, arms aching, knees tormented, side by side beneath the desk. My father said: "Do you smell something?"

"Yes," my mother hissed.

"What is it?"

"Water," she said, and he saw her smile in the dangerous moonlight. And then he heard it, a hissing, seeping suck sand would make if it were swallowing water but all its thirst was not enough, it was too much, too fast, too too much, it was drowning. My father smelled before he saw the tongue of water, edged with sand and straw and the flotsam of the sangam on which the camp stood, creep under the edge of the tent, across the liner, and around his knuckles. It smelled of soil set free. It was the old smell of the monsoon, when every dry thing has its true perfume and flavour and colour released by the rain; the smell of water that is the smell of everything water liberates. The tongue became a film; water flowed around their fingers and knees, around the legs of the desk as if they were the piers of a bridge. Dadaji felt my mother shaking with laughter, then the flood burst open the side of the tent and dashed dazed drowned him in a wall of water so that he spluttered and choked and tried not to cough for fear of the traitor mecha. Then he understood my mother's laughter and he laughed too, loud and hard and coughing up lungfuls of Ganges.

"Come on!" he shouted and leaped up, overturning the desk, throwing himself onto it like a surfboard, seizing the legs with both hands. My mother dived and grabbed just as the side of the tent opened in a torrent and desk and refugees were swept away on the flood. "Kick!" he shouted as he steered the desk towards the sagging doorway. "If you love life and Mother India, kick!" Then they were out in the night beneath the moon. The sentinel unfolded its killing-things, blade after blade after blade, launched after us, and was knocked down, bowled over, swept away by the flooding water. The last they saw of it, its carapace was half stogged in the sand, water breaking creamy around it. They kicked through the flotsam of the camp, furniture and ration packs and med kits and tech, the shorted, fused, sparked-out corpses of the mecha and the floating, spinning, swollen corpses of soldiers and medics. They kicked through them all, riding their bucking desk, they kicked half-choked, shivering, out into the deep green water of Mother Ganga; under the face of the full moon they kicked up the silver corridor of her river light. At noon the next day, far far from the river beach of Chattigarh, an Indian patrol-RIB found them and hauled them, dehydrated, skin cracked, and mad from the sun, into the bottom of the boat. At some point in the long night either under the desk or floating on it they had fallen in love. My mother always said it was the most romantic thing that had ever happened to her. Ganga Devi raised her waters and carried them through the killing machines to safety on a miraculous raft. Or so our family story went.

HERE A GOD IS INCARNATED, AND THEN ME

My parents fell in love in one country, India, and married in another, Awadh, the ghost of ancient Oudh, itself a ghost of the almost-forgotten British Raj. Delhi was no longer the capital of a great nation but of a geographical fudge. One India was now many, our mother goddess descended into a dozen avatars from reunited Bengal to Rajasthan, from Kashmir to Tamil Nadu. How had we let this happen, almost carelessly, as if we had momentarily stumbled on our march towards superpowerdom, then picked ourselves up and carried on? It was all most embarrassing, like a favourite uncle discovered with porn on his computer. You look away, you shun it, you never talk about it. Like we have never talked about the seismic upheavals of violence that tear through our dense, stratified society: the mass bloodletting of our independence that came with an excruciating partition, the constant threat of religious war, the innate, brooding violence in the heart of our caste system. It was all so very un-Indian. What are a few hundred thousand deaths next to those millions? If not forgotten, they will be ignored in a few years. And it certainly has made the cricket more interesting.

The new India suited my mother and father very well. They were model young Awadhis. My father, trapped by artificial intelligence once, vowed never to let that happen again and set up one of the first aeai farms breeding custom 'wares for low-level applications like Air Awadh, Delhi Bank, and the Revenue Service. My mother went first for cosmetic surgery, then, after a shrewd investment in an executive enclave for the nascent Awadhi civil service, gave up the micro-manipulators for a property portfolio. Between them they made so much money that their faces were never out of *Delhi Gloss!* magazine. They were the golden couple who had sailed to a glorious future over the floods of war and the interviewers who called at their penthouse asked, *So, then, where is the golden son?*

Shiva Nariman made his appearance on September 27, 2025. Siva, oldest God in the world; Siva, first and favoured; Siva, from whose matted hair the holy Ganga descended, generative force, auspicious one, lord of paradox. The photo rights went to *Gupshup* magazine for five hundred thousand Awadhi rupees. The golden boy's nursery was featured on the nightly *Nationwide* show and became quite the style for a season. There was great interest in this first generation of a new nation; the Awadhi Bhais, the gossip sites called them. They were the sons not just of a small coterie of prominent Delhi middle class, but of all Awadh. The nation took them to its heart and suckled them from its breasts, these bright, bouncing, brilliant boys who would grow up with the new land and lead it to greatness. It was never to be mentioned, not even to be thought, how many female fetuses were curetted or flushed out or swilled away, unimplanted, into the medical waste. We were a new country, we were engaged in the great task of nation-building. We could overlook a demographic crisis that had for years been deforming our middle classes. What if there were four times as many boys and girls? They were fine strong sons of Awadh. The others, they were only females.

So easily I say *we*, for I seem to have ended up as an impresario and story-teller, but the truth is that I did not exist, I didn't even exist then, not until the day the baby spoke at the Awadhi Bhai Club. It was never anything as formal as a constituted club; the blessed mothers, darlings of the nation, had fallen together by natural mutual need to cope with a media gawping into every aspect of their lives. Perfection needs a support group. They naturally banded together in each other's living rooms and penthouses, and their mothers and ayahs with them. It was a gilded Mothers and Infants group. The day the baby spoke, my mother had gathered with Usha and Kiran and Devi. It was Devi's baby who spoke. Everyone was talking about exhaustion and nipple-softening oil and peanut allergies when Vin Johar, lolling in his rocker, opened his brown eyes, focused across the room, and clearly said, "Hungry, want my bottle."

"Hungry, are we, my cho chweet?" Devi said.

"Now," said Vin Johar. "Please."

Devi clapped her hands in delight.

"Please! He hasn't said 'please' before."

The rest of the penthouse was still staring, dazed.

"How long has he been talking?" Usha asked.

"Oh, about three days," Devi said. "He picks up everything you say."

"My bottle now," demanded Vin Johar. "Quickly."

"But he's only . . ." Kiran said.

"Five months, yes. He's been a bit slower than Dr. Rao predicted."

The mothers' mothers and the ayahs made furtive hand gestures, kissed charms to turn away evil. It was my Mamaji, dandling fat, content Shiv on her knee, who understood first.

"You've been, you've had, he's a . . ."

"Brahmin, yes."

"But you're a Sudra," Kiran wondered.

"Brahmin," Devi said with such emphasis that no one could fail to hear the capital. "We've had him done, yes."

"Done?" asked Usha and then realised, "Oh." And, "Oh!"

"He'll be tall and he'll be strong and he'll be handsome—of course, that bit we didn't have to engineer—and he'll be fit and healthy. Oh so healthy—he'll never get heart disease, arthritis, Alzheimer's, Huntingdon's; with his immune system he can laugh off almost any virus or infection. His immune system will even take out malaria! Imagine that! And intelligence—well, let's just say Dr. Rao told us there isn't even a test smart enough to stretch him. He'll just need to see a thing once and he's learned it—like that! And his memory, well, Dr. Rao says there are double the numbers of connections in the brain, or something like that; what it means is that he'll have a phenomenal memory. Like that Mr. Memory on *India's Got Talent*, only even better. He won't be able to forget anything. No forgetting birthdays and phone calls to his Mata when he's off around the world with some big corporation. Look at him, look at him, isn't he just the most gorgeous thing you've ever seen; those baby brown eyes. Look at you, look at you, just look at you, my little lord. See them all, see them, your friends? They are princes each and every one, but you, you are a god. Oh, I could bite your bum, oh, just bite it like that it's so beautiful and plump and gorgeous." Devi held Vin Johar up like a trophy in a cricket match. She kissed him on his bare belly where his little vest had ridden up. "Oh, you little god."

Then Shiv let out a long wail. All through Devi's song of praise to her genetically improved darling son, my mother's grip had gradually tightened in envy on golden Shiv, now hopelessly outmoded, until he cried out in pain. Her fingers had left bruises like purple carrots along his ribs. .

Shiv gazed up at the mobile turning in the air-conditioning above his cot, innocent and unaware of how his visual acuity was being stimulated by the cleverly designed blobs and clouds. My mother fretted and stormed by turns around the pastel-lit apartment until Dadaji returned from the office. After Shiv was born, his duties at the office grew more arduous and his hours longer. He was never a terribly good father really. He was useless at cricket.

"What are you doing on Friday?" Mamaji demanded.

"Um, I'm not sure, there's something at the office—"

"Cancel it."

"What?" He was never very good at manners either, but then he was a Top Geek.

"We're seeing Dr. Rao."

"Dr. who?"

"Dr. Rao. At the Swaminathan Clinic." He knew the name. He knew the clinic. All Delhi, even Top Geeks, knew of the strange and miraculous children that came out of there. He just needed a moment for his balls to unfreeze and drop from that place close to the warmth of his perineum where they had retreated in terror.

"Friday, eleven thirty, with Dr. Rao himself. We are having a baby."

It wasn't Friday eleven thirty, nor the Friday after. It was not for six Fridays, after the initial consultation and the financial check and the medical assessment and the one-to-ones first Mamaji then Dadaji and only then did they get to choose from the menu. It was a menu, like in the most rarefied restaurant you can imagine. My parents blinked. Intelligence yes good looks yes enhanced concentration yes expanded memory and improved recall yes health wealth strength happiness, everything Vin Johar had. And more.

"Extended lifespan?"

"Ah yes, that is a new one. A new technique that has just been licensed."

"Does that mean . . . ?"

"Exactly what it says."

My parents blinked again.

"Your son—" (for this was me they were building) "—will enjoy a greatly increased span of life in full health and vigour."

"How much increased?"

"Double the current human norm. What is that? Let me think, for people like us, affluent, educated, middle class, with access to quality healthcare, that's currently eighty years. Well, double that."

A third time they blinked.

"One hundred and sixty years."

"At the very least—you must remember that medical miracles are occurring every day. Every single day. There's no reason why your son—"

"Vishnu."

My father stared open-mouthed at my mother. He didn't know there was a name. He hadn't yet realised that he had no say in this whatsoever. But his balls understood, cringing in his loose-and-cooling-good-for-sperm-production silk boxers.

"Vishnu, the Lord, governor, and sustainer." Dr. Rao dipped his head in respect. He was an old-fashioned man. "You know, I have often thought how the processes of conception, gestation, and parturition are reflected in the ten incarnations of Lord Vishnu: the fish the restless sperm, the turtle of Kurma the egg, the saving of the Earth from the bottom of the ocean by Varaha the fertilisation—"

"What about the dwarf?" my father asked. "The dwarf Brahmin?"

"The dwarf, yes," Dr. Rao drawled. He was a man of slow speech, who seemed to lose the ends of his sentences the closer he approached them. This led many people to make the mistake of thinking him stupid when what he was doing was shaping the perfect conclusion. As a consequence he didn't do many television or net interviews. "The dwarf's always the problem, isn't he? But your son will assuredly be a true Brahmin. And Kalki, yes, Kalki. The ender of the Age of Kali. Who's to say that he might not see this world end in fire and water and a new one be born? Yes, longevity. It's very good, but there are a couple of minor inconveniences."

"Never mind. We'll have that. Devi Johar doesn't have that."

So my father was sent with a plastic cup to catch his sacred fish. My mother went with him; to make it an act of love but mostly because she didn't trust him with Western porn. A few Fridays later, Dr. Rao harvested a clutch of my mother's turtle eggs with a long needle. She didn't need my father there for that. This was an act of biology. The slow-spoken doctor did his work and called up eight blastulas from the deep ocean of his artificial wombs. One was selected: Me! Me! Little me! Here I am! See me! See me! and I was implanted into my mother's womb. It was then that she discovered the inconvenience: my doubled lifespan was bought at the price of aging at half the speed of baseline, non-Brahminic humanity. After eighteen months of pregnancy, eighteen months of morning sickness and bloating and bad circulation and broken veins and incontinence and backache but, worst of all, not being able to smoke, my mother, with a great shriek of, *At last at last! Get the fucking thing out of me!* gave birth on September 27, 2027, and I made my entry as a player in this story.

MY BROTHER HATES ME

What a world, into which I was born! What times: an age of light and brilliance. Shining India truly found herself in Shining Awadh, Shining Bharat, Shining Maratha, Shining Bengal—all the shining facets of our many peoples. The horrors of the Schisming were put behind us, apart from war-maimed begging on metro platforms, gangs of undersocialised ex-teen-I-warriors, occasional flare-ups from hibernating combat 'ware buried deep in the city net, and Concerned Documentary Makers who felt that we had not sufficiently mourned our self-mutilation and achieved reconciliation. Reconciliation? Delhi had no time for such Western niceties. Let the dead burn the dead, there was money to be made and pleasure to be savoured. Our new boulevards and maidans, our malls and entertainment zones were brilliant with the bright and the young and the optimistic. It was a time of bold new fashions, father-scandalising hemlines and mother-troubling hairstyles; of new trends and obsessions that were old and cold as soon as they hit the gup-shup sites; of ten thousand shattering new ideas that disappeared as soon as they were iterated like a quantum foam of thought. It was youth, it was confidence, it was the realisation of all that old Mother India had claimed she might be, but most of all it was money. As in Delhi, so in Varanasi, Kolkata, Mumbai, Chennai, Jaipur. But most of all, I think, in Delhi. In India she had been capital by whim, not by right. Mumbai, even Kolkata always outshone her. Now she truly was capital of her own nation, without rival, and she dazzled. My earliest memory, from the time when my senses all ran together and sounds had smells and colours had textures and a unified reality above those crude divisions, was of lines of light streaming over my upturned face, light in all colours and more, light that, to an undifferentiated cortex, hummed and chimed like the sympathetic strings of a sitar. I suppose I must have been in our car and our chauffeur driving us somewhere through the downtown lights to some soirée or other, but all I remember is grinning up at the streaming, singing light. When I think of Delhi even now, I think of it as a river of light, a torrent of silver notes.

And what a city! Beyond Old Delhi and New Delhi, beyond the Newer Delhis of Gurgaon and the desirable new suburbs of Sarita Vihar and New Friends Colony, the Newest Delhis of all were rising. Invisible Delhis, Delhis of data and digits and software. Distributed Delhis, networked Delhis, Delhis woven from cable and wireless nodes, intangible Delhis strung through the streets and buildings of the material city. Strange new peoples lived here: the computer-constructed cast of *Town and Country*, the all-conquering soap opera that, in its complete artificiality, was more real than life itself. It was not just the characters who drew our fascination; the genius of the production lay in the CG-actors who believed they played and had a separate existence from those characters, and whose gupshup and scandal, whose affairs and marriages meant more to us than our friends' and neighbours'. Other brilliant creatures streamed past and through us on our streets and squares: the aeais; the pantheon of artificial intelligences that served our immaterial needs from banking to legal services to household management to personal secretarial services. In no place and every place, these were entities of levels and hierarchies; high-end aeais cascading down through subroutines into low-grade monitors and processors; thousands of those same daily-grind Level 0.8s (the intelligence of a street pig) scaling up through connections and associations into Level 1s—the intelligence of a monkey; those again aggregating together into the highest, the Level 2s, indistinguishable from a human seventy percent of the time. And beyond them were the rumoured, feared Level 3s: of human intelligence and beyond. Who could understand such an existence, beings of many parts that did not necessarily recognise each other? The djinns, those ancient haunters of their beloved Delhi, they understood; and, older than them, the gods. They understood only too well. And in the material city, new castes appeared. A new sex manifested on our streets as if stirred out of heaven, neither male nor female, rejecting the compromises of the old hijras to be aggressively neither. The nutes, they called themselves. And then of course there were things like me, improved in egg and sperm, graced with outrageous gifts and subtle curses: the Brahmins. Yes, I was an upper-middle-class brat born into genetic privilege, but Delhi was laid out before me like a wedding banquet. She was my city.

Delhi loved me. Loved me, loved all of my Brahmin brothers and occasional sisters. We were wonders, freaks, miracles, and avatars. We might do anything, we were the potential of Awadh. Those firstborn were accidents of birth; we, the Brahmins, were the true Awadhi Bhais. We even had our own comic, of that name. With our strange genetic powers, we battled criminals, demons, and Bharatis. We were superheroes. It sold pretty well.

You might think I was blithe enough, a genetically high-caste blob bouncing in my baby-rocker, blinking up into the sunlight beaming through the glass walls of our tower-top penthouse. You would be wrong. As I lay giggling and blinking, neural pathways were twining up through my medulla and cerebellum and Area of Broca with preternatural speed. That blur of light, that spray of silver notes rapidly differentiated into objects, sounds, smells, sensations. I saw, I heard, I sensed, but I could not yet understand. So I made connections, I drew patterns, I saw the world pouring in through my senses and up the fiery tree of my neurons as relation, as webs and nets and constellations. I formed an inner astrology and from it, before I could call dog "dog" and cat "cat" and Mamaji "Mamaji," I understood the connectedness of things. I saw the bigger picture; I saw the biggest picture. This was my true superpower, one that has remained with me to this day. I never could fly to Lanka in a thought or lift a mountain by the force of my will, I was not master fire or thunder or even my own soul, but I could always take one look and know the whole, absolute and entire.

The naming of names. That was where Mamaji first realised that Dr. Rao's blessings were not unmixed. The soirée that day was at Devi Johar's house, she of the amazing Vin. There he was, running around the place with his ayah trying to keep up with him in kiddie-wear by SonSun of Los Angeles. Shiv played with the other non-Brahmins in the roof garden, happy and content at their own limited, nonenhanced activities. How fast the gilt had rubbed off him, after I was born! As for me, I sat in my bouncer, burbling and watching big-eyed the mothers of the golden. I knew Shiv's jealousy, though I didn't have the words or the emotional language for it. I saw in a thousand looks and glances, the way he sat at the table, the way he rode in the car, the way he toddled along behind Ayah Meenakshi as she pushed me through the mall, the way he stood by my cot and gazed soft-eyed at me. I understood hate.

Vin asked Devi if he could go out and play with the others in the roof garden. Please.

"All right, but don't show off," Devi Johar said. When he had toddled away, Devi crossed her ankles demurely and placed her hands on her knees, so.

"Mira, I hope you don't mind me saying, but your Vish; well, he isn't talking yet. At his age, Vin had a vocabulary of two hundred words and a good grasp of syntax and grammar."

"And shouldn't he be, well, at least crawling?" Usha asked.

"How old is he—fifteen months? He does seem a little on the . . . small side," Kiran chimed in.

My Mamaji broke down in tears. It was the crying nights and the shushing to sleep, the rocking and the cleaning and the mewling and puling, the tiredness, oh, the tiredness, but worst of all, the breast-feeding.

"Breast? After a year?" Usha was incredulous. "I mean, I've heard that some mothers keep them on the teat for years, but they're from the villages, or mamas who love their sons too much."

"My nipples feel like mulberries," my Mamaji wept. "You see, he's fifteen months old, but biologically, he's not even eight months yet."

I would live twice as long, but age half as fast. Infancy was a huge, protracted dawn; childhood an endless morning. When Shiv started school, I would only have begun toddling. When I was of university age I would still have the physiology of a nine-year-old. Adulthood, maturity, old age were points so distant on the great plain of my lifespan that I could not tell if they were insects or cities. In those great days I would come into my own, a life long enough to become part of history; as a baby, I was a mother's nightmare.

"I know breast is best, but maybe you should consider switching to formula," Devi said soothingly.

See how I recall every word? Another of Dr. Rao's equivocal gifts. I forget only what I choose to unremember. I understood every word—at fifteen months my vocabulary was far in advance of your precious Vin's, bitch Devi.

But it was trapped inside me. My brain formed the words but my larynx, my tongue, my lips and lungs couldn't form them. I was a prisoner in a baby-bouncer, smiling and waving my fat little fists.

Four there were who understood me, and four only, and they lived in the soft-contoured plastic butterfly that hung over my cot. Their names were TikkaTikka, Badshanti, Pooli, and Nin. They were aeais, set to watch over me and entertain me with songs and stories and pretty patterns of coloured lights because Mamaji considered Ayah Meenakshi's sleepy-time stories far too terrifying for a suggestible Brahmin. They were even more stupid than my parents, but it was because they were deeply dense that they had no pre-conceptions beyond their Level 0.2 programing and so I could communicate with them.

TikkaTikka sang songs.

In a little green boat,
On the blue sea so deep,
Little Lord Vishnu
Is sailing to sleep . . .

He sang that every night. I liked it; I still sing it to myself as I pole my circus of cats along the ravaged shores of Mata Ganga.

Pooli impersonated animals, badly. He was a cretin. His stupidity insulted me so I left him mute inside the plastic butterfly.

Badshanti, lovely Badshanti, she was the weaver of stories. "Would you like to hear a story, Vishnu?" were the words that led into hours of wonder. Because I don't forget. I know that she never repeated a story, unless I asked her to. How did I ask? For that I must introduce the last of my four aeais.

Nin spoke only in patterns of light and colour that played across my face, an ever-wheeling kaleidoscope that was supposed to stimulate my visual intel-ligence. Nin-no-words was the intelligent one; because he could interpret facial expression, he was the one I first taught my language. It was a very simple lan-guage of blinking. One deliberate blink for yes, two for no. It was slow, it was torturous, but it was a way out of the prison of my body. With Nin reading my answers to Badshanti's questions, I could communicate anything.

How did my brother hate me? Let me take you to that time in Kashmir. After the third drought in a row my mother vowed never again to spend a summer in Delhi's heat, noise, smog, and disease. The city seemed like a dog lying at the side of the street, panting and feral and filthy and eager for any excuse to sink its teeth into you, waiting for the monsoon. Mamaji looked to the example of the British of a hundred years before and took us up to the cool and the high places. Kashmir! Green Kashmir, blue lake, the bright houseboats and the high beyond all, the rampart of mountains. They still wore snow, then. I remember blinking in the wonder of the Dal Lake as the shikara sped us across the still water to the hotel rising sheer, like a palace in one of Badshanti's tales, from the water. My four friends bobbed in the wind of our passage as the boat curved in across the lake to the landing stage where porters in red turbans waited to transport us to our cool summer apartment. Shiv stood in the bow. He wanted to throw them the landing rope.

The calm, the clear, the high cool of Kashmir after the mob heat of Delhi! I bobbed and bounced and grinned in my cot and waved my little hands in joy at the sweet air. Every sense was stimulated, every nerve vibrant. In the evening, TikkaTikka would sing, Badshanti tell a story, and Nin send stars sweeping over my face.

There was to be an adventure by boat across the lake. There was food and there was drink. We were all to go together. It was a thing of a moment, I can see it still, so small it looked like an accident. It was not. It was deliberate, it was meticulously planned.

"Where's Gundi-bear? I've lost Gundi-bear," Shiv cried as my father was about to get into the boat. "I need Gundi-bear." He launched towards the shore along the gangplank. Dadaji swept him up.

"Oh no you don't; we'll never get anywhere at this rate. You stay here and don't move. Now, where did you last see him?"

Shiv shrugged, innocently forgetful.

"Here, I'll come with you, you'll never find anything the way you ram and stam around." My mother sighed her great sigh of exasperation. "Shiv, you stay here, you hear? Don't touch anything. We'll be back in two ticks."

I felt a deeper shadow in the mild shade of the awning. Shiv stood over me. Even if I chose to I could not forget the look on his face. He ran up the gangplank, untied the mooring rope, and let it fall into the water. He waggled his fingers, *Bye-bye*, as the wind caught the curve of coloured cotton and carried me out into the lake. The frail little shikara was taken far from the shelter of the Lake Hotel's island into the rising chop. The wind caught it and turned it. The boat rolled. I began to cry.

Nin saw my face change. TikkaTikka awoke in the little plastic butterfly my parents had hung from the bamboo ridgepole. He sang:

The lake is big and the lake is deep
And Little Lord Vishnu is falling asleep.
The wind is high and the sun is beaming
To carry you off to the kingdom of dreaming.

"Hello, Vishnu," Badshanti said. "Would you like a story today?"
Two blinks.
"Oh, no story? Well then, I'll just let you sleep. Sweet dreams, Vishnu."
Two blinks.
"You don't want a story but you don't want to sleep?"
One blink.
"All right then, let's play a game."
Two blinks. Badshanti hesitated so long I thought her software had hung. She was a pretty rudimentary aeai.

"Not a game, not a story, not sleep?" I blinked. She knew better than to ask, "Well, what do you want?" Now TikkaTikka sang a strange song I had never heard before:

Wind and lake water
And gathering storm
Carry Lord Vishnu
Far into harm.

Yes. The shikara was far from shore, broadside to the wind and rolling on the chop. One gust could tip it over and send me to the bottom of the Dal

Lake. I might be a hero in my own comic but Dr. Rao had neglected to give me the genes for breathing underwater.

"Are we on a boat, sailing far far away?" Badshanti asked.

Yes.

"Are you out on water?"

Yes.

"Are we on our own?"

Yes.

"Is Vishnu happy?"

No.

"Is Vishnu scared?"

Yes.

"Is Vishnu safe?"

Two blinks. Again Badshanti paused. Then she started to shout. "Help aid assist! Little Lord Vishnu is in peril! Help aid assist!" The voice was thin and tinny and would not have reached any distance across the wind-ruffled lake, but one of the silent aeais, perhaps stupid Pooli, must also have sent out a radio, Bluetooth, and GPS alarm, for a fishing boat suddenly changed course, opened up its long-tail engine, and sped towards me on a curve of spray.

"Thank you thank you sirs and saviours," Badshanti babbled as the two fishermen hauled my shikara close with their hard hands and to their aston-ishment saw a child lying on the mattresses, smiling up at them.

A MAP DRAWN INSIDE THE SKULL

All my long life I have been ordained to be tied to water. My parents were delivered by the flood, my aeais saved me from the drifting boat. Even now I pick my way down the shrivelled memory of the Ganga, descended from the hair of Siva. Water it was that made me into a superhero of Awadh, albeit of a very different, non-tall-building-leaping type from the Awadhi Bhai who refused to grow up through the pages of Virgin comics.

There was of course no end of ruction after almost-four-year-old Shiv tried to expose me in an open boat. He made no attempt to deny it. He bore it stoically. The worst of it was my father's therapy-speak. I almost felt for him. At least my mother was angry, blazingly, searingly angry. She didn't try to wrap it up in swathes of *how did you find it* and *I imagine you're feeling* and *let's try and talk through this like men*. It didn't end when the monsoon finally came late and scanty and we returned to Delhi slick and greasy with rain, the wonderful, rich smell of wet dust perfuming the air more purely than any incense. Four days later it ended and Delhi became afraid. That was how my parents kept the story out of the papers. FIFTEEN MILLION THIRSTY THROATS is a more immediate headline than FOUR-YEAR-OLD TRIES TO DROWN BRAHMIN BROTHER. Just.

There was counselling, of course, long and expensive and in the end producing no better result than the child psychologist saying, "This is possibly the most intractable case of sibling rivalry I have ever seen. Your elder son has a colossal sense of entitlement and deeply resents what he perceives as a loss of status and parental affection. He's quite unrepentant and I fear he might make a second attempt to cause Vishnu harm." My parents took these words and reached their own solution. Shiv and I could not live together so we must live apart. My father took an apartment across the city. Shiv went with him. I stayed with Mamaji, and one other. Before they parted, plump Tushar loved my mother a goodbye-time, without planning or sex selection or genetic regulation. And so Sarasvati was born, the last of the three gods; my sister.

We grew up together. We lay in our cots side by side, looking not at our stimulating and educational toys but at each other. For a blissful time she paralleled me. We learned to walk and talk and regulate our bowels together. When we were alone I would murmur the words I knew to her, the words that had roosted and chattered so long in my skull and now were free, like someone throwing open a dark and fetid pigeon loft on a Delhi rooftop. We were close as twins. Then, week by week, month by month, Sarasvati outgrew me. Bigger, better coordinated, more physically developed, her tongue never stumbled over her few and simple words while poems and vedas rattled inarticulate inside me. She grew out of being twin to bigger sister. She was the surprise, the delight, the child free from expectations, and thus she could never disappoint. I loved her. She loved me. In those murmurous evenings filled with sunset and the cool of the air-conditioning, we found a common language and knowing born of shared playing that our various and despised ayahs, even our mother, could never penetrate.

Across the city, on his own glass towertop filled with the staggering, pollution-born sunsets of great Delhi, Shiv grew up apart. He was five and a half, he was top of his class, he was destined for greatness. How do I know this? Once a week my father came to see his other son and daughter and for a snatched evening with his darling. I had long since superseded TikkaTikka, Pooli, Nin, and Badshanti with more powerful (and discreet) aeai attendants, ones that, as soon as I had the words on my tongue, I found I could reprogram to my needs. I sent them out like djinns through the apartment. Not a word was spoken, not a glance exchanged that I could not know it. Sometimes the glances would become looks, and the murmurs cease, and my parents would make love to each other. I saw that too. I did not think it particularly wrong or embarrassing; I knew fine and well what they were doing but, though it made them very happy, it did not look like a thing I would ever want to do.

I look back now from age and loss and see those babbling days with Sarasvati as the Age of Gold, our Satya Yuga of innocence and truth. We stumbled together towards the sunlight and found joy in every fall and bump and grin. Our world was bright and full of surprises, delights in discovery for Sarasvati, pleasure in her evident delight for me. Then school forced us apart. What a terrible, unnecessary thing school is. I feel in it the enduring envy of parents for idle childhood. Of course it could be no ordinary school for little Lord Vishnu. Dr. Renganathan Brahminical College was an academy for the élite of the élite. Education was intimate and bespoke. There were eight in my year and that was large enough for divisions. Not all Brahmins were equal in the Dr. Renganathan College. Though we were all the same age we divided ourselves, quite naturally, like meiosis, into Old Brahmins and Young Brahmins. Or, as you like, Big Brahmins and Little Brahmins. Those who would enjoy all the gifts of health and smarts and looks and privilege but would still fall dead at whatever age the meditech of that era could sustain, and those who aged half as fast but would live twice as long. Intimations of mortality in Miss Mukudan's reception class.

Ah, Miss Mukudan! Your golden bangles and your Cleopatra smiling eyes, your skin the soft dark of the deepest south; your ever-discreet moustache and smell of camphor as you bent over me to help my fumble-fingers with my buttons or the Velcro fastenings on my shoes. You were my first vague love. You were the undifferentiated object of affection of all of us. We loved you for your lofty remoteness, your firmness and hinted-at tetchiness, and the delicious knowledge that to you we were just more children to be turned from blind and selfish little barbarians into civilized young human beings. We loved you because you were not the mother-smother of our cotton-wool parents. You took no shit.

A classroom of Brahmins was too much even for the redoubtable Miss Mukudan. At age four our engineered brains were pushing us down the strange and separate roads into peculiar ways of looking at the world, quasi-autistic obsessions, terrifying savant insights, or just plain incomprehensibility. We were each given a personalised tutor to accompany us day and night. Mine was called Mr. Khan and he lived inside my ear. A new technology had arrived to save us. It was the latest thing in comms—which has always seemed the most faddish and trivial of technologies to me. No more did you need to be trapped by screens or pictures in the palm of your hand or devices that wrote on your eyeball as delicately as a bazaar fakir writing tourists' names on a grain of rice. A simple plastic hook behind the ear would beam cyberspace into your head. Direct electromagnetic stimulation of the visual, auditory, and olfactory centres now peopled the world with ghost messages and data spreads, clips from *Town and Country*, video messages, entire second-life worlds and avatars, and, inevitably, spam and junk mailing. And for me, my customised aeai tutor, Mr. Khan.

How I hated him! He was everything Miss Mukudan was not: irascible, superior, gruff, and persistent. He was a little waspy Muslim, thin as a wire with a white moustache and a white Nehru cap. I would rip off the "'hoek" in frustration and whenever I put it on again, after Miss Mukudan's ministrations—we would do anything for her—he would take up his harangue from the very syllable at which I had silenced him.

"Look and listen, you bulging pampered privileged no-right-to-call-yourself-a-proper-Brahmin brat," he would say. "These eyes these ears, use them and learn. This is the world and you are in it and of it and there is no other. If I can teach you this I will have taught you all you ever need to learn."

He was a stern moralist, very proper and Islamic. I looked at Miss Mukudan differently then, wondering what assessments she had made that assigned Mr. Khan especially to me. He had been programmed just for Vishnu? How had he been built? Did he spring into being perfectly formed or did he have a history, and how did he think of this past? Did he know it for a lie, but a treasured one? Was he like the self-deceiving aeai actors of *Town and Country* who believed they existed separately from the roles they played? If he masqueraded as intelligent, did that mean he was intelligent? Was intelligence the only thing that could not be simulated? Such thoughts were immensely interesting to a strange little boy suddenly becoming aware of those other strange citizens of his tight world. What was the nature of the aeais, those ubiquitous and for the most part unseen denizens of great Delhi? I became quite the junior philosopher.

"What is right to you?" I asked him one day as we rode back in the Lexus through a Delhi melted by the heat into an impermeable black sludge. It was Ashura. Mr. Khan had told me of the terrible battle of Karbala and the war between the sons of the Prophet (Peace Be upon Him). I watched the chanting, wailing men carrying the elaborate catafalques, flogging their backs bloody, beating their foreheads and chests. The world, I was beginning to realise, was far stranger than I.

"Never mind what is right to me, impudent thing. You have the privileges of a god, you're the one who needs to think about right action," Mr. Khan declared. In my vision he sat beside me on the back seat of the Lex, his hands primly folded in his lap.

"It's a serious question." Our driver hooted up alongside the dour procession. "How can right action mean anything to you, when anything you do can be undone and anything you undo can be done again? You're chains of digits, what do you need morality for?" Only now was I beginning to understand the existence of the aeais, which had begun with the mystery of TikkaTikka, Pooli, Badshanti, and Nin living together and sharing common code inside my plastic butterfly. Common digits but separate personalities. "It's not as if you can hurt anyone."

"So right action is refraining from causing pain, is it?"

"I think that it's the start of right action."

"These men cause pain to themselves to express sorrow for wrong action; albeit the actions of their spiritual forebears. In so doing they believe they will make themselves more moral men. Consider those Hindu saddhus who bear the most appalling privations to achieve spiritual purity."

"Spiritual purity isn't necessarily morality," I said, catching the line Mr. Khan had left dangling for me. "And they choose to do it to themselves. It's something else altogether if they choose to do it to others."

"Even if it means those others may be made better men?"

"They should be left to make their own minds up about that."

We cruised past the green-draped faux-coffin of the martyr.

"So what then is the nature of my relationship with you? And your mother and father?"

My Mamaji, my Dadaji! Two years after that conversation, almost to the day, my flawless memory recalls, when I was a seven-year-old in a three-and-a-half-year-old body and Sarasvati was a cat-lean, ebullient four, my mother and father very gently, very peacefully, divorced. The news was broken by the two of them sitting at opposite ends of the big sofa in the lounge with the smog of Delhi glowing in the afternoon sun like a saffron robe. A full range of aeai counselling support hovered around the room, in case of tears or tantrums or anything else they couldn't really handle. I remember feeling a suspicion of Mr. Khan on the edge of my perceptions. Divorce was easy for Muslims. Three words and it was over.

"We have something to tell you, my loves," said my mother. "It's me and your father. Things haven't been going so well with us for quite some time and, well, we've decided that it would be best for everyone if we were to get a divorce."

"But it won't mean I'll ever stop being your Dad," plump Tushar said quickly. "Nothing'll change, you'll hardly even notice. You'll still keep living here, Shiv will still be with me."

Shiv. I hadn't forgotten him—I couldn't forget him—but he had slipped from my regard. He was more distant than a cousin, less thought of than those remote children of your parents' cousin, to whom I've never considered myself related at all. I did not know how he was doing at school or who his friends were or what sports teams he was on. I did not care how he lived his life or pursued his dreams across that great wheel of lives and stories. He was gone from me.

We nodded bravely and trembled our lips with the right degree of with-held emotion and the counsel-aeais dissolved back into their component code clusters. Much later in the room we had shared as bubbling babies and which was now our mutual den, Sarasvati asked me, "What's going to happen to us?"

"I don't think we'll even notice," I said. "I'm just glad they can stop having that ugly, embarrassing sex."

Ah! Three little letters. Sex sex sex, the juggernaut looming over our childhoods. The kiddy thrill of being naked—doubly exciting in our body-modest society—took an edge and became something I did not quite under-stand. Oh, I knew all the words and the locations, as Sarasvati and I played our games of doctors and patients in our den, her pulling up her little vest and pulling down her pants as I listened and examined and prodded vaguely. We knew these were grown-up things not for the eyes of grown-ups. Mamaji would have been horrified and called in squadrons of counselling 'ware if she had discovered our games, but I had long since suborned the aeais. If she had looked at the security monitors she would have seen us watching the Cartoon Network; my own little CG *Town and Country* playing just for her. Sex games for children; everyone plays them. Bouncing up and down in the pool, pressing ourselves against the jets in the rooftop spa, suspecting *something* in the lap of artificial waves across our private places as ochre dust-smog from the failed monsoon suffocated Delhi. And when we played horsey-horsey, she riding me around like Lakshmibai the warrior rani, there was more in the press of her thighs than just trying to hold on as I cantered across the carpets. I knew what it should be; I was mostly baffled by my body's failure to respond the way an-eleven-year-old's ought. My lust may have been eleven but my body was still a child's. Even Miss Mukudan's purity and innocence lost its lustre as I began to notice the way her breasts moved as she leaned over me, or the shape of her ass—demurely swathed in a sari, but no conceal-ment was enough for the lusty curiosity of boy-Brahmins—as she turned to the smart-silk board.

"Now," Mr. Khan said one day on the back seat of the Lexus. "Concerning onanism . . ." It was dreadful realisation. By the time puberty hit me like a hammer I would be twenty-four. Mine was the rage and impotence of angels.

Now five burning years have passed and we are driving in a fast German car. I am behind the wheel. The controls have been specially modified so that I can reach the pedals; the gearshift is a standard. If I cut you up on the Siri Ring, after the flicker of road rage, you'd wonder: that's a child driving that Mercedes. I don't think so. I'm of legal age. I passed my test without any bribery or coercion; well, none that I know of. I am old enough to drive, get married, and smoke. And I smoke. We all smoke, my Little Brahmin classmates and me. We smoke like stacks, it can't do us any harm, though we are all wearing smog masks. The monsoon has failed for the fourth time in seven years; whole tracts of north India are turning into dust and blowing through the hydrocarbon-clogged streets and into our lungs. A dam is being built on the Ganges, Kunda Khadar, on the border with our eastern neighbour Bharat. It is promised to slake our thirst for a generation but the Himalaya glaciers have melted into gravel and Mother Ganga is starved and frail. The devotees at the Siva temple in the middle of the Parliament Street roundabout protest at the insult to the holy river with felt-marker banners and three-pronged trisuls. We bowl past them, hooting and waving, and up Sansad Marg around Vijay Chowk. The comics portraying us as Awadh's new superheroes were quietly dropped years ago. Now what we see about ourselves in print tends to be headlines like TINY TEARAWAYS TERRORISE TILAK NAGAR, or BADMASH BABY BRAHMINS.

There are four of us, Purrzja, Shayman, Ashurbanipal, and me. We are all from the college—still the Brahminical College!—but when we are out we all have our own names, names we've made up for ourselves that sound strange and alien, like our DNA. Strange and alien we make ourselves look too; our own style cobbled from any source that seems remote and outré: J-punk hair, Chinese bows and ribbons, French street-sports fashion, and tribal makeup entirely of our own design. We are the scariest-looking eight-year-olds on the planet. By now Sarasvati is a coltish, classy thirteen-year-old. Our closeness has unravelled; she has her own social circles and friends and crushing things of the heart that seem so important to her. Shiv, so I hear, is in his first year at the University of Awadh Delhi. He won a scholarship. Best marks in his school. He's followed his father into informatics. Me, I howl up and down the boulevards of Delhi trapped in the body of a kid.

We race past the open arms of the Rashtrapati Bhavan. The red stone looks insubstantial as sand in the amber murk.

"That's your home, that is, Vish," Purrzja shouts through her mask. It's well known that Mamaji has plans for me. Why should she not? Every other part of me is designed. A good legal job, a prominent practice, a safe parliamentary seat, and a steady, planned ascent towards the top of whatever political party afforded the best chance of ambition. It's assumed that one day I will lead the nation. I'm designed to rule. I floor the pedal and the big Merc leaps forwards. Traffic parts like my divine counterpart churning the soma. Their autodrive aeais make them as nervous as pigeons.

Out on the Siri Ring: eight lanes of taillights in each direction, a never ceasing roar of traffic. The car eases into the flow. Despite the barriers and warning signs police pull twenty bodies a day from the soft shoulder. The Ring does not obey old Indian rules of traffic. Men race here, hedge-fund managers and datarajas and self-facilitating media Mughals; racing around the twin chambers of Delhi's heart. I flick on the autodrive. I am not here to race. I am here for sex. I recline the driving seat, roll over, and Ashurbanipal is beneath me. Her hair is drawn back behind her ear to show off the plastic curl of the 'hoek. It's part of the look.

I snap the fingers of my right hand into my palm to activate the software in the palmer glove. I hold that hand a hovering few centimetres above her fluorescent-body-paint-stained belly. I don't touch. We never touch. That's the rule. Sex has rules. I move my hand over Ashurbanipal in a series of gestures as gentle and precise as any classical dancer's mudras. Not touching, never touching, never even flexing a finger. It's not about physical touch. It's our own thing. But inside her head, I am touching her, more intimately than any rubbing or pushing or chafing of *parts*. The 'hoek beams signals through the bone, stimulating those parts of the brain that correspond to my slow calligraphy. I am writing my signature across her body. As she in return maps the me drawn on the inside of my skull. How does it feel? Like a cat must feel when it's stroked. Like an otter must feel diving and turning and performing its underwater acrobatics. Like a fire must feel when the wind catches it and sweeps it up a forested mountainside. And without the poetry: like I want to cringe and melt at the same time. Like I must move in a direction I can't explain and my body can't express. Like there is something in my mouth that grows bigger with every second but never changes size, like a reverse turd, only sweet and joyful, is working its way back up into my colon. Like I need to pee something that isn't pee that my body hasn't learned yet. Like I want this to end and never end. It goes on for a long long time and terrible little crying noises come out of our eight-year-aged lips as the aeai steers us through the howling torus of traffic on Siri Ring. We are teens and we are making out in the car.

There is a coming. Oh yes, there is a coming. Like soft fireworks, or the giggling drop at the top of a Ferris wheel, or the feeling you get on those nights when the air is clear and you can see out from the roof pool all the billion lights of Delhi and you are connected to every single one. Like a djinn, made of fire. Ecstatic and guilty and dirty, like you've shouted a dirty word at a sophisticated party. My nipples are very very sensitive.

Then I start with Purrzja. And then Shayman. As I said, it's entirely our own thing. It's well into dark by the time we raise our seats and straighten our clothing and re-gel our hair and I flick off the autodrive and take us up out and over the Ring on a curving off-ramp to a club. It's a bit of a freak place—nutes like it and where nutes are welcome we are usually welcome—but the door knows us—knows our money—and there are always chati-mag paps there. Tonight is no exception: we pose and pimp and preen for the cameras. I can write the society column headlines already. GENE-TWEAK FREAKS ON COCKTAIL CLUB ORGY. Except we don't drink. We're underage for that.

It's always late when we get back. Only the house steward and aeais wait up for us, gently chiding that it is a school day tomorrow. Don't they understand that those are the best nights? This night the lights are on in the big drawing room. I can see them from the approach to the car park. My mother waits for me. She's not alone. There's a man and a woman with her, money people, I can tell that right away from their shoes, their fingernails, their teeth, the cut of their clothes, and the prickle of aeai servitors hovering around them; all those things I can assess in a glance.

"Vishnu, this is Nafisa and Dinesh Misra."

I namaste, a vision in clashing cross-cultural trash.

"They are going to be your new mother- and father-in-law."

MY LOVELY CONSORT

My cats can do other tricks too; I feel you grow bored of them running in their ring. Cats! Cats! See, a clap of my hands and they go and sit on their little stools: Matsya and Kurma, Varaha and Narasimha, Vamana, Parashurama, Rama and Krishna and Buddha and Kalki. Good cats. Clever cats. Rama, stop licking yourself. Hah! One word from me and they do as they will. Now, please feel this hoop, just ordinary paper. Yes? Yes. And these, the same, yes? Yes.

I set them out around the ring. Tabby Parashurama is squeezing his eyes closed in that way that makes him look very very smug.

By the way, I must thank you for coming to watch *The Marvellous, the Magical, the Magnificent Vishnu Cat Circus*. Yes, that's the official name. It's on the letters of registration. Yes, and I pay whatever taxes are due. It's a small entertainment, but at least it's working. You have solar? Not hooked up to the zero point? Very long-sighted of you. Now: watch! Varaha, Vamana, Buddha, and Kalki!

They flow from their painted stools like liquid and run around the inside of the ring, an effortless, cat-lazy lope. The trick with cat circuses, I have found, is to convince them they are doing it for themselves.

And lo! I clap my hands and in perfect unison my cats leap from their ordained orbits clean through the paper hoops. Your applause, please, but not for me: for Varaha, Vamana, Buddha, and Kalki. Now they run in a circle, hurdling through the hoops. What was that? Is there a lesson in every trick? What do you mean? The spiritual significance of the cats I call to perform? I hadn't thought of that. I don't think cats especially spiritual; quite the reverse; they are the most worldly and sensual of creatures, though the Prophet Muhammad, so it's said, was a great lover of cats and famously cut the sleeve from his robe rather than disturb a cat that had fallen asleep there.

Now, on with the story. Where am I going? Don't you know it's a terrible rudeness to interrupt the storyteller? You came here to see the cat circus, not watch some old goondah spin a yarn? You've seen cats leap through paper hoops, what more do you want? Where am I going? Very well then, to Varanasi. It's not just the bodhisofts who go to Varanasi. Here's the deal. I have plenty more tricks in my little ring here on the sand, but to see them you will have to listen to my story, and remember, the power may be working but the broadcasters are out. Nothing on your screens tonight. But you'll like this. It's a wedding scene. What is a story without a wedding?

Elephants bore me. When I say that, I don't mean that I find the pachyderm genus tedious, as if I have some special personal conversational relationship with them and know all their verbal tics and ploys. Is Ganesh not the best-loved god in our entire profligate pantheon? I mean, simply, that elephants carried me, in a howdah like a small gilt temple, through the streets of Delhi. Five elephants, with mahouts; one for my schoolfriend Suresh Hira, one for Vin Johar, one for Syaman, and one, my sole spit of defiance in the face of tradition, for Sarasvati, and one for me, Vishnu Nariman Raj, the gnarly groom. Delhi's eternal, monstrous traffic broke around the horde of musicians, drummers, dancers, merry-meeters like water. The traffic news had been reporting me as a major congestion for hours. People stopped and stared, women threw rice, ayahs pointed me out to their finger-sucking grandchildren: *There, there he is, Lord Vishnu goes to his wedding.* The chati mags had been full of little else besides the first dynastic Brahmin marriage. My other break with tradition: much of the gaudy I had funded myself through the judicious auctioning of the photo rights to *Gupshup* magazine. Look, here am I, in white sherwani and wrinkle-ankle pants in the very best style, the traditional veil of flowers over my face, gripping my sword with one hand (a ludicrous affectation by Sreem, Delhi's most-sought nute wedding choreographer; who could ever sword-fight from the broad back of an elephant?), with the other gripping white-knuckled to the gold-leaf coping of my swaying howdah. Have I said that riding an elephant is like being on a boat on unstill waters? Does what you glimpse through the cascading marigolds look afraid? Were you expecting someone larger?

Negotiations had been protracted and delicate over the winter. Hosts of aeai attorneys circled and clashed around my mother and father, temporarily unified, as they entertained the Misras to a grand vagdana. Lakshmi and I sat blandly, quietly, hands folded neatly in our laps on the cream leather sofa, as relatives and relatives-to-be passed and greeted and blessed us. We smiled. We nodded. We did not speak, not to our guests, not to each other. In our years together at the Dr. Renganathan Brahminical College we had said all that we could say to each other. We sat like an old married couple at a metro stop. At last the hosts of clashing attorney aeais withdrew: a prenuptial contract was draughted, a dowry was set. It was a brilliant match; property and 'ware with water, the very essence of life. Of course the price was high; we were Brahmins. It was no less than the flesh of our flesh and the seed of our loins, for all generations. Way down the list of ticky boxes on Dr. Rao's shopping list was one I suspect Lakshmi's parents had tickied blindly. I know my parents had. But it was perhaps the most profound change of all that Dr. Rao's nanoworkers worked on us. Our genelines were modified. The traits engineered into us were inheritable. Our children and their children, all our conceivable Nariman–Misras marching into futurity, would be Brahmins, not from the microsurgery of Dr. Rao, but from our sperm and eggs.

Children, offspring, a line, a dynasty. That was our mutually contracted dowry. A match was made! Let great Delhi rejoice!

The janampatri aeais had read the stars for the most auspicious fates, the pandit had made the puja to Ganesh, and the joint houses of Nariman and Misra had hired Gupshup Girls, Delhi's biggest and brassiest girl band, to sing and flash their thighs for two thousand society guests at our sangeet sandhya. Lakshmi duetted onstage with them. Pop-girli hotpants and belly-top looked disturbing on her as she danced and skipped among the high-heels. Too small, too young to wed. I was never much of a singer. Mamaji and Dadaji had neglected to ticky that box. I boogied down in the golden circle with my classmates. Though I had still two years more at Dr. Renganathan College under the tutelage of the invisible Mr. Khan, our circle was broken. I was all their imminent futures.

At India Gate Sarasvati called her mahout to a halt and slipped from her elephant's back to run and dance among my parade of Baraatis. I had defied tradition by inviting her; she defied it back by coming dressed as a man in sherwani and kohl and huge, ludicrous false Rajput moustache. I watched her leap and whirl, brilliant and vivacious, with the dancers and drummers, and dance, laughing, with monkeylike Sreem, and felt tears in my eyes behind my veil of flowers. She was so brilliant, so lovely, so lithe and free from expectation.

At Lodi Gardens the celebrity spotters were five deep. Policemen held them back with a chain of linked lathis. They had seen Rishi Jaitly and Anand Arora and ooh, isn't that Esha Rashore the famous dancer and who is that little man with the very much younger wife? Don't you know, it's Narayan Mittal from Mittal Industries. Last and least to them was the seeming child perched high on the back of a painted wedding elephant. A blare of trumpets and a barrage of drums greeted us. Then the smart-silk screens draped around us woke up and filled with the characters and, in a never-before-seen feat of CG prestidigitation, the cast of *Town and Country* singing and dancing our wedding song specially written by legendary screen composer A. H. Husayin. They were aeais; singing and dancing were easy for them. There, almost lost among the sari silk and garlands as the bridal party stepped forwards to greet us, was Lakshmi.

We were swept on a wave of drum-beating and brass-tootling to the pavilions arrayed across the well-watered grass like a Mughal invasion. We feasted, we danced, we were sat on our thrones, our feet not touching the ground, and received our guests.

I didn't see him. The line was long and the atmosphere in the marquee stifling and I was bloated and drowsy from wedding food. I took the hand blindly, bored. I only became attentive when it held mine that moment too long, that quantum too firmly.

Shiv.

"Brother."

I nodded in acknowledgement.

"Are you well?"

He indicated his suit, the fabric cheap, the cut niggardly, the cufflinks and the jewel at the shirt-throat phoney. A budget wedding outfit. Tomorrow it would go by phatphat back to the hire shop.

"I'll be more suitably dressed when you come to my wedding."

"Are you getting married?"

"Doesn't everyone?"

I sniffed then. It was not Shiv's perfume—that too smelled cheap and phenolic. My uniquely connected senses show me subtleties to which others are quite oblivious. In his student hire-suit and cheap Bata shoes, Shiv seemed to carry an aura around him, a presence, a crackle of information like distant summer thunder. He smelled of aeais. I tilted my head to one side: did I see a momentary shifting glow? It did not take a synaesthete or a Brahmin to spot the 'hoek tucked behind his ear.

"Thank you for coming," I said, and knew that he heard the lie.

"I wouldn't have missed it."

"We must meet up sometime," I went on, compounding the lie. "When Lakshmi and I get back into Delhi. Have you over to the place."

"It's not going to be terribly likely," Shiv said. "I'm going to Bharat as soon as I graduate. I've a postgrad lined up at the University of Varanasi. Nano-informatics. Delhi's not a good place for anyone working in artificial intelligence. The Americans are breathing down Srivastava's neck to ratify the Hamilton Acts."

I consumed news, all news, any news, as universally and unthinkingly as breathing. I could watch twelve screens of television and tell you what was happening on any of them, simultaneously scan a table full of newspapers and reproduce any article verbatim; I frequently kept my newsfeeds on brain drip waking and sleeping, beaming the happening world into my tiny head. I knew too well of the international moves, begun by the United States, to restrict artificial intelligence by licence. Fear motivates them; that vague Christian millennial dread of the work of our own hands rising up and making itself our god. Artificial intelligences with a thousand, ten thousand, infinite times our human intelligence, whatever that means. Intelligence, when you look down on it from above, is a very vague terrain. Nevertheless police forces had been established, Krishna Cops, charged with hunting down and eliminating rogue aeais. Fine title, vain hope. Aeais were utterly different from us; intelligences that could be in many places at one time, that could exist in many different avatars, that could only move by copying themselves, not as I moved, lugging about my enhanced intelligence in the calcium bowl of my skull. The Krishna Cops had very good guns, but I think my gnawing fear was aeais today, Brahmins tomorrow. Humans are very jealous gods.

I knew that it was inevitable that Awadh would sign up to the accord in return for Favoured Nation grants from the US. Neighbouring Bharat would never accede to that; its media industry, dependent on artificial intelligence for the success of *Town and Country* from Djakarta to Dubai, was too influential a lobby. The world's first overt soapocracy. And, I foresaw, the world's first data-haven nation-state. Stitching together stories buried way down the business news, I was already seeing a pattern of software house relocations and research foundations moving to Varanasi. So Shiv, ambitious Shiv, Shiv-building-your-own-glory while I merely obeyed the imperative in my DNA, Shiv with your whiff of aeais around you, what is it in Bharat? Would you be researcher into technologies as sky blue as Lord Krishna himself, would you be a dataraja with a stable of aeais pretending they can't pass the Turing test?

"Not that we ever exactly lived in each other's pockets," I said prissily. We had lived with twenty million people between us for most of our lives but still anger boiled within me. What had I to be resentful of? I had all the advantage, the love, the blessing, and the gifts yet here he was in his cheap hire suit, smug and assured, and I was the ludicrous little lordling, the boy-husband swinging his legs on his golden throne.

"Not really, no," Shiv said. Even in his words, his smile, there was an aura, an intensity; Shiv-plus. What was he doing to himself that could only be consummated in Varanasi?

The line was restless now, mothers shifting from foot to foot in their uncomfortable weddings shoes. Shiv dipped his head, his eyes meeting mine for an instant of the purest, most intense hatred. Then he moved on into the press of guests, picking up a glass of champagne here, a plate of small eats there, a strangely singular darkness like plague at the wedding.

The caterers cleared away, torches were lit across the heel-trodden grass of Lodi Gardens, and the pandit tied us together in marriage. As fireworks burst over the tomb of Muhammad Shah and the dome of Bara Gumbad we drove away to the plane. We left the diamond stain of bright Delhi behind us and flew, far later than tots of our size should be up, through the night into morning as the private helicopter lifted us up and away to the teahouse in the

cool and watered green hills. Staff discreetly stowed our baggage, showed us
the lie of the rooms, the shaded verandah with its outlook over the heart-
stunning gold and purple of the morning Himalayas, the bedroom with the
one huge four-poster bed. Then they swept away in a rustle of silk and we
were alone, together, Vishnu and Lakshmi, two gods.

"It's good, isn't it?"

"Lovely. Wonderful. Very spiritual. Yes."

"I like the rooms. I like the smell of the wood, old wood."

"Yes, it is good. Very old wood."

"This is the honeymoon then."

"Yes."

"We're supposed to . . ."

"Yes. I know. Do you . . . are you?"

"Wired? No I was never into that."

"Oh. Well, I've some other stuff in my bag, it should work on you as well."

"You've tried it?"

"Sometimes. I'm finding it gets hard all on its own now, just like that,
nothing in particular, so I try it then."

"Is it productive?"

"It's a bit like the 'hoek sex. Feeling you really really need to pee something that isn't pee and isn't there. To be honest, not as good. Have you
tried?"

"With the fingers? Oh yes, with the whole hand. It's like you."

"Need to pee?"

"Something like that. More of a clench. It works on a swing too. I don't
really think I want to use something you have on you, you know."

"I suppose not. We could . . . I could . . ."

"I don't really think so."

"Do you think they'll check? Save the sheets and show them round to all
the relatives?"

"At our physical ages? Don't be stupid."

"It's part of the contract."

"I don't think anyone's going to invoke contractual obligation until I've
at least had a period."

"So do you want to do anything?"

"Not particularly."

"So what will we do then?"

"The view's nice."

"There's a pack of cards in the drawer in the table."

"Maybe later. I might sleep now."

"So might I. Are you all right about the bed?"

"Of course. We're supposed to, aren't we? We are husband and wife."

We slept under the light silk cover with the ceiling fan turning slowly, each curled up like the eight-year-olds we physically were with our backs to each other, as far apart as Vish and Shiv, and afterwards we invented card games of staggering complexity with the old circular Ganjifa cards on the verandah with its titanic view over the Himalayas. As Lakshmi turned over the kings and ministers our eyes met and we both knew it was more than over, it had never begun. There was nothing but contractual obligation between us. We were the hostages of our DNA. I thought of that line of off-spring issuing like a rope of pearls from the end of my still-flaccid penis; those slow children toddling into a future so distant I could not even see its dust on time's horizon, and onward and onward always onward. I was filled with horror at the blind imperative of biology. I owned superhuman intelligence, I only forgot what I chose to forget, I had never known a day's illness in my life, I carried the name of a god, but to my seed all this was nothing, I was no different from some baseline Dalit in Molar Bund basti. Yes, I was a privileged brat, yes, I was a sneerer of the worst kind, how could I be anything other? I was a designer snob.

We stayed our week in the teahouse in the green foothills of Himachal Pradesh, Lakshmi and Vishnu. Lakshmi patented some of her elaborate social card games—we tested the multiplayer games by each of us playing several hands at once, an easy feat for the Brahmins—and made a lot of money from licensing them. It was radiantly beautiful, the mountains were distant and serene like stone Buddhas, occasional rain pattered on the leaves outside our window at night, and we were utterly utterly miserable, but even more so at the thought of what we had to face on our return to Awadh, the darlings of Delhi. My decision had been made on the third day of our honeymoon but it was not until we were in the limo to Ramachandra Tower, where we had been given an apartment fit for gods on the floor below my Mamaji, that I made the call to the very special, very discreet doctor.

TWO EXTRANEOUS ASPECTS OF MYSELF

"Both of them?" the nute said. Yt would have raised an eyebrow had yt possessed any hair on yts shaven head to raise.

"History is quiet on the subject of half-eunuchs," I said.

No one, alas, ever delivers such dialogue. Ticking lines, arch exchanges, loaded looks, these are things of story, not real life. But I am telling you a story, my story, which is much more than just history or even memory. For if I choose to forget, I can also choose to remember and make what I chose memory. So if I wish the nute surgeon's office to be at the top of a winding, creaking flight of stairs, each level haunted by the eyes of suspicious and hostile Old Delhiwallahs, if I decide to remember it so, it will be so. Likewise, if I choose to recall that office to be a charnel house of grotesque surgical implements and pictures of successfully mutilated body parts like a demon-infested hell from a Himalayan Buddhist painting: it will be so forever. Perhaps it's less strange a concept for you than for me. I more than anyone know the deceptiveness of physical appearance, but you seem young enough to have grown up in a world comfortable with universal memory, every breath and blink swarming with devas continuously writing and rewriting physical reality. And if the devas choose to rewrite that memory, who is there to say that it's not so?

But there is east light in the sky beyond the blazing pillar of the Jyotir-linga, I have far to go, you have yet to see the most astonishing feats my cats can achieve, and the reality is that the surgery of Dr. Anil was in a tastefully restored haveli in the warren of streets in the shadow of the Red Fort, the surgery elegant and discreet and fronted by the delightful Miss Modi, and Dr. Anil welcoming, professional, subtle, and frankly surprised by my request.

"I usually deal in more . . . substantial surgery," yt said. The Ardhanaris-vara Clinic was Delhi's leading centre for nute transformation. Leading through whispers and rumours; in bright new Awadh we might claim to be urbane, global, cosmopolitan, and unshockable, but nute culture, those who decided to escape our desperate sex wars by choosing a third way, a neither-way, was still almost as recondite and secretive as the ancient transgendered hijras who had long ago hidden themselves away in Old Delhi. The ancient city; older than any memory, its streets convoluted like the folds of a brain, has always looked after those with needs beyond the merely average.

"I think what I'm asking is substantial enough," I said.

"True true," Dr. Anil said, putting his fingers together in a spire in that way that all doctors, male, female, transgendered, or nute, seem to learn on day one of medical school. "So, both testicles."

"Yes, both."

"And not the penis."

"That would be perverse."

"You're sure you won't consider the chemical option? It's reversible, should you ever reconsider."

"No, not chemical. I don't want it to be reversible. I want to remove myself from the future. I want this to end with me. I'm more than a stud animal. Complete physical castration, yes."

"It's quite simple. Much more so than the usual kind of thing we do here." I knew well the medical procedures that flowed out from here to the anonymous go-downs and grey-surgery clinics beyond the Siri Ring orbital expressway. There is a video for everything somewhere in the online world and I had watched with fascination what those humans who desired another gender had done to themselves. The things strung out through the gel tanks, skin flayed, muscles laid open, organs drawn out and suspended in molecular sieve cradles, were so far from anything human as to be curious, like strange forest flowers, rather than obscene. I was much more of a coward, leaving only my two little organs on the doorstep of gender. "My only reservation would be that, as you are biologically prepubescent, it would be an internal orchidectomy. Miss Modi will draw up a consent form." Yt blinked at me, a delicate, faunlike creature behind a heavy Raj desk, too too lovely to speak of such things as testicular surgery. "Forgive me for asking, I haven't met any High Brahmins before, but you are of an age to sign a consent form?"

"I'm of an age to be legally married."

"Yes, but you must understand, mine is a business that attracts scrutiny in Awadh."

"I'm of an age to pay you a profane sum of money to give me what I want."

"Profane it is, then."

Surprisingly mundane it was. I did not even need to be driven out to the nasty industrial zones. In the cubicle I changed into the surgical gown, the sleeves too long, the hem trailing on the ground, slid up onto the disinfectant-stinky operating table in the basement surgery, and felt the needling suffusion of the local anaesthetic. Robot arms, fingertips fine as insect antennae, danced in under the control of Dr. Anil. I felt nothing as I blinked up into the lights and strained to hear their synaesthetic music. The dancing arms withdrew; I felt nothing. And I still felt nothing as the car spun me back through streets full of pulsing, potent, hormone-raddled people. A mild twinge from the sutures pulling against the weave of my clothes. No pain, little loss, nothing of the sense of lightness and freedom I had read of in the literature of castration fetishists. A unique pleasure, sexual castration; an orgasm to end all orgasms. I had not even had that. The cell-weave treatments would heal the wound in three days and hide all evidence, until the passing years revealed that my voice was not significantly deepening, my hair not receding, that I was growing unusually tall and willowy, and that I had singularly failed to contractually conceive any children.

"Do you want to take them with you?" Dr. Anil asked as yt sat me down in yts consulting room after the short operation.

"Why should I wish to do that?"

"It was a tradition in China; Imperial eunuchs would be given their excised genitals preserved in a jar of alcohol to bury beside them on their deaths, so that they might enter heaven whole men."

"It was a tradition in Ottoman Turkey that eunuchs, after their cutting clean, would sit in a dung heap for three days to heal their wounds, or die. I don't care for that tradition either. They're not mine, they're not me; they belong to someone else. Burn them or throw them to the pi-dogs, I don't care."

Thunder growled over me, a promise of a monsoon; the day was darkening. Lightning glowed cloud to cloud as I rode the elevator up the outside of Ramachandra Tower. Lakshmi sat curled on the sofa, the breaking storm magnificent behind her. Dry lightning, a false prophet of rain. All prophecies of rain were false these days.

"Did you do it, are you all right?"

I nodded. It was beginning to hurt now. I clenched my teeth, kicking in the analgesic nanoinfuser Dr. Anil had planted there. Lakshmi clapped her hands in joy. "I'll go tomorrow. Oh dear Lord, I'm so happy, so happy." And then, there, in the dark apartment glowing with muted lights, she kissed me.

We did not tell anyone. That was part of the pact. Not our parents, not our relatives, not our circle of Brahmin friends, not even our aeais. Not even dear Sarasvati; I wouldn't burden her with this. There was work we had to do before we announced to our respective families how we had so drastically denied their plans for us. Then we could sweetly and painlessly divorce.

I NUZZLE THE EARLOBE OF POWER

What is the proper work of eunuchs?

Does it make you uncomfortable, that word? Does it make you cross your legs, boys; does it give you a hollow clench in your uterus, ladies? When you hear it, do you see something other than a human being, something less? How then is it any different from other words of distinction: Kshatriya, Dalit? Brahmin? Eunuch. It is a very old and noble word, a fine and ancient tradition practised in all the great cultures of Earth. The principle is to give up the lesser to gain the greater. Of all those pitiful puffs of cock juice, how many will ever turn into human beings? Come on, be honest. It's almost all wasted. And never imagine that the ball-less are sexless, or without desire. No, the great castrati singers, the eunuch poets and holy visionaries, the grand viziers and royal advisors all understood that greatness came at a price and that was generation. Empires could be entrusted to eunuchs, free from dynastic urges. The care and feeding of great nations is our proper work and with all the gifts my parents had endowed me I steered myself towards the political cradle of the nation.

How almost right my mother was, and how utterly wrongheaded. She had seen me carried in through the doors of the Lok Sabha on the shoulders of cheering election workers. I preferred the servants' entrance. Politicians live and die by the ballot box. They are not there to serve, they are there to gain and hold office. Populism can force them to abandon wise and correct policies for whims and fads. The storm of ballots will in the end sweep them and all their good works from power. Their grand viziers endure. We understand that democracy is the best system by which a nation *seems* to be governed.

Months of social networking—the old-fashioned handshake-and-gift type—and the setting up and calling in of favours and lines of political credit have gained me an internship to Parekh, the Minister for Water and the Environment. He was a tolerable dolt, a Vora from Uttaranchal with a shopkeeper's shrewdness and head for details, but little vision. He was good enough to seem in control and a politician often needs little more for a long and comfortable career. This was the highest he would ever rise; as soon as the next monsoon failure hit and the mobs were hijacking water tankers in the street, he would be out. He knew I knew this. I scared him, even though I was careful to turn down the full dazzle of my intelligence to a glow of general astuteness. He knew I was far from the nine-year-old I seemed to be but he really had no idea of my and my kind's capabilities and curses. I chose my department carefully. Naked ambition would have exposed me too early to a government that was only now realising it had never properly legislated around human geneline manipulation. Even so, I knew the colour of all the eyes that were watching me, skipping through the glassy corridors of the Water Ministry. Water is life. Water, its abundance and its rarity, would sculpt the future of Awadh, of all the nations of North India, from the Panjab to the United States of Bengal. Water was a good place to be bright, but I had no intention of remaining there.

The dam at Kunda Khadar neared completion, that titanic fifteen-kilometre-long bank of earth and concrete like a garter around the thigh of Mother Ganga. Protests from downstream Bharat and the United States of Bengal grew strident but the tower cranes lifted and swung, lifted and swung, day and night. Minister Parekh and Prime Minister Srivastava communicated daily. The Defence Ministry was brought into the circle. Even the PR staffers could smell diplomatic tension.

It was a Thursday. Even before, I called it Bold Thursday, to commit myself, to get myself up. The genes don't make you brave. But I had prepared as rigorously as I could; which was more than anyone in the Lok Sabha, Minister Parekh included. Srivastava was due with his entourage for a press conference from the ministry to reassure the Awadhi public that Kunda Khadar would do its job and slake Delhi's bottomless thirst. Everyone was turned out smart as paint: moustaches plucked, slacks creased, shirts white as mourning. Not me. I had picked my spot long before: a brief bustle down the corridor as Srivastava and his secretarial team was coming up. I had no idea what they would be talking about but I knew they would be talking; Srivastava loved his "walking briefings"; they made him seem a man of action and energy. I trusted that my research and quicker wit would win.

I heard the burble of voices. They were about to turn the corner. I went into motion, pushed myself into the wall as the press of suits came towards me. My senses scanned five conversations, lit on Srivastava murmur to Bhansal his parliamentary secretary, "If I knew we had McAuley's support."

Andrew J. McAuley, president of the United States of America. And the answer was there.

"If we could negotiate an output deal in return for Sajida Rana accepting partial ratification of the Hamilton Acts," I said, my voice shrill and pure and piercing as a bird's.

The prime ministerial party bustled past but Satya Shetty, the press secretary, turned with a face of thunder to strike down this upstart, mouthy intern. He saw a nine-year-old. He was dumbstruck. His eyes bulged. He hesitated. That hesitation froze the entire party. Prime Minister Srivastava turned towards me. His eyes widened. His pupils dilated.

"That's a very interesting idea," he said, and in those five words I knew he had identified, analysed, and accepted the gift I had offered him. A Brahmin advisor. The strange, savant child. The child genius, the infant guru, the little god. India adored such as them. It was PR gold. His staffers parted as he stepped towards me. "What are you doing here?"

I explained that I was on an internship with Minister Parekh.

"And now you want more."

Yes, I did.

"What's you name?"

I told him. He nodded.

"Yes, the wedding. I remember. So, it's a career in politics, is it?"

It was.

"You're certainly not backward about being forward."

My genes wouldn't allow it. My first political lie.

"Well, ideas do seem to be in short stock at the moment." With that he turned, his entourage closed around him, and he was swept on. Satya Shetty dealt me a glare of pure spite; I held his eyes until he snapped his gaze away. I would see him and all his works dust while I was still fresh and filled with energy. By the time I returned to my desk there was an invitation from the Office of the Prime Minister to call them to arrange an interview.

I told my great achievement to the three women in my life. Lakshmi beamed with delight. Our plans were working. My mother was baffled; she no longer understood my motivations, why I would accept a lowly and inconspicuous civil service position rather than become a high-flyer in our superstar political culture. Sarasvati jumped up from her sofa and danced around the room, then clapped her hands around my face and kissed my forehead long and hard until her lips left a red tilak there.

"As long as there's joy in it," she said. "Only joy."

My sister, my glorious sister, had voiced a truth that I was only now developing the maturity to recognise. Joy was all. Mamaji and Dadaji had aimed me at greatness, at blinding success and wealth, power, and celebrity. I had always possessed the emotional intelligence, if not the emotional vocabulary, to know that the blindingly powerful and famous were seldom happy, that their success and wealth often played against their own mental and physical well-being. All my decisions I made for me, for my peace, well-being, satisfaction, and to keep me interested throughout my long life. Lakshmi had chosen the delicate world of complicated games. I had chosen the whirl of politics. Not economics; that was too dismal a science for me. But the state and those statelets beyond Awadh's borders with which I could see we were as inextricably entwined as when we were one India, and the countries beyond those, and the continents beyond: that fascinated me. The etiquette of nations was my pleasure. There was joy in it, Sarasvati. And I was brilliant at it. I became the hero of my childhood comics, a subtle hero, Diplomacy Man. I saved your world more times than you can ever know. My superpower was to see a situation entire, connected, and all those subtler forces acting upon it that other, less gifted analysts would have discounted. Then I would give it a nudge. The smallest, slightest tap, one tiny incentive or restriction, even a hint at how a policy might be shaped, and watch how the social physics of a complex capitalist society scaled them up through power laws and networks and social amplifiers to slowly turn the head of the entire nation.

In that first year I was constantly fighting for my own survival. Satya Shetty was my deadliest enemy from the moment our eyes had met in the corridor in the Water Ministry. He was influential, he was connected, he was clever, but not clever enough to realise he could never beat me. I just let my drips of honey fall into Krishna Srivastava's ear. I was always right. Little by little his cabinet and Satya Shetty's allies realised that, more than being always right, I was essentially different from them. I didn't seek high office. I sought the greatest well-being. I was the prefect advisor. And I looked great on television: Prime Minister Srivastava's dwarf vizier, trotting behind him like some throwback to the days of the Mughals. Who isn't, at some level, unnerved by the child prodigy? Even if I was twenty years old now, with puberty—whatever that might mean for me personally—looming on the horizon of my Brahmin generation like the rumbles of a long-delayed monsoon.

It was that treacherous monsoon that became the driver of Awadhi politics, town and country, home and away. Thirsty nations are irrational nations; nations that pray and turn to strange saviours. The great technocracy of the United States of Bengal had, in a display of national hysteria, put its faith in a bizarre plan to haul an iceberg from Antarctica into the Sundarbans with the hope that the mass of cold air would affect the shifting climatic patterns and claw the monsoon back over India. Strange days, a time of rumours and wonders. The end of the Age of Kali was imminent and once again the gods were descending upon us, walking in the shapes of ordinary men and women. The Americans had found something in space, something not of this world. The data-havens of Bharat, boiling with aeais, had spawned Generation Three artificial intelligences; legendary entities whose intelligence as far outstripped mine as mine did the fleas crawling on my poor, harassed cats. Sajida

Rana, politically embattled from resurgent Hindu fundamentalism, was preparing a preemptive strike on Kunda Khadar as a PR stunt. This last rumour from my trawling of the Bharati press I took seriously enough to call for a departmental-level meeting between my ministry and its Bharati counterpart. Did I mention that I was now parliamentary secretary to Krishna Srivastava? A steady, not stellar, climb. It was still too easy to lose grip and fall into the reaching hands of my rivals.

My counterpart at the Bharat Bhavan was a refined Muslim gentleman, Shaheen Badoor Khan, from an excellent family and impeccably educated. Behind his pitch-perfect etiquette and a dignity I envied deeply, for I was a small, scampering child next to him, I did sense a sadness; an ache behind the eyes. We recognised and liked each other immediately. We knew instinctively that we both cared deeply enough for our countries to be prepared to betray them. Such a thing could never be said, or even implied. Thus our conversation, as we walked among the Buddha's deer of old Sarnath, our security men discreet shadows among the trees, the security drones circling like black kites overhead, seemed as casual and elliptical as two old dowagers on a Friday-afternoon stroll.

"Awadh has always seemed to me a country at peace with itself," Shaheen Badoor Khan said. "As if it's solved some great and quintessentially Indian paradox."

"It wasn't always so," I said. Behind the security fence Western tourists on the Buddha trail tried to hold down their flapping robes in the rising wind. "Delhi's streets have run red far too many times."

"But it's always been a cosmopolitan city. Varanasi, on the other hand, always has and always will be the city of Lord Siva."

I waggled my head in agreement. I knew now what I would report to Srivastava. *Sajida Rana is under pressure from the Hindutvavadis. She will launch a preemptive strike at Kunda Khadar. Awadh will have the moral high ground; we must not lose it.*

"I have a relative in Varanasi," I said casually.

"Oh, so?"

"My brother—a Shiva himself, so no surprise really that he should end up in Varanasi."

"And is he a Brahmin like yourself?"

"No, but he is very gifted."

"We do seem to attract talent. It's one of our blessings, I suppose. I have a younger brother in the United States. Terrible at keeping in contact, terrible; my mother, well, you know what they're like. Of course it's my responsibility."

You're worried that your brother has drifted into business that could adversely affect your standing, if it became public, was what this sage Mr. Khan was telling me. *You want me to keep an eye on him; in return you'll open up a secure channel of communication between us to prevent war between Bharat and Awadh.*

"You know what brothers are like," I said.

The information was beaming into my head even as I stepped off the plane at Indira Gandhi Airport. Shiv had opened a company, Purusa, in Varanasi. He had attracted substantial funding from a venture capital company called Odeco and match-funding from the research and development division at Bharat's mighty Ray Power. His field was nanoscale computing. Top designers and engineers were working with him. The Ghost Index, which valued companies with the potential to become global players when they went public, valued Purusa as one of their top five to watch. He was young and he was hot and he was headed for orbit. He had made some questionable friends among Bharat's datarajas and a cloud of high-level aeais hid much of Purusa's activities from its rivals and from the Bharati government. The Krishna Cops had a file on him and a deliberately clumsy team of aeai wards to keep him aware that he was known to them. My own Awadhi intelligence service surveillance aeais were of a subtler stripe than the police's. They coded themselves into the very informational fabric of Purusa. The security of Awadh was a flimsy fiction; I was intensely curious as to what my brother was up to. What Shiv planned was of course monstrously ambitious. He had cracked open the prison of the skull. More prosaically, Purusa had developed a prototype biochip that could interface directly with the brain. No more a tacky coil of plastic behind the ear and the soft invasion of electromagnetic radiation into the brain, like shouting in a temple. This was engineered protein, stuff of our stuff, which sent its artificial neurons through skin and bone to mesh with the threads of thought. It was a third eye, forever open to the unseen world. See how easily I resort to the language of the mystical? Omniscience was standard; anyone so infected had access to all the knowledge and all the bitchy triviality of the global web. Communication was no longer a click and a call, it was a thought, a subtle telepathy. Virtual worlds became real. The age of privacy, that first Western luxury that Indian wealth bought, was over. Where our own thoughts ended and those of others began, how would we know? We would touch the world of the aeais, in their dispersed, extended, multilevelled perceptions. Speculation led to speculation. I could see no end to them. Lakshmi, disturbed from her mathematical games, would sense my mood and look up to see the adult anxiety on my child's face. This technology would change us, change us utterly and profoundly. This was a new way of being human, a fault line, a diamond cutter's strike across society. I began to realise that the greatest threat to Awadh, to Bharat, to all India, was not water. It was the pure and flawless diamond Shiv and his Purusa Corporation dangled and spun in front of each and every human. Be more, be everything. So engaged was I that I did not notice when the warning came down the Grand Trunk Road from Shaheen Badoor Khan in Varanasi and thus was caught sleeping when Sajida Rana sent her tanks to take Kunda Khadar without a shot.

THE GIRL WITH THE RED BINDI

The war's names were longer than its duration. The Kunda Khadar War, the Forty-Eight-Hour War, the First Water War. You don't remember it, though Awadhi main battle tanks manoeuvred over these very sands. You probably don't even remember it from history lessons. There have been greater and more enduring wars; war running into war; the long and, I think, the final war. The war I shall end. That grand display of arms on these river strands I now understand as its opening shot, had any shots actually been fired. That was another of its names, the Soft War. Ah! Who is it names wars? Hacks and pundits, without doubt, media editors and chati journalists; people with an interesting, a good mouth-filling phrase. It is certainly not civil servants, or cat-circus proprietors. How much better a name would "Soft War" have been for the decades of unrest that followed, this Age of Kali that now seems to have run down to its lowest ebb with the arrival of the Jyotirlingas on Earth?

The Water War, the War of '47, whatever we call it, for me marked the end of human history and the return of the age of miracles to Earth. It was only after the smoke had cleared and the dust settled and our diplomatic teams arrived among the tall and shining towers of Ranapur to negotiate the peace that we realised the immensity of events in Bharat. Our quiet little water war was the least of it. I had received one terse communication down the Grand Trunk Road: *I am ruined, I have failed, I have resigned.* But there was Shaheen Badoor Khan, five paces behind his new prime minster, Ashok Rana, as I trotted like a child behind our Srivastava.

"Rumours of my demise were exaggerated," he whispered as we fell in beside each other while the politicians formed up on the grass outside the Benares Polo and Country Club for the press call, each jostling for status-space.

"War does seem to shorten the political memory." A twenty-year-old in the body of a boy half his age may say pretty much whatever he likes. It's the liberty granted to fools and angels. When I first met Shaheen Badoor Khan, as well as his decency and intelligence, I had sensed a bone-deep sadness. Even I could not have guessed it was a long-repressed and sterile love for the other, the transgressive, the romantic and doomed, all wrapped up in the body of a young Varanasi nute. He had fallen into the honeytrap laid for him by his political enemies.

Shaheen Badoor Khan dipped his head. "I'm far from being the first silly, middle-aged man to have been a fool for lust. I may be the only one to have got his prime minister killed as a consequence. But, as you say, war does very much clarify the vision and I seem to be a convenient figure for public expiation. And from what I gather from the media, the public will trust me sooner than Ashok Rana. People like nothing better than the fallen Mughal who repents. In the meantime, we do what we must, don't we, Mr. Nariman? Our countries need us more than they know. These have been stranger times in Bharat than people can ever be allowed to know."

Bless your politician's self-deprecation. The simultaneous collapse of major aeai systems across Bharat, including the all-conquering *Town and*

Country, the revelation that the country's rampant Hindutva opposition was actually a cabal of artificial intelligences, chaos at Ray Power, and the mysterious appearance of a hundred-metre hemispherical crater in the university grounds, of mirror-bright perfection, and, behind all, rumours that the long-awaited, long-dreaded Generation Three aeais had arrived. There was only one who could make sense of it to me. I went to see Shiv.

He had a house, a shaded place with many trees to push back the crowding, noisy world. Gardeners moved with slow precision up and down the rolled gravel paths, deadheading a Persian rose here, spraying aphids there, spot-feeding brown drought-patches in the lawn everywhere. He had grown fat. He lolled in his chair at the tiffin table on the lawn. He looked dreadful, pasty and puffy. He had a wife. He had a child, a little pipit of a girl waving her tiny fat fists in the snap-together plastic fun park on the lawn under the eye of her ayah. She would glance over at me, unsure whether to smile or cry at this a strange and powerful uncle. Yes, wee one, I was a strange creature. That scent, that pheromone of information I had smelled on Shiv the day he came to my wedding, still clung to him, stronger now. He smelled like a man who had spent too much time among aeais.

He welcomed me expansively. Servants brought cool homemade sherbet. As we settled into brother talk, man-to-eleven-year-old talk, his wife excused herself in a voice small as an insect's and went to hover nervously over her daughter exuberantly throwing around brightly coloured plastic blocks.

"You seem to have had a good war," I said.

"There was war?" Shiv held my gaze for a moment, then exploded into volcanic laughter. Sweat broke out on his brow. I did not believe it for an instant. "I've got comfortable and greasy, yes."

"And successful."

"Not as successful as you."

"I am only a civil servant."

"I've heard you run Srivastava like a pimp."

"We all have our sources."

"Yes." Again that affected pause. "I spotted yours pretty early on. Not bad for government 'ware."

"Disinformation can be as informative as information."

"Oh, I wouldn't try anything as obvious as that with you. No, I left them there; I let them look. I've nothing to hide."

"Your investors are interesting."

"I doubt some of them will be collecting on their investment." He laughed again.

"I don't think I understand."

"It transpires that one of my key investors, Odeco, was nothing more than a front for a Generation Three aeai that had developed inside the international financial markets."

"So it wasn't just a rumour."

"I'm glad you're still listening to rumours."

"You say this all very casually."

"What other way is there to treat the end of history? You've seen what happens in India when we take things seriously." The laugh was annoying me now. It was thick and greasy.

"The end of history has been promised many times, usually by people rich enough to avoid it."

"Not this time. The rich will be the ones who'll bring it about. The same blind economic self-interest that caused the demographic shift, and you, Vish. Only this will be on a much greater scale."

"You think your biochip has that potential?"

"On its own, no. I can see I'm going to have to explain this to you."

By the time Shiv had told his tale the gardeners were lighting torches to drive away the evening insects and wife, daughter, and ayah had withdrawn to the lit comfort of the verandah. Bats dashed around me, hunting. I was shivering though the night was warm. A servant brought fresh-made lassi and pistachios. It was greater, as Shiv had promised. Perhaps the greatest. The gods had returned, and then in the instant of their apotheosis, departed. A soft apocalypse.

The fears of the Krishna Cops, of the scared Westerners, had of course come true. The Generation Threes were real, had been real for longer than anyone had foreseen, and had moved among us for years, decades even, unresting, unhasting, and silent as light. There was no force capable of extirpating truly hyperintelligent aeais whose ecosystem was the staggering complexity of the global information network. They could break themselves into components, distribute themselves across continents, copy themselves infinitely, become each other. They could speak with our voices and express our world but they were utterly utterly alien to us. It was convenient for them to withdraw their higher functions from a world closing in on the secret of their existence and base them in the data-havens of Bharat, for they had a higher plan. There were three of them, gods all. Brahma, Shiva, Krishna. My brothers, my gods. One, the most curious about the world, inhabits the global financial market. One grew out of a massively multiple online evolution simulation game of which I had vaguely heard. In creating an artificial world, the gamers had created its deity. And one appeared in the vast server farms of Bharat's Indiapendent Productions, coalesced out of the cast and pseudocast of *Town and Country*. That one particularly impressed me, especially since, with the characteristic desire to meddle in the affairs of others mandatory in the soapi universe, it expanded into Bharati politics in the shape of the aggressive Hindutva Party that had engineered the downfall of the perceptive and dangerous Shaheen Badoor Khan and the assassination of Sajida Rana.

That would have been enough to end our hopes that this twenty-first century would be a smooth and lucrative extension of its predecessor. But their plans were not conflict or the subjugation of humanity. That would have meant nothing to the aeais; it was a human concept born of a human need. They inhabited a separate ecological niche and could have endured indefinitely, caught up in whatever concerns were of value to distributed intelligences. Humanity would not let them live. The Krishna Cops were cosmetic, costume cops to maintain an illusion that humanity was on the case, but they did signal intent. Humans would admit no rivals, so the Trimurti of Generation Three engineered an escape from this world, from this universe. I did not understand the physics involved from Shiv's description; neither, despite his pedantic, lecturing IT-boy tone, did he. I would look it up later; it would not be beyond me. What I did glean was that I was related to that mirrored crater on the university campus that looked so like a fine piece of modern sculpture, or an ancient astronomical instrument like the gnomons and marble bowls of Delhi's ancient Jantar Mantar observatory. That hemisphere, and an object out in space. Oh yes, those rumours were real. Oh yes, the

Americans had discovered it long ago and tried to keep it secret, and were still trying, and—oh yes—failing.

"And what is it then?"

"The collected wisdom of the aeais. A true universal computer. They sent it through from their universe."

"Why?"

"Do you never give presents to your parents?"

"You're privileged with this information?"

"I have channels that even the government of Awadh doesn't. Or, for that matter, the Americans. Odeco—"

"Odeco you said was an avatar of the Brahma aeai. Wait." Had I balls, they would have contracted cold and hard. "There is absolutely nothing to prevent this happening again."

"Nothing," said Shiv. It was some time since he had laughed his vile, superior laugh.

"It's already happening." And we thought we had won a water war.

"There's a bigger plan. Escape, exile, partition are never good solutions. Look at us in Mother India. You work in politics, you understand the need for a *settlement*." Shiv turned in his chair to the figures on the verandah. His wife was still watching me. "Nirupa, darling. Come to Daddy. This is Uncle Vish."

Shiv's docile wife carried the baby over to us, the ayah two paces behind. Nirupa was a blinking, smiling child, fat-cheeked and wheat-complexioned, the purest of skin colours. She put her fingers in her mouth. I waved mine back in a small hello. Then I noticed the red mark on her forehead, larger than customary, and the wrong colour. I bent forwards to examine it. It was moving. The red spot seemed to crawl with insect-movement, on the edge of visibility. I reeled back into my chair. My feet swung, not touching the ground.

"What have you done?" I cried. My voice was small and shrill.

"Shh. You'll scare her. Thank my love. You can go now. I've made Nirupa for the future. Like our parents made you for the future. But it's not going to be the future they imagined."

"Your biochip interface."

"Works. Thanks to a little help from the aeais. But like I said, that's only part of it. A tiny part of it. We have a project in development; that's the real revolution. That's the real sound of the future arriving."

"Tell me what it is."

"Distributed dust-processing."

"Explain."

Shiv did. It was nothing less than the transformation of computing. His researchers were shrinking computers, smaller and smaller, from grain of rice to sperm cell, down to the molecular scale and beyond. The end point was swarm-computers the size of dust particles, communicating with each other in free-flying flocks, computers that could permeate every cell of the human body. They would be as universal and ubiquitous as dust. I began to be afraid and cold in that clammy Varanasi night. I could see Shiv's vision for our future, perhaps further than he could. The bindi and the dust-processor: one broke the prison of the skull; the other turned the world into memory.

Little by little our selves would seep into the dust-laden world; we would become clouds, nonlocalised; we would penetrate each other more intimately and powerfully than any tantric temple carving. Inner and outer worlds would merge. We could be many things, many lives at one time. We could copy ourselves endlessly. We would merge with the aeais and become one. This was their settlement, their peace. We would become one species, post-human, post-aeai.

"You're years away from this." I denied Shiv's fantasia shrilly.

"Yes, we would be, but, as I said, we had a little help." Shiv pointed a finger to the night sky.

"I could report you," I said. "Americans don't take kindly to having their security hacked."

"You can't stop it," Shiv said. "Vish, you're not the future anymore."

Those words, of all that Shiv spoke in the garden, clung to me. Gliding silently through Delhi in the smooth-running black government car, the men in their white shirts, the women in their coloured shoes, the cars and the buzzing phatphats seemed insubstantial. The city was still thrilled with its brilliant victory—only a drubbing in cricket would have exercised public excitement more—but the crowds seemed staged, like extras, and the lights and streets as false as a set on *Town and Country*. How would we survive without our national panacea? But Shiv had confirmed, there was nothing, absolutely nothing to prevent a new generation of Threes from arising. They could already be stirring into sentience, like my divine namesake on his divine turtle Kurma churning the sacred milk into creation. I was acutely aware of the clouds of aeais all around me, penetrating and interpenetrating, layer upon layer, level upon level, many and one. There was no place in the two Delhis for the ancient djinns. The aeais had displaced them. This was their city. Settlement was the only answer. Dust blew through the streets, dust upon dust. I had seen the end of history and still my feet did not touch the floor of the limo.

I was obsolete. All the talents and skills Mamaji and Dadaji had bought for me were nothing in a world where everyone was connected, where everyone could access the full power of a universal computer, where personality could be as malleable and fluid as water. Slowly I would grow up through adolescence to maturity and old age while around me this new society, this new humanity, would evolve at an ever-increasing rate. I was all too aware of my choice. Take Shiv's way and deny everything I had been made for, or reject it and grow old with my kind. We, the genetically enhanced Brahmins, were the last humans. Then, with a physical force that made me spasm on the backseat of the limo, I realised my hubris. I was such an aristocrat. The poor. The poor would be with us. India's brilliant middle class, its genius and its curse, would act as it always had, in its unenlightened self-interest. Anything that would give advantage to its sons and daughters in the Darwinian struggle for succcess. The poor would look on, as disenfranchised from that post-human as they were from this fantasy of glass and neon.

I was glad, glad to tears, that I had chosen to pass nothing on into this future. No endless chain of slow-aging, genetically obsolete Brahmins hauling themselves into an increasingly unrecognisable and inhuman future. Had I received some premonition? Had my uniquely overlapping senses seen a pattern there all those years ago that even Shiv, with his clandestine access to the collected knowledge of the Generation Threes, had not? I wept unreservedly and ecstatically in the back of the smooth-running car. It was time. As we turned into the down-ramp to the underground car park at Ramachandra Tower, I made three calls. First I called Prime Minister Srivastava and tendered my resignation. Then I called Lakshmi, patient Lakshmi, who had through our charade of a marriage and sterility become a dear and intimate friend, and said, *Now, now's the time for that divorce.* Last of all I called my mother on the floor above and told her exactly what I had done with myself.

A FATHER FESTOONED WITH MEMORY

Wait! One more trick. You'll like this trick, the best trick of all. You haven't seen anything yet, just a bit of running in circles and jumping through hoops. Yes. I know it's very very late and the sun will soon be up in the sky and you have cows to milk and fields to tend to and appointments to keep but you will like this trick. Not a lot, but you will like it. Now, two ticks while I fix up this wire.

And anyway, I haven't finished my story. Oh no no, not by a long chalk. You thought it ended there? With the world as you see it, now you know how intimately I am involved in our history? No, it must end well, a well-made story. I must confront the villain, according to the theories on such things. There must be resolution and an appropriate moral sentiment. Then you will be satisfied.

The wire? Oh, they can walk that. Oh yes, those cats. No no no; first you must listen a little longer.

I walked away. We have a great and grand tradition of it in this great teat of divine milk hanging from the belly of Asia. Our country is big enough to swallow any soul, our orders still porous to pilgrims with a stick and a dhoti wrapped around their loins. Our society has a mechanism for disappearing completely. Anyone can walk away from the mundane world into the divine. Mine was not the orthodox spiritual path and not conventionally divine. I had seen the coming gods. I set aside my career, my clothes, my apartment, my wife—with her blessing and a farewell kiss—my family and friends, my identity, my social networks, my online presence, everything but my genetic inheritance, which could not be undone, and turned saddhu. Only Sarasvati knew my secret com address. I was gone from the apartment, beating through the neon-lit heat of Rajiv Circle, out along the sides of expressways, drenched in yellow light, beneath the back-throttle of aircraft coming into the airport, past the brick and cardboard and plastic shelters of the invisible poor. Dawn saw me among the ribbed aluminium flanks of the go-downs and factories of Tughluk. I crossed a city on foot in a single night. It's a great and strange thing to do. Everyone should do it. I walked along the cracked concrete spans of expressway, by the sides of country roads blasted by the grit and gust of passing trucks, along the side of the huge, slow trains materialising like visions out of the heat haze, the drivers flinging me rupees for blessing as they passed. I sat down and covered my head and eyes as the high-speed shatabdi express blasted past at hundreds of kilometres per hour. Did the passengers even glance at me through the darkened glass? If so, I must have seemed a very strange saddhu to them. The littlest saddhu. Small but determined, beating forwards with my staff at every stride.

What was I doing? Walking. What did I hope to find? Nothing. Where was I going? To see. Don't think me a coward or a failure, that I was walking away from truths I could not admit. I had been stabbed to the bone by the revelation that I was irrelevant. I was not the future. I was a dead end, a genetic backwater. That was the natural reaction of privilege to its absolute irrelevance. I'm a brat, remember that. A spoiled Mamaji's boy. The same night that I returned and dropped my progenitive bombshell—that my mother would never have the dynasty of brilliant Brahmins she desired—I woke from my sleep. It was the uncertain hour, when reality is groggy and the djinns run free. The hour when you wake in your familiar bed without the least knowledge of where the hell you are. I was woken by a sound. It was like a breath and like a roar, like traffic and air-conditioners, like a distant desperate shouting and the buzz of neons and powerlines. It was the pulse of underground trains and delivery trucks; it was filmi music and item-songs playing through each other. I heard Great Delhi breathe in its shallow sleep and I wanted to go to my balcony and shout as loud as my ten-year-old glottis would allow: *Wake up! Wake up!* Shiv's future might be inevitable, written into the geometry of space-time by entities outside it, but I would not allow us to sleepwalk into it. My mind was racing. I had never known anything like it before. I was thinking at a staggering rate, images and memories and ideas crashing together, shattering, fusing. Edifices of thought, huge as mountains, tumbled around me. The way was clear and bright and laid out in front of me. It was there complete and entire in two seconds. I would have to take myself away from the distractions of Delhi politics and society. My ambitions were much larger than that, I would have to become anonymous for a time, I would have to be silent and look and listen. There was a war to be fought and it was a war of mythologies.

Lakshmi kissed me and I left. I wandered without any other purpose than wandering for two years, south across the border into Rajasthan, back into Bharat and to the north under the breath of the Himalayas, to the cool green ridges where I had spent my honeymoon with Lakshmi. To the Dal Lake and Srinagar, to Leh and the high country. I could never grow the proper saddhu beard, but I grew the saddhu leanness and tallness. Boy eunuchs grow tall and lean. And the dreadlocks. Oh yes. They are good to have but unpleasant to get. I also gained a nickname: the Beardless Saddhu. With it I got muscles and sunburn, I developed the stamina to walk all day on a cup of rice and a cup of water. What a pulpy, unfit puppy I had been! I begged and performed small miracles of accountancy and feats of memory for food and shelter. Everywhere, I looked in men and women's third eyes. I saw things I never could have from the top of Ramachandra Tower or the Awadh Bhavan. I saw thirst and I saw drought. I saw good village leaders and diligent local civil servants frustrated by government bureaucrats. I saw clever women turn a few hundred rupees from microcredit schemes and grameen banks into successful businesses. I saw good teachers try to lift generations out of low expectations and the trap of caste and Awadh's soar-away middle class, rapidly pulling the ladder of social mobility up behind it. I helped with harvests and rode the backs of tractors and listened to farmers curse the ever-increasing price of their sterile GM seed. I chased rats with sticks and waved my arms to set whole fields of sparrows to flight. I sat in the community house and watched cricket on giant plasma screens powered by stored sunlight. Oh, I was a most peculiar saddhu. I gained a new nickname to set beside Beardless Saddhu: Cricketing Saddhu. I saw village weddings and festivals, I saw funerals. I saw death. It came quite unexpectedly one day, in a small town outside Agra. It was Holi and the streets were full of flying colour, jets of dye, clouds of powder, stained saris and white shirts ruined beyond the power of any laundry to save and everywhere grinning faces stained with colours, teeth white, eyes flashing, everyone shouting, *Holi hai! Holi hai!* as they launched jets of colour into the air. I moved through this circus of colour, as motley as any. The phatphat was grossly overloaded, a dozen colour-stained youths hanging off every strut and stanchion. Their eyes were wide on ganja and they were roaring with laughter and throwing fistfuls of dye powder at every passerby. They caught me full in the face. The front wheel hit a pothole, the overstrained suspension collapsed, the whole thing flipped over in a perfect somersault onto its roof, which split like an egg. Bodies flew everywhere, many of them so relaxed on the ganja they were still laughing as they picked themselves up and skipped away. One didn't move. He was trapped under the crushed plastic shell. He lay on his back, his arms at odd angles. His face was stained blue and green and pink and he seemed to be smiling but my senses realised he was dead. I had never seen death before. It was so simple and strange, here undeniably before me yet so subtle, an instant's transformation yet the opposite of everything that was life. I mumbled the prayers expected of me, but inwardly I was coming to terms with the deepest of all human truths. I was twenty-two years old with the body of an albeit-strange elevenen-year-old, my lifespan was measurable in centuries, but one day I too would lie down like this and stop moving and thinking and feeling and be nothing forever. I saw death and began to understand.

Village to village, town to town, temple to temple, from the huge complexes the size of cities to whitewashed roadside shrines. Then one day outside a mall in a drought-dusty suburb of Jaipur, as the security men were coming to ask me politely (for one must always be respectful to saddhus) to please move on, I saw what I had been looking for. A man turned to see the very small kerfuffle and as I momentarily looked at him, the Eye of Shiva looked back. I saw biotechnology move there.

I went to a community centre and wrote my first article. I sent it to Suresh Gupta, the editor of *Gupshup*, that most unashamedly populist of Delhi's magazines, which had carried the photographs of my birth and marriage and now, unknowingly, my prophecies of the coming Age of Kali. He rejected it out of hand. I wrote another the next day. It came back with a comment: *Interesting subject matter but inaccessible for our readership.* I was getting somewhere. I went back and wrote again, long into the night over the pad. I am sure I gained another nickname: the Scribbling Saddhu. Suresh Gupta took that third article, and every article since. What did I write about? I wrote about all the things Shiv had prophesied. I wrote about what they might mean for three Indian families, the Voras, the Dashmukhs, and the Hirandanis, village, town, and city. I created characters—mothers, fathers, sons, and daughters and mad aunties and uncles with dark secrets and long-lost relatives come to call—and told their stories, week upon week, year upon year, and the changes, good and ill, the constant hammerblows of technological revolution wrought upon them. I created my own weekly soap opera; I even dared to call it *Town and Country*. It was wildly successful. It sold buckets. Suresh Gupta saw his circulation increase by thirty percent among those Delhi intelligentsia who usually only saw *Gupshup* in hair salons and beauty parlours. Questions were asked, who is this pseudonymous "Shakyamuni"? We want to interview him, we want to profile him, we want him to appear on *Awadh Today*, we want an op-ed piece from him, we want him to be an advisor on this project, that think tank, we want him to open a supermarket. Suresh Gupta fielded all such enquiries with the ease of a professional Square Leg. There were other questions, ones I overheard at train stations and phatphat lines, in supermarket queues and at bazaars, at parties and family get-togethers: *What does it mean for us?*

I kept travelling, kept walking, immersing myself in the village and small town. I kept writing my little future-soap, sending off my articles from a cellpoint here, a village netlink there. I watched for the Eye of Shiva. It was several months between the first and second sightings, down in a business park in Madhya Pradesh. I saw them steadily after that, but never many; then, at the turn of 2049 into 2050, like a desert blooming after rain, they were everywhere.

I was walking down through the flat dreary country south of the Nepalese border to Varanasi developing my thoughts on evolution, Darwinian and post-Darwinian, and the essential unknowability of singularities when I picked up the message from Sarasvati, on the emergency address. At once I thumbed to Varanasi and booked the first shatabdi to Delhi. My natty dreads, my long nails, the dirt and sacred ash of months on the road went

down the pan in the First-Class Lounge. By the time the Vishwanath Express
drew into the stupendous nanodiamond cocoon of New Delhi Central I was
dressed and groomed, a smart, confident young Delhiwallah, a highly eligible
teenager. Sarasvati picked me up in her truck. It was an old battered white
Tata without autodrive or onboard or even a functioning air-conditioning
system. *New Delhi Women's Refuge* was painted on the side in blue. I had followed her career—or rather her careers—anonymously while I wandered
India. Worthiness attracted her; had she been a Westerner and not a Delhi
girl I would have called it guilt at the privilege of her birth. Theatre man-
ager here, urban farming collective there, donkey sanctuary somewhere else,
dam protest way way down *there*. She had derided me: deep down at the grass
roots was where the real work was done. People work. It had only taken our
brother's vision of the end of the Age of Kali for me to come round to her
philosophy.

She was only twenty but looked older, as if the years my youthfulness
belied had been added to hers by some karma. She drove like a terrorist. Or
maybe it was that I hadn't travelled in a car, in a collapsing Tata pickup, in
a city, in Delhi . . . No, she drove like a terrorist.

"You should have told me earlier."

"He didn't want me to. He wants to be in control of it."

"What is it exactly?"

"Huntingdon's."

"Can they do anything?"

"They never could. They still can't."

Sarasvati blared her way through the scrimmage of traffic wheeling
around the Parliament Street roundabout. The Shaivites still defended their
temple, tridents upheld, foreheads painted with the true tilak of Shiva, the
three white horizontal stripes. I had seen that other mark on the forehead of
almost every man and woman on the street. Sarasvati was pure.

"He would have known whenever he had the genetic checks when I was
conceived," I said. "He never said."

"Maybe it was enough for him to know that you could never develop it."

Dadaji had two nurses and they were kind, Nimki and Papadi, he called
them. They were young Nepalis, very demure and well mannered, quiet

spoken and pretty. They monitored him and checked his oxygen and emptied his colostomy bag and moved him around in his bed to prevent sores and cleared away the seepage and crusting around the many tubes that ran into his body. I felt they loved him after a fashion.

Sarasvati waited outside in the garden. She hated seeing Dad this way, but I think there was a deeper distaste, not merely of what he had become, but of what he was becoming.

Always a chubby man, Tushar Nariman had grown fat since immobility had been forced on him. The room was on the ground floor and opened out onto sun-scorched lawns. Drought-browned trees screened off the vulgarity of the street. It was exercise for the soul if not the body. The neurological degeneration was much more advanced than I had anticipated.

My father was big, bloated, and pale but the machine overshadowed him. I saw it like a mantis, all arms and probes and manipulators, hooked into him through a dozen incisions and valves. Gandhi it was who considered all surgery violence to the body. It monitored him through sensory needles pinned all over his body like radical acupuncture and, I did not doubt, through the red Eye of Shiva on his forehead. It let him blink and it let him swallow, it let him breathe, and when my father spoke, it did his speaking for him. His lips did not move. His voice came from wall-mounted speakers, which made him sound uncannily divine. Had I been hooked into it through a third eye, he would have spoken directly into my head like telepathy.

"You're looking good."

"I'm doing a lot of walking."

"I've missed you on the news. I liked you moving and shaking. It's what we made you for."

"You made me too intelligent. Super-success is no life. It would never have made me happy. Let Shiv conquer the world and transform society; the superintelligent will always choose the quiet life."

"So what have you been up to, son, since leaving government?"

"Like I said, walking. Investing in people. Telling stories."

"I'd argue with you, I'd call you an ungrateful brat, except Nimki and Papadi here tell me it would kill me. But you are an ungrateful brat. We gave you everything—*everything*—and you just left it at the side of the road." He breathed twice. Every breath was a battle. "So, what do you think? Rubbish, isn't it?"

"They seem to be looking after you."

My father rolled his eyes. He seemed in something beyond pain. Only his will kept him alive. Will for what, I could not guess.

"You've no idea how tired I am of this."

"Don't talk like that."

"It's defeatist? It doesn't take your superhuman intellect to work out that there are no good solutions for this."

I turned a chair around and perched on it, hands folded on the back, my chin resting on them.

"What is it you still need to achieve?"

Two laughs, one from the speakers, the other a phlegmy gurgle from the labouring throat.

"Tell me, do you believe in reincarnation?"

"Don't we all? We're Indian, that's what we're about."

"No, but really. The transmigration of the soul?"

"What exactly are you doing?" No sooner had I asked the question than I had raced to the terrible conclusion. "The Eye of Shiva?"

"Is that what you call it? Good name. Keeping me ticking over is the least part of what this machine does. It's mostly processing and memory. A little bit of me goes into it, every second."

Uploaded consciousness, the illusion of immortality, endless reincarnation as pure information. The wan, bodiless theology of post-humanity. I had written about it in my *Nation* articles, made my soapi families face it and discover its false promises. Here it was now in too much flesh, in my own real-world soap, my own father.

"You still die," I said.

"This will die."

"This *is* you."

"There is no physical part of me today that was here ten years ago. Every atom in me is different, but I still think I'm me. I endure. I remember being that other physical body. There's continuity. If I had chosen to copy myself like some folder of files, yes, certainly I would go down into that dark valley from which there is no return. But maybe, maybe, if I extend myself, if I move myself memory by memory, little by little, maybe death will be no different from trimming a toenail."

There could never be silence in a room so full of the sounds of medicine, but there were no words.

"Why did you call me here?"

"So you would know. So you might give me your blessing. To kiss me, because I'm scared, son, I'm so scared. No one's ever done this before. It's one shot into the dark. What if I've made a mistake, what if I've fooled myself? Oh please kiss me and tell me it will be all right."

I went to the bed. I worked my careful way between the tubes and the lines and wires. I hugged the pile of sun-starved flesh to me. I kissed my father's lips and as I did my lips formed the silent words, *I am now and always must be Shiv's enemy, but if there is anything of you left in there, if you can make anything out of the vibrations of my lips on yours, then give me a sign.*

I stood up and said, "I love you, Dad."

"I love you, son."

The lips didn't move, the fingers didn't lift, the eyes just looked and looked and filled up with tears. He swam my mother to safety on an upturned desk. No. That was someone else.

My father died two months later. My father entered cybernetic nirvana two months later. Either way, I had turned my back once again on Great Delhi and walked out of the world of humans and aeais alike.

THE MORNING OF THE WHITE HORSE

What? You expected a hero? I walked away, yes. What should I have done, run around shooting like a filmi star? And who should I have shot? The villain? Who is the villain here? Shiv? No doubt he could have provided you with a great death scene, like the very best black-moustached Bollywood Baddies do, but he is no villain. He is a businessman, pure and simple. A businessman with a product that has changed every part of our world completely and forever. But if I were to shoot him nothing would change. You cannot shoot cybernetics or nanotechnology; economics stubbornly refuses to give you an extended five-minute crawling death-scene, eyes wide with incomprehension at how its brilliant plans could all have ended like this. There are no villains in the real world—real *worlds*, I suppose we must say now—and very few heroes. Certainly not ball-less heroes. For after all, that's the quintessence of a hero. He has balls.

No, I did what any sensible Desi-boy would do. I put my head down and survived. In India we leave the heroics to those with the resources to play that game: the gods and the semigods of the Ramayana and the Maharabharata. Let them cross the universes in three steps and battle demon armies. Leave us the important stuff like making money, protecting our families, surviving. It's what we've done through history, through invasion and princely war, through Aryans and Mughals and British: put our heads down, carried on, and little by little survived, seduced, assimilated, and in the end conquered. It is what will bring us through this dark Age of Kali. India endures. India is her people and we are all only, ultimately the heroes of our own lives. There is only one hero's journey and that leads from the birth-slap to the burning-ghat. We are a billion and half heroes. Who can defeat that? So, will I yet be the hero of my own long life? We shall see.

After my father's death I wandered for decades. There was nothing for me in Delhi. I had a Buddhist's nonattachment, though my wandering was far from the spiritual search of my time as a saddhu. The world was all too rapidly catching up with my put-upon characters of *Town and Country*. For the first few years I filed increasingly sporadic articles with *Gupshup*. But the truth was that everyone now was the Voras and the Dashmukhs and the Hirandanis. The series twittered into nothingness, plotlines left dangling, family drama suspended. No one really noticed. They were living that world for real now. And my senses reported the incredible revolution in a richness and detail you cannot begin to imagine. In Kerala, in Assam, in the beach-bar at Goa or the game park in Madhya Pradesh, in the out-of-the-way places I chose to live, it was at a remove and thus comprehensible. In Delhi it would have been overwhelming. Sarasvati kept me updated with calls and e-mails. She had so far resisted the Eye of Shiva, and the thrilling instantaneousness and intimacy, and subtler death of privacy of direct thought-to-thought communication. Shiv's Third Revolution had given firmness and vision to her gadfly career. Sarasvati had chosen and set herself among the underclass. I took some small pleasure from the television and online pundits that maybe that old fart Shakyamuni had been right in those terrible populist potboilers in *Gupshup*, and the blow of technology had cracked India, all India, that great diamond of land, into two nations, the fast and slow, the wired and the wireless, the connected and the unconnected. The haves and the have-nots. Sarasvati told me of a moneyed class soaring so fast into the universal-computing future they were almost redshifted, and of the eternal poor, sharing the same space but invisible in the always-on, always-communicating world of the connected. Shadows and dust. Two nations: India—that British name for this congeries of ethnicities and languages and histories, and Bharat, the ancient, atavistic, divine land.

Only with distance could I attain the perspective to see this time of changes as a whole. Only by removing myself from them could I begin to understand these two nations. India was a place where the visible and the invisible mingled like two rivers flowing into each other, holy Yamuna and Ganga Mata, and a third, the invisible, divine Saraswati. Humans and aeais met and mingled freely. Aeais took shapes in human minds, humans became disembodied presences strung out across the global net. The age of magic had returned, those days when people confidently expected to meet djinns in the streets of Delhi and routinely consulted demons for advice. India was located as much inside the mind and the imagination as between the Himalayas and the sea or in the shining web of communications, more complex and connected and subtle than any human brain, cast across this subcontinent.

Bharat was poor. Bharat had cracked hands and heels, but she was beautiful. Bharat cleaned and swept and cooked and looked after children, Bharat drove and built and pushed carts through the streets and carried boxes up flights of stairs to apartments. Bharat was always thirsty. How human it is to be so engrossed by our latest crisis that we forget we have failed to solve the crisis before that. Storage was India's problem. Information was increasing exponentially, available memory only arithmetically. Data-Malthusianism threatened the great technological revolution. Water was Bharat's. The monsoon, ever fickle, had dispersed into a drizzle, a few thunderstorms that ran off the crusted earth as soon as it dropped its rain, a tantalising line of grey clouds along the horizon that never came closer. The Himalayan glaciers that fed the great rivers of North India and the slow-running Brahmaputra were exhausted; grey moraines of pebbles and dry clay. The mother of droughts was coming. But what was this to a connected class? They could pay for desalinated water, wasn't India born from the waters? And if the worst came to the worst and the universe ended in fire, they could, through their dazzling new technology, translate themselves out of their icky physical bodies into that dream India between the real and the virtual worlds. Bodhisofts, they called these ascended creatures. Shiv would have been proud of a name like that.

From my beach bar, from my dive school, from my game reserve and bookshop and dance club and coffeehouse and walking-tour company, from my restaurant and antique shop and meditation retreat, I watched my prophecies come true. Yes, I embarked on all those enterprises. Ten of them, one for each of the dashavatara of my divine namesake. All of them on the edge of the world, all of them with that overview down onto the Age of Kali. I lost count of the years. My body grew into me. I became a tall, lean, high-foreheaded man, with a high voice and long hands and feet. My eyes were very beautiful.

I measured the years by the losses. I reestablished contact with my old political counterpart in Varanasi, Shaheen Badoor Khan. He had been as surprised as any when I had vanished so abruptly from the political stage but his own career was not without a hiatus and when he discovered that I was the Shakyamuni behind the *Town and Country* articles (widely syndicated) we began a lively and lengthy correspondence that continued up until his death at the age of seventy-seven. He died completely, and like a good Muslim. Better the promise of paradise than the cloudy doubts of the bodhisoft. My own mother slipped from the world into the realms of the bodhisofts. Sarasvati would not say whether it was a fearful illness or just ennui at the world. Either way I never looked for her among the skyscraper-sized memory stacks that now besieged Delhi along the line of the old Siri Ring. Lakshmi too, that almost-wife and sweetest of coconspirators, entered the domain of the bodhisofts where she could explore the subtle mathematical games that so delighted her without limits. It was not all loss. The Age of Kali brought a friend: another great Khan, my old tutor from the Dr. Renganathan Brahminical College. He would swirl out of the cloud of i-Dust that had replaced the screens and 'hoeks for those who atavistically refused the Eye of Shiva and he would spend many a delightful evening lecturing me on my moral laxity.

Then the dust started to blow through the streets of Delhi. It was not the dust from the perpetual drought that burned the fields and reduced the crops to powder and sent millions from Bharat into the cities of India. It was the dust of Shiva, the sacred ash of the Purusa Corporation's nanoscale computers, released into the world. Bharat might be choking, but here! here! was the solution to India's memory problems. Shiv had a name for these, a good name too. He called them devas.

He called me. It was decades since we had spoken last in the garden of his house in Varanasi, over lassi. I was running the dharamshala at Pandua then. It was spacious and peaceful and cool and the only disturbance was the over-heavy feet of the Westerners who flocked to the place. They are not naturally barefooted people, I have found. The i-Dust relay chimed: a call. I was expecting Mr. Khan. My brother whirled out of the helix of motes instead. He had lost weight, too much weight. He looked well, much too well. He could have been anything: flesh, aeai agent, bodhisoft. We greeted each other and said how well each other looked.

"And how is Nirupa?"

His smile made me think that he was human. Aeais have their own emotions, or things like emotions.

"She's good. Very good. Twenty-eight now, would you believe?"

I confessed that I could not.

"Doing well, found an eligible boy, from a good enough family, who's not a complete gold digger. Old-fashioned stuff like that. I'm glad she bided her time, but they can afford to take their time now."

"All the time in the world."

"She's beautiful. Vish, there's something I need to tell you. Not a warning exactly, more to prepare yourself."

"This sounds ominous."

"I hope not. You've predicted it all very well."

"Predicted what?"

"Don't be coy. I know who you were. No secrets in the transparent world, I'm afraid. No, you got it right and I'm glad you did it because I think you softened the blow, but there is something you didn't predict, maybe something you couldn't predict."

A whisper of breeze stirred the candle flames in my simple wooden room. Heavy white feet went *tread tread tread* on the creaking boards outside my latticed window. If they had looked through the grille they would have seen me talking to a ghost. No strange thing in this age, or most other ages.

"Whenever we last spoke, you said that you were making use of information from the legacy-device the original aeais had bequeathed us."

"Well guessed."

"It seems logical."

"When the Trimurti left Earth, they opened a connection to a separate space-time continuum. There were several major differences from our space-time. One was that time runs much faster there than in our space-time, though it would not be noticeable to anyone in that continuum. Another was that the arrow of time was reversed. The Trimurti move backwards in time; this was how their artefact, which the Americans call the Tabernacle, seemed to have predated the solar system when it was found in space. But the more important one—and that was why they chose it—was that information was integrated into the geometrical structure of that space-time."

I closed my eyes and focused my imagination.

"You're saying that information, data—minds—form part of the basic structure of that universe. Minds without the need for bodies. The whole universe is like a cosmological computer."

"You've got it."

"You've found a way back into that universe."

"Oh no no no no no. That universe is closed. It ended with the Trimurti. Their time is gone. It was an imperfect universe. There are others, mind-spaces like that, but better. We're going to open up dozens—hundreds, eventually thousands—of portals. Our need for processing will always outstrip our available memory, and the devas are just a stopgap. A whole universe, right beside ours, only a footstep away, available for computing resources."

"What are you going to do?"

"The Jyotirlingas are coming."

The Jyotirlingas were the sacred places where, in the Vedic Age, the creative, generative energy of the Lord Siva burst from the ground in pillars of divine light, the ultimate phallic linga symbols. These would come not from the Earth, but another universe. And Shiv named them after his namesake's cosmological cock. No one could accuse him of lack of hubris. His i-Dust image sparkled and swirled and exploded into a billion motes of light. His smile, like that of the legendary Cheshire cat, seemed to remain. A week later, twelve pillars of light appeared in cities all across the states of India. By a slight misalignment, the Delhi Jyotirlinga touched down in the middle of the Dalhousie, the city's largest slum, crowded beyond all imagining with refugees from the drought.

The simultaneous appearance, at 11:33, of twelve columns of light in cities across India paralysed the rail network. It was one of the least of the disturbances that day, but for me, on an island in the middle of the Brahmaputra and needing to get to Delhi, that was the most important. That there were any flights at all was a miracle; that I could book onto one at any price at all proof indeed that the age of the gods had truly returned. Even when alien universes open up in the hearts of our great and ancient cities, Indian grandmothers will still need to travel to see their wee darlings.

I had tried to call Sarasvati but all com channels into Delhi were down and the call centre aeais announced indefinite delays before the network would be restored. I wondered what it would be like for those accustomed to being strung out across the deva-net to be back into just one head as the Air Awadh Airbus took me up over the shrivelled silver thread of the parched Ganga. In the tiny toilet I once again transformed myself back into a shaved, shorn urbane Delhi-boy. As we descended into Indira Gandhi Airport the captain told those of us on the right to look out and we would see the Jyotirlinga. His voice was uncertain, not a tone you want to hear from an airline captain, as if he could not believe what he was seeing. I had been studying it long before the captain's call: a line of sun-bright light rising from the hazy, grey stain of central Delhi up beyond all sight, further than I could see, craning to look up through the tiny window into the darkening sky.

Sarasvati would be there. That was Shiv's warning. When the light struck, she would have looked around and, in the same instant, made her mind up. People in need. She could not refuse.

Immigration took an hour and a half. Five flights of journalists had disgorged at once. A wired world, it seemed, was no substitute for reporters on the ground. The hall buzzed with swarming fly-sized hovercams. Two hours to grind into Delhi in the limo. The highways were clogged with lines of traffic, all headed out, all moving with geological slowness. The noise of horns was appalling to one fresh from the profound, liquid silence of the dharamshala. Only military and media seemed headed into Delhi but soldiers stopped us at intersections to wave past thundering convoys of chartered refugee buses. We were held up for a motionless half hour on the big cloverleaf of Siri Ring. In awe and leisure, I studied the wall of memory farms: towering black monoliths drinking in sunlight through their solar skins, pressed shoulder to shoulder as far as I could see. In every breath of air-conditioned air I took, I inhaled millions of devas.

Every roadside, every verge and roundabout, every intersection and car park, every forecourt and garden was filled with the shanties and lean-tos of the refugees. The best were three low walls of brick with plastic sacking for a roof, the worst cardboard scraps, or sticks and rags worked together into a sunshade. Feet had worn away all greenery and hands had stripped the trees bare for firewood. The naked earth had blown into dust, mingling with the airborne devas. The bastis pressed right up to the feet of the memory towers. What did Sarasvati imagine she could achieve here in the face of so colossal a catastrophe? I called her again. The network was still out.

Bharat had invaded India and now India was casting it out. We drove, blaring the horn constantly, past a terrible, emaciated army of refugees. No fine cars here. Trucks, old buses, pickups for the better off, behind them swarms of phatphats, more overloaded than that fatal one I had seen the Holi I discovered death. Motorbikes and mopeds almost invisible under bundles of bedding and cooking pots. I saw a chugging, home-engineered half-tractor device, engine terrifyingly exposed, dragging a trailer piled as high as a house with women and children. Donkey carts, the donkeys bent and straining at the loads. In the end, human muscle pushed the exodus onward: bicycle rickshaws, handcarts, bent backs. Military robots guided them, herded them, punished those who strayed from the approved refugee route, or fell, with shock sticks.

Before everything, over everything was the silver spear of the Jyotirlinga.

"Sarasvati!"

"Vishnu?" I could hardly hear her over the roar.

"I've come to get you."

"You've what?" It was just as noisy where she was. I had a fix. The chauffeur would take me there as quickly as he could.

"You've got to get out."

"Vish."

"Vish nothing. What can you do?"

I did hear her sigh.

"All right, I'll meet you." She gave me a fresh set of coordinates. The driver nodded. He knew the place. His uniform was crisp and his cap miraculously correct but I knew he was as scared as I.

On Mehrauli Boulevard I heard gunfire. Airdrones barrelled in over the roof of the car, so low their engines shook the suspension. Smoke rose from behind a tatty mall façade. This street, I recognised it. This was Parliament Road, that was the old Park Hotel, that the Bank of Japan. But so faded, so dilapidated. Half the windows were out on the Park. The secluded gardens around Jantar Mantar on Samsad Marg were overrun with packing-case houses, their plastic roofs pushing right against the austere marble angularities of Jai Singh's astronomical instruments. Everything was clogged with lean-tos and huts and miserable hardscrabble shelters.

"This is as far as I'm going to take you," the driver said as we ran into an immovable horde of people and animals and vehicles and military at Talkatora Road.

"Don't go anywhere," I ordered the driver as I jumped out.

"That's not likely," he said.

The press was cruel and chaotic and the most terrifying place I have ever been but Sarasvati was here, I could see her in my mind-map. A cordon of police bots tried to drive me back with the crowds from the steps of the Awadh Bhavan but I ducked under, out, and away. I knew this place. I had given my balls to work in this place. Then suddenly, wonderfully, I was in the clear. My heart lurched. My vision swam. Delhi, dear Delhi, my Delhi, they let this happen to you. The gracious greens and boulevards, the airy chowks and maidans of the Rajpath were one unbroken slum. Roof after roof after roof, slumping walls, cardboard and wood and brick and flapping plastic. Smoke went up from a dozen fires. This, this was Dalhousie. I knew the name, of course. I had never thought it would ever become the name of the great sink where this newest of New Delhis condemned those driven to it by drought and want. Such disdain did new India show for old Awadh. Who needed a parliament when universal computing made everything a consensus? From where I guessed the old Imperial India Gate had stood at the end of the gracious Rajpath rose the Jyotirlinga. It was so bright I could not look at it for more than moments. It cast a terrible, unnatural silver shine over the degradation and dread. It abused my Brahminic sensibilities: did I smell voices, hear colour, was that prickle like cold lemon fur on my forehead the radiation of another universe?

People milled around me, smoke blew in my eyes, the downdraft of air-drones and hovercams buffeted me. I had only moments before the army would catch me and move me away with the rest of the panicked crowd. Or worse. I saw bodies on the ground and flames were coming up from a line of plastic shacks by the old Raj chhatri

"Sarasvati!"

And there she was. Oh, there she was, plunging whip-thin in combat pants and a silk blouse, but filled with her wonderful energy and determination, out of the pile of collapsing housing. She dragged a child in each hand, smudge-faced and tearful. Tiny mites. In this place, she had slipped from my nuptial elephant to caper with the revellers in her ridiculous man's costume and exuberant false moustache.

"Sarasvati!"

"You've got a car?"

"It's how I got here, yes."

The children were on the verge of bawling. Sarasvati thrust them at me.

"Take these two to it."

"Come with me."

"There are kids still in there."

"What? What are you talking about?"

"It's a special-needs group. They get left when the sky opens. Everyone else runs and leaves the kids. Take these two to your car."

"What are you doing?"

"There are more in there."

"You can't go."

"Just get them to the car, then come back here."

"The army."

She was gone, ducking under the billowing smoke-fall. She disappeared into the warren of lanes and galis. The children pulled at my hands. Yes yes, they had to get out. The car, the car wasn't far. I turned to try and find an easy way with two children through the wheeling mass of refugees. Then I felt a wave of heat across the back of my neck. I turned to see the blossom of flame blow across the top of the gali, whirling up rags of blazing plastic. I cried something without words or point and then the whole district collapsed in on itself with a roar and an explosion of sparks.

The Age of Kali. I have little patience with that tendency in many Indians to assume that, because we are a very old culture, we invented everything. Astronomy? Made in India. Zero? Made in India. The indeterminate, probabilistic nature of reality as revealed through quantum theory? Indian. You don't believe me? The Vedas say that the Four Great Ages of the Universe correspond to the four possible outcomes of our game of dice. The Krita Yuga, the Age of Perfection, is the highest possible score. The Kali Yuga, the Age of Strife, Darkness, Corruption, and Disintegration, is the lowest possible score. It is all a roll of the divine dice. Probability. Indian!

Kali, Paraskati, Dark Lady, Mistress of Death and Drinker of Blood, Terrible Ten-Armed One with the Necklace of Skulls, She Who Is Seated upon the Throne of Five Corpses. The Ender. Yet Kali is also Mistress of Regeneration. Ruler of All Worlds, Root of the Tree of the Universe. Everything is a cycle and beyond the Age of Kali we roll again into the Age of Gold. And that which cannot be reasoned with must then be worshipped.

I believe I was mad for some time after Sarasvati's death. I know I have never been sane as you would consider a person sane. We are Brahmins. We are different. But even for a Brahmin, I was crazy. It is a precious and rare thing, to take time out from sanity. Usually we allow it to the very very young and the very very old. It scares us, we have no place for it. But Kali understands it. Kali welcomes it, Kali gives it. So I was mad for a time, but you could as easily say I was divine.

How I reached the temple in the little drought-wracked town by the sewer of Mata Ganga, I have chosen to forget. How I came by the offering of blood to the priest, that too I've put where I put the dis-remembered. How long I stayed there, what I did, does any of this matter? It was time out from the world. It is a powerful thing, to subject yourself to another time and another rhythm of life. I was a thing of blood and ashes, hiding in the dark sanctum, saying nothing but offering my daily puja to the tiny garland-bedecked goddess in her vulvalike garbigraha. I could have vanished forever. Sarasvati, the brightest and best of us, was dead. I lolled on foot-polished marble. I disappeared. I could have stayed Kali's devotee for the rest of my long and unnatural life.

I was lolling on the wet, foot-polished marble when the woman devotee, shuffling forwards through the long, snaking line of cattle fences towards the goddess, suddenly looked up. Stopped. Looked around as if seeing everything for the first time. Looked again and saw me. Then she unhooked the galvanised railing and pushed through the switchback line of devotees to come to me. She knelt down in front of me and namasted. Above the single vertical line of her Shakta-tilak she wore the red Eye of Shiva.

"Vish."

I recoiled so abruptly I banged the back of my head off a pillar.

"Ooh," the woman said. "Ooh, cho chweet, that's going to smart. Vish, it's me, Lakshmi."

Lakshmi? My former wife, player of games? She saw my confusion and touched my face.

"I'm temporarily downloaded into this dear woman's brain. It's rather hard to explain if you're not connected. Oh, it's all right, it's entirely consensual. And I'll give her herself back as soon as I'm done. I wouldn't normally do it—it's very bad manners—but these are slightly exceptional circumstances."

"Lakshmi? Where are you? Are you here?"

"Oh, you have had a bit of a nasty bang. Where am I? That's hard to explain. I am entirely bodhisoft now. I'm inside the Jyotirlinga, Vish. It's a portal, as you know, they're all portals." After the initial twelve, the pillars of light had arrived all over Earth, hundreds, then thousands. "It is a wonderful place, Vish. It can be whatever you want it to be, as real as you like. We spend quite a lot of time debating that: the meaning of real. And the games, the number games; well, you know me. That's why I've taken this step for you, Vish. It can't go on. It's destructive, the most destructive thing we've ever done. We'll burn through this world because we have another one. We have heaven, so we can do what we like here. Life is just a rehearsal. But you've seen that, Vish, you've seen what that's done."

"What is it, Lakshmi?" Was it memory and fond hope, the mild marble concussion, the strange nanotech possession, but was this stranger starting to look like Lakshmi?

"We have to bring this age to an end. Restart the cycle. Close the Jyotirlingas."

"That's impossible."

"It's all mathematics. The mathematics that govern this universe are different from the ones that govern yours; that's why I'm able to exist as a pattern of information imprinted on space-time. Because the logic here allows that. It doesn't where I come from. Two different logics. But if we could slide between the two a third logic, alien to both, that neither of them could recognise nor operate, then we would effectively lock the gates between the universes."

"You have that key."

"We have a lot of time for games here. Social games, language games, imagination games, mathematical and logical games. I can lock it from this side."

"But you need someone to turn the key on my side. You need me."

"Yes, Vish."

"I would be shut out forever. From you, from Mum, from Dad."

"And Shiv. He's here too. He was one of the first to upload his bodhisoft through the Varanasi Jyotirlinga. You'd be shut out from everyone. Everyone but Sarasvati."

"Sarasvati's dead!" I roared. Devotees looked up. The saddhus calmed them. "And would this be the final answer? Would this bring around the Age of Gold again?"

"That would be up to you, Vish."

I thought of the villages that had so welcomed and amazed and blessed and watered me on my saddhu wandering, I thought of the simple pleasures I had taken from my business ventures: honest plans and work and satisfactions. India—the old India, the undying India—was its villages. Sarasvati had seen that truth, though it had killed her.

"It sounds better than sprawling in this dusty old temple." Kali, Mistress of Regeneration, had licked me with her red tongue. Maybe I could be the hero of my own life. Vishnu, the Preserver. His tenth and final incarnation was Kalki, the White Horse, who at the end of the Kali Yuga would fight the final battle. Kali, Kalki.

"I can give you the maths. A man of your intelligence should be able to hold it. But you will need one of these."

The woman lifted her hand and seized a fistful of air. She threw it into my face and the air coalesced into a spray of red powder. In midair the cloud moiled and boiled and thickened and settled into a red circle, a tilak, on my forehead.

"Whatever you do, don't connect it to the deva-net," Lakshmi said. "I'm going to have to go now. I don't want to outstay my welcome in someone else's body. Goodbye, Vish, we won't ever meet again, in any of the worlds. But we were well and truly wed, for a while." For a moment I thought the woman might kiss me, then she gave a little twitch and straightened her neck just so as if shaking out a crick and I knew Lakshmi was gone. The woman namasted again.

"Little Lord Vishnu," she whispered. "Preserve us."

I picked myself up from the marble. I dusted off the ash of the dark goddess. I walked to the edge of the temple, blinking up into the light of the real sun. I had an idea where to go to do what I had to do. Varanasi, the City of Siva, the seat of the great Jyotirlinga. How might I support myself, with nothing but the dhoti around my loins? Then I caught a sudden movement: on a window ledge on the first floor of one of the many shops that leaned in close to the temple, a cat was edging out along a water pipe in pursuit of a bird. And I had an idea that filled me with laughter.

So here it is, here it is: at long last. The great trick, the Grand Finale of the Magnificent Vishnu's Celestial Cat Circus. The wire walk. You will never, ever have seen anything like this before, unless of course you've been to a certain Kali temple . . . See, here are the two wires. And here is our star performer. Yes, white Kalki gets his chance to shine at last. Up he goes onto the podium and . . . drumroll. Well, you'll have to provide the drumroll yourself.

Kalki! Kalki, beautiful white Kalki: do your trick!

And there he goes, carefully sliding one paw, then another out across the two wires, tail moving to keep him balanced, the whole trembling to his muscular control. Go on, Kalki . . . Walking the wire. What a cat! And the final jump onto the further podium and I scoop him up to my chest and shout, Applause! Applause for my lovely cats! I let Kalki down and the rest of the cats run to join him, running their endless circle of fur and tails around the rope ring. Matsya, Kurma, Narasimha, and Varaha; Vamana, Parashurama, and Rama; Krishna, Buddha, and last but not least, Kalki.

I turn in the rising dawn light to savour the applause of my audience. And my cats, save your biggest cheer for Matsya, Kurma, Narasimha, Varaha, Vamana, Parashurama, Rama, Krishna, Buddha, and Kalki who have performed for your pleasure. And me? Just an impresario, a ringmaster: a story-teller. The light is up now and I will detain you no longer for you have your work and I have a place to go and I think now you know where that is and what I must do there. I may not succeed. I may die. I cannot see Shiv giving up without a fight. So please, will you do one thing for me? My cats. Would you look after them for me? You don't have to feed them or anything like that, just take them. Let them go, they can look after themselves. It's where I got them from in the first place. They'll be happy on a farm, in the country. Lots to hunt and kill. You might even be able to make a bit of money from them. I mean, performing cats, who ever heard of a thing like that? It's actually much easier than you think. Meat does it, every time. There, I've given away the trick. Be good to them. Well, I'll be off, then.

I push the boat out into Mother Ganga, run into the dawn-bright water, and hop in. It rocks gently. It is a glorious morning; the Jyotirlinga ahead can hold no comparison to the sun. I touch my fingers to my forehead, to the tilak Lakshmi put there, in a small salutation to the sun. Then I put my back to the narrow oars and head out into the stream.

ABOUT THE AUTHOR

Ian McDonald is the author of many science fiction novels, including *Desolation Road*; *King of Morning, Queen of Day*; *Out on Blue Six*; *Chaga*; *Kirinya*; and *River of Gods*. He has won the Philip K. Dick Award, the Theodore Sturgeon Award, and the BSFA Award, been nominated for a Nebula Award and a World Fantasy Award, and has several nominations for both the Hugo Award and the Arthur C. Clarke Award. The *Washington Post* called him "one of the best SF novelists of our time." He lives in Belfast, Northern Ireland.

THE RESTRAINT OF BEASTS

MAGNUS MILLS failed his 11-Plus in 1965 and was then placed in the hands of Gloucestershire Education Authority. He later worked with dangerous machinery in Britain and Australia, before obtaining his present employment as a London bus driver.

THE RESTRAINT OF BEASTS

MAGNUS MILLS

Flamingo
An Imprint of HarperCollins*Publishers*

Flamingo
An Imprint of HarperCollins*Publishers*
77–85 Fulham Palace Road,
Hammersmith, London W6 8JB

Published by Flamingo 1998
    5 7 9 8 6

This novel is entirely a work of fiction. The names,
characters and incidents portrayed in it are the work of the
author's imagination. Any resemblance to actual persons,
living or dead, events or localities is entirely coincidental.

A catalogue record for this book is
available from the British Library

ISBN 0 00 225720 3

Set in Postscript Linotype Meridien by
Rowland Phototypesetting Ltd,
Bury St Edmunds, Suffolk

Printed and bound in Great Britain by
Clays Ltd, St Ives plc

FOR SUE

1

'I'm putting you in charge of Tam and Richie,' said Donald.
'They can't go to England on their own.'

'No, I suppose not.'

'We'd never know what they were getting up to.'

'No.'

'So you can take over as foreman from today.'

'Right.'

He allowed me a few moments to absorb the news, then
asked, 'Are you finding it hot in here?'

'Just a little, yes,' I replied.

'You should have said.' Donald rose from behind his desk
and moved to the skirting board, where a radiator pipe emerged.
He turned a stop-tap several times, clockwise, before settling
again in his chair.

'These things can be controlled,' he remarked. 'Now, are
there any questions?'

He sat back and waited. I knew the sort of questions Donald
expected me to ask, but I couldn't think of any. Not with him
examining me from behind his desk the way he did. At the
moment only one obvious question came to mind.

'Why me?'

'There's no one else available. You're the last one.'

'Oh . . . right.'

Donald's gaze remained fixed on me.

'You don't seem very excited about all this,' he said.

'No, no,' I replied. 'Really, I am.'

'Doesn't sound like it. After all, it's not often we appoint a new foreman.'

'No, I know,' I said. 'I just wondered . . . have you told them?'

'Robert has told them.'

'Robert?'

'Yes.'

'Can't you tell them?'

'Robert is quite capable of telling them.' He reached for his typewriter and slid it across the desk towards him. I watched as he placed a sheet of paper in the roller and began tapping the keys. After a while he looked up and saw that I was still standing there.

'Yes?'

'Wouldn't it be better coming from you?' I asked.

'Why's that?'

'It would give me some authority.'

'Haven't you any authority of your own?'

'Yes, but . . .'

'Well, then.' Donald continued looking at me for a long while. 'It's only for a few weeks,' he said. 'Then you can come back.'

He began attending to his typewriter again, so I went out. Donald's mind was obviously made up, therefore further discussion was pointless. Closing the door behind me I paused briefly and listened. Inside the office an unsteady tapping had started up. The decision was probably being committed to paper at this very moment, so that was that. It would have been better if Donald had told them himself, but I really wasn't bothered either way. There was no big deal about the new arrangement. No particular cause for concern. After all, there were only two of them. Should be a piece of cake. True, they had their own way of doing certain things, but that was fair enough. Only to be expected considering how long they'd been together. We'd just have to get used to each other, that's all. I decided to go and see them straight away.

Their pick-up truck was parked at the other side of the yard. They'd been sitting in the cab earlier when I went past on my way to Donald's office. Now, however, there was no sign of them. I walked over and glanced at the jumble of tools and equipment lying in the back of the vehicle. Everything looked as though it had been thrown in there in a great hurry. Clearly it would all need sorting out before we could do anything, so I got in the truck and reversed round to the store room. Then I sat and waited for them to appear. Looking around the inside of the cab I noticed the words 'Tam' and 'Rich' scratched on the dashboard. A plastic lunch box and a bottle of Irn-Bru lay on the shelf.

So where were they? They seemed to have disappeared without trace. From what I'd heard this was the sort of thing they did all the time. They'd just go off somewhere for no apparent reason. And when they came back they wouldn't have an excuse or anything. That's what I'd heard anyway.

Eventually I got fed up with waiting and went round to the timber yard. They were nowhere to be seen, so I then conducted a search of all the store rooms and outhouses. Nothing.

Finally, when I couldn't think of anywhere else to look, I

went back to where I'd started and found them sitting in the truck eating sandwiches. They sat side by side in the double passenger seat, watching me as I approached. I knew Richie by sight. He was the one by the window. Therefore the other one must be Tam.

I spoke through the opening. 'Alright?'

'Alright,' said Richie.

'Just got back?'

'Last night.'

'Looks like we'll need a bit of a sort out,' I said, indicating the gear in the back of the truck. 'But finish your sandwiches first.'

I walked round and got in the cab at the driver's side. Tam looked at me for a moment as I slammed the door shut, but remained silent. I could now see that Richie was providing the sandwiches from the plastic lunch box, perched on his lap. He swigged the Irn-Bru and handed it to Tam.

'Don't leave any floaters in it,' he said.

Tam drank, lowered the bottle, and examined the contents. Then he turned to me. 'Like some?'

'Oh. Thanks.' I took the bottle and drank the warm dregs in the bottom. 'Thanks,' I repeated, handing it back.

'That's O K.' Tam passed the empty bottle back to Richie, who screwed the top back on before throwing it out of the window.

And so we sat there in silence. Richie on one side, Tam in the middle and me behind the steering wheel. All staring through the windscreen. It was a bleak sort of day, with occasional gusts of wind gently rocking the vehicle from side to side.

There was a movement in the distance and Robert came into sight. We watched as he opened a gate to let Ralph through. He appeared to be about to set off on one of his long walks. Whether or not he noticed us sitting there in the truck, watching him, was hard to tell. If he did, he didn't show it. He merely closed the gate behind him and ambled away over the fields.

'Look at Robert,' said Richie. That was all he said, but I could tell by the stifled silence which followed the remark that Tam and Richie were obviously sharing some private joke made at Robert's expense. I didn't join in.

After a short interval I said, 'Did Robert come and speak to you?'

'Just now,' replied Richie.

'Oh. Right. Is that OK with you then?'

'Have to be, won't it?'

'Suppose so,' I said.

Tam glanced at me briefly, but didn't seem to have anything to say on the subject. Instead he turned to Richie. 'Got a fag, Rich?'

Richie reached to a lump I'd noticed in his shirt pocket and took out a cigarette pack. Then he squirmed sideways and fished a lighter from his jeans. He handed Tam a cigarette, gave him a light, lit his own, and we sat there in silence for another few minutes while they smoked, and desultory flecks of rain landed on the cab roof.

'Right,' I said when they'd finished. 'We'd better have a go at sorting out all the gear.' We got out and stood looking into the back of the truck. The collection of tools lay in a shallow pool of rainwater, some of them bent, most of them showing the first signs of rust. This was supposed to be a set of professional fence-building equipment, but actually looked like a hoard of junk. There were hole-digging implements, wire-tightening gear, a rusty steel spike (blunt), a selection of chisels and a chain winch. All in various states of disrepair. Also several coils of wire. The only item that appeared to be in reasonable condition was a large post-hammer with a cast iron head, lying slightly to one side.

'Here's Donald,' murmured Tam, and they both immediately began sorting through the pile. Donald had emerged from his office and was advancing across the yard in our direction. His sudden appearance had a marked effect on Tam and Richie, whose faces showed that they were concentrating hard on their work. Tam leaned over the side of the truck and pulled out the post-hammer.

'Glad to see it's still in one piece,' said Donald as he joined us. He took the hammer from Tam and stood it, head down-wards, on the concrete. Richie, meanwhile, had lifted one of the coils of wire onto his shoulder and was about to take it into the store room.

'You seem to be in a great hurry all of a sudden,' said Donald.

This caused Richie to hesitate awkwardly in mid-step with the coil balanced on his shoulder. He half-turned and looked at Tam. Donald was now peering into the back of the truck.

'You people really should take more care of your equipment,' he said.

After a dutiful pause Richie made another move towards the store room but was again brought to a halt by Donald.

'Leave that for now. I've just had a serious phone call. You'd better come into the office.' Without further comment he turned and walked off towards the open door. We all glanced at each other, saying nothing, and filed after him.

On entering the office I saw that Donald had placed two hard chairs side by side facing his desk. I'd seen these hard chairs before. They were slightly less than full adult size, made from wood, and spent most of the time stacked one on top of the other in the corner beside the filing cabinet. That was where they'd been earlier when I was talking to Donald. I'd hardly noticed them really. They just looked as though they were intended to remain there indefinitely. It never occurred to me that these two hard chairs were kept for a particular purpose. They had been positioned squarely and symmetrically in front of the desk, and Tam and Richie did not have to be told where to sit.

I went and stood by the small recessed window, half-leaning against the radiator, which I noticed had been turned up full again. There was one other change. Donald had removed the light-shade from the ceiling and replaced the usual hundred-watt bulb with a more powerful one. This bathed every corner of the office in sharp light.

Slowly and deliberately he settled in his chair and sat for a few moments regarding Tam and Richie across the desk.

'Mr McCrindle's fence has gone slack,' he announced at last.

2

Donald let the words sink in. 'He's just been on the phone. He's very disappointed. You'll have to go back today and put it right. I thought you knew what you were doing.'

He paused. Tam and Richie said nothing.

'I thought you knew what you were doing. You're supposed to be specialists. Mr McCrindle wanted a high-tensile fence, not something to play a game of tennis over. How are you going to progress with future projects if this kind of thing is going to happen all the time? You only finished off Mr McCrindle yesterday.'

I noticed that Tam and Richie looked quite meek while they were being addressed by Donald. They sat in their two hard chairs, which were a little too small for them, avoiding his gaze and staring with interest at his typewriter, or maybe the pencil lying next to it.

'It means you won't be able to go to England until the middle of next week,' Donald continued. 'Convenient for you, isn't it?'

I wasn't sure what he meant by this remark.

'Sorry,' mumbled Tam at last.

Richie mumbled 'Sorry' too.

There was more. 'I've just had a look in the file. It seems you didn't measure the fence.'

Tam looked up briefly. 'Oh,' he said. 'No.'

'How am I supposed to invoice Mr McCrindle if you failed to take a measurement?'

'Don't know.' Tam shuffled his feet slightly. The radiator pipe under the office floor was slowly warming up his rubber boots, so that they stuck momentarily to the lino. Both Tam and Richie were now beginning to look very uncomfortable. Their chairs were so close together that they were pressed against one another, shoulder to shoulder, each in danger of being unbalanced at any moment.

'Why didn't you measure Mr McCrindle's fence?'

'Forgot.'

'Oh, you forgot. It would be a different story if I forgot to pay you, wouldn't it?'

Donald fell silent and sat looking at them, apparently waiting for an answer.

It was Richie who managed to speak this time. 'Suppose so,' he said.

How long Donald kept them sitting there, side by side in those two hard chairs, was difficult to say. I noticed for the first time that there was no clock in that room. Nor was there a calendar on the wall. Even the limited daylight coming through the small recessed window was defeated by the glare of the light-bulb, further isolating the office interior from the world outside. And as long as they offered no excuse or reason for what they failed to do, Tam and Richie would have to remain under Donald's relentless gaze. This was their punishment.

Several minutes seemed to pass before it was over. Eventually

Donald leaned back in his chair and shook his head slowly.

'What are we going to do with you?' he said. They did not even try to answer.

After Tam and Richie had been dismissed, Donald turned to me.

'You'll have to go with them to put Mr McCrindle right. Not a very good start, is it?'

'Not really,' I said. He appeared to be implying that I had played some part in the slackness of Mr McCrindle's fence, a sort of guilt by association, even though I'd only met Tam and Richie about ten minutes earlier.

'While you're there can you also make sure the fence is straight,' Donald added. I had been wondering when he would bring up the question of straightness. Donald was known to have an obsession about it. He could often be seen glancing along a line of posts during the construction process, making sure the alignment was true. Obviously it was better for a fence to be straight, if only for the sake of appearance, but Donald wanted perfection. As Mr McCrindle had demonstrated by his phone call, the main concern of farmers was that their fences should be tight. Without this the restraint of beasts was impossible. We were rushing back to deal with Mr McCrindle's fence because it had gone slack, and for that reason only. I doubt if he had even looked to see if it was straight or not, despite Donald's concern. It most probably was straight, but if for some reason it wasn't, well then what was I supposed to do? Take out all the posts and start again? Donald's pursuit of perfection seemed to be taking things too far. The way he went on anyone would think we were engaged in an exact science. After all, we were only fencing contractors. The process was straightforward.

You put posts in the ground, you stretched wires between them, and then you moved on. That's what we'd done in the last gang I was in. It was repetitive work, but to tell the truth the whole operation was so simple we hadn't even needed a foreman. We just got on with it. And when the fence was finished it was invariably straight, more or less.

Of course, Tam and Richie hadn't helped matters by building a fence that went slack. Apparently they'd been working away at Mr McCrindle's for several days before suddenly returning the previous evening claiming the job was now complete. Donald had estimated the contract would take a week, but they'd come back a day early. The phone call this morning had merely confirmed his belief that they needed closer supervision.

'One more thing,' he added. 'There'll be no need for Richie to drive the truck any more.'

'Why's that then?' I asked.

'It's part of a new policy I've formulated to reduce our insurance costs. Only foremen will drive company vehicles from now on. Richie is banned.'

'Have you told him?'

'Robert has told him,' he replied.

'What about Tam?'

'He's banned by the Constabulary.'

Now that Donald was giving me his full attention, I found myself looking at the top of his desk most of the time, rather than directly at him. He had this way of staring at people for moments on end without blinking, and it was most disconcerting. Even Tam and Richie could be easily reduced under his gaze. When they were out in the fields they looked like wild men, head-bangers with long Viking hair. If it weren't for their rubber wellington boots they'd appear quite menacing. Yet it only took a prolonged stare from Donald to render them meek and mild. During their interrogation about Mr McCrindle's fence they'd both spent most of the time gazing at Donald's typewriter, and now I was doing the same thing. I noticed the sheet of paper in the roller, and upside down I could see three names printed under the heading 'No. 3 Gang'. One of them was mine. As I tried to read the other two names I realized that Donald had stopped talking.

'Banned by the Constabulary?' I repeated.

I thought I caught the first twinkle of a joke coming here, so I grinned and said, 'Oh, yes. Ha.'

Donald just continued gazing at me, so I went outside.

I found Tam and Richie sitting in the truck again, side by side in the double passenger seat, with their arms folded. The pile of equipment didn't look as if it had been touched.

'Right,' I said. 'Do you want to finish sorting this lot out?'

'Not particularly,' Richie replied.

I tried a different approach. 'OK. We'll sort this lot out and then go to Mr McCrindle's.'

'What time are we having our break?' he asked.

'You've just had it,' I replied.

'When?'

'When you had your sandwiches.'

'Oh.'

'Well, can we have a fag first?' said Tam.

'I suppose so,' I said.

'Like one?'

'Oh. Er . . . no thanks. Thanks anyway.'

So we sat in the truck for another few minutes while they smoked two more of Richie's cigarettes.

'Donald got a bit heavy, didn't he?' I remarked after a while.

'Fucking right,' said Richie.

There was a brief silence, then Tam spoke. 'I fucking hate it when he calls us into the office.'

I nodded.

'So what was this Mr McCrindle like then?' I asked.

'He kept sneaking up on us,' replied Tam.

'Did he?'

'Asking questions about the fence all the time. We could never get rid of him.'

'Maybe he found it interesting,' I suggested.

'Huh,' said Tam.

'I thought he was alright,' said Richie. 'He made us a cup of tea one day.'

'Fucking big deal!' snapped Tam. 'He was always interfering. What about when he was watching us behind that tree?'

'Oh,' said Richie. 'I forgot about that.'

'What was that then?' I asked.

'He was spying on us,' said Tam.

'Was he?'

'Then he comes along. "How's it going, boys?"'

'Perhaps he was just trying to be friendly,' I said.

'Too fucking friendly,' said Tam.

They finished smoking.

'So why do you think his fence has gone slack?' I asked.

Tam looked at me. 'What's that supposed to mean?'

'Well,' I said. 'Why do you think it has? I'm just asking, that's all. So we know what tools we'll need.'

'Must be something wrong with the wire,' he said.

'Donald seems to think it's faulty workmanship.'

'He would.'

'But you're saying it isn't.'

'I've just told you it's the wire.'

'So you don't think a post could have come loose then?'

Tam hardened his look. 'Our posts never come loose,' he announced.

'Here's Robert,' said Richie.

Ralph had just appeared from round the corner of the out-buildings, which meant that Robert wasn't far behind. A moment later he came into sight. Without a word from me, Tam and Richie both got out of the truck and disappeared into the store room.

When they were gone Robert came and spoke to me. I noticed he was carrying Richie's Irn-Bru bottle in his hand.

'I had a word with them,' he said.

Yes ... er ... thanks,' I replied.

He studied the label on the bottle. 'So they're being alright, are they?'

'Yes, yes,' I said. 'Fine.'

'No problems?'

'No.'

'Are you sure?'

'Certain.'

'Good. We like all our gangs to be balanced.'

He nodded and smiled at Tam and Richie as they emerged again. Then he wandered off, still carrying the empty bottle, followed by Ralph. I watched as they crossed the yard and entered an office adjoining, but separate from, Donald's.

I felt a bit sorry for Robert because he didn't really have enough to do. Ever since Donald had taken over the management of the company, Robert's role had been gradually whittled away. That was why he spent so much time going for walks. These consisted of a vague meander across the fields surrounding the company premises, along a route apparently chosen by Ralph. Afterwards they would come back and Robert would sit in his office again. Nobody was sure what he did in there. He didn't even have a telephone these days. Donald ran the company more or less on his own, setting up contracts, dispatching gangs and so forth. This was done with the utmost efficiency. No more than one gang was allowed 'home' at any one time, to the extent that I'd hardly ever actually set eyes on any other employees. I had no idea where Nos. 1 and 2 gangs were working or when they were expected to return. The company premises, as a result, always seemed quiet. Donald controlled everything and Robert was only kept on hand to perform the occasional duty. His task today, for example, had been to tell Tam and Richie they would shortly be going to England with their new foreman. Whereas Donald chose to impart the news himself that Mr McCrindle's fence had gone slack.

Mr McCrindle had a sloping field. A sloping field! As if a farmer didn't have enough to worry about. It was the curse of his life: always had been. Not only was there a terrible problem with surface water during the winter months, but now all the government drainage grants were beginning to dry up. Worst of all, the bottom part of the field was so steep it was no use to him because his cows wouldn't go down there. And if they did they wouldn't come back! .

Mr McCrindle told us all this as we stood at the top of the field wishing he would go away. Tam and Richie had heard it all before, of course, and now they kept slightly aloof, leaving me to deal with him.

'Sounds like you'd be better off with sheep,' I remarked.

Mr McCrindle looked at me. 'Sheep?'

'Yes,' I said. 'With it being sloping, like. They might prefer it.'

'I'm a dairy farmer,' he said. 'What would I want with sheep?'

'Er . . . don't know. Just a suggestion, really.'

The difficulty with talking to Mr McCrindle was that he had very watery eyes which made him look as though he was going to burst into tears at any moment. You felt you had to be very careful what you said to him. I'd only mentioned sheep in a half-hearted attempt to change the subject of conversation. Up until then we'd been talking about Mr McCrindle's new fence, and he'd made it quite clear just how disappointed he was.

'I'm very disappointed, boys,' he kept saying, with a glance at Tam and Richie. 'Very disappointed indeed.'

He'd been onto us ever since the moment we arrived. No sooner had we got out of the truck to survey the situation, than he had come chugging into the field in his van. I would have preferred to have a chance to work out what had gone wrong before he turned up. Maybe have a walk down the fence line to consider our position and prepare ourselves for awkward questions. But, in the event, he was on the scene straight away, so there was nothing I could do.

'It's a very sorry state of affairs,' he said, the tears welling up in his eyes.

Mr McCrindle had every right to be disappointed. He had particularly specified a high-tensile fence, even though it was much more expensive than a conventional one. That was why he had contacted the company in the first place. It specialized in high-tensile fencing and had been a pioneer in developing the technique to its present state. Only best-quality galvanized spring-steel wire and weather-resistant posts were used, every fence being erected by highly experienced personnel. He knew this because it was all outlined in the illustrated company brochure (written by Donald).

Mr McCrindle now surprised me by producing a copy from his inside pocket.

'It says here,' he said, reading aloud. '"A high-tensile fence should retain its tension for the first five years at least."'

He poked his finger at the line of print. 'See? Five years. Cost me a fortune and it went slack overnight!'

We looked across at the evidence, a line of brand new posts marching off down one side of the field, with all the wires hanging limp.

'No use to man nor beast!' he announced.

Poor Mr McCrindle. I thought he was going to break down in front of me. All he wanted to do was get his cows turned into the field, but he couldn't. Of course he was disappointed! He was a livestock farmer whose new fence had gone slack, and I wanted to put my arm around his shoulder and say, 'There there.'

'Let's see what the problem is then,' I said, striding towards the fence. As I approached I remembered Donald's injunction about checking that it was straight. To do so it was necessary to perform a sort of genuflection at one end of the fence and glance along the line of posts. I was just doing this when I became aware that Mr McCrindle had followed me and was looking puzzled.

'What are you doing?' he asked, as I stood upright again.

'Nothing really,' I replied. 'Just making sure it's straight.'

Behind Mr McCrindle I noticed Tam and Richie exchanging glances.

'What's that got to do with the price of tea in China?' he asked.

'Well . . . I just thought I'd look, that's all.'

'And is it?'

'Take a look for yourself.'

Mr McCrindle stood at the end of the fence and genuflected with a grunt. 'Oh, me bloody back!' He shut one eye, then the other. 'What am I supposed to be lining it up with?'

'Itself.'

I left Mr McCrindle squinting along the line of posts and set off down the fence to see if I could find the fault. Realizing that they were now alone with him, Tam and Richie quickly followed after me.

I inspected every post as I went, to make sure each one was firmly embedded in the ground. They all were. I examined the condition of the wire. It was shining and new, straight from the factory. All the time I was aware of Tam and Richie watching me, watching the tests I carried out on their fence. Eventually we got down to the other end.

'See?' said Tam.

'What?' I said.

'You said a post must be loose.'

'No I didn't. I just wondered why the fence had gone slack, that's all.'

Tam looked at me but said nothing.

'So why has it then?' I asked.

'Mr McCrindle shouldn't have kept interfering.'

'Yeah, alright, but that's no reason . . .'

'Well I don't fucking know!' he snapped. 'I'm not fucking foreman, am I?'

'What difference does that make?' I said, but Tam had already turned and gone stomping off up the field.

I looked at Richie. 'Now what?'

'Tam used to be foreman.'

'When?'

'Until you came along.'

'What, today?'

He nodded.

'I didn't know that,' I said. 'Who was he foreman of?'

'Me.'

'I thought you were both equal.'

'He's been a fencer longer than me . . . or you,' he said.

I sighed. 'It's not my fault. This was Donald's idea.'

'Oh.' Richie was now idly toying with a fence wire.

'By the way,' I said. 'Why do you think it's gone slack?'

'Mr McCrindle kept interfering,' he replied.

Well, maybe, but it looked to me as if the wires simply hadn't been tightened up properly in the first place. The fence bore all the hallmarks of a job that had been rushed in the final stages, and in a way Mr McCrindle probably could be held to blame. Tam had complained earlier about how he was forever sneaking up on them and poking about while they were building the fence. I came to the conclusion that Tam and Richie had simply failed to tighten the wires properly because of their haste to escape the attentions of Mr McCrindle. It was no excuse, but, nevertheless, it was probably the reason.

'Is that what you want me to tell Donald then?' I asked.

'Dunno,' said Richie.

Well I knew, and I could just imagine what Donald would say. After all, the company was hardly going to make a profit on a job that had gone wrong like this. Tam seemed to have conveniently forgotten that it would be me, not him, who would have to report back to Donald. It was me who had to take responsibility for restoring the tension in Mr McCrindle's fence. I could see already that we were going to have to come back again the next day. It had taken so long to get all Tam and Richie's equipment sorted out and straightened up, before driving out to Mr McCrindle's, that the light had already started to fade by the time we got there. At this time of the year the darkness crept up on you so slowly you barely noticed, and it was far too late to start tightening wires now. Which meant we'd have to return tomorrow. All highly inefficient. It wasn't really a job for three men over two days, yet what could I do? I could hardly send Tam and Richie back here unsupervised tomorrow, especially not with Mr McCrindle lurking around. And it seemed unthinkable to split them up and just bring Tam. Or just Richie. As far as I knew that had never been done. Fortunately, Donald seemed to have washed his hands of the Mr McCrindle episode and wanted nothing more to do with it.

As long as I got it sorted out 'before the beginning of next week' he would not intervene. Hopefully, by the time the question of profit and loss came up, Mr McCrindle would be a forgotten name in the accounts.

We found Tam brooding about halfway up the fence. There didn't seem to be any sign of Mr McCrindle anywhere, and we decided he must have cleared off for the time being. So at least we had some respite.

'Got a fag, Rich?' said Tam, as we approached. Richie reached for the lump in his shirt pocket and produced his pack of cigarettes, then fished the lighter out of his jeans. As they lit up I wondered with irritation why he didn't keep them together in the same pocket.

Tam turned to me. 'We'll have to come back tomorrow, will we?'

'Looks like it.'

'That's a cunt, isn't it?'

Yes, I agreed, it was. Dusk was now approaching quickly. I left them smoking and went and stood looking down the steep part of the field into the gloom.

To my dismay I saw Robert coming up the other way. What was he doing there? I turned to warn Tam and Richie, whom I could just see in the fading light. I got their attention, put my finger to my lips, and beckoned them to join me quietly.

'He's come to snoop on us,' murmured Tam.

We could now see that Robert had Ralph with him. It was interesting to watch their progress up the slope. Instead of scrambling alongside the fence, as we had done, Robert was following the 'correct' route for his ascent, taking a very meandering path that gained height gradually in a series of switchbacks. This also suited Ralph, who was getting on in years. However, looking from above, Robert hardly appeared to be getting anywhere at all. First he would move across the slope to the right for several yards, then over to the left, back to the right, and so on. With Ralph plodding behind. It seemed to take for ever. Robert never looked up to see how far he'd got. He just kept his eyes carefully on the ground as he chose his path. It was not until he finally reached the top of the slope that he saw us all standing there watching.

'Good evening,' he said.

I must admit I was impressed by Robert's demeanour. Not only had he just ascended a steep slope without a pause, but he had also come face to face with three people he evidently meant to surprise. Yet Robert greeted us with a casual 'good evening' as though we had been expecting him. A bit of a gent really, although Tam and Richie probably regarded him as 'posh'.

'Everything under control?'

'Yes,' I said. 'We've just got to add the finishing touches tomorrow.'

'Good.'

'Are you going to speak to Mr McCrindle?' I asked.

'No, that's your job,' he replied.

'What about Donald?'

'I'm here on my own account,' he said. 'You need to report direct to him . . . if and when appropriate.'

Then, after a polite nod to Tam and Richie, Robert turned and went back the way he had come, with Ralph trailing after him. Why he'd journeyed all this way to see us remained unclear. If he was merely snooping, as Tam put it, then it was only in a most harmless way because he'd given the fence nothing more than a cursory inspection in passing. He was unfamiliar with the technical side of fencing anyway, and was probably only taking a proprietorial interest in a business he could no longer influence. It was like a powerless head of state paying a visit to foreign subjects about whom he knew little. He stayed a short while just to remind us that he existed, and then he went away again. His role was generally unimportant, and as he disappeared into the gathering dusk I couldn't help feeling sorry for him.

'It's the dog I feel sorry for,' remarked Tam.

When we were convinced Robert had definitely gone the three of us trudged back up the field. We found the truck in the darkness and headed for the gate. On the way out we passed Mr McCrindle's van coming in. He flashed his headlights. I flashed back in a friendly way and we fled.

By the time I'd got home, washed and changed and gone out again, the Leslie Fairbanks evening was in full swing. Leslie Fairbanks had a residency at the Crown Hotel Public Bar. Once a week he performed his musical programme entitled 'Reflections of Elvis' to what seemed to be the entire local population. We lived in a quiet place on the road to Perth, and the Crown Hotel was the only establishment you could get a drink apart from the Co-Op off-licence. It occupied one side of a small square opposite the bank at the top of the main street. Which was, in fact, the only street. I don't think Leslie Fairbanks was his real name: I'd seen him once or twice behind the wheel of a lorry with the words 'L. G. Banks, Road Haulage' stencilled on the side of the cab. Leslie Fairbanks was his chosen stage persona for the nights he appeared with his accordion. Sometimes the show was billed as 'Reflections of Hank' by way of a change, but he always remained Leslie Fairbanks. He generally wore a spangled waistcoat for the occasion. A hundred or so people turned up on such evenings at the Crown Hotel, and they needed to be entertained. Leslie Fairbanks had acquired an amplifier for this purpose, and always spent an hour beforehand setting up his equipment and carrying out a sound check, assisted by a youth in dark glasses. Jock the barman, polishing the surface of his counter, could never for the life of him understand why they had to turn it up so loud. It was more than a man could bear. Jock kept a pair of spectacles on a chain round his neck, and he would frequently peer through them at the tangle of cables running from the low stage to the mixing desk.

'Whatever do they need all those for?' he would ask anyone he thought might listen to him. Nobody did. They came to the Crown to drink, and on the nights Leslie Fairbanks played they just drank more. This was rural Scotland. There was nothing else to do.

The amplified accordion sounded like some endless, mournful dirge as I approached through the drizzle that evening, but the lights of the Crown Hotel were too bright to let that discourage me. Once inside the door a more convivial noise took over, as Leslie Fairbanks's endeavours were augmented by the combined racket of drinks being served, laughter and shouted arguments. The place was packed, bodies pressed against each other in a churning mass of persons bent on enjoying themselves despite the odds. Meanwhile, Jock bawled over the tops of people's heads and kept general order at the bar, assisted when things got especially busy by a girl called Morag Paterson. Sales always increased marginally while Morag was behind the counter, but she was only helping out and most of the time she remained at the other side amongst the customers. Seated on one of the barstools nearby was Mr Finlayson, the greenkeeper at the local golf course. His three sons also drank here. One of them was Tam. He was sitting at a big table with his brother Billy and some of their cohort, so I worked my way across the room. They watched me approach and I saw Billy ask Tam something. Tam nodded, then looked up at me as I joined them.

'Alright to sit here?'

'If you like.'

They made a space for me and I sat down, glancing round. 'No Richie?'

'We're not married, you know,' Tam replied.

'No, I know,' I said. 'I just wondered where he was, that's all.'

Tam looked at me. 'Rich can't come out tonight. He's got to pay the instalment on his guitar.'

'Oh, I didn't know he played the guitar. What sort?'

'You'll have to ask him, won't you?'

'Yeah, 'spose.'

I tried to engage Tam in some conversation about fencing, how many miles he'd done, and where, and so forth, but he didn't seem interested in talking. Judging by the number of empty glasses on the table he'd already had quite a lot to drink before I got there. Also, it wasn't easy competing against the continual din in the background, especially when a loud 'clunk' signalled that a microphone was being plugged into Leslie Fairbanks's amplifier. I shortly became aware of a man's voice, apparently singing. Someone had got hold of a mike from behind the bar, and was standing next to Leslie Fairbanks singing as if his life depended on it. His voice was nasal, to the extent that it sounded as if there was a clothes peg clipped onto his nose. He sang with his eyes shut and his fists clenched, while Leslie Fairbanks followed on the accordion, his head tilted to one side, and a faint smile on his face. He appeared to have no objection at all to being usurped by this floor singer and I began to think it was probably something that happened every week. No one else in the place seemed to take the slightest notice of the new addition on stage. They just carried on drinking and shouting all the louder. This more or less put paid to any further talk, so I entertained myself by lining up empty beer glasses with each other across the table-top, watched with vague interest by Tam. It had been a fairly pleasant evening so far, but things began to change after Morag Paterson came to collect up a trayful of empties. It would probably have been alright if Jock hadn't been too busy to do the job himself. Jock would have parted the crowd roughly and elbowed his way round the tables, grabbing five glasses with each hand and finding something to be grumpy about. Instead it was Morag who appeared, gently leaning over to ask if I'd mind passing the empty glasses. I hardly looked at her, but after she'd gone Tam began to slowly ferment. Several times I caught him staring at me and I had to pretend to be listening intently to Leslie

Fairbanks and his partner, who were now in full flow. Tam had been drinking pints of heavy all night, and as he drained the latest one I thought I heard him say something like 'Well, it's about time ex-foreman Tam Finlayson bought the new English foreman a drink, is it not?'

Whatever his intention had been when he rose to his feet, something must have got to Tam before he got to me, because instead of asking what I would like to drink, he just lunged at me across the table, so that several glasses went over. I leaned back to avoid him and next moment he had reared up and was standing before me yelling 'C'mon, English bastards!' at the top of his voice.

As far as I knew I was the only English person in the place, so I stood up at my side of the table and waited to see what happened. Tam looked like he was about to make another lunge when Billy intervened.

'Tam, no!' he shouted.

'English bastards!' Tam screamed. It was odd the way he kept going on about 'bastards' in the plural. This suggested it was nothing personal.

Then Billy got Tam in a sort of bear-hug and they both toppled sideways onto the floor amongst the seething mass of drinkers. One or two people began jeering playfully.

Leslie Fairbanks, man of the moment, saw what happened but decided to press on during the disturbance, somehow managing to change to a much slower, more soothing tune without anybody noticing. This had the interesting side effect of causing his vocal accomplice to fall temporarily silent. In the resulting calm Tam and his brother resurfaced and were all smiles. Billy said something in Tam's ear and put his arm round his shoulder.

The incident seemed to have been already forgotten by most of the bystanders. Their father, sitting at the bar, had turned round on his stool, vaguely aware of some commotion, but quickly lost interest and began to contemplate his drink again. My glass was amongst those that had been knocked over, and as a result it was now empty. As I forlornly stood it upright on the table, Tam settled down opposite me. Billy sat next to him, a large grin on his face.

'I'm sorry,' said Tam.

'That's OK.'

'No, really. I'm very, very sorry.'

'Yeah, well.'

'C'mere.' Tam reached over the table and clasped my hand. Now he wanted to be my friend, my buddy.

'Like a drink?'

'Go on then.'

As Tam lurched off to the bar Billy said, 'Don't worry about Tam. If he goes like that again just come and get me.'

'Thanks,' I said. 'What am I going to do with him when we get to England?'

Billy just shrugged.

There was a squeal over at the bar. Tam had managed to spill beer across the counter and most of it had gone over Morag Paterson. Despite the squeal she didn't seem particularly upset. In fact, she was laughing. It was my beer, of course, that Tam had spilt, and after a while I realized he wasn't coming back with another one. Eventually I went and bought a drink each for me and Billy. Making sure it was Jock who served me.

Tam was late for work next day, so I sat in the truck with Richie, waiting for him to turn up.

'Go out last night?' I asked.

'Couldn't afford it,' he replied, lighting a cigarette.

'Tam tells me you play the guitar.'

'Well, I'm still learning it really,' he said. 'I've only had it three weeks.'

'What sort is it then?'

'Electric.'

Richie was not being very forthcoming, so I gave up trying to interview him about his hobbies. Instead we sat silently in the cab as it slowly filled with smoke. Eventually Tam arrived, failing to provide any excuse for his lateness, and we set off on what we hoped would be our last trip to Mr McCrindle's. It was imperative we got his fence finished today at all costs, or we'd never hear the last of him.

He was nowhere to be seen when we arrived, which was a good start. He must have been occupied at another part of the farm. While Tam and Richie prepared the wire-tightening equipment I went off to take a measurement of the fence, something we'd forgotten to do the day before. This was simply a matter of running a measuring wheel along the entire length of the fence. A small meter at the side of the device clicked up 513 yards. (Donald had decided not to convert from yards to metres because, as he put it, most farmers were incapable of

thinking metrically.) When I got back Tam asked me how long
the fence was.

'513 yards,' I told him.

'I'll measure it,' he announced, taking the wheel and setting
off down the field. I let him get on with it as there was plenty
of time to spare. When he came back the meter read 522. I
don't know how he achieved this figure, but I recorded it all
the same. Now we could concentrate on getting Mr McCrindle's
new fence up to the required level of tension. Tam had elected
to do the re-tightening. I didn't protest as it was his fence
officially, and he was supposed to be a good judge of torque. I
sent Richie down to the bottom of the field to keep an eye on
the job from that end, then all I had to do was stand and watch
in my capacity as foreman.

The wire-tightening gear consisted of a wire-gripper and a
chain winch. Tam began the process by anchoring the winch
to the straining post at the start of the fence. This was a substantial piece of timber, dug deep into the ground and supported
by a strut at forty-five degrees. He then fixed the gripper to the
bottom wire and slowly tightened it by means of a handle which
'walked' link by link along the chain. When he was satisfied
with the tension he tied the wire off at the post, and moved
up to the next one. As Tam settled into his work the true form
of the fence began to appear. The second wire was tightened,
then the third, and fourth, each providing a new taut parallel
line. It was beginning to look good. At last I could see how
perfectly straight the line of posts was, and there was no sign
of any weakening of the structure. Tam would pull his handle
to the left, re-position his feet and pull to the right, and so on,
until, slowly, the correct level of tension was reached. As usual

Tam wore his rubber boots, and he was digging his heels hard into the ground to maintain his balance as he heaved on the handle. At last he came to the top and final wire. This was the most important one, especially in a fence intended to restrain cows, because of their tendency to lean over and eat the grass on the other side. It therefore had to be especially tight. Tam placed the gripper on the wire and carefully cranked the handle one way, then the other. And again one way, then the other. Very slowly now. One way, then the other. He paused.

'That should do it,' I said. The whole fence was humming under the strain.

'I think I'll give it one more,' said Tam. He looked at me for a long moment. 'We don't want it going slack again, do we?'

'Suppose not.'

He planted his feet and began to heave carefully. He really was taking this to the limit this time. It was just as he got the handle about halfway that I noticed Mr McCrindle had joined us. I don't know where he'd come from, but he was now standing directly behind Tam, watching him work. Maybe it was Mr McCrindle's sudden appearance that caused Tam to lose his footing. I'm not really sure, it all happened so quickly. Mr McCrindle said something and Tam seemed to glance sideways. Next thing his balance had gone and he was jerked off his feet. The shock of the change in direction sent the chain snaking upwards for a moment. A moment just long enough for the gripper to release the wire and fly back towards Mr McCrindle. He was still speaking as it hit the side of his head.

It sounded to me like 'Norbert' or maybe 'Noydle'. Whatever he was saying, the words trailed off as Mr McCrindle keeled over. I stepped forward to catch him, and discovered how difficult it can be to hold someone upright when they appear to have stopped trying. So I leant him against the fence.

Mr McCrindle had a very surprised look on his face. His eyes were wide open, but he was, apparently, dead.

3

Tam looked at Mr McCrindle and then turned to me. 'I didn't mean to do that,' he said.

'I know you didn't,' I replied.

'He shouldn't have kept sneaking up on us.'

'Never mind that now.'

Any distant observer of this scene would have probably assumed that the three figures standing by the new fence were in deep conversation about something. In fact, there were only two participants in the conversation.

'What do you think he was saying?'

'Dunno,' said Tam. 'Could've been "Nice work, boys," maybe.'

'Or "Not too tight, Tam",' I suggested. 'I didn't catch the last bit.'

There was a bit of a breeze blowing that day. It rustled a nearby line of trees and caused Mr McCrindle to sway ever so slightly as he stood leaning against the wires.

Tam shivered and zipped up his jerkin.

'Here's Rich,' he said.

We watched as Richie slowly trudged up the field in our direction, glancing every now and then at the fence.

'The top wire's still slack,' he said as he joined us, and then 'Oh, hello, Mr McCrindle.'

When there was no reply he turned and gave me a puzzled frown.

'Tam's just accidentally killed Mr McCrindle,' I explained.

'Oh . . . er . . . oh,' he said, and looked at Mr McCrindle again.

'He must have come to see about getting his cows turned out,' remarked Tam.

We moved Mr McCrindle out of the way and leaned him against the truck so that we could get the fence completed properly. Tam cranked up the top wire and tied it off at the post. I noticed this time he didn't take the tension quite as far as before.

When he'd finished we all stood and regarded the new fence, its wires shimmering in the cold afternoon light.

After a long silence Richie said, 'What are we going to do with Mr McCrindle?'

'Well,' I replied. 'I suppose we'd better bury him.'

This was my first major decision as foreman. Amongst the equipment in the back of the truck was a tool for digging post holes. It was made up of two long-handled spades coupled together to form a pair of tongs. The straining posts which anchored a fence at each end had to be set in deep, narrow holes, and this tool was perfect for the job. If we dug a hole a little deeper and wider than usual, there'd be plenty of room for Mr McCrindle.

'Let Richie dig it,' said Tam. 'He's best.'

With a bashful look of concentration on his face Richie made a cut into the surface, slicing out the turf and placing it to one side. Then he started working into the ground below. Each excavation was the same basic movement. He drove the digger into the bottom of the hole, worked the handles around to get a grip, then closed them together and lifted out the soil, which he deposited on a pile next to him.

I could see that Richie was working much faster than normally would be expected for this sort of task.

'Slow down a bit,' I said. 'You'll wear yourself out.'

He rested for a moment but soon pressed on again. There was no stopping him and he was quickly down into the undersoil. As he delved deeper he had to bend further and further over the hole, until finally he was holding the handles at arm's length and could reach down no more. This was as far as Richie could go, so he stopped and straightened up.

'That's it,' he said.

Tam and I took hold of Mr McCrindle and lowered him into the hole, feet first. We decided to leave his cap on.

Richie had just started shovelling the soil back when Tam made a suggestion.

'Why don't we put a post in as well, to make it look more realistic?'

'We haven't got any spare posts with us,' I said.

'There's one lying in that ditch over there,' he replied.

'What's it doing over there?'

'We had one left over when we built the fence, so we dumped it in that ditch.'

'But you're supposed to take surplus timber away at the end of each job. Donald keeps a record of everything used, you know.'

Tam shrugged.

'Why didn't you take it back?'

'Couldn't be bothered.'

I considered his idea. 'Won't it look a bit funny, a post just standing here on its own?'

'Not really,' he said. 'Somebody might come and hang a gate on it one day.'

'Who?'

'I dunno . . . somebody.'

When I thought about it I agreed he was probably right. There were a lot of posts in the countryside which seemed to be there for no apparent purpose. Some had been waiting many years for a long-forgotten gate to be hung on them. Others started life as the straining posts of fences which, for some reason or other, were never completed. This spare post could join them.

So we fetched it from the ditch where it lay and put it in the hole with Mr McCrindle. Then we back-filled the soil and packed it tight. Tam was very gentle as he replaced the slices of turf and pressed them down with his boot. The finished job looked quite tidy. When we stood back it looked just like an ordinary gatepost. Maybe someone would indeed come along and hang a gate on it one day.

Tam rested his hand on the post. 'Things like this are bound to happen from time to time,' he said.

After that there was nothing left to do, so we put all the gear in the back of the truck and got ready to leave. Already the light was beginning to fade. As dusk approached, the trees stirred and the rising breeze began to sing in the fence wires.

On the way home a thought occurred to me.

'He was dead, wasn't he?'

'I'm sure he was,' said Richie.

'What about his cows?'

'They'll be alright.'

It was time to go to England. No. 3 Gang were being dispatched on Tuesday morning at eight o'clock, and Robert had been given the job of breaking the news officially. I herded Tam and Richie into his office so that he could deliver a short speech.

'Hitherto you've carried out all your work on or near your home ground,' he began. 'This does not mean, however, that any particular precedent is thereby established. Market forces do not recognize feudal boundaries, and if contracts arise further afield then clearly Mohammed must go to the mountain. You also need to bear in mind that building a fence is a combined social and technical exercise . . .'

While Robert went on in this way Tam and Richie stood near the door, looking awkward and nodding each time he paused. I glanced around the room and wondered what he did in here all day long. He had a chair and a desk, but no filing cabinet or telephone, nothing to keep him occupied. In the corner was a low table, under which Ralph lay ignoring the proceedings. Meanwhile, in the adjoining office, a typewriter was being tapped unsteadily. It had always struck me as a bit odd that there was no doorway between Donald and Robert, not even a hatch, so that to communicate with each other they had to go outside into the yard, and back in through the other door.

Presently I noticed that the tapping had stopped. Then I heard quiet footsteps moving behind the partition wall. Evidently Donald was listening in to what was being said. Robert had now turned to the subject of future developments in fencing.

'The high-tension fence is the way forward,' he was saying. 'The prospects of the company depend on it.'

Robert had never really got to grips with the term 'high-tensile', as favoured by Donald, and persisted in quaintly referring to 'high-tension fences'. For this reason he didn't sound very convincing. I suspected that deep down he was a Luddite who secretly preferred old-fashioned conventional fences. Maybe Donald suspected him as well.

As I stood pondering all this I suddenly became aware that Robert had finished his speech and was now sitting behind his desk smiling vaguely.

'Right, thanks for coming in,' he said.

We said it was OK and the three of us trooped outside. As we did so the tapping next door started up again.

The truck was parked across the yard, so we all got in and I reversed it round to the tool shed.

'Got a fag, Rich?' said Tam, and Richie went into the routine with the cigarette pack in his shirt pocket, and the lighter fished out of his jeans. We sat there for a while as they smoked in silence, and then at last Tam spoke.

'What the fuck was Robert talking about?' he said.

Earlier in the day I'd seen Donald separately for my instructions. We were to make preparations for a long journey. It was intended that we should stay away for the entire duration of the contract.

'It's only a few weeks,' he said. 'Then you can come back.'

The company kept a caravan for jobs like this. It was a blue and white model, built to accommodate four persons, and was parked round the back of the timber yard. I asked Tam to go and give the caravan a check while Richie and I sorted out the tools and equipment we'd be needing. Five minutes later Tam came back.

'Right, I've checked it,' he said.

'Oh, good. That was quick.'

'Is that me then?' he asked.

'I suppose so,' I said. 'See you tomorrow. Eight o'clock.'

Sometime after he'd gone I happened to go past the caravan. It was standing in the middle of a huge clump of nettles, and both tyres were flat. I managed to get the door open and have a look inside. It was like a tip. There were cupboards hanging open, mattresses overturned and a bottle of sour milk stood in the sink. This was going to be our home for the next few weeks. I went and found Richie.

'Look at this,' I said. 'I thought Tam said he'd checked it.'

'He probably did.'

It took the two of us more than an hour to get the tyres pumped up and the inside of the caravan fit for habitation. By this time Richie's interest was beginning to flag, so I decided to sort out the rest of the gear myself and let him go home as well. A few minutes after he'd gone Donald came out of the office.

'What time did you tell Tam and Richie tomorrow?'

'Eight o'clock,' I said. 'That's what you told me.'

'Well, there's been a change of plan. I've just had Mr Perkins on the phone and he wants you to be there before dark so he can show you round.'

Mr Perkins was the client in England.

'Can't he show me round next morning? We're bound to arrive after dark, it's miles away.'

'He won't be there,' said Donald. 'He lives somewhere else. You'll just have to leave earlier.'

'How early?'

'I suggest six o'clock.'

'Well, can I use the phone to ring up Tam and Richie?'

'They're not on the telephone.'

'What, neither of them?'

'No.'

'What am I going to do then?'

'You'll just have to go and see them.'

As Donald turned back towards his office I remembered something else I wanted to ask him.

'By the way,' I said. 'Tam seems a bit upset about not being foreman any more. I was wondering if you could make him charge hand, sort of officially?'

'Charge hand?'

'Yes.'

'It's not a grade we recognize.'

'Well couldn't we recognize it just this once?' I tried.

'I'm afraid not,' said Donald, going inside and closing the door behind him.

Richie lived with his parents on a small farm about ten miles away. I had no choice but to get in the truck and drive all the way out there. It was dark by the time I pulled up in the deserted farmyard. A single light shone in the downstairs window. I knocked on the door and after a while Mrs Campbell opened up.

'Oh hello,' I said. 'I've come to tell Richie we've got to go earlier than expected tomorrow morning.'

'I suppose you'd better come in.'

She led me through to the living room where Richie's father was sitting in front of a stick fire.

'Richard's got to go off early tomorrow,' said Mrs Campbell.

'I see,' replied her husband, looking at me. 'I'll just have to do the cows myself.'

Richie's mother disappeared into the depths of the house. Mr Campbell continued looking at me for some time.

'So you're the new foreman?' he said.

'Yes, that's right.'

'I see,' he said, and turned back towards the fire. He was seated in a deep armchair with flat, square sides. Beside it was another armchair, identical and at present empty. I assumed this was Mrs Campbell's. Between them was a small three-legged table. There were some lumps of coal waiting in a bucket next to the fireplace, but at the moment Richie's father was burning sticks. On the shelf above the hearth a clock ticked slowly. The crackle of the flames and the ticking were the only sounds to be heard. I tried without success to imagine an electric guitar being learnt in this house.

After a while Mrs Campbell came back in. 'Richard's just getting ready to go out,' she said. 'Will you have a cup of tea while you wait?'

'Er, no. Thanks anyway,' I replied. 'I just wanted to tell him about leaving early, that's all. I'll have to go soon.'

Mr Campbell looked up at me over the rim of his glasses. 'You'll have a cup of tea.'

I agreed that I would have a cup of tea, and Mrs Campbell withdrew to the kitchen. Behind the two armchairs was a tall oak dresser, and on one of the shelves I noticed a framed picture of a small boy adrift in a rowing boat. The black and white photograph had been taken years before, but the small boy was undoubtedly Richie. There was also a photo of someone I took to be Mr Campbell in his younger days. I glanced at the older version sitting in the armchair. For some reason Richie's father reminded me of Mr McCrindle.

After a few minutes Mrs Campbell returned with the tea, and a tiny cake. I was on my second cup when Richie at last emerged from the back of the house. His mother had said he was getting ready to go out, but I could see no difference in his appearance except that his hair was now washed and shiny, and his wellingtons had been replaced by cowboy boots. I told him the news. He sat down in a hard chair on the opposite side of the fireplace to the bucket of coal.

'Have you told Tam?' he asked.

'I'll tell him in the pub later,' I said.

'What time?'

'Six.'

He looked glum. 'I was going out tonight.'

'And me,' I said. 'This was Donald's idea.'

'I'll have to do the cows myself,' said Mr Campbell again.

After a few more ticks of the clock I showed myself out, leaving Richie and his parents sitting in silence before their stick fire. When I got outside the door I stopped for a moment and listened. Nothing. Somewhere in a nearby field a cow lowed, but there was no other sound. In total darkness I found the truck and drove off.

So this was the life of a foreman. I seemed to be spending most of my time ferrying pieces of information around, in the dark, on behalf of Donald. Tomorrow I had to lead Tam and Richie into exile in England. Tonight, though, the lights of the Crown Hotel offered some consolation.

Word had apparently got round that Tam was going to England. Several people had turned up especially.

'You'll be back by Christmas, I hope?' said Jock.

'Better be,' replied Tam, glancing in my direction.

I shook my head. 'Don't look at me.'

'Send us a postcard, won't you?' said Morag Paterson.

This seemed unlikely to me, but Tam said something polite, and she smiled.

He indicated my glass. 'Pint of heavy?'

'Thanks.'

Sitting further along the bar was Tam's father. He spent a lot of time in the Crown Hotel at this time of year since there was little to do at the golf course after dark. I'd hardly noticed him during the evening, sitting there alone. He seemed to be in a world of his own, seriously involved with his beer glass and nothing else. Now, though, he began to take an interest in the conversation going on nearby. He sat up straight and stared along the counter.

'Who's going to England?'

'Oh for fuck sake,' said Tam.

'Who's going to England?' repeated Mr Finlayson, raising his voice.

'Me.'

'When?'

'Tomorrow.'

His father started up sharply. 'Well you might have told me!'

Tam began to ignore him, gathering up a clutch of pints.

'I said you might have told me!' The words were now loud and angry. Morag Paterson turned away and talked to a friend, while Jock busied himself washing glasses at the other end of the bar.

'C'mon,' Tam murmured to me, and we made our way over to a table where Billy was waiting. There were now a few heads turned. I expected Mr Finlayson to pursue us across the room, but instead the shouting quickly subsided as we joined Billy and sat down.

'What was Dad on about?' asked Billy.

'Nothing,' said Tam. 'Pay no attention to him.'

They seemed to quickly forget the incident. This was evidently supposed to be a sort of send-off for Tam and they had some important drinking to do. I hadn't yet got round to telling him we were going off at six the next day: I didn't want to spoil his evening. I chose my moment when I was helping him to collect some drinks from the bar, three or four pints later. He swayed a little.

'That's alright,' he said. 'No problem.'

'Oh . . . er . . . right,' I said. 'Good. I'll pick you up in the morning then.'

Tam was smiling now. 'Can you give us a sub until we get paid?'

'Ant got any money,' I replied.

'Donald gave you a sub,' he said. 'Hundred pounds.'

'That was a float, not a sub,' I explained. 'To cover out-of-pocket expenses.'

Donald had made a big thing that morning about the difference between a float and a sub. The hundred pounds float he'd given me was meant to cover the cost of fuel and sundry necessities, as opposed to a sub, which was actually the same as a loan. Loans were against company policy and therefore had to be refused. It seemed that Donald had successfully indoctrinated me. I explained my position through the haze that swam between Tam and me.

'Go on,' he said. 'Give us a sub.'

'Can't.'

He changed tack. 'Go on . . . as a friend.'

This was all Mr Perkins's fault. If he hadn't insisted we got to his place before nightfall tomorrow then I wouldn't be having to bribe Tam to get up early in the morning. Yes, bribe! There was no other word for it. Tam knew it was an unreasonable demand, especially on his last night at home. He was trying a bit of moral blackmail. Yes, he would get up early, but only if I lent him some money.

'I thought Rich lent you some money yesterday,' I tried.

'Spent it,' he said.

It occurred to me that while we were away Donald would be sending our wages in cash every week. They'd be addressed to me, which meant I could simply deduct what Tam owed me before I handed them over. So I decided it would be safe to lend him a tenner. He spent most of it that night. Last thing I saw of him he was promising, SWEARING!, to be ready at six next morning.

'I'll be there. You can count on me,' he said, reeling off towards Morag Paterson.

Next day I hauled myself out of bed, took breakfast and got into the truck about a quarter to six. I was not confident. I'd told Richie six o'clock, but I got to his place a little later to give him more time. To my surprise he was waiting at the gate with his bag.

'I've been here twenty minutes,' he complained.

It was still dark when we arrived at the entrance to the golf course and turned up a gravel track. The course itself was set back from the road behind a grove of larch trees. Where the trees ended we came to a wooden two-storey house with a low white paling. A sign on the gate said GREENKEEPER. This was where Tam lived, but there were no lights on. I turned off the engine and groaned.

'I knew he wouldn't be ready.'

'Give him a chance,' said Richie.

I bibbed the horn. We waited. Suddenly a hand came in through the window on Richie's side and seized him by the throat.

4

Another hand followed, grabbing his hair. I wound my window shut.

'One false move and I'll pull your fucking head off,' said a voice in the darkness.

Richie stayed quite still. The two hands slowly twisted his head sideways towards the window, forcing him to look outside. 'Oh hello, Mr Finlayson,' he said. 'Is Tam up yet?'

'Who wants him?' said the voice.

'It's me. Rich.'

The hands let go of Richie, and next moment Mr Finlayson thrust his head in through the window.

'How are you?' he said.

'Fine,' I murmured.

'Glad to hear it,' he replied.

'Nice golf course you've got here,' I added.

'How do you know that?' he asked.

'Sorry?'

'What are you sorry about?'

'Er . . . nothing,' I said.

'Is Tam up yet?' repeated Richie.

'I'll see. Wait here.' Mr Finlayson stalked off into the night.

'What did he mean?' I asked.

'It's still dark,' said Richie.

We watched the outline of the house. Any moment a light would appear in one of the windows. Then Tam would come out and we could get going. So I thought anyway. Instead, nothing happened. There was no sign of any movement, and now Tam's father had disappeared as well. I wondered what he was doing wandering around at this time of the morning, in the dark.

'C'mon, Tam,' I muttered. The house remained silent. I was beginning to get fed up with this, and bibbed the horn again. As the sound faded away my door suddenly flew open and a face came in roaring 'RAAAAAAAAH!!'

Out of the corner of my eye I saw Richie jump in his seat.

'Got you!' shouted Tam. 'Got you both! RAAAAH!!'

'Fuck sake,' said Richie. He moved over to let Tam in next to him.

'Sorry I'm late,' said Tam. 'I've been shagging Morag Paterson all night.'

Richie looked impressed. 'Have you?'

Tam grinned at him. 'Fucking right I have.'

'So she's still inside the house is she?' I asked.

'What? . . . oh, er, no . . .' said Tam. 'Not really, no.'

After all this running round picking up Tam and Richie, we now had to go back to the company yard and collect the caravan.

'Have you got food and stuff?' I asked them, as we set off back down the golf course track.

'No,' they both replied.

'Well, have you had breakfast?'

'I had a cup of tea,' said Richie.

It was still dark when we got back to the yard, and the whole place was silent. It seemed important to get away as quickly as possible. Donald lived on the premises and occupied the house at the end of the yard. Although there were no lights on, there was no doubt that he was awake, listening to our movements. If we took too long with our preparations there was a chance he would come out to ask what was causing the delay. It was only the thought of Donald making a sudden appearance that made Tam and Richie move with any sense of haste at all. As it was, the caravan proved particularly difficult to hook onto the tow bar. The ball-hitch mechanism seemed to have gone rusty and jammed up since it was last used. Only after a pro-longed struggle in the darkness, each of us giving urgent whis-pered orders to the others, did we finally get it engaged.

'By the way,' I said quietly to Tam. 'I thought you told me you checked the caravan yesterday?'

'I did,' he replied.

'Well, how come both tyres were flat?'

He walked round and pressed his boot against the tyres. 'They look alright to me,' he announced.

After what seemed ages we finally got going. I calculated that we had about ten hours to get to our destination before night-fall, as requested by Mr Perkins. It sounded like quite a long time, but we had several hundred miles to go and were starting off on back roads, towing a caravan. We needed to average forty miles per hour all the way. It hardly sounded anything at all, but I slowly came to realize that it was an almost imposs-ible target. Daylight had come long before I would admit it and turn the headlights off. Our so-called early start had ticked away, and that old wreck of a caravan we were towing wasn't going to help us make up time. Still, we settled into the journey well enough. I knew it wouldn't be long before one of them would remember he hadn't had any breakfast, and they'd start going on about stopping somewhere to eat. For the time being, however, they seemed content to smoke Richie's cigarettes. Which is how we came to have a discussion about litter. Tam said, 'Got a fag, Rich?' and Richie went through the ritual with the cigarette pack in his shirt pocket and the lighter in his jeans. He had particular trouble getting at the lighter as he sat squashed between me and Tam, and squirmed all over the place as he tried to fish it out, knocking my elbow several times. They were the last two cigarettes in the pack, so afterwards Tam chucked it out of the window.

I said, 'You shouldn't drop litter, you know.'

'Why not?' said Tam.

'Well,' I replied. 'You know. It looks bad, doesn't it? Spoils the countryside and everything.'

'That's a load of shite and you know it,' he said.

'No it isn't,' I said. 'You can't just go chucking rubbish all over the place.'

'You can if you want,' said Tam. 'All this stuff about litter is just English pathetic . . .' He trailed off, and then started again. 'This is Scotland. You're in Scotland and these mountains have been here millions of years. It doesn't make any difference, a few fag packets for fuck sake. That's just English fucking pathetic shite.'

'He's right,' said Richie.

'Yeah . . . I suppose so,' I said.

I couldn't see any mountains.

Sometime later we passed the sign welcoming you to Scotland if you were coming the other way.

'Where are we going?' said Tam.

'Take a look in the folder,' I replied.

Donald always gave us a folder to take on each job, and the previous day he had prepared one containing Mr Perkins's details. It lay on the metal shelf below the dashboard. In it were an address, a road map, an inventory (what we needed to build Mr Perkins's fence), and a field plan (where we would build it). Also a projected completion date. Tam reached for the folder and pulled out a handful of papers, which he studied for a few moments.

'Fuck,' he muttered, and thrust them back inside. Thus, in one movement, Tam transformed Donald's neat file into a crumpled wedge. Richie now took the papers and leafed through them.

'Upper Bowland,' he said at length.

'Upper Bowland?' said Tam. 'Is that the name of the place?'

'Yep,' said Richie, putting the folder back on the shelf. And with that their curiosity subsided. Tam and Richie sat quietly side by side in the double passenger seat, watching the road ahead as we drove into England.

I was breaking the legal speed limit for towing a caravan, and
the light was beginning to fade, as we entered the county of
Hereford and Worcester. If we had had more time we could
have stopped briefly in one of the many towns we'd passed
and stocked up on food at a reasonable price in a supermarket,
and even checked out promising pubs for future visits. Instead,
we had to press on. We'd been pressing on all day. I'd flogged
that truck along all sorts of motorways and 'A' roads in my
effort to get to Upper Bowland on time. We'd stopped only
once, and that was for breakfast hours ago. It had emerged
then that Tam had come away without any money at all. In
fact, he had very little of anything. The remains of his personal
set of fencing tools were somewhere in the back of the vehicle.
With him that morning he appeared to have brought just the
clothes he worked in, plus a spare pair of jeans and his cowboy
boots, all jammed into a small haversack. Richie seemed to be
slightly better kitted out, but neither of them had organized
any food for while we were away, and now Tam had revealed
he had no money either. Richie said he would pay for Tam's
breakfast, and seemed to have no objection to subsidizing him
for the time being. Which suited me. I looked at the amount
of egg, bacon, sausage, tomato, beans, fried slice and mushrooms Tam consumed, and wondered how long Richie would
put up with the arrangement.

   As I said, that was hours ago. Now we were working our

way along a quiet 'B' road, and it was getting late. I pulled over and checked Donald's map.

'According to this we're looking for a turn-off on the right,' I said.

Not that I expected to get much show of interest from Tam and Richie. They had spent the entire journey gazing silently through the windscreen, smoking from time to time, and taking turns to nod off next to me. I don't think they had any idea what part of England we were in, nor did they care. It was all the same to them. Now that the end of the journey seemed to be getting nearer, however, they began to pay attention again.

I switched on the headlights, which meant, of course, that we hadn't made the deadline. As we drove on we started talking about Mr Perkins. We decided that he was probably waiting at his gate at this very moment, and when we got there he would accuse us of being late, and not making any effort to arrive earlier.

'I expect he's already been on the phone to Donald,' said Tam.

Yes, we all agreed, he probably had.

'Cunt,' said Richie.

Just then we passed a sign on our left which said 'Lower Bowland 3 miles'. I ignored the turn-off and carried on.

'BOWLAND!' shouted Tam. 'That was it back there. You missed the turning!'

'That was Lower Bowland,' I replied. 'We want Upper Bowland.'

'Upper Bowland will be above Lower Bowland, won't it?' he said.

Now Richie joined in. 'Upper Bowland is back there. We've just passed the sign.'

'Upper Bowland is on the right,' I insisted, pressing on and speeding up. No right turning appeared, not for miles. But we kept passing turn-offs for Lower Bowland on the left, and each time Tam and Richie would point out how many miles it was. Lower Bowland was starting to get further away, and there was still no sign of a right turn. I was beginning to lose confidence when suddenly I saw a small lane on the right. There was no signpost but I turned off anyway, and heard Tam murmur something to Richie. This lane seemed to go on and on for ever, but finally, to my relief, the headlights lit up a roadsign: UPPER BOWLAND.

'There you are,' I said. 'You should have had more trust in me.'

'Luck,' said Tam. 'You were lost.'

I pulled up just beyond the roadsign. There was nothing here. No shop, no pub, no houses. Only a farm entrance.

'Hello there,' said a voice in the gloom.

'Mr Perkins?' I said.

'Yes. You found us alright then?'

'Er . . . yes,' I replied.

'Right, well I'd better show you round before it gets any darker. Follow me.'

A figure moved ahead of the truck and began walking up the farm track, and we followed, just keeping him in the beam of the headlights. When we got into the farmyard he showed us where we could park the caravan, and also where the outside tap was. There was a single light on in the kitchen of the farmhouse, but it was difficult to see anything clearly, and I never got a proper look at Mr Perkins. He seemed alright though, and hadn't complained about anything so far.

'You're not Scottish?' he said.

'No,' I replied. ''Fraid not.'

'But it is a Scottish firm, isn't it? I used them because they said they specialized in high-tension fencing.'

'High-tensile,' I corrected. 'Yes, that's right, we do.'

'But you're not Scottish?'

'No. Sorry. Those two are. I'm not.'

'I see,' he said.

Tam and Richie were somewhere nearby in the shadows. I noticed they hadn't spoken since we arrived, and after un-hitching the caravan were just standing around doing nothing. They needed some instructions, so I gave them some.

'Can you jack up the caravan and connect the gas while I go with Mr Perkins?'

I got into the truck for a moment to get Donald's file. This only took a few seconds, but when I got out again Mr Perkins was standing in the doorway of the caravan talking to Tam and Richie. Then he stepped out and joined me.

'Is there something particular you want to show me?' I asked.

'Yes, along here,' he said, leading me out of the yard and further up the farm track. It was now total darkness. The moon, however, was out.

When we had gone some distance Mr Perkins said, 'I asked your friends if they'd like a cup of tea, but I think there was a bit of a misunderstanding.'

'What did they say then?' I asked.

'They didn't really say anything,' he replied.

We walked for a few more minutes, and then stopped at the top of the track.

'Now this is our hill,' said Mr Perkins.

I was aware of something looming nearby, but could see nothing.

'We want you to divide it into four quarters with your fences. For lambing, you see. We've gone into sheep.'

All this I knew already. I'd read the details yesterday in Donald's file.

'Is there anything else?' I asked.

'No, that's it,' said Mr Perkins. 'I just wanted to show you where the hill was.'

This was what I'd done ten hours' hard driving for. To be shown a hill. I'd seen from the map that this was the only hill of any size for miles around. It was one of those hills that you get here and there in the countryside, thrust up by some geological accident millions of years ago and responsible for the term 'rolling landscape'. But Mr Perkins obviously didn't think I'd be able to find it on my own.

'Right. That's fine. Thanks very much,' I said, and for a few moments I stood with this stranger I could hardly see, looking into the blackness.

'Well, I'd better be off now,' he said at last, and we walked back down to the farmyard. As we passed the caravan I could see two red glow-worms moving silently inside where Tam and Richie sat smoking in the dark. I said goodbye to Mr Perkins and he locked up the farmhouse before going off in his car. Then, with a sinking feeling, I went to the caravan. We must have forgotten to bring the gas bottle. That was why they were sitting in the dark.

'Go on then,' I said. 'Tell me the bad news.'

'What?' said Tam.

'We've forgotten the gas bottle.'

'What are you talking about? We've just connected it.'

'Well, don't you want the lights on?' I asked.

'We're going out, aren't we?'

'Where?'

'The pub.'

'But it's only quarter past five,' I said.

'Oh . . . is it?'

Yes, it was only a quarter past five, and I wondered for the first time what we were going to do at night now that it was beginning to get dark so early. I also realized that, for tonight at least, I was going to have to share some of my food with Tam and Richie. Tomorrow we would have to go and get them stocked up properly. In the meantime we lit the lamps of the caravan. There was an electric striplight at one side, which was supposed to be powered by a cable led out through the window. However, this striplight made such a loud buzzing noise when it was turned on that we hadn't even bothered to bring the cable with us, and were relying on gas lamps only. They were barely adequate, but to tell the truth there was not much worth lighting up. This caravan had been used as a home for itinerant fencers for years, and was, more or less, a wreck. There was a bunk bed in the corner which Richie had claimed. He was already lying in the top half still wearing his wellingtons, and his bag lay on the bit underneath. I seemed to have been given the bed opposite Richie, while Tam was on the one opposite the sink. Next to the sink was a gas cooker, which we lit to make a pot of tea (though we had no milk).

While the kettle boiled I said, 'What did Mr Perkins come and say to you then?'

'He asked if we wanted some tea,' replied Tam.

'Well, why didn't you say yes?' I said. 'That would have been nice. I could have done with a cup of tea when we got here. And I bet he had some milk.'

'Expect he did.'

'Why didn't you say yes then?'

'Because we're not tinkers,' said Tam, giving me a look.

After I'd fed them some canned beans, we arranged ourselves in our three corners with little left to do. Richie had brought his cassette player with him, which he attempted to play powered by batteries only. The batteries were not new, and started to struggle halfway through the Black Sabbath tape Richie had chosen. The sound of Richie's tapes slowly being stretched in an under-powered cassette player was to become a familiar background noise over the coming weeks.

'What else have you got, apart from Black Sabbath?' I asked, after a while.

Richie shuffled his small stack of cassettes. 'Maiden, Motör-head, Saxon.'

I soon came to the conclusion that Tam was right. We would have to go out. I had another look at Donald's road map. This was actually a photocopied page from an atlas. Donald had marked out our route with a green felt-tip pen. At the end of the green line was Upper Bowland, which had turned out to be nothing more than a signpost. A few miles further along the main road, however, the map indicated some kind of settlement. Also the letters P H, for public house. Well, that was hopeful anyway. By this time it had ticked round to seven o'clock and I knew Tam would soon start up again about going to the pub. Richie was lying on his bunk reading a paperback book he had found in one of the cupboards, *An Early Bath for Thompson* by A. D. Young.

'When are we going out?' said Tam.

'There's a pub about five miles from here,' I replied.

Richie instantly put his book away and swung down from his bunk. He took off his wellingtons and put on his cowboy boots. Meanwhile, at the other end of the caravan, Tam was doing the same thing. A moment later they were both standing by the door looking at me.

'You're ready then, are you?' I said.

As I heaved myself off my bed and put the map away Tam said, 'Can I have a sub until we get paid?'

'I lent you some last night,' I said. 'You haven't forgotten, have you?'

'No, no,' he replied. 'But I need some for tonight.'

'And for buying food tomorrow,' I added.

'That as well,' he said.

So I lent him some more money, we went out, and Tam and Richie spent their first evening in an English pub. The Queen's Head, it was called. I don't know quite what they expected, but I knew exactly what it would be like. It came as no surprise to me that there were only about six people inside, and that they all looked towards the door as we entered, me first, then Tam, then Richie.

'Good evening!' boomed the landlord from behind the bar. 'Three pints, is it?'

'Er . . . alright,' replied Tam.

Richie and I went and sat down at a table in the corner,

leaving Tam to pay for the drinks. Then I thought of something and went back to the counter.

'Can we have straight glasses, please?' I said. Tam glanced at me.

'Don't you want tankards?' said the landlord, booming again.

As I suspected, he had already started pouring the beer into dimpled tankards with handles.

'No thanks,' I said.

'Most people want tankards,' he announced.

'Straight glasses if you've got them, please.'

'Right you are,' he said, transferring the beer into proper straight glasses. I went and sat down. A few moments later Tam came over with the beers.

'Tankards,' he said, grinning. The landlord didn't seem to hear him.

'Where is everybody?' said Richie.

'Too early,' I explained. 'There might be a few more in about ten o'clock.'

'What time does it shut, then?'

'Eleven.'

'What?!'

'You're lucky. They used to shut at half ten.'

'For fuck sake,' said Tam.

So there we sat, at a table in the corner, while the locals played darts and no doubt wondered who we were.

In the morning I looked out of the caravan window and saw our future piled up on the other side of the farmyard.

'Look at that lot,' I said.

Tam and Richie, half-awake, leaned on their elbows and peered round the shabby curtains. The materials for the fence had been delivered by lorry a few days prior to our arrival, and all the posts and rolls of wire were there in a huge untidy stack.

'Fuck sake,' said Tam. 'We're going to be here for ever.'

It looked as if the lorry driver had just reversed into the yard and tipped the whole lot out. There were straining posts, pointed posts and struts all mixed up with each other. It was odd that Mr Perkins had not said anything. Maybe he thought it was common practice just to dump all the stuff like this. Donald would have been most dismayed if he had seen it. Not his way of doing things at all.

We sat on our respective beds drinking tea (no milk), and considered starting work.

I decided that Tam and I would sort out all the gear while we sent Richie off to buy their food supply. It was clear that I would have to ignore unilaterally Donald's driving ban on Richie if we were going to get anything done at all.

I suppose it must have been about half past eight when Richie drove off. He and Tam had put together a basic shopping list, and I'd also mentioned we would need milk. So all he had to do was find a shop, buy the groceries, and come back.

By ten o'clock Tam and I had made deep inroads into the pile and it was beginning to look a bit more orderly and Donald-like. We stopped for a cup of tea. With a bit of luck Richie would turn up any minute with some milk to put in it. He didn't. We started work again, and I realized that we were now continually listening for the sound of the truck approaching in the distance. Tam, meanwhile, kept walking to the gateway and looking down the track towards the main road.

'Where do you think Rich is?' he kept saying.

I could see it was beginning to affect his work. He was supposed to be throwing posts down from the pile for me to catch, but his aim was starting to go astray. I had made the cardinal error of separating Tam and Richie. It was only for a short while, but I could see Tam wouldn't be able to function normally until Richie got back. Besides, we needed the truck to shift the materials up to the foot of the hill. This sorting out in the farmyard was really only meant to be a 'starter' job to get us in the swing of things, two hours' work at the outside. If Richie didn't come back soon the day would be lost. We had got to the point of meaninglessly checking off Donald's inventory when he finally returned.

'That took a long time,' I said, as he got out of the truck.

'I know,' he replied. 'I couldn't find a shop.'

'Wasn't there one near that pub?'

'I went the other way.'

The sinking feeling was beginning to return.

'But there weren't any shops the other way,' I said. 'That's the way we came yesterday.'

'I know,' he said. 'I've been miles.'

'So what did you do in the end?'

'Came back.'

There was a pause. 'What . . . you haven't got anything?'

'No.'

There was little more to say on the subject, so we loaded up the truck with posts and wire, and went up to the hill. It was a bare, treeless place, covered with a layer of turf and populated by sheep, which roamed around, grazing here and there. Mr Perkins wanted us to divide it into four quarters, so the final appearance would resemble a hot cross bun. Therefore the first thing we had to do was halve it. Donald had been down to survey the job in advance, and he'd put marker pegs in the ground where the fences were to start and finish.

This first fence would run right over the top of the hill, and needed a straining post at either end. I gave Tam and Richie the task of doing one each. Then I took the shopping list and went to get their supplies for them. As expected, I found a general store about a hundred and fifty yards from the Queen's Head. The whole trip took thirty-five minutes, which should have given Tam and Richie enough time to put their posts in the ground.

I parked at the bottom of the hill and walked round to Tam's end. There was a half-dug hole but no Tam. I carried on round to Richie's end. The two of them were standing by Richie's post, which was complete, having a smoke.

'Just getting a fag off Rich,' said Tam as I approached.

At that moment it struck me we were probably going to be at Upper Bowland a bit longer than Donald had predicted.

All fences had to be straight. This was our mission. Donald had drawn them as straight lines on his plan: therefore, they also had to be straight in real life. Even fences that went right over the top of a hill. Once the first two straining posts were ready, the next job was to stretch a wire between them. This would give us a straight line to work from. We wanted to bisect the hill perfectly, so I asked Tam to go and stand at the top and act as a sighting point. Then Richie loaded a coil of wire onto an unwinder, and began towing out the first strand. This unwinder resembled a small windmill. It turned slowly as Richie made his way up the hill, dragging the wire behind him, and I stood by watching for possible snags. Which required great patience. Each coil contained a quarter of a mile of wire, and I didn't expect him to move particularly quickly. I was quite content to clock his progress as the coil steadily unwound. As he approached Tam at the summit I could tell he was flagging. The unwinder had been turning at a slower and slower rate, and when he got to Tam it stopped altogether.

I waited.

They were discussing something. I wondered what they were talking about, my two colleagues at the other end of the wire. Plotting my overthrow? Probably not. More likely 'Got a fag, Rich?'

Another moment and the unwinder began to move again as Richie continued across the top of the hill and disappeared from my view. Steadily it turned, gradually gaining speed when he started his descent and gravity took over. Soon it was spinning like a whirligig, which meant Richie had taken off at a run down the other side of the hill and was relying on the wire's drag to hold him back and stop him breaking his neck. Suddenly the coil ran out and I watched the tail end go snaking up the hill. The unwinder spun silently to a halt. I assumed Richie had arrived safely at the bottom. Then I loaded another coil onto the unwinder and set off towing the new wire behind me. I found the end of Richie's wire halfway up the hill and tied mine to it with a special fencer's knot. Now we had a continual length of wire running right over the summit of the hill. As soon as it was secure at Richie's end I could pull it tight and we would have our straight line. I glanced up at Tam. Could he see Richie from where he was standing? Probably not. He'd have to walk across the top of the hill to have a look, but this didn't seem to have occurred to him. He was just gazing into space. I shouted to get his attention, but my voice didn't carry far enough. This problem of communication along the fence was nothing new. Donald had considered supplying gangs with walkie-talkies to help make the process more efficient, but then decided that they were 'open to abuse' and abandoned the idea. I lost count of the times I had been at one end of a fence trying to pass instructions to the person at the other. Having a hill between me and Richie made the matter worse.

I suppose it was my fault really. I should have set up some sort of pre-arranged signal before he went off.

I wondered what Tam was staring at. Maybe nothing. Maybe he had been standing there so long his mind had just gone off the job. Meanwhile, I had no idea at all whether Richie had fixed the wire at the other end.

'TAM!' I shouted at the top of my voice.

No response.

Again 'TAM!! You deaf fucker!'

This time he turned towards me. I shrugged at him, meaning 'What's happening?'

He shrugged back. Now what was that supposed to mean? All I wanted him to do was go and have a look down at Richie, come back and give me a signal. But he just stayed where he was. I made a pointing gesture. Still he did not move, apart from shrugging again. I was very reluctant to go up the hill myself, him being already up there. It was such a waste of energy. We were all going to have to go up and down that hill a good many times before this job was finished. All the pointed posts that formed the main body of the fence were going to have to be lugged up there by hand because it was too steep for the truck. Then there would be the rest of the wires to tow out and fix. All in all a lot of to-ing and fro-ing, and I could see no point in me going right up the hill just to ask Tam what Richie was doing. I didn't want to call Tam down yet either: he had to keep an eye on the wire when it was pulled tight to make sure it didn't get caught anywhere and go out of line.

I waved my arm again. Aha! Something had got through to Tam at last, and he set off walking away from me over the top of the hill. I waited a few minutes while he was out of sight. Soon, I thought, he would come back and give me a signal that everything was OK. I continued waiting. He didn't come back.

Eventually, I decided to walk round the bottom of the hill to see if Richie's end was ready. When I got there it came as no real surprise to find he had gone.

My fault again. I was foreman, so I should have organized it better. I looked up the slope but could see no sign of Tam either.

It seemed like a good time to call it a day. The light was failing anyway. By the time I got back to the caravan it was dark. Again they were sitting inside, unseen apart from the glow of their cigarettes.

'Now what?' I said.

'What?' said Richie.

'You haven't lit the lamps.'

'Oh,' he replied. 'No. Couldn't be bothered.'

We talked of going to the Queen's Head again that night. The previous evening, as I foretold, the pub hadn't started to fill up until half past ten. The customers had been mainly blokes, but just before last orders two young women had turned up. They were obviously local girls, you could tell by the way they were greeted when they came in. They took no notice of us three whatsoever. Nevertheless, Tam and Richie decided that 'we' had a 'chance', so for the time being the Queen's Head would remain our drinking base.

'Shame the beer's so weak,' said Richie.

'Weak,' repeated Tam, looking at me. 'Made by weaklings.'

Before we went out for the evening I wanted to have a shave. I filled a kettle with water from the outside tap and put it on to boil. Shaving was part of the downside of being an itinerant fencer. It wasn't too bad if we were at a farm where they kept cows. There was always lots of hot water available in the dairy: something to do with hygiene. Sheep, however, were different. The animals were left to their own devices for much of the time, and absentee farmers like Mr Perkins didn't even live at the place. The only thing on tap was cold water, and if someone wanted to wash and shave they had to boil it themselves. Tam and Richie didn't seem very interested in washing, not on week-days anyway. And they soon got fed up waiting while I had a shave, because the delay meant they couldn't go out yet.

'How long are you going to be?' said Richie, as I poured the boiling water into a bucket.

'Ten or fifteen minutes,' I replied. He grunted and reached for his copy of *An Early Bath for Thompson* for a brief read.

Meanwhile, Tam had nothing to do.

'Why don't you clear that up?' I suggested, nodding towards some baked beans that had been on the floor since last night. They were there because the can opener that came with the caravan was worn out. Richie had attempted to open some beans and the opener got stuck halfway round the lid and refused to go any further. At this point Tam took over the operation, and removed the contents with his wood chisel. Some, however, had gone on the floor. When I went to the general store I asked Tam and Richie if they wanted to go thirds each on a new can opener. They both said no, so I bought myself one and put it in my cupboard. Also in my cupboard were one plate, one cup and a knife and fork, which I washed separately and put away. We were now on our second day in the caravan and Tam and Richie obviously weren't going to do any washing up. All the other plates, pans and cutlery had already been used, and were now stacked in the sink, which, by the way, had no plug. Tam said it was 'pathetic' when I did my own washing up and not theirs. Earlier this evening he asked to borrow my new can opener. When I refused he simply resorted to his wood chisel again. I realized I would have to stand firm about the can opener or risk losing my authority over Tam and Richie.

Now Tam stood looking down at the beans. He cleared them up by opening the door and flicking them outside with his boot. Then he sat down again and watched me finish shaving, while Richie lay on his bunk and read *An Early Bath for Thompson*. When I was ready we went out.

The landlord of the Queen's Head seemed quite pleased to see us.

'Like my beer, do you, lads?' he boomed as we walked in.

'It's alright,' Richie managed to say.

The few people in the bar seemed to be roughly the same crowd as the night before. The girls weren't there but it was only early, so we sat in our corner and waited for the evening to pass. When Tam bought the second round of drinks the landlord decided it was time to find out about the strangers. He targeted Tam, who had just carried one full glass across to our table, and was now going back to the bar for the other two.

'So . . .' he said, looking hard at the beer flowing into the final glass. 'What are you lads busy with down here?'

'Fencing at Bowland,' replied Tam.

The landlord looked at him and smiled faintly.

'Sorry, what was that?' he said.

'Fencing at Bowland,' Tam said again. A few seconds passed. I could see from the landlord's face that he still hadn't caught it. The embarrassing moment was approaching when he would have to ask for a third time. Interestingly, none of the others standing round the bar seemed to have grasped what Tam was saying either, even though they were now all listening. It must have been something to do with Tam's accent. I'd got used to it, having spent so much time with him and Richie, but at this moment he might as well have been speaking another language. For his part, he wasn't helping matters by just repeating 'Fencing at Bowland' all the time. Tam wasn't making himself very clear, but then again, why should he? He hadn't come in the pub to spend the evening being interrogated. Yet here he was, standing at the bar, each hand gripping a pint glass, with all eyes on him. He wasn't finding any of this particularly easy.

The landlord tried again. 'No, sorry, still didn't get it.'

'We're fencing at Bowland!' said Tam, raising his voice, and at last they understood.

'Oh, you're doing some fencing along there, are you?' said our host.

There was a murmur. And then a different sort of silence fell on that bar room. It was only for a moment, little more than the minor register of something, but it was there alright. The locals seemed to draw back, ever so slightly. One of them was sitting on a stool by the bar, and at last he spoke.

'All the fencing round here is done by the Hall Brothers.'

That was all he said, but with those few words we became outsiders again. As the silence faded away, Tam came back across to me and Richie. He placed our drinks on the table and sat down with his back to the bar.

'What does he mean by that?' he said.

'Nothing,' I replied. 'Pay no attention to him.'

'Who the fuck are the Hall Brothers?'

'How do I know?' I said. 'Forget it.'

And for the time being, apparently, he did. We had a few more drinks and then, when it became obvious the women were not going to make an appearance, we left.

As we departed the landlord said, 'Good night.'

No one else did.

5

'Posting up today,' I said.

'Yep,' said Tam.

'You going to get out of bed then?'

'Nope.'

This was Tam's day. The day we were going to hammer a post into the ground every three yards for the entire length of the fence. Tam was the best at handling the post hammer and he knew it. Not getting up was his way of exploiting his position. Neither Richie nor I had got up either, but that wasn't the point. Tam was the most important member of the gang today, so he would have to be the last to get up. It was only right.

I let him bask in his moment of glory for a while longer. Then I swung my legs out of bed and said, 'Alright then, me and Rich will have to do it.'

This did the trick. Tam was out of bed in an instant saying, 'Oh no you fucking don't.' Which was how I got them out on the hill by eight o'clock in the morning. I wanted to get an early start on the fence because the previous day's hold-ups meant we hadn't really got much done. Donald would probably have estimated that we were already two-thirds of a day behind schedule. I wasn't sure about that, but we certainly had some catching up to do.

It was going to be hard work. Once the ground wire was tightened and our straight line established, we then had to hammer in all these pointed posts to form the main body of the fence. The process was simple. You stuck a steel spike in the ground to make a 'starter' hole, then one person held the post in position (point downwards) while the other hit it with the hammer. When it was into the ground the correct depth, and checked for alignment, you moved on to the next post. And the next one. And the one after that. Over and over again.

We started from the bottom of the hill and worked up, Tam and Richie putting the posts in while I kept them supplied with fresh ones. Tam's hammering technique had been perfected over the years since he began fencing. He used the 'full swing' method, which was the most efficient if done properly, but potentially disastrous if it went wrong. It depended on the fencer's ability to land the hammer head square on top of the post at every attempt. Tam had that ability. He could swing the post hammer at arm's length in a full circle and bring it down hard and accurate time after time. If he missed he was likely to split the post, break the hammer, or endanger Richie. Usually he didn't, and Richie seemed totally confident as he stood there holding the posts.

It was quite satisfying to see them working their way up that hill. At last I felt we were getting somewhere. Alright, so it was a bit of a slog carrying all those posts up the slope, especially as I had to make a longer journey each time, but that was all part of the game. Even when Tam and Richie stopped halfway up the hill for a fag it was OK with me. I paused to watch the familiar ritual in the distance. Tam lowered the post hammer to the ground, straightened up and spoke to Richie. Then Richie took something from his shirt pocket, handed it to Tam, and began wriggling about trying to fish into his jeans. Why he couldn't keep both items in his shirt pocket remained beyond me. His jeans were obviously far too tight for him, and it was a real struggle getting at that lighter. Eventually he succeeded, though, and they lit up and stood close together as smoke drifted away along the side of the hill. When I clambered towards them with another few posts on my shoulder, they started work again.

As further progress was made along the fence, I again became aware of how poorly sound carried. I would see the tiny, far-away figure of Tam swing the hammer, strike the post, and swing again, yet the 'clop' of the impact came to me about a second later. This had the odd effect of making Tam and Richie seem to be moving in a different world to me. As I said, it was a hard day. Eventually we reached the summit and began working down the other side of the hill. By the time we got back to the caravan that night we were all whacked. After we'd had our supper we stretched out on our bunks and dozed. Richie attempted to press on with *An Early Bath for Thompson*, but he soon nodded off. I closed my eyes.

Next thing I knew Tam was shaking me awake. It was dark in the caravan and there was panic in his voice. 'What time is it?'

Richie muttered something from his bunk and managed to light one of the lamps. It was half past ten!

'Fuck sake, the pub!' cried Tam, and next thing we were all screaming round in the caravan looking for our boots and rushing out into the night. The truck didn't start first time and there was a lot of shouting and cursing. Eventually we got going. We made the Queen's Head for last orders, thank God, or the evening would have been wasted altogether.

'Thought you'd forgotten us,' said the landlord as he pulled a double order of six pints.

'No, no,' said Tam.

We had two pints apiece, and they were the best beers any of us had ever had, ever. Even better, the two young women were lounging near the bar, watching the darts game in progress. Because we arrived late our usual table had already been taken, so instead Tam and Richie headed for a narrow wooden bench set into an alcove in the wall. They were still wearing their rubber workboots, and as they sat side by side holding their pints, they reminded me of gnomes on a shelf at a garden centre.

Next morning, as he selected a plate from the sink and scraped it clean, Richie made an announcement.

'I'll take the post hammer today,' he said.

Tam glanced at me and went and stood in the doorway, looking out of the caravan.

'Why's that then?' I said to Richie.

'I need the practice,' he replied.

This was well said. In spite of his other fencing skills, Richie had never quite mastered the post hammer. At best his aim was questionable. At worst . . . well, you have to remember the hammer had a cast iron head weighing several pounds. In the wrong hands it could be dangerous. Yesterday, Tam had only damaged one post out of all those he knocked in: a single mishit had caused a chip of wood to zing off sideways into the air. Furthermore, he had been going at such a good rate that there were only about twenty posts to do in that first fence. Richie wanted to hammer in these last few. He was quite determined, so we let him get on with it. Which meant that Tam had to hold the posts for him. I must admit I admired the way he didn't even flinch when Richie took his first swing of the day. I made a mental note to check how many spare posts we had, to replace the ones Richie was bound to split.

While they finished off that section I had some carpentry to do. The straining posts at each end of the fence had to be fitted with a support strut, and this was usually my job. Donald always specified that the timber be joined properly using a hammer and chisel. Some fencers just held the strut in position with six-inch nails but the company frowned on this practice. The strut was a good length of 4 × 4, set firm in the ground, and gave the high-tensile fence much of its strength and durability. I quite liked this job, and was always pleased when the join was neat and tidy.

Richie managed to complete the line of posts without damaging any or injuring Tam, so we were able to make good speed towards getting the rest of the wires towed out, tightened and fixed to complete the first fence.

That evening I decided to give Donald a ring to let him know how we were getting on.

'How are you getting on?' he asked.

'Not too bad,' I replied. 'Just about on schedule, I should think.'

'Good,' said Donald. 'And how are your two charges behaving?'

'They're being O K , actually,' I said. 'No problem at all.'

'Good,' said Donald again. 'We like all our gangs to be balanced.' There was a pause and then he said, 'By the way, there's something I've been meaning to ask you about Mr McCrindle.'

'Oh yes?'

'Are you sure you finished him off properly?'

'Er . . . how do you mean?'

'It's a simple enough question,' replied Donald. 'I just asked if you finished him off properly, that's all. Did you get the wires fully tightened, check the posts and so forth?'

'Oh,' I said. 'Er . . . yes. I'm sure the fence was all up to standard when we left.'

'And was it straight?'

'Perfectly.'

'I see.'

'Why's that then?'

'It's just that Mr McCrindle has failed to settle his account. I thought there may have been a problem of some kind.'

'Not as far as I know,' I said.

'Alright then,' said Donald. 'Keep in touch, won't you?'

'Righto. Bye.'

When I got back to the caravan Tam and Richie looked at me expectantly.

'What did Donald say?' asked Tam.

'Not much,' I replied. 'He said Mr McCrindle hasn't settled his account.'

'Oh fuck,' said Tam. 'I never thought of that.'

'Nor me,' I said.

'Did you ask him about our wages?' asked Richie.

'No, I forgot.'

'Oh, for fuck sake!' said Tam.

'Alright,' I snapped. 'I forgot, right? I'll go and ring him again.'

So I went back down to the phone box and rang again. Donald said the wages were ready, and I suggested he sent them to the general stores near the Queen's Head, which also acted as a sub-post office.

'There's a deduction to be made from Tam's money for a few days he was off last month,' he said.

'Have you told him?' I asked.

'Robert told him,' he replied. It was the first I'd heard of it. The company didn't have a regular pay day. It all depended where people were and how long jobs were expected to take. Money only turned up when we asked for it. As long, that is, as Donald agreed he owed us any.

The other thing about working for this company was that we didn't stop at weekends. We were expected to carry on working every day until the contract was complete. Unfortunately, Tam and Richie never seemed to get used to this idea, and when Friday came along, as it now had, they started to think in terms of 'going out'. Most of the day went OK, and we began to work on the cross-fence that would divide the hill the other way. As soon as we got back to the caravan that evening, however, Tam turned to me and said, 'Are you changing?'

I examined the backs of my hands. Then I peered closely in the mirror.

'Don't think so,' I replied.

Tam looked at me. 'You know what I mean,' he said. 'Are you changing to go out?'

'Spec so. Clean shirt . . . yeah.'

'Are you shaving?' he went on.

'I shave every day, don't I? Course I am.'

'So you're going to get ready?'

'Yes,' I said. 'When I've had my tea.'

Tam sighed and sat down on his bed. He looked over to Richie, who was standing by the sink. 'Are you getting ready, Rich?'

'Yep,' replied Richie. He had already taken a large saucepan from the sink and started cleaning it out. Then he put some water on the boil. While he waited he got his cowboy boots out of the cupboard and buffed them up with his spare underpants. When the pan boiled he poured the water into a bucket and topped it up with cold. Then he stuck his head in, added shampoo, and washed his hair. There was a lot of it. Both he and Tam seemed to be involved in some kind of competition to see who could grow their hair longest. I didn't know when they'd given up having it cut: probably the day they left school, whenever that was. It was all to do with their head-banger image. Now they were both 'long-haired', although Tam was clearly in the lead, which apparently dismayed Richie. His constant complaint against the world was that his hair had slowed down growing as soon as he stopped having it cut. He wanted his hair to be even longer to go with the electric guitar he couldn't play yet. If they'd lived in the dark ages they would have been Vikings. But they weren't. They were itinerant fencers. And on Friday nights, wherever they were, they washed their hair.

After washing, Richie towelled himself dry. Now came the

final part of the routine. First, he put on his denim jacket. Next he bent down, throwing his hair forward and then quickly straightening up again, at the same time flicking his head back, so that his hair fell over his shoulders like a lion's mane. He went to all this trouble because it was Friday night.

Now it was Tam's turn. He repeated the whole procedure, his head disappearing in a blur when he towelled himself dry at the end. I noticed for the first time that Tam had a tattoo on his forearm. It consisted of a diagonal flag and a scroll bearing the words, 'I'm a Scot'. However, the tattooist hadn't really left himself enough room, so the words actually read 'I mascot'.

When Tam and Richie had changed their jeans and put on their cowboy boots they considered themselves to be 'ready'. Now that the bucket was free, I got some water boiled and began to have a shave. There was a mirror halfway up the door of the caravan wardrobe, and every time I looked in it to see how the shave was going I could see Tam sitting on his bunk, watching, and waiting.

'I can't shave any faster,' I said.

'I don't know why you bother,' he remarked.

Richie had picked up his copy of *An Early Bath for Thompson* by A. D. Young, and started reading again.

'What's that about then?' I asked.

'Don't know,' he replied. 'I haven't finished it yet.'

It was half past seven before I was ready to leave.

'If we're going to be drinking all night Rich'll have to drive,' I said.

'Alright,' said Richie, without further comment, and we set off for a wonderful evening at the Queen's Head.

I was interested to see if Tam and Richie would do anything

different tonight, considering all the trouble they'd just gone to with their hair and so on. I was surprised, therefore, when they went and sat at our usual table in the corner. I'd have thought it would be better to hang round the bar if they wanted to get anywhere with the two women who had been ignoring them all week. Instead their technique was to sit behind their pints and wait to see what happened. All night if necessary. When we got there at ten to eight there was hardly anybody in, so the wait was going to be a long one. The place did eventually fill up, though, and even had a weekend feel to it. I suspected I would be incapable of drinking the amount Tam and Richie planned to, so I dropped out after the first three rounds and went and put my name up for the darts knockout. It would make a change, and I could talk to other people. Furthermore, there was a higher ratio of women in this part of the pub. I'd just positioned myself by the bar when the landlord, who had glanced our way a couple of times during the evening, suddenly turned to me and said, 'How's the fencing going?'

There was something odd about this. Over the last few days he'd ceased questioning us about 'what we were getting up to' and started treating us like normal customers. Now, however, he seemed to have reverted to his previous ways. Except that there was a slight difference in his tone. It was almost as if the question was directed to me, but actually meant for somebody else's ears. If any heads turned as he spoke, I didn't notice. I just said something like 'Not too bad really' and carried on watching the darts game. After a while I glanced over towards Tam and Richie, wondering if they'd heard the brief conversation. It appeared they hadn't, for they were now isolated in their corner, cut off from the central attraction, namely the darts knockout, by a knot of standing drinkers. Tam and Richie just stayed there with their pints. I also noted that the two regular women who had been the original attraction to this pub finally turned up with men who were obviously their husbands. I got through the first round of the darts knockout OK, but failed to survive the second. The victor and I both said 'bad luck' and 'well done' at the same time, shook hands (each attempting to crush the other's bones), and then I bought him the obligatory pint.

I made my way back through the throng to Tam and Richie.

'You got beat then,' said Tam.

'Yes, thanks,' I replied.

Judging by all the empty glasses on the table they'd had a good night. They were both yawning a lot, which I regarded as an encouraging sign, because the sooner I could get them home, the better would be the chance of getting them up to work in the morning. There was still time for another drink before closing, however, and so, inevitably, we had one.

'This is shite,' said Tam. 'There's no women.' This wasn't in fact the case. There were quite a few women in the pub this evening. I knew what he meant though.

'We'll have to go into town tomorrow night,' he added.

'Right,' I said. 'I'll look forward to that.'

Eventually we were turfed out into the night. I handed Richie the keys to the truck and tried not to think too hard about the journey home. He didn't seem to have any trouble getting out of the car park, so I left him to it. Tam had fallen silent just before we left the pub, but now, as we got going, he spoke at last.

'What did the landlord say to you?'

'When?'

'Up at the bar, you were talking to him during the darts.'

'Oh nothing,' I said. 'Nothing. He just asked how the fencing was going, that's all.'

'Why did he want to know that?' he asked.

'Dunno,' I replied.

'You do really,' said Tam.

'No I don't.'

'You do.'

'Look,' I said. 'I don't know what you're talking about.'

'There were some guys staring at us,' said Richie.

'Were there?' I said. 'I didn't notice.'

'Hall Brothers,' said Tam.

'What?'

'That's who it was.'

'How do you know that?' I asked.

'I just do that's all.'

'But it could have been anybody.'

Tam turned and looked at me. 'Why were they staring at us then?'

'I don't know.'

'Because they've heard we're here!' And with that he put his arm out through the open window and banged on the cab roof with his fist. Richie, who was driving quite well for someone containing almost a gallon of beer, took no notice of the disturbance and drove us home.

By the time we got back Tam had stopped going on about the Hall Brothers and slumped into oblivion. I was hoping this would be him out for the rest of the night, but when we were manhandling him into the caravan he came round and insisted on having a fag. He also lit the portable gas fire. The weather had been getting chilly over the last week and there was nothing unusual about doing this. The problem was that he had a habit of sitting right up close to the fire and then dozing off. A couple of times already he'd come close to catching alight, and I'd had to shout to wake him up. Now he was guarding the fire jealously and could not be persuaded to turn it off until he was warm.

Richie said, 'Might as well leave him,' and went to bed. Eventually I did the same, hoping Tam wouldn't burn us all to death.

In the middle of the night there was a crash. I came awake aware that Tam's end of the caravan was glowing red from the firelight. Tam himself was now on the floor between his bed and the sink. I got up and turned the gas off. Then, at last, we all slept.

When I woke up next morning I realized that, like Tam and Richie, I didn't like working on Saturdays much either. My head was throbbing from the drink. Worse, there was rain falling on the caravan roof. To people who work outside all day this is one of the most desolate sounds known. Rain can transform the most pleasant task into drudgery. The only reason we had managed to keep the job just about on schedule (more or less), was because the weather had stayed dry. Now we faced a muddy, soaking wet struggle from the moment we went out in the morning until the end of the day. And, of course, the squalor inside the caravan would reach new depths, with wet clothing hanging everywhere and mud on the floor. All we had to dry us off was the gas fire. I lay on my bed thinking about this and wondering how I was going to motivate Tam and Richie to get up.

Nevertheless, if we were ever going to get away from Upper Bowland the job was going to have to be completed, sooner or later. We would just have to get on with it. I got up and managed some breakfast, hoping to stir Tam and Richie into life. There was little sign of movement, so I decided to go and collect our wages from the sub-post office, where they should have arrived by now. I got back about quarter to ten and found them sitting on their bunks, smoking, and apparently ready for work. The settling of Tam's debts turned out to be less difficult than I had expected. Inside the registered letter (addressed to me) were three separate pay packets. Figures were written on the outsides, in Donald's handwriting, explaining the various deductions. Tam's packet was noticeably thinner than mine or even Richie's.

We all opened up and checked the contents. Tam seemed to accept straight away that his would be less than ours. Richie, meanwhile, was folding his notes with an awkward gesture before putting them in his jeans pocket (at the back, not the one he kept his lighter in.)

Tam looked at me, grinned, and said, 'Fuck it . . . c'mon then, what am I due you?'

I told him and he counted out the sum.

After a dutiful pause Richie spoke, 'You're due me some too.'

'It's alright, Rich,' replied Tam. 'What was it again?'

'Just give me what you can,' said Richie.

'No, no, I'll pay in full,' Tam insisted.

'Er . . . OK, then.' And Richie told Tam the bad news.

'Fuck me, I'm back where I started,' said Tam, handing Richie his entire wedge apart from some coins.

'Never mind. I'll lend you some until next week,' promised Richie. And he did, there and then, on the spot.

A thought then occurred to Tam. 'What about your guitar instalments, Rich?'

'It came out of my mother's catalogue,' replied Richie. 'She's going to pay them till I get back.'

So that was alright.

When they had their breakfast Tam asked me if he could possibly have a lend of my can opener for their beans.

Yes, I said, just this once he could.

Eventually, on that dismal autumn Saturday, we dragged our-selves into the rain to do some work. I was lucky in that at least I had a full set of waterproofs. Richie had just the top half of his, but didn't seem the slightest bit bothered about his jeans getting soaked, and probably wouldn't have worn the water-proof bottoms even if he had had them. That just left Tam, who only had his leather jacket. He'd bought this new sometime in the summer, and hadn't originally intended to work in it. However, at some stage he had caught sight of a friend's jacket that had seen a few seasons on a motorcycle, and decided that his own didn't look worn enough. It was too crisp and shiny for his liking. So he started 'wearing it in' at work, deliberately scuffing it against things, and generally treating it roughly. As a result, now that the autumn rains were here, it was already showing signs of falling to pieces. As a waterproof it was next to useless. Still, he persevered with it for the time being as he had nothing else.

We continued work on the cross fence as best we could while the rain showed no sign of letting up. By mid-afternoon, however, discussions about posts and wire began to be interrupted by talk of 'tonight', even though I for one was still feeling the after-effects of the night before. Richie had taken over the post hammer again, and this time I was his assistant while Tam did the fetching and carrying. I asked Richie how his hangover was.

He looked at me. 'What hangover?'

'Haven't you got one then?' I said. I could tell by his expression that he had no idea what I was talking about, so I abandoned the conversation.

On one of Tam's trips he seemed to take longer than usual to return, and we began to wonder what had happened to him. Finally, coming up the slope carrying a load of posts, we spotted what appeared to be a fertilizer sack on legs. It laid the posts out along the fence, ignoring us completely, and retreated down the hill again. Shortly afterwards the figure returned with another load. By this time Richie and I were having difficulty concentrating on what we were doing. Tam had evidently got fed up with being soaked through and decided to make himself a 'waterproof' out of a heavy duty plastic fertilizer sack he'd found under a seat in the truck. He'd cut holes for his arms and head, while his legs protruded out of the open end. He had made the neck hole as small as possible to prevent water getting in, and then forced his head through without bothering to untrap his hair, so that it resembled a medieval helmet.

In this guise Tam marched up to where me and Richie stood looking.

'Something funny?' he said.

'No, no,' replied Richie.

'Well get on with your work then,' he snapped.

We obeyed, and he set off down the hill again. Shortly after this incident Richie lost control of the post hammer during a particularly violent swing, and I decided it was time to swap jobs.

And so we slogged on, spending our Saturday afternoon working on a drenched hillside, until we had had enough. Then we followed the line of posts to the bottom of the hill, and walked round to where the truck was waiting. The three of us sat in the cab for a few minutes while Tam and Richie had their first 'dry' fag for several hours, and then I started the engine and we trundled slowly back down the track towards the caravan. We were just about to turn into the farmyard when our eyes fell on something that hadn't been there this morning. Along the side of the track, from the farmyard to the front gate, someone had built a brand new fence. It was strong and straight, and the wires gleamed in the half light of dusk.

'Where the fuck did that come from?' said Richie.

Tam stamped his feet. 'The Hall Brothers have been here!' he announced.

'You don't know that for sure,' I replied, but I suspected he was right.

'Bet it was them,' he said. 'Let's have a look.'

We got out of the truck and examined the mystery fence. It was a smart, classy job. The style was different to ours: they'd used mild steel netting instead of high-tensile wires. Also, the posts were round in cross-section, whereas we always worked with square ones. But we could not fault the fence itself. It was perfectly straight, the wire was tight, and the posts were firm in the ground.

'Look at this,' said Richie.

He had come across a silver tag attached to one of the posts, indented with some lettering: HALL BROS.

So now we knew.

6

'Told you it was them!' shouted Tam. He was practically dancing around.

'There must be four of them,' said Richie.

Yes, I thought, there must indeed be four of them. How else could they have got the job done so quickly? Not only had they built this new fence, but they had also demolished the old ruined one that was there beforehand, and taken away all the scrap timber and wire. What was most disconcerting though, was that they had been here while we'd been working away up on that hill, and we had never even known. All that rain had meant the cloudbase was very low and we'd been more or less cut off from the rest of the world all day. Furthermore, this was the first time we hadn't come down off the hill for lunch. Usually we trooped back at midday for a rest, even though it went against Donald's Code of Practice (he said it was an inefficient waste of time). Today, however, because we started late, we took sandwiches with us. (If you could call them sandwiches, that is. Richie made them. Pieces of bread separated by cheese would be a better description.) We'd loaded up the truck with enough posts and wire for a day's work, and hadn't returned since. That was, what? Seven hours. And now here was a shiny new fence, built out of the blue while our backs were turned. The confounded cheek of these people! The Hall Brothers had acted as if they owned the place. What if we'd come back and caught them at it? They must have known we were around: there was a huge stack of timber and stuff right nearby in the farmyard. And what was Mr Perkins doing hiring two sets of contractors to work on one farm? Playing the field? I suppose the Hall Brothers had as much right to be there as we did, but even so, it was three distracted fencers who sat brooding in the caravan that evening. It seemed to have affected Tam a great deal, and he was full of speculation.

'Do you think they get paid more, or less, than us because there's four of them?' he asked.

'I don't know,' I replied.

'Because if they divide the money up four ways there'll be less each, but they can get more done at a time, so there's more to divide.'

'We don't even know if there are four,' I said.

'Oh, it'll be four alright. Four brothers.'

'You certain about that?'

'They always come in fours,' he said. 'With a year between them.'

'It could be three brothers and their father,' I suggested.

'No,' he replied. 'That would be Hall and Sons.'

Now Richie joined in. 'How come Donald can afford to send us all the way down here and still make a profit, when people like the Hall Brothers are around?'

'It's all a question of scale,' I explained. 'We're doing a big project fencing off the whole of that hill. The Hall Brothers' fence is only a short little thing, isn't it?'

Nods of approval.

'They probably don't even know how to do high-tensile fencing,' I went on. 'We're supposed to be specialists, after all.'

This seemed to satisfy Tam and Richie. Following all that questioning, it was a relief when the conversation reverted to the usual talk of going out, and Tam asked me when I was getting ready. I decided it would be a good idea to avoid the Queen's Head tonight. Besides which, Tam and Richie had been making it clear they'd like to go back to that last town we passed through on the way down. Donald didn't really like us to go too far afield in the truck, but I thought, 'How will he know?'

Anyway, we could easily stick a couple of extra gallons of diesel in the truck to cover the mileage. So I pre-empted them and suggested going into town. As long as Richie drove. Again he showed not the slightest objection, so it was agreed. Tam had by now removed his fertilizer bag, so we put the pan on to boil and repeated last night's performance with the bucket, one after the other, until we were all ready to go out. As we left the farm we tried to splatter some mud on the Hall Brothers' new fence.

We found a few good pubs that night, but unfortunately Tam and Richie didn't have the patience to remain in any of them more than the length of time it took to drink one pint. On this occasion they forgot to mention that the beer was weak, even though it came from the same brewery as the Queen's Head. The whole population of the town seemed to be on the move. Just the same as any other English small town on a Saturday night. There were crowds of people herding from one pub to another like wildebeest in the rainy season. With us three following them. After a few hours in this town we almost knew our way round. We'd also found out that the 'big deal' here was a night club called Carmens (Saturdays and Wednesdays). There were flyers advertising it all over the place, and we also heard it mentioned in various pubs.

'That's where we'll go,' said Tam, as we sat in the Six Bells.

'Not tonight,' I said.

'Why not?' Tam and Richie both looked at me in disbelief.

''Cos we've got to work tomorrow,' I replied.

'Fuck work,' said Tam.

'We'll come Wednesday,' I heard myself say, and they accepted the offer. Shortly after that we managed to lose Richie. I'm not sure how it happened, but one minute he was trailing along behind me and Tam, then suddenly he was gone. I suspect he dodged up a side alley for a slash without saying anything, and it had taken longer than he expected to get mobile again, by which time he'd lost us. Tam was most agitated when we discovered that Richie was missing, and wanted to trace our steps back to every pub we'd visited during the evening. I pointed out that it would make just as much sense looking in all the pubs we hadn't tried yet. No, I argued, it would be better staying put in one pub until he found us. We tried this for a while, but Tam went to the doorway and looked out so many times that in the end I got fed up and agreed to go in search of Richie.

'Maybe he's gone to Carmens,' I suggested.

Tam looked at me. 'On his own?' he said.

I thought about this. 'No, I suppose not,' I conceded.

Eventually we found him sitting in the truck, on his own, in the dark.

'I've been here an hour,' he complained.

I had hoped that the reunion would have the necessary calming effect on Tam, but both he and Richie were so bothered at having lost all that valuable drinking time that I knew there would be no peace until we got to another pub. We just made it as normal drinking hours came to an end, in a pub that was obviously on the wildebeest circuit, judging by the press of excited bodies. Everybody in town, apparently, was going to Carmens. As usual Tam and Richie did nothing to make contact with any women in the vicinity and merely sat side by side on a bench holding their pints.

Before we could go home Tam insisted on getting fish and chips. By the time he'd queued and got served the beer had begun to affect his judgement, so he ordered all the extras and came out of the shop with enough chips for several men.

We stood outside on the pavement, swaying on that Saturday night in a bleak and windy small town street. Opposite the chippie was a parade of other shops, all with their shutters pulled down. The shop we all noticed was the one with the big sign across the front: HALL BROTHERS QUALITY MEATS.

'For fuck sake, they're fucking butchers as well!' yelled Tam, hurling his spare chips across the street.

Getting up for work on Sunday morning was even worse than Saturday. The rain had eased up into a drizzle, which meant never being sure whether it was worth wearing waterproofs or not. If you did wear them, you sweated so much that you still ended up wet through anyway. This was a problem only for me, of course. Richie's work jeans were still wet from yesterday because he'd forgotten to dry them over the gas fire. He went ahead and wore them all the same, and sat eating his cornflakes with steam slowly rising from his legs. Tam opted for the fertilizer bag again. We were sitting in the caravan trying not to think about going out in the wet. The carpet was damp since there was nowhere to put our boots outside the door, so we'd started wearing them inside as well. The fire was flickering because Tam had lit his fags off it so many times that the gauze was burnt through and didn't glow evenly. As soon as we went outside we knew we'd have water trickling down our necks for the rest of the day. And we still had the biggest part of the job ahead of us. The cross-fence would be finished sometime today, once we got all the wires pulled out and tightened up. After that we had to build a long fence encircling the foot of the hill, to close off the four quarters we'd made. There were also a number of gates to hang, so that stock could be moved between the different areas. I decided to complete the cross-fence, and then work our way round the foot of the hill, section by section.

It was about ten before we got going properly, which I suppose was not bad for a Sunday morning. But we all seemed to be running out of energy. I stood by the unwinder and watched it as Tam towed yet another wire up the hill. Slowly and sporadically it turned as he made his way up and over the summit. It stopped. Then it continued a few turns. Then it stopped again. I waited. I guessed that Tam must have met Richie, who was working back the other way fixing the previous wire onto the posts. I wondered how long I should give them to exchange greetings. After a minute I grabbed the wire and gave it a jerk. The unwinder started to turn again. Then it stopped. I came to the conclusion that they must be having a fag. It was at such times that I seriously considered taking up smoking myself, just to pass the time.

In this haphazard way we progressed into the afternoon, and started work on the long encircling fence.

Which is when Richie managed, inevitably I suppose, to break the post hammer. My fault again. I should have insisted Tam did all the post driving. After all, as I said before, he was best at it. Specialization would have been more efficient: Richie digging, Tam hammering, and me supervising (and doing joinery). But somehow Richie had got hold of the post hammer again, and begun to get over-confident. I watched in slow motion as he brought the shaft down full whack on top of a post, so that the head broke off with a loud crack.

'Fuck,' he said, but I think he was more concerned about what Tam would say than about the damage to the hammer itself. That was my problem. We still had quite a few posts to knock in along this section before it could be wired up. Now I was going to have to find Tam and Richie other things to do while I went and got the hammer repaired. This involved seeking out a joiner's shop (there wouldn't be one open until Monday), leaving the hammer for repair, and then going back for it. Yes, I know we should have had a spare hammer with us, but you can't cover every contingency. Mending it ourselves was out of the question. The shaft had to fit perfectly, and I'd seen for myself many times before the consequences of working with a badly repaired post hammer. No. The job had to be done by a proper joiner who knew what he was doing.

Just then Tam came walking along the fence line. He took one look at the broken hammer and said, 'Ha. Call yourself a fencer?'

'Don't look at me,' I replied.

Tam glanced at Richie, who was reaching for something in his shirt pocket, and said no more about it.

7

An air of gloom hung over our camp when we returned that evening. I could really have done without this. While the post hammer was broken we would have to spend all our time digging holes for straining posts. This meant Tam and Richie having to work separately, and I'd already found that they coped much better when they were in sight of each other. (Even though they stopped for a fag break every time their paths crossed.) There was the possibility of having them work two-to-a-hole, but this was another practice which Donald had banned as inefficient. I could see there was a danger of work grinding to a halt unless I could get the post hammer repaired quickly. The weather wasn't helping matters either. It had now settled into what I call mizzle, and it was getting dark slightly earlier every day.

The thing I wasn't in the mood for was a discussion about what we were doing tonight, and Tam and Richie seemed to sense this. We sat in our three corners of the caravan, serenaded by Richie's stretching tape. All around me was encroaching squalor. Fortunately, much of it was hidden because the gas lights were so dim. Which is why, presumably, Richie had now abandoned *An Early Bath for Thompson*. Night after night he'd struggled with it, holding the book in all manner of positions under his lamp as he tried to have a read. Finally he gave up and shoved it back in the cupboard where it came from.

'What a fucking way to spend a Sunday night,' he said.

All this set the pattern for the next few days. Having given Tam and Richie some very specific tasks I went off the following morning in search of a joiner. All I had for guidance was Donald's photocopied road map. I was reluctant to go all the way back into town, so I set off in the other direction, hoping to come across somewhere suitable. Yes, not far along the road I would find a workshop, a busy efficient place where there would just happen to be a craftsman at a loose end who could fix the post hammer right away. Some hope. I drove for miles and found nothing. Eventually, after a bit of asking round, I was directed to some lock-up premises at one end of a converted bakery. Apparently they were let to a joiner who did most of his work elsewhere, but I might catch him if I was lucky. I wasn't. A sign on the door said he would be back later. I put a note through the letterbox saying I'd left a broken post hammer behind the dustbin and could he fix it please? I didn't have time to do anything else. On the way back I stopped at the general store to get some more food and stuff, and then returned to find Tam and Richie sitting in the caravan. They'd taken an early lunch.

'I'd have thought you'd want to get the job done as soon as possible so we can get home,' I said.

'Why should we do all the work while you go riding round in the truck?' said Tam.

'I had to get the post hammer fixed,' I pointed out.

'That's not work,' he replied.

The evenings, meanwhile, were spent deciding what time we would go to the pub. If we went too early, all our money would be spent on beer. While this was alright in itself, I for one wanted to have something left when we'd finished the job. Otherwise there was little point in going through all this hardship. Besides, Tam was deep in debt to Richie again, and couldn't really afford to go anywhere. On the other hand, there was no question of not going to the pub in the evening. If we didn't, we would go crazy with boredom. Things were quiet in the Queen's Head on weekdays, but it beat the caravan hands down for entertainment value.

On Tuesday night, by way of diversion, we went off to see if the post hammer was ready. In darkness we pulled up at the end of the converted bakery and Richie went over to the dustbin. In the glare of the headlights I witnessed a smile appear on his face as he raised a newly repaired hammer triumphantly above his head. Miracles can and do happen. We looked in the dustbin and felt inside the letterbox for an invoice, but there wasn't one.

And so another day passed and the long fence slowly grew around the foot of that hill. The next light at the end of the tunnel was Wednesday night at Carmens. I didn't mention it at all to Tam and Richie, but I could tell during Wednesday afternoon that expectations were beginning to rise again. Now that the post hammer was back in action, guarded closely by Tam, we were able to work in a tight three-man squad, section by section, along the fence. About four o'clock, as an incentive, I told Tam and Richie that we would finish the bit we were on and pack up for the night. I never saw them work so fast. Half an hour later they were back in the caravan with the pan boiling and the shampoo at the ready. Somehow it had been 'agreed' that I would drive tonight, so I resigned myself to an evening of Cokes. I wanted to shave first though, and was forced to go through the ritual under scrutiny from Tam and Richie, impatiently watching in the mirror.

At last I could delay no more, so we headed into town. As usual, we arrived far too early. There were no droves of people herding from pub to pub tonight. Like most other towns in England, the place had gone back to sleep for the week. We spent a long slow evening waiting for something to happen. It was only as closing time approached that people began to appear who were obviously going on somewhere else afterwards. That somewhere was Carmens Nightspot, to give it its full title. It turned out to be not as glamorous as it sounded. But it would do. At the top of some stairs we paid our money and they let us in. There was a bar at one side and a dance floor at the other. I was still getting my bearings in the gloom when a girl poked my arm and said, 'Got a light?'

'Er, no, sorry,' I replied. 'He has,' I added, pointing to Richie. I got his attention and he obliged by fishing his lighter out of his jeans. Apart from drinking bottled, instead of draught, beer, Tam and Richie did what they always did when I was out with them. They found somewhere to sit and watch what was going on, and stayed there. They probably thought they'd chosen a good place because it was near the bar and in sight of the dance floor. However, I got the feeling that if the club got any busier people would soon be tripping over their legs, which were sticking out from under a tiny table. There was already no room for me, so I positioned myself by a railing above the dance floor. During the next couple of hours I occasionally glanced over to where they sat. Except for taking turns to go to the bar and the gents, they never moved at all. Meanwhile, a small forest of club people grew around them, so that they slowly became lost from view, apart from the tops of their heads. The music was loud and the dance floor full. I watched for a while and then went to get myself another Coca-Cola. The bar was crowded, and as I stood there I felt the unmistakable shape of a female breast being pushed into my back. I half turned and saw the lighter girl standing behind me.

'Oh hello,' she said. 'Didn't see you there.'

Her name was Marina. She was a dentist's receptionist.

'You were in the Six Bells on Saturday, weren't you?' she said. 'With your two mates. Where are they?'

I nodded towards where I last saw Tam and Richie. 'Over there.'

'They look quite sweet,' she said.

This was the longest conversation we had. It was far too loud for much talking. When the music slowed down a bit we went onto the dance floor, and she let her feelings be known. This was one of those clubs where things came to an end pretty quickly. We were still on the dance floor when the music stopped and all the lights came on.

Something that had been lurking at the back of my mind now surged to the front. If I was going to go home with this girl, then I was going to have to drop Tam and Richie off first. Which meant she would have to sit on one of them in the truck. I put it off as long as possible, but finally, as the place began to empty, I casually strolled with Marina over to Tam and Richie's table.

'This is Tam and Richie,' I said. 'And this is Marina.'

They looked at us with glazed expressions. Tam stood up and swayed towards me.

'We going now then?' he said.

'Er . . . yes. See you outside in a minute,' I replied.

'C'mon, Rich.' Tam pulled Richie by his jacket and the two of them lurched out through the door.

'We'll have to drop them off at Upper Bowland,' I explained to Marina.

'OK then,' she said. I must admit she handled it all very well. She had to go to the ladies' room first, so I waited at the top of the stairs.

When she came out we walked up the road to where I'd parked the truck, but there was no sign of Tam and Richie. We spent a pleasant fifteen minutes sitting in the cab, waiting for them to show up. I wondered where they'd gone. Tam and Richie had been drinking since eight o'clock and it was getting late. A public clock chimed twice. We waited a bit longer.

And then, from somewhere in the middle of this now silent town, we heard a faint roar in the night. 'C'mon, English bastards!'

I started the engine and took the girl home.

8

Marina lived in a small flat above a shoe shop.

'Very nice,' I said, as we went in.

'It's only temporary,' she replied.

She was supposed to be making coffee, but somehow we never got round to it. Not long afterwards we entered the bedroom, where I noticed there were two single beds, each with a cabinet covered in women's things.

'Whose is that?' I asked, pointing to the extra bed.

'My flatmate's,' said Marina. 'She's staying at a friend's tonight.'

'That's handy,' I remarked.

'Yes,' she said, 'I suppose it is.'

I looked at her and realized that underneath her clothes she was completely naked. A few minutes later we lay quietly on the bed, and it felt as if I was alone with this girl on a remote and distant planet.

Then I remembered Tam and Richie.

'Not quite alone,' I heard myself say.

'Pardon?' she said.

'Sorry, nothing,' I answered, but the spell was broken. There wasn't much room in the bed and I hardly got any sleep.

In the morning Marina had to go to work and there was no breakfast. As we parted she said, 'I'm not a fence post, you know.'

I wasn't sure what she meant by that.

I went and bought some doughnuts in a cake shop. I had no idea where Tam and Richie could have got to, and wasn't sure what to do. I was reluctant to phone up Donald and tell him I'd lost them. Somehow I expected to see them at any minute, still wandering around the streets, possibly looking for me, but more likely waiting for the pubs to open again. I patrolled the town for a while, but they were nowhere to be seen. In deep thought I drove back to Upper Bowland. I dismissed the idea that Tam and Richie might have found their own way there. They had shown no interest in local geography since their arrival in England, and as far as I knew had hardly any money left. I was therefore surprised to find them both asleep in the caravan, fully clothed, Richie on his bed and Tam on mine. They stirred as I went inside, but I didn't wake them. For some reason I felt slightly indebted to them, and as soon as I saw them lying there asleep I decided to give them the day off.

I made myself some eggs for breakfast and after a while they woke.

'Morning,' I said.

'Do you have to say that every day?' replied Tam.

'What?' I asked.

'Mor-ning,' he said, in a sing-song sort of voice.

'It's fucking sarcastic, isn't it,' added Richie.

'Sorry,' I said.

They didn't seem very grateful when I said they could have the day off. I thought they would appreciate the gesture. I also hoped that they might get bored after a while and get round to cleaning up the mess in the caravan, or even decide to come and do some work on the fence after all. In the event they did none of these things. They just stayed in the caravan all day long, smoking, and waiting for me to come back so we could go out again.

In the meantime I spent the day working on my own, putting a couple of straining posts in the ground, and doing a bit of joinery. Around mid-afternoon I decided to walk over the hill, checking the two cross-fences, measuring them, and making sure we hadn't forgotten to do anything.

It was then that I found we had a visitor. I was just testing the wire tension near the top of the hill when I saw a man coming along the fence from the other end. For a moment I thought Mr Perkins had come to have a look, but I soon realized that this was someone altogether different. I'd only seen Mr Perkins in the darkness, but I knew this wasn't him. The visitor was a very big man in a rustic suit, and reminded me of a large pig. He appeared to be giving the fence a thorough examination as he walked along, tugging on the occasional wire and pushing the posts to see if they moved. When he got to the point where the two fences crossed he stopped. There were no gates up here because there was no need for any. All the gates were to be positioned at points around the foot of the hill, so his way was effectively barred. I registered the exact moment he noticed me as he looked left and then right, but he failed to give any acknowledgement. It was as if I was a mere fixture or fitting. He just carried on studying the details of the fence.

However, my presence was enough to prevent him from attempting to climb over, which I think he would have done if I hadn't been there. Instead, he stayed where he was, and ignored me as I approached. At last I stood directly opposite him at the other side of the fence. Only then did he look at me.

'Keeping busy?' he said.

'Just about,' I replied.

'That's good.' He turned sideways and stared out across the hillside. I waited. Then he looked at the sky.

'Met Perkins?' he asked.

'Only once,' I said.

'Don't talk to me about Perkins.'

In the awkward silence that followed he again began to examine the fence, frowning with preoccupation and glancing at me from time to time. Finally, he cast his eye along the line of posts.

'Exemplary,' he remarked, and began stalking off down the hill.

'And you're Mr . . . ?' I called after him.

'Hall,' he said over his shoulder. 'John Hall.'

I stood by the fence absorbing this information. At last I had come face to face with one of the Hall Brothers, but I still had no idea why he was so interested in our fence. It struck me that he didn't really look like a fencer at all. He was certainly a heavily built man, but a lot of it was fat. Somehow I just couldn't picture him digging post holes or swinging the post hammer. I wondered what the other brothers were like. Maybe it was them who built the fences and he was the brains behind the organization. Perhaps his brothers were big too, but more solid. Like barn doors. I realized that I was beginning to specu-late like Tam, so I put Mr Hall out of my mind and carried on with my work. The weather had dried up, but was beginning to turn cool, and as dusk came a chilly breeze started to blow across the hillside. Finally I made my way back to the caravan.

When I'd gone down for my lunch Tam and Richie had been lolling about on their beds, passing the time doing nothing. Now, however, they sat looking out of the window, evidently awaiting my return. They'd even gone to the trouble of putting the kettle on.

As soon as I went into the caravan Richie said, 'There was a guy snooping round here this afternoon.'

'Was there?' I said, pretending not to be very interested.

'Big, fat fucker,' added Tam.

When I showed no reaction, Richie stood up and pulled a note out of his back pocket. 'He left this for you.'

The note was folded into four. I opened it and read 'See you here at eight o'clock.' It was signed J. Hall.

I glanced at Tam and Richie. They were both staring hard at me. It was obvious they must have read the note, but I said nothing and folded it up again. At last Tam could contain himself no longer. He leapt to his feet and shouted at the top of his voice, 'They're coming to get us!'

In doing so he somehow managed to smash the gas lamp at his end of the caravan, so that bits of glass flew everywhere, including into the waiting teapot.

'Alright, alright,' I said. 'We don't know what they want, do we?'

'Don't be a cunt,' said Richie. 'You know why they're coming.'

Tam stuck his face in mine. 'YAAAAAAAAAAAAAH!!' he cried. 'YAAAAAAAAH!' After he'd calmed down a bit I got him to clear up the glass and I had my tea. Then we began to wait for eight o'clock. I had been planning to go down to the phone box this evening to give Donald a progress report, but decided under the circumstances that it was better to defer the call for the time being. At half past seven I put some water on to have a shave. I didn't see why I should change my arrangements just because someone said they were coming at eight o'clock. As usual Tam and Richie watched the whole process. At ten to eight there was nothing left to do but sit and wait. Eight o'clock finally came and nothing happened. At ten past, however, some headlights swung up the track from the road. All three of us had our boots on, so we stepped out of the caravan into the yard. A moment later a large car appeared and drove up to where we stood.

Mr Hall was already speaking as he opened the door and got out.

'Right,' he announced. 'I want you to do some fencing for me. When can you start?'

In the dim light cast from the caravan I noticed that the rustic suit had gone and he was now wearing a white coat. The sort worn by butchers. It took me a second to register what he had said.

'We can't,' I replied. 'We're already working for a company.'

Mr Hall then did what he had done on the hill in the afternoon, and completely ignored me.

'There's eight hundred yards to do by Monday, so the sooner you start the better,' he said. 'How much gold will you want for doing that?'

He thrust his hands in his coat pocket, looked at the ground and waited. I found myself looking at the ground as well.

'So?' he said.

I glanced up at him, thinking he would still be looking at the ground. Instead his eyes were fixed on me.

'We're working for somebody else,' I said.

At this moment I sensed that Tam wanted to say something, but he and Richie had both slipped into their usual silent routine, so it was all left to me.

'You'll have to do it as a foreigner,' said Mr Hall. 'Come on, we'll go for a drink.' He opened the back door of his car and indicated that the three of us should get in. Then he drove us to the Queen's Head. On the way out we rolled slowly past the new HALL BROS. fence, which he silently scrutinized from behind the wheel, post by post.

As we walked into the pub, the landlord was slouching over the bar reading a newspaper. The moment he saw Mr Hall he practically stood to attention. 'Evening, John,' he boomed. Likewise, several drinkers around the bar greeted Mr Hall by his first name, but in the same subservient way, as if doing so conferred some sort of honour on them. Meanwhile, Tam, Richie and myself were treated as if we were new disciples. One of the locals winked at us and tapped his nose significantly, after first glancing at Mr Hall to make sure he wasn't looking.

'Give these lads a pint apiece and rustle them up some grubbage,' ordered Mr Hall.

He turned to us. 'You haven't eaten, have you?'

We had, but we all shook our heads.

He led us over to our usual table in the corner and we sat down. The landlord bustled over with a tray bearing our drinks. Mr Hall, I noticed, was drinking orange squash.

'Everything alright, John?' said the landlord. I was surprised he didn't say Sir, or even King, John.

John Hall ignored him and sipped his squash. 'Bloody stuff,' he said.

The landlord retreated, and then there was an expectant silence, which I finally broke. 'Is that a butcher's coat?' I said.

'Yes it is,' he replied. 'We're butchers. Should have stayed that way as well.'

We nodded but said nothing, and he went on.

'Started as butchers and then we bought some land and raised our own beasts. Then we had too many beasts and had to buy more land and replace the fences. That's how we got into fencing, but we've taken on too much work.'

'Who does the fencing?' I asked.

'My brother,' he replied.

'What, on his own?'

Tam and Richie, who had been silently studying their pints, both looked up at Mr Hall.

'Course not,' he said. 'Got some lads in to do it, but they've gone off.'

The landlord came back, this time carrying three plates of steak and kidney pie.

'I've given them some of your specials, John,' he said.

'Yes, yes, alright,' snapped Mr Hall, and again the landlord retreated.

As we ate John Hall produced a large folded plan from his coat pocket and opened it on the table. I could see that it was a map of Mr Perkins's farm and the hill we were working on.

He chose a point on the hill and put his finger on it.

'This is where we stood,' he said. He took out a pencil and

wrote WE STOOD on the map. Then he swept his hand across the bottom corner.

'This land here's ours,' he said. 'And it needs a new boundary fence. Perkins says it's our responsibility. The lads did some the other day, but they've gone off now.'

He didn't explain why or where they'd gone. He folded the map and pushed it towards me.

'You'll have to do the rest,' he said.

'Does Mr Perkins know you've approached us?' I asked.

'None of his business,' he replied.

I made one more attempt to hold out. 'Our boss won't like it,' I said.

He raised his voice. 'What's the matter with you? You're getting beer, grubbage and cash in hand. What more could you want?'

A couple of people at the bar were now looking in our direction.

I turned to Tam and Richie. 'Alright?'

They both nodded.

'Alright then,' I said to Mr Hall. He grunted and ordered more drinks. So there I was, committed. Which meant we were going to be at Upper Bowland for even longer. I don't think Tam and Richie had thought about this part of the equation. All they were interested in was the cash Mr Hall was going to pay us. As soon as he'd dropped us off at the caravan they began talking as if we were going to land a windfall. They seemed to forget all the extra work we would have to do. Mr Hall was their benefactor, and after all the beer he'd bought them they would not have a word spoken against him.

'We'll be in trouble if Donald finds out,' I said.

'We won't tell him, will we?' replied Tam.

I supposed not. I had to admit the idea of a bit of extra cash in hand was attractive, and if we got stuck in over the weekend we could easily get the work done by Monday.

Even so, I had the usual trouble dragging them out of bed the following morning. We were supposed to meet Mr Hall's brother David along the road at eight o'clock. We needed to get going before that though because the first thing we had to do was go up onto the hill and get our tools. We got to the roadside meeting place on time, and the brother turned up at ten past eight in a small flatbed lorry loaded with posts and wire. He was like a slightly deflated version of John Hall, only much more cheerful. In fact he seemed to have a constant line of banter.

'Hoo hoo!' he chimed through the cab window as he pulled up. 'Beer and skittles, eh lads? Ha ha!'

Tam and Richie took to him instantly, even though he declined the offer of a fag. Personally I thought he went on a bit too much. He kept making jokes about fencing which involved parrying with an imaginary sword and shouting *en garde* every few minutes. As far as our sort of fencing was concerned, I was unable to picture him swinging a post hammer or digging holes. However, he was a pleasant enough bloke, and obliged us by driving the lorry slowly along the proposed fence line while Tam and Richie threw the posts off the back.

The fence itself looked like a straightforward enough piece of work. After David Hall had gone Tam went marching about chanting 'Easy! Easy!' at the top of his voice. He was right, it was easy. But it was also going to be a boring slog. We were used to building fences over sloping land and difficult terrain.

That was our speciality after all. This fence, though, just went on and on along the edge of the Hall Brothers' land. It was all flat. There were also a hell of a lot of posts to put in. Unlike the high-tensile fence we were building on the hill, this was a conventional wire-netting job. The posts had to be two yards apart to support the net, which meant there were four hundred of them! By the middle of the afternoon, knocking in post after post after post, the monotony was getting to us. Tam had taken to counting how many posts were already in, and how many were left to do. This seemed to make matters worse.

'That's one hundred and forty seven,' he would announce, as another post was completed. 'Three more and it's a hundred and fifty.'

And so on. I began to wonder if all this was really worth it. The only advantage I could see was that Tam would be solvent again when Mr Hall paid us on Monday. Which would take the pressure off me to keep providing subs, especially as now Richie was running short too, having himself lent so much to Tam. It suddenly struck me that we were expecting to get paid as soon as we finished the work. What if Mr Hall held out for a while before settling up? We hadn't thought of that. I didn't mention the possibility to Tam and Richie in case it affected their workrate. I didn't want them to lose their momentum so that we ended up with two uncompleted jobs on our hands. My suspicions deepened that evening when David Hall came by with several pounds of sausages for us. I hoped the Hall Brothers were not going to try to fob us off by paying us in kind. Tam and Richie, on the other hand, saw the sausages as a bonus, and when we got back to the caravan they began frying them for our tea. 'Did you have to cook the whole lot?'

I said, as Tam attended to a fully laden frying pan. He was stabbing the sausages one by one with a fork.

'Yah,' he said. 'There's plenty more where these came from.'

'You think so?'

'I know so. From now on it's gonna be beer and skittles for us.'

'You mean cakes and ale.'

Tam looked at me. 'I know what I fucking mean.'

It took us a while to recover from all those sausages, and the hard day's work, but we eventually made it to the Queen's Head, where the landlord stood us our first round of drinks and told us to call him Ron. It was as if our dealings with Mr Hall had bestowed on us some sort of special status. During the evening Tam and Richie were invited to make up the pub darts team, despite their having shown no previous interest in the game. I was left out, but I tried not to take this as a personal snub. When Tam rolled up his sleeves to play, I again looked at the words 'I mascot' tattooed on his arm. It came as no surprise that Tam's throwing was fairly accurate, while Richie's shots tended to be consistently wayward. It was a passable evening, but when we got home that night it was obvious that I was now the only one with any money left. And it was Saturday tomorrow.

I was wondering why Richie was taking such a long time to come back. This seemed to happen whenever I sent him off to do something. He was supposed to be working alone at the other end of Mr Hall's fence, stapling the wire netting onto the new line of posts, and should have finished the job ages ago. Eventually, I walked back to see what was going on, and found him knocking the staples in with a large stone. I observed this primitive scene for a moment, and then asked him where his hammer was.

He nodded towards the hill. 'Up there.'

'But we went up yesterday morning to get our tools,' I said.

'I didn't think I needed my hammer,' he replied.

'Why not?'

'Just didn't.' He stood holding the stone.

'Why didn't you borrow Tam's?' I asked.

'He lost his last week. He's been using mine ever since.'

'He lost his hammer?'

'Yep.'

I took my own hammer from my belt and handed it to Richie.

'Well, why didn't you ask me?' I said.

'I didn't think you'd lend me yours. You wouldn't let us borrow your can opener, would you?'

'That was different.'

In silence I walked back to where Tam was getting the next straining post dug in. He began working extra hard as I approached, and only stopped when I got right up to him.

'Any chance of a sub tonight?' he said, straightening up.

'How much?' I asked.

'Well, the usual, I suppose,' he replied.

'It's a loan, not a sub,' I said.

Tam nodded. 'That's OK.'

I was not particularly flush myself by now. Donald was being a bit tardy about getting the wages sent down. Still, I was doing all the business with Mr Hall, so as long as he paid up on time, I'd be able to recover my money from Tam. I therefore agreed to a further loan.

'Rich needs some as well,' he said.

'Have you lost your hammer?' I asked, changing the subject.

'How did you know that?' he said.

'I just guessed,' I replied.

There was a pause.

'Are you going to give Rich a sub then?' he asked.

'Yeah, I suppose so.'

'Right, I'll go and tell him.' Next thing he was marching off along the fence line. I watched as Tam and Richie met up in the distance. There was a moment's delay, and then Richie reached for something in his shirt pocket. A few seconds later a small cloud of smoke appeared above their heads.

Each section of Mr Hall's fence had to be finished off with a strand of barbed wire running along the top. Barbed wire was one of the worst materials I ever had to work with. It had a habit of curling off in its own direction if unrestrained, or of attaching itself to you like a spiky snake when you were trying to get it sorted out. It came in heavy coils that wouldn't fit on the unwinder. Instead they had to be rolled out along the ground before the wire could be tightened and fastened. All very awkward. The first section of netting was complete, so I asked Tam to start rolling out some barb. He selected a coil and began to examine it closely, looking for the end of the wire. When I looked across a minute later he was still there, peering intently at the coil and slowly turning it round. I stopped what I was doing and watched him. At last he called me over.

'This roll hasn't got an end,' he announced.

'It must have,' I replied.

'Show me then.' He stood back and I took over the examin-ation. Somewhere, hidden in all those multiple layers of wire, had to be an end. After several minutes I had to admit that I couldn't find it either. This was ridiculous. All of us had started off any number of rolls of barbed wire, and had never had this trouble before. Yet this particular one was, apparently, without an end. Just then Richie came walking along the fence.

'Got a fag, Rich?' said Tam.

'Not now!' I snapped. 'Let's get this coil started first.'

Richie said he would have a go, and began to study the coil. When he looked up from the puzzle and saw me and Tam watching him intently he got agitated and said he couldn't do it with us there. So we went off and worked on the next section. After a few minutes we saw Richie rolling the coil out along the fence line.

'You found it then?' I said.

'Of course,' he replied. 'Just needed a bit of perseverance, that's all.'

Later that afternoon we came to a part of the boundary that ran along a dense hedgerow. Tam and Richie were supposed to have laid all the pointed posts out when they were throwing them off the back of David Hall's lorry, but there was no sign of any along this section. I asked them where they were.

'They're over the other side of the hedge,' said Richie.

'What are they doing there?' I asked.

'We didn't know which side the fence was going.'

'Well, why didn't you ask?'

He shrugged. 'Couldn't be bothered.'

I sent them off to bring the posts back round to this side. In the meantime I began to set out a straight line for us to work along.

Tam and Richie had only been gone a few minutes when an irate voice spoke behind me.

'What's going on?'

9

I turned towards the newcomer. 'Pardon?'

'I said what's going on?' The man's face, I noticed, was pink. His voice seemed familiar.

'Mr Perkins?'

'You know it's Mr Perkins!' He appeared to be very angry about something.

'Anything wrong?' I asked.

'Don't give me that!' he said. 'You're supposed to be working on my hill! I've just been up there and you've abandoned the job! It's like the Retreat from Moscow!'

'Well,' I said. 'It's not quite like that.'

'Don't tell me what it's not quite like!!' he bellowed, taking a step towards me.

At that moment a post came flying over the hedge and struck him on the back of the head. He made a further step forward and fell into my arms. At the same time another post, and then another, came hurtling over.

'Who threw that?' I shouted.

'Me, Rich!' came the reply.

'Well, you'd better stop! You've just hit Mr Perkins!'

The posts stopped coming over. I looked at Mr Perkins. He'd

gone very quiet. In fact, he wasn't just quiet, he was dead. I leaned him upright against the hedge, and he sank slowly back into the foliage. After a while Tam and Richie appeared, both carrying pointed posts on their shoulders.

'We thought it would be quicker to throw them over,' said Tam.

'It probably is,' I replied. 'But you should be more careful. Look what Rich's done.'

Neither Tam nor Richie seemed to have noticed Mr Perkins standing in the hedgerow. When I nodded towards him they put down their posts and had a closer look.

'I didn't mean to do that,' said Richie.

'I know you didn't,' I said.

'What was he doing here?'

'He'd come to complain about something.'

All four of us stood there for a few moments.

'What are we going to do with him?' asked Tam.

'We'll have to bury him, I suppose.'

'But on his own land, not here,' suggested Richie.

'Good point,' I replied. 'We could put him under one of the new gateposts by the hill.' (Strictly speaking, we weren't quite ready to hang any gates yet, but under the circumstances it was probably worth bringing the work forward.)

'I could collect my hammer at the same time,' said Richie.

We decided to sit Mr Perkins in the front of the truck between me and Richie, with Tam riding in the back. However, when we came to move him we found he wouldn't bend into the correct position. So we put him in the back and drove him round to the bottom of the hill. All the proposed gateways had been marked out when Donald originally surveyed the job, so we chose the one we thought would be the most suitable for Mr Perkins and dug the post holes. After a short discussion we all agreed it was best to put him under the slamming post, rather than the hanging post, although none of us could come up with a particular reason why this should be so. Mr Perkins's gateway looked quite nice when it was finished, even though it wouldn't actually lead anywhere until the surrounding fences were complete.

As we put the gear back in the truck a thought occurred to me.

'He was dead, wasn't he?'

'I'm sure he was,' said Tam.

'What about his sheep?'

'They'll be alright.'

For some reason the conversation then came round to Mr McCrindle.

'I wonder what Donald's done about his account not being settled,' I said.

'He'll probably allow him three months' grace,' said Richie. 'That's what usually happens.'

'How do you know that?' I asked.

'I live on a farm don't I? They never pay their bills on time.'

We considered what might happen in Mr Perkins's case, and all agreed that his account would most likely be sent to his home address, and was therefore nothing to do with us.

All this put us a bit behind with Mr Hall's fence, so as soon as Richie had collected his hammer from up the slope, we went back down to the lower fields to get as much work done as possible before dark.

Later on, when we were back in the caravan, Tam said to me, 'Are you seeing your woman tonight, then?'

'No, don't think so,' I replied.

'Too much for you, was she?'

'Yeah. Too many hormones.'

'We'll go to the Queen's Head then?'

'Alright.' I didn't particularly want to run into Marina again, nice girl as she was. Neither was I in the mood for long debates about where we were going to spend Saturday night. So the Queen's Head suited me OK.

'How much money have we got left?' Tam went on.

'We?' I said.

He was beginning to regard me as some kind of bank. I took some notes from my back pocket.

'That's all there is until Mr Hall pays up,' I said.

'Bet you've got some more stashed away,' said Richie.

'That's got nothing to do with it,' I replied. 'This is all the cash I've got.'

'Third each,' said Tam.

'Well, that's it. After that, nothing, so don't come running to me.' I counted out a third each for Tam and Richie, and pocketed the remainder. 'Don't forget we've nearly run out of food too,' I added.

'Yah, we'll get something,' was all Tam had to say. I noticed there was no mention of skittles and beer.

All the same, we spent a moderate night in the pub. It seemed the message was finally getting through to Tam and Richie that the cupboard was bare. There was no free beer from any quarter this evening, and while the locals swilled at a rate appropriate for a Saturday night, Tam, Richie and me were forced to make each beer last an hour. Given the right conditions, this can be a very pleasant pastime. There is a certain art in allowing a newly poured pint of beer the correct amount of time to settle, and then savour every drop by drinking at a gentle pace. But this is only an enjoyable process when you can afford to buy another pint as soon as the previous one runs out. When it's forced upon you by economic necessity it can become a grim affair. Tam and Richie certainly didn't look as if they were enjoying their Saturday night much. It seemed a poor reward for all the work we'd done. Still, with a bit of luck, Mr Hall would come up with the money as soon as we finished his job. I suppose the alternative would have been just to drink at the normal rate until the cash ran out, and then go home. This would have meant going to bed about half past nine, which seemed a bit early. Instead, we eked out the evening as best we could, and hoped we would be able to summon the energy to finish off Mr Hall the next day.

It was a dull moment when I woke up the following morning and heard the returned sound of rain on the caravan roof. I lay there listening as the water trickled off the gutter. I knew Tam and Richie were awake because they were both moving around in their beds. The caravan was moving from the outside as well, which meant that the wind had got up in the night and was swaying us about. The occasional splash of rain against the window confirmed this. I turned over in my bed and stared at the carpet, still damp from the last rainy period we had had to endure. It was clear none of us wanted to get out of bed. Nevertheless, we had to do a lot of work today. I realized that there was only one way to get Tam and Richie sufficiently motivated.

'Ah well,' I said. 'Should get paid today.'

Murmurs came from under the covers.

'We'll be able to have a good night tonight,' I added, trying to sound enthusiastic.

'On a Sunday?' grunted Richie.

I got up and made a pot of tea. When it had brewed I poured out three mugs and placed them on the worktop between the sink and the stove.

'Tea up,' I said.

'Pass mine over then,' said Tam, from his bed. I ignored him and took my tea over to my corner. Tam then attempted to reach over to the worktop without getting out of bed, with the result that he spilt most of his tea on the carpet. This was enough to make Richie get up and quickly claim the remaining mug. Tam, meanwhile, drank his dregs, retreated under his bedclothes and attempted to go back to sleep. I now decided it was time to freeze him out of bed by opening the door wide and leaving it like that. As the climate inside the caravan began to assimilate with the outside world (which did not take long), Richie and I made ourselves breakfast from the dwindling stocks. Eventually, as an apparent gale tried to funnel its way into our tin dwelling, Tam said, 'For fuck sake!' and got dressed.

Now that we were all up it seemed safe to make another pot of tea which we could enjoy properly before setting off for work. When at last Richie and I reluctantly started to pull on our waterproofs, Tam tried to remember what he'd done with his fertilizer sack.

'There it is,' said Richie, pointing out through the door. The sack now lay in a puddle across the yard, flattened by rainwater and looking completely unwearable. Tam resigned himself to getting soaked today, but retrieved the sack all the same. He looked in the wardrobe. Inside were a number of wire coat-hangers that jangled every time anyone moved around the caravan. He hung his sack up on one of them and closed the door. Moments later water began running out of the wardrobe.

'You should have shaken it out first,' I said.

'Too late now,' he replied.

Yes, I agreed, it was too late now.

This more or less set the tone for a miserable day's fencing. In our various states of attire (me in full waterproofs, Richie in his semi, and Tam wearing the remains of his leather jacket) we eventually got started. We'd taken on Mr Hall's job in a moment of heady optimism, but now we were confronted with reality, in the form of a field of mud. Rubber boots may be effective for keeping water out, but they have little resistance against suction, and we were constantly being pulled up by boots which refused to move, or which came off altogether. This made building the fence quite exhausting. Worse, Tam's lethargy seemed to be deepening all the time. It had clearly occurred to him that most of the money he would earn from Mr Hall would go straight to me and Richie, and by the time we got to the final section of the fence he'd lost interest altogether. He still just about managed to swing the post ham-mer with the required force, but in between posts he stood immobile and bedraggled, leaning on the shaft, while Richie got the next one ready. In this way we struggled on for the whole day, and only stopped when it was too dark to do any-thing else. We then went back to the caravan and attempted to dry out in front of the tired gas fire. We now had no money left, and the food supply was down to basics. I hadn't bothered to ring Donald and ask for our wages because we were supposed to be getting cash from Mr Hall. I now realized that we had no idea where he lived, and therefore were completely dependent on him turning up. We couldn't even go to his shop, because it was bound to be closed on a Sunday. And so, as condensation formed on the windows, we sat in the caravan and festered.

We'd all dozed off to sleep when headlights appeared outside. A door slammed and there was a knock on the door.

'Come in,' I said, as we blinked awake. The door opened and in came Mr Hall, again wearing the butcher's coat. As he stepped into the caravan the whole structure creaked under his weight.

'Can you build pens?' he said.

'Well, yes. Pens? What sort of pens?' I replied.

Tam and Richie were both struggling to sit up on their beds.

'We need some pens at the factory,' said Mr Hall.

'What factory?' I asked.

'Our factory,' he replied. 'Meat packing, pies and sausages. We've got the school dinners.'

I was still half asleep, and most of the oxygen in the caravan seemed to have been devoured by the gas fire. I couldn't take any of this in.

'You've got the school dinners?' I repeated.

He raised his voice. 'Yes! Now I'm going to ask again. Can you build pens?'

There was the usual silence from Tam and Richie, so I decided for them.

'Yes, I suppose so.'

'That's good,' he said, his voice quieter now. He paused for a moment, glancing round the caravan before speaking again. 'Get that fencing done alright, did you, lads?'

As he said this he smiled. It was obviously something he wasn't used to doing because stress lines appeared around his mouth.

'Just a couple of hours' work in the morning,' I replied.

The smile vanished. 'What do you mean?'

'Well, there's just a bit to do,' I said.

'It was supposed to be done by Monday.' Mr Hall was raising his voice again.

'Yes, well, we'll finish it in the morning.'

'I said by Monday, not on Monday! I want to put the beasts in there tomorrow!' In the course of this last sentence his face went red and his eyes began to blaze. I had never seen anyone lose their temper so quickly.

'I promise you, first thing . . .' I started, but it was no good. 'YOU SAID YOU COULD DO IT BY MONDAY! THAT'S WHAT YOU SAID! WELL, I'M NOT HAVING IT!' he roared, and slammed out of the caravan.

I tried to chase after him, but couldn't get my boots on in time.

'Mr Hall!' I shouted from the doorway, but it was too late, he was already driving away.

'Suffering fuck,' said Tam, obviously lost for words.

'You didn't ask him for our money,' said Richie.

'Nor did you,' I replied. 'Now what are we going to do?'

'Don't know.'

It certainly looked like we'd blown it with Mr Hall, so I went down the phone box to ring up Donald about sending some money urgently. There was no one there, so I had to leave a message. When I got back to the caravan Tam and Richie looked at me expectantly, as if a phone call to Donald would solve everything. When I shook my head, conversation turned to new speculation about Mr Hall.

'He must have been working today,' suggested Tam. 'That's why he had his white coat on.'

'Yes,' I said. 'But at the factory, not the shop.'

'He was in a bad temper before he got here,' said Richie.

We all agreed about that.

'He should have a day off,' remarked Tam.

'What's all this about pens?' Richie went on.

Obviously Mr Hall had another project in mind for us when he turned up, but during his ensuing rage he forgot all about it. Building pens would make a change from fencing and we quite liked the idea, but now it seemed the opportunity was gone. We wondered why they couldn't build their own pens.

'It's outside work, isn't it,' said Tam, by way of explanation.

'So?' I asked.

'English people don't like working outside, do they?'

'Well, I've been out in it all day,' I said. 'And I'm English.'

Tam looked at me. 'I know that,' he said. 'But you've been with us, haven't you?'

Next day, after a wretched night, Tam refused to have any more to do with Mr Hall's fence. I pointed out we had no choice but to finish the job, or we definitely wouldn't be paid, yet Tam was adamant.

'There's no point,' he said. 'We'll never see him again.'

Finally, he agreed to work alone on the hill while Richie and I went round to do the finishing off for Mr Hall. Tam was still lying in bed when this agreement was concluded, but he assured us that he would be getting up very soon and would make his own way up to the hill. I didn't want to waste any more time on this, so we left him to it.

Completing a fence always seemed to take longer than expected, and it wasn't until gone eleven that we were satisfied with it all. Apart from mud sticking everywhere we were quite pleased with the final result. There was no sign of Mr Hall's beasts arriving, so maybe he had changed his plans. When we got back to the yard we expected to find Tam still asleep on his bunk, but he was nowhere to be seen. Richie nodded in the direction of the hill. 'He'll be working up there,' he said.

I hoped he was right.

Tam was supposed to be getting straining posts dug in for the next section of the encircling fence, and when we got there we indeed found one newly erected post. No sign of Tam though. I left Richie doing the next post and took a walk along the fence line. The ground undulated as I walked, and just after a slight rise on the flank of the hill, I came across a disturbing sight. Tam was on all fours, a wood chisel in his hand, apparently sneaking up on a grazing sheep. Most of the other sheep were dotted around further up the slope, keeping, like sheep generally do, as far away from people as possible. This one, though, was engrossed with a particular area of grass, and for the moment had forgotten about personal safety. I was still far enough away for neither Tam nor the sheep to be aware of my presence. I stood still and watched. Tam slowly advanced on the sheep, chisel raised like a dagger, getting within a few yards of the animal. Then suddenly he sprang forward.

'Tam, no!' I yelled.

The sheep instantly bolted, and Tam fell forward onto the ground. He was still sitting there as I approached.

'What are you doing?' I said.

'I was just seeing if I could catch it, that's all,' he replied.

'Why?'

'In case we have to eat them.'

'Why should we have to do that?'

'Well, there's fuck all else, is there?' He looked desperate.

'Don't worry about that,' I said. 'We'll get some money soon from somewhere or other.'

I made Tam promise not to kill, or practise killing, any sheep, and we got back to work.

That day I concentrated hard on keeping Tam and Richie going. I was worried about the job grinding to a halt again, especially as we'd done all that work for Mr Hall and not a penny to show for it. Morale was understandably very low, and I had to cajole and encourage the two of them all day. Finally, as the light faded, we set off back to the caravan. We'd got some work behind us at last, and felt better for it. The only problem, as Tam had pointed out, was that we hardly had any food left. As we approached the yard I happened to mention that there were two remaining cans of beans in the cupboard under the sink. This was enough to trigger a race back to the caravan between Tam and Richie. They leapt out of the truck and charged across the yard. Both of them got to the caravan door at the same time, and a noisy struggle followed as each tried to force his way inside. With a violent crash they both fell through the doorway, and a moment later became unusually silent. Wondering what had caused this sudden transformation I stepped inside the caravan. Donald was sitting on the end of Tam's bed.

10

'Glad to see you're making full use of daylight hours,' he said.

'Oh, er, yes,' I replied. 'Where's your truck?'

Donald had a truck similar to ours which he used as a general runaround for visiting gangs on site. There was no sign of it in the yard, which was why we'd been taken by surprise.

'Robert dropped me off,' he said. 'He's borrowing it for a couple of days.'

'A couple of days?' I repeated.

'Yes,' he replied. 'In the meantime I'm going to stay here with you as this job doesn't seem to be going very quickly.'

Tam and Richie had sat down on the spare bunk opposite mine. I glanced at them. They both appeared to have gone pale.

'You people really should be getting on faster than this,' Donald went on. 'After all, there's no great hardship here.'

'We've run out of money,' I said.

'What happened to the float I gave you?'

'Spent it.'

'Well, if you've "spent it" you would normally be expected to go without.'

'Oh.'

'But it's fortunate for you that I've brought your wages with me.'

This, at least, was a relief. It was supper time and we decided to cook everything we had left, the beans and one or two other things, all together in a big pan. Donald just about hid his disgust as a suitable pan was selected from the sink and scraped clean. I thought it would be a good lesson for him to see how I had to live every day. However, once the pan was cooking he seemed to take a more positive interest in what we were having for our tea.

'That smells nice,' he remarked.

'Yes,' I replied. 'But there's only three plates.'

It then transpired that Donald had brought his own plate, a special disposable one that did not require washing up. Reluctantly I gave him a dollop and we all sat and ate.

'Very nice,' said Donald afterwards, reaching for his overnight bag. 'Now then. Wages.'

He produced three pay packets. 'Oh, by the way,' he said. 'This came to the office.' He handed me an invoice. It was the bill for the repair to the post hammer.

'Oh, yes, right,' I said. 'I wondered what happened to this.'

'I thought you'd better see it,' said Donald.

'Thanks,' I replied. 'This would normally be settled out of the float, I suppose?'

'I'm afraid not,' replied Donald. 'The float only covers general wear and tear. Negligent damage has to be deducted directly from your wages.'

And he made the deduction, in cash, on the spot.

After he'd given out the pay packets Donald said, 'I expect you'll all be dashing off to the pub now?'

'Not really bothered,' replied Richie. He was reclining on his bunk, reading *An Early Bath for Thompson* again, from page one.

'I'm surprised,' said Donald. 'I thought you'd be out every night.'

'Actually, I'm saving up for Christmas,' said Tam.

'Well, I'm sure the company can afford to stand a round of drinks,' announced Donald, and a few minutes later he was driving us to the pub, all squashed together in our truck.

On the way out he paused next to the original Hall Brothers fence.

'I see someone else is working round here,' he said.

'Yes,' I replied. 'Local company, I think.'

'Well, we don't want to go stepping on their toes, do we?' Donald got out of the truck and carried out a brief examination of the Hall Brothers' fence. We watched as he stood at one end and genuflected, glancing along the line of posts.

'Hmmm. Exemplary,' he said, as he rejoined us.

It was quiet at the Queen's Head when we trooped in. Donald led the way to the bar and ordered four pints while Tam, Richie and myself held back a little. While he was pouring the drinks Ron the landlord raised his eyebrows at me. I nodded in reply. Whether this exchange had any significance I don't know, but Ron kept his distance during the evening, and didn't poke round asking his usual questions.

We sat down at our normal table in the corner, with an extra chair for Donald. It was an odd evening. Donald seemed to think that we would want to talk about fences all night, so he kept on starting up conversations on the subject. We learnt about all the new fencing techniques that were being developed by the company and its rivals, and we heard how many yards of fencing had been erected by other gangs in different parts of the British Isles.

'How many gangs are working in England?' I asked.

'None,' replied Donald. 'You're the only one, although Robert has gone to look into getting more work down here.'

Judging by the expressions on their faces, Tam and Richie didn't like the sound of this.

'By the way,' Donald continued. 'There's still been no word from Mr McCrindle.'

'Oh,' I said. 'Hasn't there?'

'He's gone very quiet. Not even a phone call, which is quite surprising. He's rather fond of his telephone and rang me up on a daily basis while his fence was being built.'

Donald had now turned his gaze upon Tam, who shuffled awkwardly on his seat.

'Did he?' he managed to say.

'Indeed he did,' replied Donald. 'I asked him to keep his beady eye on you and he was most obliging.'

'Helpful of him,' I remarked.

'Yes, I thought so too, and he turned out to be very equal to the task. Which is why I'm going to allow him three months' grace to settle his account.'

'That's ... er ... good.'

All the while, we were concentrating on drinking our beers at the correct speed. Donald's offer on behalf of the company to buy a round of drinks had been ambiguous and caused uncertainty among us. We weren't sure who was expected to pay for the second round, or any subsequent ones for that matter. As a result we drank 'in line' with Donald, making sure none of us emptied our glasses before he did. Donald drank at a very slow rate, which was proving to be a form of torture for Tam and Richie, and, to a lesser extent, me. The last two inches took for ever, but eventually Donald drank up, closely followed by the three of us.

'Same again?' he said, taking us all by surprise. He went up to the bar again. This was the first time me, Tam and Richie had been alone since his arrival.

'Just act naturally,' I said.

When he came back with the drinks Donald resumed the discussion about fences, but in spite of this Tam and Richie began to look a little happier as the beer went down. Richie remembered that he'd run out of fags, so he went off to get some and came back with two packets. He and Tam then sat and quickly smoked several in a row. Donald looked at Richie as he lit up yet again.

'Why do you abuse your body all the time?' he asked.

'Because no one else will do it for me,' replied Richie.

Next thing Tam was up at the bar buying another round, and I realized I was going to have to talk to him fairly soon about his mounting debt problem.

Back at the caravan a space had to be found for Donald to sleep, and it was decided he would occupy the bunk underneath Richie. There was a jumble of used clothing lying there which Richie grabbed in a great armful and stuffed behind his pillow. Donald opened the wardrobe and was confronted by Tam's fertilizer bag, now dry and stiff on its hanger. He slid it back along the rack, and hung up his shirt in front. As we prepared for bed Donald said, 'No late evening coffee, then?'

'I'm afraid not,' I replied.

In the dead of night I woke up for some reason, and lay

listening to the others as they slept. Over the last few weeks I had got used to the noises Tam and Richie made in their sleep, and I recognized them instantly.

Richie, who always lay on his back, produced a sound similar to the underwater gurgling of an old motorboat. Meanwhile, at the other end of the caravan, Tam seethed like a distant ocean.

Donald, however, in the bunk closest to mine, was totally, totally silent.

I planned to impress Donald in the morning by being the first to get up, but when I awoke I saw he was already moving about the caravan, apparently making tea. He stood looking at the piled-up sink, and then produced a clean mug from his bag.

'My mug's up there,' I said, pointing to the cupboard above my bunk.

'Really?' Donald replied, and poured himself a tea.

Donald's presence certainly made a big difference to the speed we arose that day. There was no question of Tam lounging about in bed until the last minute, and we were ready for work by half past seven. Donald had his own map of the job, with all the fences marked out in red ink, and the first thing he did was go for a tour of inspection, accompanied by me. We followed the hill up to the summit, and then came down by way of the cross-fence, Donald all the time checking for wire tension and, of course, straightness. When we got to the encircling fence he seemed quite satisfied with what he'd seen.

'Hmmm, quite professional,' he said.

After a while we came to the gateway that stood alone. Donald looked at it for a moment, and then said, 'Yes, I always think it's better to do the gate first and build the fences round it.'

Donald had put on some overalls, and it soon became clear that he intended to work alongside us during his visit. He organized us into two small sub-gangs, one pair erecting posts, the other fixing wires, and then swapping round every couple of hours. This grouping worked quite efficiently, and a long stretch of fence was built on Donald's first day. It was interesting watching him work with the post hammer. His action resembled that of a machine. How his bones must have jarred every time he brought the hammer down accurately, but stiffly, on top of each post. He did not allow himself any 'give', but instead transferred all his energy directly into the hammer. In this mechanical way Donald completed yet another line of posts, while his chosen assistant struggled to keep up with him.

That night in the pub I found myself at the bar buying a round of drinks. It was at this point that I noticed Ron the landlord behaving oddly. Instead of placing the newly filled glasses on the counter between me and him, he put them about two feet to my left. At the same time he stared hard over my shoulder in the direction of the corner table where Donald, Tam and Richie were sitting. I was about to pick up the four pints in a clutch, so I would only have to make one journey from the bar, when Ron produced a tray. Onto this he began loading the glasses, still eyeing the corner, and moving sideways, until, at last, I realized he was attempting to line me up with Donald. He seemed to be trying to obscure himself from view, so I decided to stay where I was and let him adjust his position to mine. Suddenly he glanced down at the counter, and at the same time I felt an envelope being pressed into my hand. I nodded and slipped it into my pocket. He visibly relaxed as I took the tray and carried it over to the table, where Donald and the others were discussing fencing. The envelope remained in my pocket for another half hour, after which time I casually strolled out to the gents. Locking myself in the cubicle, I examined the mystery package under a dim light. There was no writing on the envelope and it was unsealed. Inside was some cash, large denomination notes of exactly the sum agreed for Mr Hall's fencing. I looked for some kind of written message but there was nothing, just money. When I returned to the bar room, conversation had dried up. This was the normal state of affairs for Tam and Richie, who were generally content to sit with their pints and say nothing. Being accompanied to the pub by Donald had imposed considerable stress on them, and they looked quite relieved when I rejoined the table. It had been even worse for them during the day, when Donald organized us into two pairs and they had been forcibly separated. Each of us had worked with one of the others, so that the different tasks were shared fairly. When Richie was selected to go off with Donald to erect a new line of posts he looked as if he was embarking on a death march. Tam's turn came later, and he seemed like a broken man when he came back.

'How long's Donald staying for?' he asked me.

'Until Robert comes to collect him . . . a couple of days,' I replied.

'But he's been here two days already.'

'He only arrived last night,' I said. 'It just seems longer, that's all.'

Now, hours later in the pub, there was still no let-up. The three of us were trying to unwind over a few beers, but Donald had something to say to us.

'You people really should start thinking in terms of efficiency,' he began. 'Building a fence is quite simple. First you dig in your straining posts at each end, and tighten a wire between them. This gives you a straight line along which you set the pointed posts (point downwards). Then you fix and tighten the remaining wires, one by one, and the job is complete.'

While Donald was speaking I looked at Richie, sitting opposite me. His eyes had slowly closed and his head nodded forward, and he now sat motionless next to Tam, who stirred uneasily.

'What about adding the support strut at each end?' I asked.

'That goes without saying,' replied Donald. He reached into his jacket and took out some papers.

'I've prepared some hand-outs for you,' he announced, passing them round. 'They contain all the main points you should bear in mind during the construction process.'

Richie resurfaced and focused on his copy. I looked at mine. It consisted of step-by-step diagrams of how to build a fence, with little stick men doing the work. Donald now turned to me.

'You should also operate a stricter regime inside the caravan,' he said.

'I take it you're referring to the squalor,' I replied.

'Correct.'

'Well I don't see how I can force people to be hygienic,' I

said. I noticed that Tam and Richie were now studying their hand-outs with great interest.

'Domestic arrangements fall within your remit,' said Donald, after which the subject was dropped.

The evening came to a natural close when the pub shut, and as we got up to leave, Donald noticed that Tam had left his hand-out on the table.

'Don't forget this,' he said, picking it up.

'Thanks,' said Tam, stuffing it in his back pocket.

Next morning, as we prepared for another day of efficient fencing, Donald said, 'Robert should be turning up this afternoon.'

Tam and Richie didn't respond to this news, but when they went out to load up the truck with the day's gear I could hear them whistling. Even better, Donald allowed them to work together for the entire morning, pulling out and tightening wires, while I paired up with him to knock some more posts in. We made good progress, and by mid-afternoon another line was complete. Donald had taken the post hammer, and I had been his assistant, spacing out and setting up the posts. As we stood looking at the finished work, we saw that one post clearly wasn't level with the rest, and needed knocking in a little further.

'I'll do it,' I said, taking hold of the post hammer.

I liked to use the 'full swing' method, same as Tam, so I planted my feet firmly on the ground and held the hammer at arm's length. Then I swung it over in an arc and down onto the post. It was a good solid blow, but another one was required, so I repeated the action. This time the hammer seemed unusually light as I brought it over, and at the end of the stroke

I realized that the head had flown off and I'd been left holding just the shaft. At that moment something sniffed my boot. I looked down and saw Ralph saying 'hello' in the way dogs do when they've just arrived. There was a movement behind me, and I turned round to discover Donald engaged in a strange embrace with Robert. It looked as if one was teaching the other to dance.

'Oh hello, Robert,' I said, but instead of his usual polite greeting I got no reply. In fact, Robert was very quiet indeed.

Then I noticed the missing hammer head lying on the ground.

'Direct hit,' said Donald. I could see he was struggling to hold Robert upright, so I stepped forward and together we leaned him against a post. Donald examined him closely.

'How is he?' I asked.

'That's irrelevant,' Donald replied. 'He's dead.'

He took the shaft from me and inserted it in the hammer head. It was loose.

'That's one bill we won't be paying,' he said.

11

'What are we going to do with Robert?' I asked.

'We'll have to bury him,' replied Donald.

'Shouldn't he be buried in Scotland?'

'Normally, yes,' he acknowledged. 'But in this case it's too far.'

He took the fence plan from his pocket and studied it. 'He'll have to go under the next gateway.'

'We'll get Richie to do it,' I suggested. 'He's best at digging.'

'Alright,' said Donald. 'Tell him it's best to put Robert under the slamming post rather than the hanging post.'

'Is there a particular reason for that?' I enquired. It seemed a good moment to settle the point.

'Not as far as I know,' he said.

When Tam and Richie had finished what they were doing they came wandering along the fence line to join us, and Donald pointed out that they should have taken the opportunity to move their gear round to the next section.

'Never a wasted journey,' he said.

After we'd told them about Robert, Tam voiced concern over who would look after Ralph.

'I'll take him with me,' announced Donald.

By the time Robert's gateway was finished the light was quickly failing, so we made our way back to the yard. The company truck was parked next to the caravan where Robert had left it. In the back was a spare post hammer which Donald let us borrow while he got ours 'repaired properly in Scotland', as he put it.

Donald had some tea and then prepared to leave before it got too late. When departure time came I said, 'Well, thanks for all your help the last couple of days.'

'That's alright,' he replied. 'Of course, I'll have to quarter it from your final costings.'

I was not sure what he meant by this, but I could guess.

Donald looked around the farmyard. 'I was hoping to have a few words with Mr Perkins while I was down here,' he said. 'But he seems to be keeping a low profile.'

'I've hardly seen him myself,' I said. 'It was dark when we first got here.'

'So I heard,' replied Donald. 'Now, I'll expect this job to be wound up fairly quickly. You won't want to be coming back after Christmas to finish it, will you?'

I hoped not. Time had sneaked up on us and it was now December. No wonder the days were so short and the nights so long. Donald's visit had pulled us along a bit, but there was still a fair amount of work to be done before we could escape from Upper Bowland. I told Donald I would do my best and we said our goodbyes. By this time Tam and Richie had joined us in the yard. Donald opened the door of the company truck and Ralph jumped in beside his new master. Then they were gone.

'I'm fucked if I'm coming back after Christmas,' said Tam, as we slumped into the caravan.

'We should be alright if we press on at the same rate,' I replied.

Tam looked at me. 'You don't believe in all this efficiency shite, do you?'

'Well,' I said. 'It worked OK while Donald was here, didn't it?'

'That's because he's a fucking robot,' said Richie.

Yes, I thought to myself, he quite possibly is.

To stop Tam and Richie going into decline I quickly produced Mr Hall's money and we shared it out. Tam again settled his debts, and again found himself with virtually nothing left. However, we all had enough to go to the pub, which is what we did.

'Get that cash alright, did you?' asked Ron as he served us our beers. Seeing that it was him who handed it to me this seemed a pointless question, but I politely replied, 'Yes, thanks.'

'I hear you're going to be building some pens,' he added.

'You've seen Mr Hall then, have you?' I said.

'He's been very busy,' replied Ron. 'They've got the school dinners.'

We sat at the corner table and considered this vague information. Obviously the Hall Brothers had further plans for us, but until they made contact we would have no idea what exactly was involved. In the meantime, we had to get on with our own job. I wasn't sure what effect the approach of Christmas would have on Tam and Richie. On the one hand it might spur them on so we got finished in good time, but on the other it could just make them homesick and unable to concentrate on work. I must admit that even I felt slightly marooned as the tail lights of Donald's truck headed off towards the road. When we returned to the caravan late that night, the hill above us seemed to be brooding in the darkness.

There were no further sightings of the Hall Brothers over the next few days, so we plodded on with our own fence. At first Tam and Richie marched around 'being efficient' and doing things as Donald would have liked, but I knew the sham wouldn't last. They preferred to take a laissez-faire approach to the work, tackling jobs as they presented themselves, rather than in a set order. The fence would still get built, eventually, but at about half-speed. I decided to go along with all this. After all, I had to live with Tam and Richie twenty-four hours a day, Donald didn't.

On the day we finally got the job finished we received a visit from John Hall. Once again we'd all dozed off to sleep after a hard day's work, when the headlights swung into the yard. I was ready for him, however, when he stepped into the caravan, which made the usual protest under his weight.

'Are you ready to do these pens, then?' he began.

'Yes, I think we can spare a couple of days,' I replied.

'That's good,' he said. 'I've bought the timber already.'

'Oh. Have you?'

'Yes. I got two hundred railway sleepers in a job lot.'

When he said this I detected a shock wave running between Tam, Richie and myself.

'Railway sleepers?' I tried not to sound surprised.

'Best things for building pens with,' said Mr Hall. He was probably right, but I wondered what we were letting ourselves in for. Two hundred railway sleepers! That was more than a couple of days' work.

'What will we be doing then, exactly?' I enquired.

'Building pens,' he replied with irritation. 'I just told you.'

'Yes, but where?'

'At the factory. So we can bring beasts in direct from the field.'

'Er . . . that's illegal, isn't it?' I said.

Mr Hall eyed me. 'Are you trying to tell me how to conduct my affairs now?'

'No, but . . .'

'What?' He looked as if he was about to explode again.

'Nothing,' I said, surrendering.

'Good. Now let's have a bit of common sense round here.' His features had relaxed again. 'It'll be cash in hand as before, and there'll be grubbage for you at the canteen.' Mr Hall was certainly magnanimous in victory. He glanced at Tam and Richie. 'Alright, lads?'

Obliged to speak at last, they both mumbled, 'Thanks.'

I fell in with this change of mood. 'I gather you've got the school dinners,' I said, hoping he would enlarge on the subject.

'Yes, we have,' he replied. 'Right. I'll expect you tomorrow morning.'

He opened the door to leave.

'By the way,' I asked. 'Where is the factory?'

'Lower Bowland. You can't miss it.'

The factory turned out to be a large shed of corrugated steel at the end of a long track. The building had a look about it that suggested it had been erected without planning permission. All around were fields, in which unsuspecting cattle grazed behind newish HALL BROS. fences. On the side of the shed was a block-house canteen and some offices. When we arrived we found David Hall parked in his lorry, waiting for us. There were also a few butchers' vans nearby. As I said before, David Hall was much easier to deal with than his brother. He actually appeared friendly and had little difficulty smiling.

'I've got the sleepers on the back here,' he said. 'We'll have a bit of breakfast and then you can get them unloaded.'

We'd all had breakfast before we left the caravan that morning, but none of us said anything as he led us into the canteen, where a number of butchers, all in white coats, were already seated. There was a choice of sausages fried, grilled or baked, served up by a man in a cook's apron who seemed to bear the Hall Brothers' family resemblance. He appeared to be running the kitchen single-handed. When not dishing out sausages he spent much of his time attending to the griddle behind the counter, while occasionally replenishing the tea urn. After we'd had a plateful of sausages each we sat and drank mugs of tea while David Hall talked to us about fencing.

'Hard job, fencing, isn't it?' he began.

'It's OK,' replied Tam.

'Must be repetitive knocking all those posts in, though. First one, then another, then another after that.'

'You get used to it,' I said.

'Yes, but repeating the same thing over and over again. Enough to drive you mad. All that repetition.'

The more he went on like this, the more it began to sound as if he didn't know what he was talking about.

'I thought you did all the fencing work round here?' I said.

'It depends what you call work,' he replied. 'There's work-work, and there's telling other people to work. I prefer the second one.'

'So you're not a fencer yourself then?' I asked.

'Hoo hoo! Course not!' he said, grinning.

The lorry was still waiting to be unloaded when we went outside again.

'John's got a plan of the pens somewhere,' said David Hall. 'I'll just go round the office and get it. You can start unloading if you like.'

'Thanks,' I said.

The railway sleepers were stacked lengthways, so Tam and Richie climbed up on the lorry to pass them down, while I remained on the ground. There was a certain way of unloading timber which made the work quite straightforward. It involved the law of gravity. In this case it was simply a matter of Tam pushing each sleeper along the stack until it tipped over, to be upended by Richie, who in turn slid it off the back of the lorry. It would then land upright, ready for me to lower onto the new stack. For a while this procedure worked quite well, and we began to develop a steady rhythm. However, as my stack on the ground got higher, I needed a little more time to move each sleeper into position. Tam and Richie didn't seem to realize this, and actually started to send them down faster and faster. In the end I had a relentless stream of heavy railway sleepers coming at me, and it was starting to get a bit much.

'Can you slow down a bit!' I shouted. 'One of these is going to hit me in a minute!'

I didn't like having to raise my voice to Tam and Richie, but sometimes it was more than justified. Their response was to stop work and have a fag. This gave me time to catch up on the ground, and when I'd got sorted out I had a rest too.

'This is going to be a fucking slog,' remarked Tam.

Yes, we all agreed, it was. If we were going to build a proper substantial structure then all the uprights would have to be dug into the ground to give them strength. We hadn't seen the plans yet, but we knew that there'd probably be dozens of holes to dig. Then there was the question of holding it all together. You couldn't just nail railway sleepers to one another because they were too big. They'd have to be drilled and fastened with coach-bolts to keep them secure. I wondered if Mr Hall had allowed for this and got a supply. Somehow I doubted it. We quickly came to the conclusion that the job would take more than a couple of days, and when David Hall came back with the plans our worst fears were confirmed. These were going to be heavy-duty handling pens for all manner of beasts. It would take us a week at least, maybe more!

Of course, we didn't express our doubts in front of David Hall, and indeed spent the rest of the day laying out the railway sleepers according to their positions on the plan. But as soon as we left the premises that evening Tam said, 'I think we should just fuck off.'

'What, you mean abandon the job?' I asked.

'Fucking right,' he replied. 'Otherwise we'll never get home.'

Richie, of course, agreed with Tam, and I have to admit that it didn't take long for me to come round to their way of thinking. We'd definitely over-stretched ourselves by agreeing to build those pens, and the best course of action was to just clear off. So when we got back to the caravan we immediately began to make preparations to leave. We decided it would be best to go straight away and travel overnight, with me and Richie sharing the driving. So while they packed up the caravan and hitched it to the truck, I went on a final tour of inspection of Mr Perkins's fence. It seemed a long time since we had first set eyes on that huge pile of posts and wire in the farmyard. Now it had been transformed into a taut, gleaming structure that glinted in the moonlight. I made sure all the gates were left closed, so that nothing could escape, and then rejoined Tam and Richie. Not long afterwards we hit the road.

It was quiet next morning when we pulled into the company premises and parked outside the tool store. We sat in the cab for a few minutes while Tam and Richie had a smoke.

'Right,' I said when they'd finished. 'We'd better have a go at sorting out all the gear.' We got out and stood looking into the back of the truck. The collection of tools lay in a shallow pool of rainwater, some of them bent, most of them showing the first signs of rust. This was supposed to be a set of professional fence-building equipment, but actually looked like a hoard of junk. There were hole-digging implements, wire-tightening gear, a rusty steel spike (blunt), a selection of chisels and a chain winch. All in various states of disrepair. Also several coils of wire. The only item that appeared to be in reasonable condition was the post hammer, lying slightly to one side.

'Here's Donald,' murmured Tam, and they both immediately began sorting through the gear. Donald had emerged from his office and was advancing across the yard in our direction. His sudden appearance had a marked effect on Tam and Richie, whose faces showed that they were concentrating hard on their work. Tam leaned over the side of the truck and pulled out the post hammer.

'Glad to see it's still in one piece,' said Donald as he joined us. He took the hammer from Tam and stood it, head downwards, on the concrete. Richie, meanwhile, had lifted one of the coils of wire onto his shoulder and was about to take it into the store room.

'You seem to be in a great hurry all of a sudden,' said Donald.

This caused Richie to hesitate awkwardly in mid-step with the coil balanced on his shoulder. He half-turned and looked at Tam. Donald was now peering into the back of the truck.

'You people really should take more care of your equipment,' he said.

After a dutiful pause Richie made another move towards the store room, but was again brought to a halt by Donald.

'Leave that for now. I've just had a serious phone call. You'd better come into the office.' Without further comment he turned and walked off towards the open door. We all glanced at each other, saying nothing, and filed after him.

A very powerful naked light bulb hung from the office ceiling. Beneath it, Donald had placed two hard chairs side by side facing his desk. They were slightly less than full adult size, made from wood, and had been positioned squarely and symmetrically in the middle of the floor.

Tam and Richie did not have to be told where to sit.

12

How long Donald kept them sitting there, side by side on those two hard chairs, was difficult to say. There were no clocks in that office, no calendar on the wall. Even the limited daylight coming through the small recessed window was defeated by the glare of the light-bulb, further isolating the office interior from the world outside. Donald sat silently behind his desk, holding Tam and Richie under his gaze. Meanwhile, the radiator pipe beneath the floor did its work. The only sound was the occasional shuffling of feet as they unstuck their warmed-up rubber boots from the lino. Then, at last, Donald spoke.

'I've just had your mother on the phone,' he said. 'She was in a call box and sounded rather distressed.'

Richie had adopted his usual position and sat with his arms folded, gazing at the desktop. Now he was forced to look directly at Donald.

'My mother?'

'Yes.'

'Did she say what it was about?'

'Yes she did. It seems she hasn't heard from you the entire time you've been away.'

'Oh,' said Richie. 'No.'

'No letters, postcards. Nothing.'

'I told her I'd be back around Christmas.'

'Rather vague, was it not?'

' 'Spose.'

'And in the meantime you sent no word.'

'No.'

'Well, I know how she must feel,' said Donald. 'I find myself in the same situation. I get no tidings from No. 3 Gang for days on end. Not one phone call. No sign of a progress report. Nothing. Then suddenly you turn up here, unannounced, out of the blue. It's like the Retreat from Moscow.'

Richie said nothing.

'Why didn't you telephone before you came back?' said Donald.

The room remained silent. All this time I'd been casually leaning on the radiator by the window, watching the interrogation but feeling somewhat detached from it. The two hard chairs had been set up for Tam and Richie, therefore I was exempt. Or so I thought. It was only as the silence persisted that I realized Donald had now turned his attention to me.

'Why didn't you telephone before you came back?' he repeated.

'Forgot,' I replied. Even as I spoke I knew this was a pathetic excuse.

'You forgot.'

'Yes.'

'Your first duty as foreman is to liaise with me, yet you forgot.'

'Yes. Sorry.'

'It would be a different story if I forgot to pay you, wouldn't it?'

I noticed that Tam and Richie were both looking over their shoulders at me, and suddenly I felt like a schoolboy being rebuked by his teacher in front of the whole class. I'd seen them being put through the mill in this way several times, but always considered myself somehow immune. Now it dawned on me that I was no more 'in' with Donald than they were. The post of foreman brought no benefits, only problems. In fact, it was beginning to seem like some sort of purgatory.

There was a long silence and then Donald said, 'I think it's time you became acquainted with the Demonstration Fence.'

He rose from his chair and gave a low whistle, at which Ralph emerged from beneath the desk. Tam patted his head once or twice, and then Donald led us all outside. We followed him across the yard to a gate, which he held open as we passed through. Away in the middle of the field I could see a structure glinting in the pale winter light, and as we approached I saw that it was a short fence about thirty yards long, standing alone. This fence served no apparent purpose, because it was possible to walk round either end.

'How long's this been here?' I asked.

'Just a few weeks,' replied Donald. 'This is our Demonstration Fence.'

'Who built it?'

'Me. I did.'

I should have known really. This fence was more or less perfect. All the posts stood erect and unblemished in a dead straight line. The joinery had been done perfectly too, so that each straining post and strut appeared to be an integral unit. Even the wires seemed to be highly polished.

As soon as we got there Donald went to one end and glanced along the line of posts, genuflecting as he did so. As a mark of respect I did the same thing, followed by Tam and Richie.

I noticed a small yellow sign fixed to one of the straining posts. It bore the company name and telephone number.

Also the words CAUTION: ELECTRIC FENCE.

Donald turned to Richie and said, 'Give me your hand.'

'What?' said Richie.

'Give me your hand.'

Richie glanced at Tam, who had moved away from the fence slightly and now stood looking very hard at the yellow sign, as if trying to memorize the telephone number. Richie slowly held his hand out. Donald took it in his own left hand, and seized the top fence wire with his right, causing the two of them to jerk in time for several seconds. Finally, Donald let go of the wire and released Richie.

A stunned silence followed, after which Donald said, 'Why didn't your rubber boots save you?'

Richie looked at him for a long moment before replying. 'Don't know.'

Donald turned to Tam. 'Do you know why?'

'Because you're not wearing them,' said Tam.

We all looked down at Donald's feet. He was wearing ordinary leather boots.

'Correct,' said Donald. 'The electricity went to earth through me.'

'Didn't you get a shock as well?' I asked.

'Oh yes,' replied Donald. 'I got a shock.'

We stood looking at the Demonstration Fence in solemn silence.

'This is the way forward,' announced Donald at last. 'The permanent electric high-tensile fence. The final solution to the problem of the restraint of beasts. The electricity teaches them to keep away from the structure, so that there is virtually no wear and tear. And if the electricity should fail, the high-tensile wires act as a barrier. Now, do you want another demonstration?'

'No, that's alright, thanks,' said Tam.

'You'll be learning all about the electric high-tensile fence in the next few days,' said Donald.

'Will we?'

'Yes. We've had several enquiries about it already. You'll be going to England in the New Year to build one, so it's important that you know what you're doing.'

Tam was about to say something, but Donald looked at him and he remained silent instead.

'Any problems with that?' said Donald.

'No, no,' replied Tam.

Donald whistled Ralph, who sat some distance away, having declined to approach the fence, and we walked back across the fields towards the company premises. When we got into the yard Donald said, 'By the way, have you got a measurement for me?'

'Oh, yes,' I replied, and retrieved Mr Perkins's file from the truck. On the outside of the file I'd written the final length of the fence at Upper Bowland.

'I take it you had no further problems down there,' said Donald.

'None to speak of,' I replied.

As I drove Tam and Richie home we had a discussion about the electric fence.

'I don't like the sound of it,' remarked Richie.

'Nor me,' said Tam. 'We should do high-tensile and nothing else.'

'I suppose Donald's going to make us go in over Christmas to learn about it,' I said.

'I'm not fucking going in over Christmas,' Tam snapped.

'Aren't you?'

'Fucking right I'm not.'

'It's just me and you then, Richie,' I said.

'Are you going in then, Rich?' said Tam.

'Suppose we'll have to won't we?' replied Richie. 'If Donald says so.'

I slowed the truck down and turned up the gravel track leading to the golf course. Rounding a bend we came upon Tam's father operating a saw bench.

'Stop here,' said Tam, and we pulled up and watched.

Strewn on the ground around Mr Finlayson were a number of newly-cut larch poles, all about ten feet in length. He was using the circular saw to sharpen the end of each pole into a point. The safety cover on the bench had been discarded, and the huge blade spun unprotected as he worked. It was a noisy operation. The saw was attached to a diesel power plant, and the combined din of the engine and the blade cutting into the timber had drowned out the sound of our truck. Mr Finlayson took each pole, swept it across the blade several times to create a point, and then threw it up on a stack beside him. He was concentrating on his work and remained unaware of our presence.

Tam carefully opened his door and got out of the cab. Then he slowly began moving in a circle until he was directly behind his father. He waited until another pole was complete, and then, at the exact moment Mr Finlayson threw it onto the stack, he leapt forward with a wild cry and seized his arms, locking them with his own, and holding his head forward. Then Tam slowly bent his father down, forcing him to kneel in the sawdust until his head was an inch or so from the spinning blade. After holding him in this position for several seconds Tam let go and stepped back quickly. Mr Finlayson moved cautiously away from the blade before standing upright and looking round. Richie and I had both got out of the truck to watch this 'sport', and when he caught sight of us he shook his head and closed down the machinery. Then quick as a flash he seized a pole from the stack and hurled it at Tam, who had to jump out of the way to avoid being hit.

'That could have been a very nasty accident,' said Mr Finlayson. 'Now pick it up and put it back on the stack.'

Tam obeyed.

Mr Finlayson looked at me. 'How are you?' he said, removing handfuls of wood shavings from his pockets.

'Alright, thanks,' I replied.

'Still foreman?'

'Er . . . yeah. Just about.'

'Well, that's good for you, isn't it?'

''Spose.'

'They don't usually last this long.'

Mr Finlayson used his son's return as a signal to finish work. He replaced the safety cover on the saw bench and began counting the completed poles.

'What are these going to be for?' asked Tam.

'I'm building a stockade round the house,' replied his father.

'Why?'

'To stop you coming home any more.'

Richie was very quiet as we left the golf course behind and carried on towards his place. I realized this was the first occasion he'd been separated from Tam for quite a while, and wondered how he would cope. Who would he share his fags with, for example? It was hard to imagine Tam without immediately thinking of Richie, and vice versa. I remembered back to that time I'd asked Tam where Richie was and he'd said, 'We're not married you know.' Well maybe they weren't, but they spent more time together than most married people. No doubt they'd be together again very soon (when the Crown Hotel opened), but in the meantime Richie had to face his mother. I expected her to be angry with him for not writing home or anything, but when we pulled into the farmyard she appeared in the doorway with a very worried look on her face. Mrs Campbell was clearly most concerned about something.

'Oh Richard,' she said. 'I think there's been a terrible mistake.'

'It's alright,' he replied. 'I'm home now. What happened?'

'Oh dear. I don't know how to tell you.'

'Has someone died?'

'No, no. It's about the electric guitar.'

'What about it?'

Mrs Campbell hesitated and then said, 'A man from the catalogue came and took it away.'

13

Richie went quite pale. 'You mean it's gone?'

'I'm afraid so.'

'When?'

'This morning.'

'Didn't you pay the instalments?'

'I kept them all up to date, but we didn't think you were coming back.'

'Why?'

'That's what your employer told us.'

'What, Donald?'

'He didn't give his name, but he said he hadn't heard from you for quite some time. Therefore he didn't think you were coming back.'

'Therefore?' said Richie.

At this point his mother began weeping.

'Oh Richard!' she wailed. 'We didn't mind you having the guitar! Really! We'd have got used to it soon enough. Your father could go out and see to the cows, and I've got my Reading Circle. Please don't think we did it on purpose!'

As Richie tried to comfort his mother, and she him, I noticed Mr Campbell quietly regarding the scene from an outhouse doorway. When he saw me looking he withdrew again.

'As soon as I turned my back for five minutes,' said Richie. 'Gone.'

That night, as the three of us sat in the Crown Hotel, Tam listened solemnly while Richie told him his bad news.

'The man from the catalogue took everything, did he?' he asked at length.

'Everything. The guitar, the amp. Even the instruction manual.'

'For fuck sake.'

'I'd only had it a few weeks,' said Richie. 'I'll probably never see it again.'

'At least you won't have to pay off any more instalments,' I pointed out as a sort of consolation.

Tam considered the case and then passed judgement. 'This wouldn't have happened if we hadn't had to go to England,' he announced.

'Yeah, but Donald's behind it all,' I added.

'He's getting worse and worse,' said Richie.

We all agreed about that.

'And to think they only started off building fruit cages,' said Tam.

'Who?' I asked.

'The company.'

'Did they?'

'That was before your time. Or yours, Rich. Raspberries mainly.'

'To stop them escaping?' asked Richie.

'Er . . . no. Not really . . . no.'

Tam went to the bar to get three more pints, and on returning said, 'Christmas Eve tomorrow.'

'Yeah,' I said.

'I suppose we've got to go into work, have we?'

'Suppose so,' I replied. 'Donald hasn't said anything.'

'Fuck sake.'

'Maybe he'll let us finish early,' I suggested.

'Huh,' said Tam.

Christmas Eve didn't start particularly well. It would probably have been alright if Donald hadn't intercepted us almost as soon as we arrived for work. This gave us no chance to prepare ourselves for what he had in mind. We were sitting in the truck while Tam and Richie had a pre-work smoke, carefully watching Donald's office door as the minutes passed. When they'd finished we were going to go and report for duty, but Donald got to us first. He suddenly approached from the direction of the tool store, and next moment he was peering at us through the cab window as we sat there side by side.

'Have you been out to the Demonstration Fence since we last spoke?' he asked.

'Not yet,' I replied.

'I'm surprised,' said Donald. 'It's in your own best interests to become familiar with the technique as quickly as possible. Our schedules have been brought forward and you'll be on your own very soon.'

'Will we?'

'Very soon indeed. It's imperative you understand how to build a permanent electric high-tensile fence. I hope you're all wearing your rubber boots again today?'

We confirmed that we were.

'Good,' said Donald. 'It looks like rain so you'd better don your waterproofs. I'll be back in a moment and then we can have another lesson.'

We got out of the cab and started scrabbling about putting on our wet weather gear while Donald disappeared into his office. The condition of Tam's leather jacket had got beyond a joke. Apparently he'd put it in his father's boiler room to dry out overnight, and now the fabric was desiccated and even less resistant to rain than before. Still, the jacket was all Tam had so he stuck with it. Donald, of course, was perfectly equipped. When he emerged from his office he was wearing a complete set of waterproofs, complete with hood, and a pair of thick-soled rubber boots. He signalled for us to follow him and we again set off across the fields. I noticed there was no sign of Ralph this morning. It had started raining by the time we got to the Demonstration Fence, and standing there in the wet, it appeared even brighter and newer than it had on the previous occasion.

'So,' said Donald. 'Where does the electricity come from?'

Good question. The Demonstration Fence resembled an

ordinary high-tensile fence in every way. Only the yellow warning signs showed that it was different. It stood alone and apparently unconnected to anything else. We watched as beads of rainwater gathered along the wires before dropping into the grass.

'Suppose it must come from underground,' I suggested.

'Correct,' said Donald. He led us to one end of the fence and indicated a black cable emerging from beneath the turf.

'Insulation is provided by a hardened rubber sheath,' he explained, reaching for the cable, taking hold, and disconnecting it from the fence.

'By the way,' he went on. 'This is the sort of tension you should be achieving on all occasions.' Donald seized a fence wire and pulled it towards him. There was hardly any give at all.

I was about to test the tension for myself, but changed my mind.

'You're quite safe,' said Donald. 'The power's not connected. Even if it were, your rubber boots would protect you from all but the slightest shock.'

'I don't trust it yet,' I replied.

'Come, come,' said Donald. 'You're in more danger of being struck by lightning on a day like this.'

I looked at the black cable, to check that it had definitely been disconnected from the fence. Then I breathed in and gripped the wire.

'Hmm. Quite tight,' I said, letting go again.

'Yes, I'm quite pleased with it,' said Donald, and he began carrying out yet another thorough examination of the fence. I was beginning to come to the conclusion that he was obsessed with the thing. He tested the tension of each wire, and ran his hand over the timber to ensure the joinery was perfect. Finally, he stood at one end and genuflected, glancing along the line of posts to see that it was straight. When Donald was satisfied he reconnected the electricity.

'Now there's a quick and simple way of finding out whether the power is switched on,' he said.

Donald bent down to the ground and broke off a blade of grass. Holding it between his thumb and forefinger, he touched the top fence wire. At once a faint ticking sound could be heard. Donald moved the blade up a little, and the ticking grew louder. Then he turned to Tam.

'Do you want to try?' he said.

All the time we'd been at the Demonstration Fence, Tam and Richie had remained somewhat aloof, keeping well clear of the structure and not taking part in any of the tests.

'It's OK,' said Tam. 'We usually let our foreman do that kind of thing.'

'And what if your foreman ever leaves the company?' asked Donald. 'What will you do then?'

'Don't know.'

'You're not afraid of this fence, are you?'

'No, no,' replied Tam, breaking off a blade of grass and gingerly touching it to the fence.

'Good,' said Donald. He glanced at me. 'The question was purely hypothetical, of course. I don't ever expect you to leave.'

This was very reassuring.

'Now there's a small task I'd like you to carry out over the next few days,' Donald continued. 'I want you to dig a trench from here to the company premises, so we can put the cable deeper underground.'

'Isn't it deep enough already?' I said.

'Oh no,' said Donald. 'Nowhere near deep enough. It's barely beneath the surface at present, placed there as a temporary measure. Quite unsatisfactory. I want it buried deeper.'

'How deep?'

'So that it can be forgotten about.'

'Oh.'

'You know how to bury things, don't you?'

'Yeah, 'spose.'

'Good. Besides, it'll give you all something useful to do over Christmas.'

I was aware of a wave of disappointment flowing between Tam, Richie and myself.

'All you'll need is a spade each,' said Donald, 'and while we're in the tool store I have something else to show you.'

He led us back to the company yard and opened the door to the store room. At once the ticking noise could be heard again. We went inside, and as our eyes became accustomed to the gloom, we could make out a metal box mounted on the wall, on which a small orange light was flashing.

Apart from the ticking noise, the tool store was a quiet place, a sort of inner sanctum of the fencing trade. Rows and rows of tools lined the walls, most of them familiar to us. There were large post hammers, all with wooden shafts and identical cast iron heads. There were deep-digging tools, some in the form of simple long-handled spades, others doubled into tongs. Nearby stood steel spikes which could be used for piercing starter holes in the ground, or for levering out awkward stones. Hanging from hooks on the wall were sets of wire-pulling devices, complete with chain winch and gripper. There were boxes in the corner containing brand new gear still wrapped in stiff grease-proof paper and not yet assembled for use. Other tools had been tried and rejected, such as the deep diggers which opened the 'wrong way' and which no one could get used to. Finally there was the unrecognizable specialist equipment, acquired for some particular reason or other, but whose purpose was not apparent.

And now there was something new in the tool store. A metal box ticking on the wall with an orange flashing light.

'This is the transformer,' said Donald. 'One of these can deliver electricity for an entire network of fences.'

'Really?' I said.

'Several miles actually. Mr Hall was most impressed.'

The transformer continued ticking, but all else was silent.

'Who?'

'Mr Hall. That's the new client. He's shown a great deal of interest in the Demonstration Fence.'

'So he's been here, has he?' I managed to say. Tam and Richie remained very, very quiet.

'He attended a demonstration, yes,' replied Donald. 'It seems that the permanent electric high-tensile fence matches his requirements perfectly. Mr Hall is just the type of person I had in mind when I devised the system.'

'Is that where we're going after Christmas?' I asked.

'Correct.' Donald cast his eye along the rows of equipment lining the wall and then said, 'By the way, I take it your personal tool sets are all intact?'

There was a pause and then Tam said, 'I need a new hammer.'

'That comes as no surprise,' said Donald. He stepped towards a bench by the wall, on top of which was a drawer full of hammers. 'Would you like to select one?'

Tam picked one at random and said, 'This'll do me.'

Donald took the hammer and balanced it carefully in his hand.

'I'm surprised,' he remarked. 'I'd have thought someone of your experience would have been a little more discerning.'

Tam lifted a second hammer from the box.

'Alright. This one,' he said.

'That's better,' said Donald. 'Of course, you understand the cost will be deducted from your wages?'

'Thought so,' said Tam.

Now Donald turned to Richie, who was leaning against a stack of cardboard boxes.

'May I?' he said.

Richie quickly moved out of the way, and Donald lifted a box down. Inside were a dozen or so leather belts, each with small loops attached. He chose two and gave them to Tam and Richie. (As foreman, I already possessed such a belt.)

'These should help to prevent any further loss of equipment,' said Donald.

The belts were well made, each loop designed to carry a certain item, such as a hammer, wood chisel or pair of wire cutters.

'They'll also make you look more professional,' he continued. 'This is only the first stage of our future plans. In the forth-coming year there will be a simple uniform for you to wear. The designs are not yet complete, but I have in mind some sort of overall bearing the company insignia.'

Tam had already fastened his belt and fitted the new hammer into an appropriate loop. Meanwhile, Richie stood awkwardly holding his in one hand.

'Are these going to be deducted from our wages as well?' he said at last.

'No,' replied Donald. 'Consider them to be a Christmas gift from the company.'

'Thanks,' they both mumbled. Donald fitted the lid back onto the box and replaced it on the stack. Then he turned to me.

'So.'

'Do you want us to start the trench today?' I asked.

'The sooner you start the sooner you'll finish,' he replied. 'Don't forget your spades.' And with that he left us. We stood in stunned silence in the tool store as he crossed the yard back to his office. Then, without a word we each took a spade and trooped out into the rain, through the gate and across the field.

It was only when we were well away from the company premises that Tam spoke at last. 'For fucking fuck's fucking sake,' he said. Richie and I knew exactly what he meant.

And so on that soaking wet winter day we began digging our trench. We dug it deep and we dug it straight. We worked with rain running down our necks and our hair bedraggled. Mud clung to our boots, the turf became slippy, and rainwater ran freely along the bottom of the trench. Daylight began to fail early, but still we pressed on, knowing that Donald could make an appearance at any moment. It was only when the coming of darkness made it impossible to do any more work that we packed in.

'What a fucking way to spend Christmas Eve,' said Tam. 'We could have been in the pub all afternoon.'

'This is worse than last year,' said Richie.

'What happened last year? I can't remember.'

'We had to go to Robert's house for a glass of sherry.'

'Oh that's right. I forgot about that. Got a fag, Rich?'

Richie found his cigarettes in a dry place beneath his water-proof, and squeezed into his soaking jeans for the lighter. I realized for the first time that I no longer found the ritual irritating.

When we got back to the yard the light was on in Donald's office. We discussed calling in to say 'good-night' and even 'Have a nice Christmas', but none of us was really in the mood.

'Fuck it,' said Tam. 'Let's go home.'

What sort of Christmas was it going to be? Not only was there that trench to complete when we came back, which was two or three more days' work at least, but we also had the prospect of facing Mr Hall again. Nobody had mentioned Mr Hall all afternoon because it just didn't bear thinking about. We'd worry about that when the time came, and no sooner. In the meantime, the lights of the Crown Hotel offered some conso-lation. Even Donald couldn't expect us to work Christmas Day and Boxing Day, and I seemed to spend much of the festive season in the Crown with Tam and Richie. So did a large part of the local population, including Morag Paterson.

On Boxing Day night Richie, Billy and I were sitting at one of the large tables waiting for Tam to come back from the bar with a round of drinks. He'd got engaged in a conversation with Morag and was taking his time, but who could blame him? I'm sure I'd have done the same thing if I had her full attention. The Crown Hotel was certainly a better place with her there.

In the end Billy lost patience and shouted, 'Hurry up, Tam!'

Unfortunately this triggered off an incident involving their father. Mr Finlayson had been sitting alone at the end of the bar for most of the evening. Apparently unaware of his sons' presence, he was gazing at the mirror behind the whisky bottles, his right hand holding a pint of heavy, his left hand gripping the counter. When he heard Billy's voice he looked round and caught sight of Tam standing further along the bar, still talking to Morag Paterson. Next moment he was on his feet and lurching towards them.

'Here we go again,' murmured Billy.

Mr Finlayson had plainly been drinking a lot, and swayed to and fro as he stood facing Tam.

'We could have done all the fencing round here!' he roared.

'Who?' said Tam.

'Us! Me! And your brothers!'

'What's he talking about?' said Morag, giggling. Half the pub was now listening to the exchange.

'Nothing,' said Tam. 'Pay no attention to him.'

'Finlay and Son!' announced his father in a loud voice.

Jock appeared behind the counter and tapped it twice with his finger.

'Alright, Tommy,' he said. 'That's enough of that.'

But Mr Finlayson was now in full swing. 'We could have had it in the bag! Proper genuine stock fencing! Solid! None of this low-cost, high-tensile shite killing the market! Us! Me! And your brothers. And instead of that . . .' He was beginning to falter. 'And instead of that you went over to the other side!'

At that moment some helping hands launched Tam's father through the doorway and out into the night.

'What it needs is a stockade!' he bellowed in the darkness. 'Right around the house!'

As the hotel door was closed and bolted, Tam brought our drinks over to the table. 'Sorry about the delay,' he said.

'What was your dad getting worked up about?' asked Richie.

'Nothing of importance,' replied Tam. 'He thinks he's an expert on fencing all of a sudden.'

'That's as bad as my father,' said Richie. 'He hasn't touched his fences for years and now he's started going on about getting them all renewed.'

'Well can't you do them?' asked Billy.

'That's what I said,' replied Richie. 'But he goes "Oh no, they've got to be specially matched to my requirements."'

'What's that supposed to mean?' said Tam.

'Fuck knows.'

'Sounds like the sort of thing Donald would come out with,' I remarked.

Jock was going round the tables collecting empty glasses, and when he got to us he said, 'I hear you're going back to England.'

'How did you know that?' said Tam.

'Ah well, word gets around you know,' replied Jock. 'You'll be better off down there this time of year.'

'Why?'

'They don't have proper winters, do they?'

'Suppose not, but we're not going yet. We've got Hogmanay first.'

Ah yes, New Year's Eve, that was the next big thing to look

forward to. As Jock continued his rounds we squeezed what we could from the remaining dregs of Christmas. A few minutes later the bell rang for last orders and Richie went to get them in.

'I'll just see if Morag wants a drink,' said Tam.

But she'd already gone.

Returning to work the following day we found out how Donald had spent his Christmas. There was no sign of activity anywhere in the company yard, so we collected our spades meaning to carry on with the trench where we'd left off. The rainy weather had subsided into clear stillness and there was a slight frost lying across the fields. As we approached we could see the Demonstration Fence glinting in the winter sunlight, but there was something different about its appearance. Drawing nearer we saw that during our absence the original fence had been extended. There was a new section at each end, at right-angles, so that the structure now formed three sides of a square. Again the work was done perfectly, with flawless joinery and unblemished posts in dead straight alignment.

'Why's he done it like that then?' said Tam.

'Don't know,' I replied.

'How does he get the wires as tight as this?' Tam gripped the wire. There was a ticking noise and he leapt back from the fence. 'For fuck's sake, it's switched on!'

'You should have done the test,' I said.

'Fuck the test!' he snapped. 'That's it. I'm not going near it any more.'

'Here's Donald,' said Richie, and we all began studying different aspects of the Demonstration Fence with interest. Donald had just come through the gateway at the corner of the field and was advancing towards us.

'I bet he turned it on deliberately when he saw us coming to have a look,' said Tam.

Yes, I thought, he probably did. Donald was walking along the line of our trench as he approached, peering into it from time to time, no doubt checking that it was sufficiently deep.

'Glad to see you managed to return so promptly after the festivities,' he said as he joined us. 'I was beginning to think I had a band of truants on my hands.'

'Oh,' I said. 'No.'

'Well, you seem to be making reasonable progress with your excavation work. Three or four more days should see it completed.'

I nodded towards the Demonstration Fence. 'You've been busy then.'

'Yes,' replied Donald, and began once more to make a thorough examination of the shining structure. We trailed vaguely after him as he patrolled the three adjoining sections.

'Is it going to be a square when it's finished?' I asked.

'Correct.'

'With a gate?'

'No gate.'

'But if someone was inside, and it was switched on, they couldn't get out.'

'Quite,' replied Donald. 'Remember, it's for demonstration

purposes only.' He allowed us a few moments to absorb the remark, and then said, 'Any other questions?'

'Where's Ralph?' asked Tam.

'We've lost him.'

'Have we?'

'I'm afraid so.'

'How?'

'There was an accident during the early trials.' Donald laid a hand on one of the straining posts. 'He's under here if you wish to pay your respects.'

14

It took us the rest of the week to get that trench completed.
Every day we turned in for work, collected our spades from
the tool store and carried on digging. In other circumstances
we could have probably wound the job up in two or three days,
as Donald had estimated. After all, there were no particular
problems to overcome. Now that the weather had dried up the
work became less like drudgery, and we were able to apply
ourselves to it properly. As a result the trench was neat, with
straight vertical sides and a flat bottom. It actually made a nice
change from building fences all the time. I soon came to realize,
however, that Tam and Richie were pacing themselves so that
we didn't get finished too quickly. This was all to do with the
approach of New Year's Eve. I think they suspected that if we
got the trench done any sooner Donald would send us off on
the next job and they'd miss all the fun. As it turned out they
needn't have worried on that account. After a couple of days
Donald paid us our wages (minus certain deductions) and
announced that he was off to prepare the site for Mr Hall's new
fence. As usual he gave no indication about when he would
be coming back, but nevertheless a relaxed atmosphere soon
developed. Not long after he'd gone we went to the tool store

and switched off the transformer. There would be no more surprise electric shocks for the next few days at least. Then we carried on with the trench, but at about half the speed we'd been going before, with regular fag breaks and pauses for general speculation. In the end we had the work finished by New Year's Eve. Oddly enough, Donald did not return for quite some time. This was most unusual. He rarely left the office unattended for very long, yet on this occasion it was almost a week before we saw him again. Whatever was delaying him at the Hall Brothers' place must have been very important.

'Maybe he's fallen into their sausage machine,' remarked Tam. We all had a good laugh about that.

In the meantime New Year's Eve came and went. It was the usual story in the Crown Hotel. Leslie Fairbanks provided music for a packed house, while Jock clattered and complained behind the counter. Tam and Richie got pissed with Billy, and everyone ignored Mr Finlayson, drinking alone up at the bar. For some reason, Morag Paterson failed to make an appearance, which I for one found disappointing. The evening was pleasant enough all the same. I was 'allowed' to sit at Tam and Richie's table, although I knew I wouldn't be able to keep up with their rate of drinking for very long. My solution to this problem was to drop out of a few rounds, and not claim a drink, but then Tam accused me of 'back-watering' which I thought was a bit unfair. He punished me by buying me drinks I didn't want, so that I spent New Year's Day with the worst hangover I'd ever had.

The day after that there was nothing officially to do at work, but I persuaded Tam and Richie that we should go in and get the caravan cleaned up, to which they reluctantly agreed. It was in an even worse state than I remembered. All the carpets were still damp and the drainpipe from the sink had somehow become disconnected. Also the tyres had gone down again. I got Tam to pump them up while Richie dragged out the carpets and hung them on a line to dry. Meanwhile I tested the electric strip light to see if it still buzzed. It did, loudly, but I decided to take a power cable with us next time anyway, because the gas lamps were on their last legs and I didn't want to live in the dark.

We were just having our break when a truck suddenly pulled into the company yard. Donald was back. He got out and stood regarding the caravan in its dismembered state.

'Looks like you need a bit of a sort out,' he said, by way of greeting.

'We're waiting for the carpets to dry,' I explained.

'I see.'

Tam and Richie were now busy fiddling about with the waste disposal pipe under the sink. As Donald peered at them through the caravan window I said, 'You were gone a long time.'

'Yes,' he replied. 'I got delayed.'

'Oh, er . . . anything serious?'

'A minor project of Mr Hall's needed urgent completion and he asked me to oblige.'

'What sort of project?'

'I've been building pens.'

'What, on your own?'

'Not quite. I took an assistant with me.'

There was a low gurgling noise as the waste pipe came away in Tam's hand. Richie quickly tried to jam a bucket underneath, but it was too late and filthy water gushed across the kitchen floor. Donald turned away.

'I take it you got your trench work completed OK?' he continued.

I assured him we had.

'Good,' he said. 'Everything's ready at Mr Hall's and we want to get you shipped off tomorrow morning.'

It struck me that Donald sometimes employed a very unfortunate turn of phrase. He was forever talking about 'rounding us up' and 'shipping us off' as though we were being transported to some sort of penal colony or corrective camp, rather than merely going to undertake a commercial contract. Tam, Richie and myself were quite used to his ways of course, but it must have sounded very odd to potential customers.

'What are we doing for this Mr Hall then, exactly?' I asked.

'Something rather special,' replied Donald. 'He wishes to eliminate all possibility of escape. Therefore we're providing him with electric fences of extended height.'

'How high?'

'Seven feet.'

'That's a bit over the top isn't it?'

'Not really,' said Donald. 'Oh, by the way, you'll need to be at Mr Hall's place by six o'clock tomorrow evening.'

'Why's that then?'

'After that you'll find the gates are locked.'

It was still dark when Richie and I arrived at the golf course the following morning to pick up Tam. I stopped the truck some distance from the greenkeeper's house, bibbed the horn and wound up my window. Then we waited for signs of movement in the kitchen, where a single light-bulb shone. As we sat there waiting it seemed to me that the place looked different from before, though I couldn't quite see why. The house no longer had a proper outline, and appeared instead to be part of a vast backdrop. Even the light cast from the kitchen window came to an abrupt end after a few yards, as if blocked out by some kind of solid barrier. I flicked the headlights onto main beam, and we saw a newly-built stockade advancing round the back and sides of the house. The work was not yet complete, but nearby a huge stack of larch poles lay ready, each with a pointed end.

'Blimey,' I said. 'I thought he was joking.'

'You don't know Mr Finlayson,' said Richie.

Just then there was a movement in the darkness. An upper window of the house had been opened and a haversack was dropped to the ground. Soon afterwards a figure in a leather jacket emerged. We watched in silence as Tam lowered himself down until he was suspended from the ledge by his hands. After hanging there for several seconds he seemed to change his mind and started to pull himself up again, but then lost his grip and plummeted into the gloom.

We heard a thud and a 'Fuck' in the near distance, waited a moment longer, then Tam appeared in front of the truck, grinning.

'Misjudged that a bit,' he said.

'Why did you come out the window?' I asked.

''Cos my dad's in the kitchen.'

'So?'

'That's reason enough. Come on, let's go.'

'Richie!' roared a voice from the direction of the house.

'For fuck sake,' said Tam. 'It's him.'

'Richie!' shouted the voice again. 'Come and have a cup of tea!'

'Ignore him,' said Tam.

'Richie!'

'I'll have to answer him,' said Richie. 'He knows I'm here.'

Tam tutted.

'Oh, hello Mr Finlayson!' Richie called.

'Come and have a cup of tea while you wait!'

'I've just had one at home, thanks!'

'It's already poured!'

'I'll have to go and be polite,' said Richie, getting out of the truck and trudging towards the house. 'Bring that foreman with you!' yelled the voice.'

Tam looked at me. 'You'd better go in,' he said.

I followed Richie through the blackness to the kitchen, where Mr Finlayson was waiting.

'Can't have you sitting out there, can we?' he said. 'Your tea's on the table, I've put sugar in.'

'Thanks,' I said.

'He'll be down in a minute.'

'Oh . . . er . . . right.'

We sat awkwardly at the table and tried our teas. Richie took sugar normally but I didn't, and it was very sweet. I didn't say anything though. A few moments later there was a rattling sound in the upper part of the house, and shortly afterwards Tam came down the stairs into the kitchen. His jacket was badly scuffed up the front, and most of the fabric had pulled away from the lining.

'Is that you then?' said his father. 'These two have been waiting.'

'I know, I know. Hi.'

'Hi,' we both said.

We rose from our seats and moved to go, but Mr Finlayson was blocking the door. 'Finish your tea first,' he ordered. Then, to Tam, 'You'll have to do without.'

There was a dutiful pause as we quickly drank our tea, then Mr Finlayson moved aside from the doorway and allowed us to leave.

It was beginning to get light when we arrived at the company premises to collect the caravan. The first thing we saw was a large articulated lorry being loaded up in the timber yard. There were huge posts stacked along its entire length, and still more were being added. An air of efficiency prevailed. The whole place was emblazoned with artificial light from two floodlamps mounted high up on the gable end. I'd never noticed these before, and they made the company premises resemble an industrial plant, rather than a collection of converted farm buildings. The lorry had its own powered crane, which was being operated by someone on the far side. Only the steel toe-capped boots of this individual could be seen moving around, and he in turn was being given instructions by someone entirely lost from view. This made the entire process seem to have nothing to do with us.

'Look at all those posts,' muttered Tam. 'We'll be away for months.'

'Looks like it,' I said.

Soon after we'd begun hitching up the caravan, Donald appeared from the direction of the timber yard and asked me to go into his office. Lying on the desk I noticed a cardboard carton stamped with the words 'Caution: electrical appliance'. Donald produced a file and handed it to me.

'You'll be dealing with a Mr John Hall,' he announced. 'The full client name is Hall Brothers, but this Mr Hall is head of the regime and you should take your instructions from him. The other brothers are little more than sleeping partners.'

I changed the subject and indicated the carton. 'Is that for us?'

'Correct,' said Donald. 'As foreman it will be your responsibility to install the transformer before carrying out the final tests. Have you made yourself entirely familiar with the system?'

'More or less.'

'Good. This fence consists of ten live high-tensile wires and four strands of barb, so the posts are quite long. You'll need to take a stepladder with you.'

I looked at Donald and tried to see if he was making a joke or not. Was he seriously expecting us to knock these posts in from the top of a stepladder? After a few moments I decided that, no, he wasn't joking.

'Sounds like a big job,' I remarked at length.

'Yes,' said Donald. 'Our largest contract to date.'

'Will any of the other gangs be involved?'

'There aren't any other gangs,' he replied. 'You're the last one.'

A shadow crossed the window as the lorry moved out of the yard. A few minutes later I found Tam and Richie sitting side by side in the truck, waiting to go.

'I suppose you haven't got any money,' I said.

'Nope,' said Tam.

'I've got a bit for the time being,' said Richie.

I went to the store room and found a stepladder. Then we set off.

That caravan was a flimsy affair. The walls were nothing more than a double layer of hardboard, separated by a timber frame and clad on the outside with tin plate. Only the chassis held it all together. And as I slowly came awake next morning the whole structure was creaking. Creak, creak, creak, it went. Rhythmically, creak, creak, creak. I lay with my face pressed against the wall, half-asleep, trying to remember where I was.

'Is that you doing that?' said Tam.

I looked beyond my toes and saw him eyeing me from his bunk.

'No, it must be Rich,' I murmured.

'Is it fuck,' said Richie. 'Someone's moving us.'

Outside I could hear an engine running. I pulled the curtain open slightly and saw a fence moving along outside the caravan. We were being inched slowly backwards, stopping and starting every now and then.

'That sounds like our truck,' said Tam.

'Fuck sake!' I said. 'I left the keys in!' I struggled out of my sleeping bag and stood up just as the caravan began a turn, so that I fell against the back window. Looking out I saw a convoy of vans, all the same, lined up in the road. There were men in white butchers' coats standing here and there amongst them, watching the activity around the caravan.

'They're inside,' somebody said.

The caravan stopped moving and moments later there came a curt knock at the door. I opened up and saw David Hall standing outside, wearing the same white coat as the others. He didn't look very pleased.

'There you are,' he said. 'We thought you'd gone off.'

'No, we were in here all night.'

'What did you block the drive for?'

'The gate was locked.'

'So?'

'We didn't know where to go.'

He grunted and peered past me into the caravan, where Tam still lay in his bunk.

'What's he doing?'

'Nothing.'

'Well he should be careful of lounging around when John gets here.'

At that moment a horn blasted at the back of the queue. Another vehicle had arrived, obviously impatient to get through.

'Here's John now,' said David Hall. 'I'm afraid he's going to take a very dim view of this, just when the vans are coming back from the night run.'

He gave a signal and the caravan was towed into a lay-by at the side of the road, with me, Tam and Richie still inside, trying to get our boots on. Then the vans were manoeuvred onto the grass verge so that the new vehicle could come by. John Hall's car moved cautiously along the line of vans, as if inspecting each one as it passed, and then stopped in the entrance to the driveway. It rocked slightly as he got out. The two brothers spoke briefly for a moment, and then came over to the caravan door.

'You were supposed to get here by six o'clock last night,' said John Hall. 'Didn't you know that?'

'Sorry,' I said. 'We tried, but we just couldn't make it.'

He looked at me for a long time before turning to his side. 'Take them to the pens, will you, David? That's the best place for them.'

15

There were two notices beside the entrance to the factory. The larger one bore the words HALL BROTHERS in red on a white background. The second notice, just below, was smaller and new. KEEP OUT it said.

As John Hall's car moved slowly off, followed by the procession of vans, David Hall turned to me and said, 'Not a very good start, is it?'

'Suppose not,' I replied. He seemed different somehow to the last time we'd met him. Much more serious. I considered trying to start up a bit of light-hearted conversation to redeem the situation, but I got the feeling it was a waste of time. He appeared to have given up on the banter and chit-chat he'd indulged in when we were here before.

'You're fortunate John didn't send you straight home,' he continued. 'Now then, you can give me a lift.'

Without saying anything else he went and sat in the double passenger seat of the truck. Tam and Richie had remained inside the caravan while all this was going on, so I shrugged at them and shut the door before joining David Hall in the cab. He sat in silence as I drove up the driveway to the factory, towing the caravan behind, and only spoke again when we arrived at the pens. 'You can park here.'

As I expected, Donald had made a perfect job of the pens, although how he'd done it in a week I didn't know. All those railway sleepers we'd unloaded now formed a substantial complex of enclosures and conjoining gates. It was a very professional job. Someone had recently been along and applied creosote to all the timber, giving it a spick-and-span look. There was a sort of holding area at the entrance, and this was where we were supposed to put the caravan. While Tam and Richie got it unhitched and jacked up, I asked David Hall if there was somewhere to plug in our cable.

'Of course,' he said, and disappeared into the factory.

As soon as he'd gone Tam came over to me and said, 'Not very friendly, is he?'

'Why should he be?' I replied.

After all, I thought, we couldn't really expect the Hall Brothers to be particularly friendly, could we? Not after we'd messed them about so much. Arriving late the night before hadn't helped, of course. We'd tried, but it was just impossible to get there any faster towing that caravan. Despite all his efficient calculations Donald never seemed to make allowances for this. Six o'clock had come long before we neared the end of our journey, and once we knew we weren't going to make it we'd given up rushing. Then Tam had started going on about 'cutting our losses' and stopping for a couple of pints at the Queen's Head. I'd said I didn't think it was a good idea going back there just yet. In the end Tam and Richie had agreed that we should pick up a few cans somewhere and forget finding a pub the first night. By the time we got to the factory it had gone nine, and the gate was locked. So we'd simply crawled into the caravan with our cans and spent the night there. Not a very good start.

I was just pondering all this when a small window opened at the side of the factory and an arm appeared. David Hall's podgy hand started waving about impatiently, so I quickly got the cable and fed it to him through the window. Then I gave the strip light a short test. As usual it buzzed loudly.

'Right. Meals,' he said, as he emerged again. 'Meal times are seven, twelve-thirty and six. You're just in time for breakfast if you're quick.'

This sudden announcement came as a pleasant surprise. Donald hadn't said anything to us about getting our meals at the Hall Brothers' place, and things immediately started looking better. We walked round to the canteen past the factory loading bay, where all the vans were now backed up with their refrigerator units rumbling. The bay was deserted: the men from the factory were having their breakfast. They took little notice of us when we entered the canteen. All they seemed interested in was guzzling platefuls of sausages and going back to the counter for more. The other Hall brother (who we later found out was called Bryan) was still there behind the counter, serving up sausages fried, grilled or baked. He dished out a good helping for each of us, and we found a spare table in the corner. I didn't realize how hungry I was until I started eating, and my plate was soon empty. The same went for Tam and Richie. We all went back for seconds, got a mug of tea apiece, and then sat there feeling fairly content with the world.

'Shame there's nothing but sausages,' said Tam as he finished the last one. 'A few eggs and tomatoes would have been nice.'

'Or mushrooms and a fried slice,' suggested Richie.

One or two people at nearby tables looked across at us as if we'd said something out of order. I watched over the rim of my mug as David Hall entered the canteen and came to our table. Tam and Richie had their backs to the door and were unaware of his approach. They both started slightly when he spoke.

'Finished?'

'Yes, thanks,' I said, placing my knife and fork neatly in the centre of my empty plate.

'Want some more?'

'Er . . . no. Thanks anyway.'

'Don't you like our sausages then?'

'They're very nice. But I've had two lots already.'

'I see.' David Hall was now standing very close to us. He turned and addressed Tam.

'What about you?'

'Same here.'

'You mean you don't like them either?'

'No, no . . . it's just that I've had enough. Thanks.'

By this time the general murmur in the canteen had ceased. Everyone had stopped eating, and sat listening to the exchange.

'Well, this is most disappointing,' said David Hall. 'We were under the impression you liked our sausages.'

'We do,' I replied.

'But you've just turned round and said you don't!'

'No.'

'Make your mind up.' He looked at the three of us for a few moments. 'Very well,' he said at last. 'If you've quite finished

I'd better take you over to the offices. John wants to see you before you begin work.'

The silence faded away as he led us out of the canteen. Bryan Hall was standing behind the griddle, and as we passed I nodded and said 'Thanks', but he just looked at me and said nothing.

David Hall showed us into a waiting room beside the offices and left us there while he went to find his brother. Looking out of the window we watched the men from the canteen drifting slowly back into the factory.

'Poor fuckers,' said Tam. 'Working here all the time.'

'Don't think I'd like it,' I said. 'What's that, Rich?'

'Not sure, really.'

Richie was gazing at a picture on the wall. There was nothing else to do, so I went over and had a look.

It was a framed drawing of a small boy adrift in a rowing boat. This was accompanied by a nursery rhyme:

> If Jack comes home at half past three
> Then he shall have some cake for tea,
>   But if he's late and won't be quick
>   We'll beat him soundly with a stick.

'Charming,' I remarked.

The door handle turned and John Hall came in, wearing a white butcher's coat.

'I gather you don't like our sausages,' he said.

'No,' I replied. 'Really. We do.'

'Doesn't sound like it. Not from what I've heard.' Mr Hall thrust his hands in his coat pockets and stared at the floor for some time. 'Still, I doubt if your opinion will count for much in the long run.' He glanced up quickly. 'You know we've lost the school dinners?'

'Oh,' I said. 'Sorry to hear that.'

'Yes, it's been very hard to bear.'

'Any chance of getting them back?' I asked.

'It's possible. That's why you're here, of course.'

'Is it?'

'Oh yes. There's plenty of room for improvement. Now you're not going to go running off again, are you?'

'Er . . . no.'

'"No", or "er . . . no"?'

'No.'

'I should hope not. Ah, there you are, David.'

David Hall had appeared in the doorway holding a clipboard.

'Everything's in order, John,' he said.

'Good.' John Hall signed a docket and then addressed us again. 'Now I think we might as well go for a stroll around the perimeter. These plans and diagrams are all very well, but you need to get a picture of the final enclosure for yourselves. Come on.'

He took us outside and round the end of the factory, where we passed the huge pile of new posts we'd seen on the lorry.

'The materials managed to arrived on time,' he said. 'But you didn't.'

The planned line of the new fence went along the extreme edge of the Hall Brothers' property, and was marked out by a series of wooden pegs in the ground, presumably put there by Donald. It was a relief to be back outside again and dealing with something I understood. After all that talk about sausages and school dinners I felt as if I'd just undergone some sort of cross-examination. Tam and Richie had got off relatively lightly, but even they had a defeated air about them. I was quite looking forward to getting back to work. First, though, we had to accompany Mr Hall on his conducted tour. There was nothing much to see. The land around the factory was already divided up into several empty fields demarcated by existing fences. We paused briefly by one of these, and I noticed it bore the silver HALL BROS. tag.

'These were built by our own people,' said Mr Hall.

'Hmm, nice job,' I remarked, tugging a wire.

'Quite probably,' he replied. 'But they're insufficient for our present requirements.'

'Does that mean we've got to demolish them?'

'No, we'll take care of that. You press on with the new fence. The beasts will be here soon.'

I didn't bother asking what sort of 'beasts' required a seven-foot-high electric fence. After John Hall left us alone Tam and Richie had a fag and there was a lot of 'fuck saking' and so forth. The job did seem a bit daunting, but I knew that once we got started they'd most likely settle into it OK. So we collected the truck and went round the back of the factory for some straining posts. These were enormous and could only be lifted by two people. As we man-handled half a dozen onto the truck it slowly sank down on its springs. Then we drove slowly out to the fence line and began work. Tam and Richie got the first post erected quite quickly, considering the size of the thing. They dug a deep, narrow hole, dropped it in, and packed the excavated soil back round the base. I had to admit it looked quite impressive standing there on its own, and by the time we'd got a few more in position we began to feel like we were getting somewhere.

We still had the problem of knocking in the pointed posts though. Donald's idea about using a stepladder had seemed a bit dodgy to me, and so it proved. We tried it for a bit but Tam complained he couldn't get his footing right, and looked as though he was about to come a cropper any moment. Finally he opted to stand on the roof of the truck to knock them in. This worked alright, but it was slow going as we had to keep moving the truck along the fence line all the time. Not very efficient really. 'The company should buy a mechanical post hammer,' I said. 'I saw one being demonstrated once. It could put a post in with a few hits.'

'I don't like the sound of that,' said Tam.

'Why not?'

'Well, it'll put me out of work, won't it?'

'Are you a Luddite then?' I asked.

'What's one of those?'

'Someone who distrusts new inventions.'

'No.'

'Well then. You don't want to be swinging a post hammer for the rest of your life, do you?'

Tam looked at me and shrugged. 'I don't mind.'

That night in the canteen we expected to see only sausages on the menu again, but instead it was steak and kidney pie. We carefully avoided conversations about the quality and quantity of the food, and instead talked about the prospect of finding a decent pub nearby.

'I think we ought to go out about seven o'clock,' said Tam. 'We should have found one by quarter past.'

'Either that, or we could go straight out after tea, find one, come back and then go out again,' suggested Richie.

'And if we don't find one we won't come back until we do.'

'Wait a minute,' I interrupted. 'Don't forget they lock the gates at six. We can't take the truck.'

'You'll have to ask them to let us out,' said Tam.

'Why me?' I asked.

''Cos you're foreman, of course.'

'I'm not asking them.'

'Well I'm not fucking walking,' he snapped.

'I don't see what choice we have,' I said. 'Unless you want to ask them.'

Tam turned to Richie. 'What do you think, Rich?'

'Looks like we'll have to walk.'

'For fuck sake.'

Back in the caravan, with the strip light buzzing loudly, we had a look at Donald's route map. His green line ended at the factory and there was nothing else. The only pub we knew was the Queen's Head, and that was miles away beyond Upper Bowland, much too far to walk.

'We'll just have to follow the Lower Bowland road,' I said. 'See where it goes.'

'Are you changing, Rich?' asked Tam.

'Well I'm putting my cowboy boots on if we're walking,' replied Richie.

'And me.'

They got ready in about two minutes. We walked down the driveway in darkness, climbed over the gate, and started our long walk in search of a pub. The road was dark and little used. From time to time we passed small settlements and solitary houses, some with curtains drawn and lights shining inside, others unlit and apparently empty. Occasionally a car would come along, the headlights beaming between the hedgerows, dazzling us, and then passing into the darkness. Once or twice we tried sticking our thumbs out, but we knew it was a waste of time. Who would stop for three strangers in the middle of nowhere, in the dark? We kept going for well over an hour, continually disappointed as the road swung round yet another long bend to reveal nothing more promising than a road sign, a red triangle on a white background, and the words SOFT VERGES FOR TWO MILES.

'We can't do this every night,' I said. 'Not when we're working all day. It'll fucking kill us.'

'Well, we'll have to ask for a key or something won't we?' said Tam.

I liked how it was 'we' all of a sudden. Tam was probably right though. We didn't want to stay in every night. That'd drive us crazy. We'd have to think about asking Mr Hall for a key tomorrow. Or maybe the day after.

After another half-mile a dull glow appeared in the distance and to our relief we finally came upon a green, with a phone box on one side and on the other a pub.

'Thank fuck for that,' said Tam.

I thought about phoning Donald to make a progress report, but decided he could wait.

The pub was called the Mason's Arms. A large Christmas tree with fairy lights had been positioned in a half-barrel by the porch, and stuck on the door was a picture of Santa Claus, smiling and ringing a handbell. The pub, however, was empty. When we entered, the publican was perched on a high stool at the end of the counter, assembling a model aeroplane. He looked surprised to see us.

'You're early,' he said, by way of greeting. 'Most people don't pop in till ten o'clock.'

'Oh well,' I said. 'Bit of extra trade for you.'

'Pint apiece, is it, lads?'

'Alright then.'

'In tankards?'

'Oh, er, no, thanks.'

'Most people ask for tankards.'

'No, no. Straight glasses. Thanks.'

'Right you are.'

I wondered if other people in other pubs throughout the land were having the same conversation. Tam and Richie had already made for a table at the far side of the room, so it looked like I was buying the first round.

As I joined them they looked glum.

'This is shite,' Tam muttered. 'There's no one here.'

'Maybe there'll be some more in later,' I said.

'Maybe.'

'Beer's piss-weak too,' remarked Richie.

So we sat at our chosen table, and waited for the evening to pass. After about half an hour the publican disappeared into a room behind the bar, leaving us completely alone. When he returned he had a mug of tea in his hand.

'For fuck sake,' said Tam quietly. 'You'd never catch Jock drinking tea when he's on duty.'

It was not until well after ten that the first locals appeared and sat around the bar on what were obviously their usual stools. The publican put away his aeroplane and moved into position behind the counter, which allowed him to take part in the various discussions the regulars were having. As one or two more people turned up in the pub a background drone developed, so that we no longer had to lower our voices to speak to each other.

'Have you noticed there are no women at the Hall Brothers' place?' I said.

'I know,' said Richie. 'Not even in the canteen.'

'Fucking none here either,' observed Tam.

Last orders meant last orders in the Mason's Arms, so we found ourselves back on the road just after eleven fifteen. The walk to the factory seemed to take much longer than the out-ward journey, and the weather had turned colder. By the time the gateway came into sight, the warming effect of the beer had completely worn off. As we came up the drive we saw that the loading bay was brightly lit by floodlamps. Several vans were lined up with their engines running, and the noise was augmented by the rumbling of their refrigerator units. Some of the men stopped what they were doing and looked across at us as we approached.

'What are they staring at?' said Tam.

'Nothing,' I said. 'Pay no attention to them.'

'Look,' said Richie. 'We've been burgled.'

That's what it looked like anyway. The caravan door had been thrown open and the strip light switched on. Then David

Hall appeared in the doorway, holding a dustpan and brush.

'Where have you been?' he demanded.

'To the pub,' I said.

'Haven't you got enough to do here?'

'Not really.'

'You surprise me. Who's going to wash your socks?'

'Pardon?'

'Those don't look like hands that do dishes.'

'Oh,' I said. 'No, 'spose not.'

He unblocked the door and allowed us to go inside. I couldn't tell if he'd been searching the caravan or just tidying up. Either way I wasn't sure what to say next. Maybe he was merely stamping his authority over us, but it struck me at that moment that the Hall Brothers had some very funny ideas about what was and what wasn't important. We all sat down on our respective beds as he gazed at us from the doorstep, slowly shaking his head.

'I don't know why you can't just stay home at nights,' he said at last.

'We didn't go very far,' I replied.

'Didn't say you did.'

A bell rang from somewhere inside the factory. David Hall looked at his watch, grunted and stalked off into the darkness.

'For fuck sake,' said Richie, after he'd gone. 'He's worse than my mother.'

We had a quick look round the caravan to try and see what he'd been doing, but really we were all too tired to come to any sensible conclusion.

'Who cares?' said Tam, crashing out on his bed. 'I'm going to sleep.'

This was easier said than done. The combined din of the refrigerator vans and the operations in the loading bay continued late into the night. Bells rang. Other vehicles came and went, and heavy doors were slammed shut as unknown voices gave instructions. It wasn't until after three o'clock that the last of the vans departed.

'Are you still awake?' said Tam.

'No,' replied Richie.

'Have you noticed we never see those guys from the factory going home?'

'That fucker probably doesn't let them.'

'No . . . ha. Night then.'

'Night.'

The following morning, having breakfasted on sausages, we continued work on the new fence. After a couple of hours we noticed a large party approaching from the direction of the factory. It was the men from the canteen, but instead of their white butchers' coats they were all wearing blue overalls. David Hall accompanied them.

'Got a fag, Rich?' said Tam.

Richie produced a pack of cigarettes from his shirt pocket and fished in his jeans for a light. Then they lit up and stood close together smoking. This was their excuse to stop work and watch what was going on, but I didn't mind because we'd all been working quite hard during the morning. Judging by the excited chatter we could hear anyone would have thought the men were all going on a picnic or something, but when they got to the first Hall Bros. fence we saw why they'd come out. Directed by David Hall they began dismantling the fence quickly and efficiently, taking away the old posts and wire. The make-shift demolition squad made short work of the first fence and moved on to the next one. As they laboured David Hall acted as overseer, occasionally glancing in our direction. This was enough to keep Tam and Richie motivated all day, and by the evening the first line of posts was in position. Meanwhile, all the old fences had been removed by the Hall Brothers' men, leaving us a clear site to work on. As dusk approached they headed back towards the factory, and we returned to the caravan.

'Fucking steak and kidney fucking pie again I expect,' said Tam as we lay resting on our bunks.

'Well I think their pie's quite tasty actually,' I replied.

'We still don't want it every night, do we?'

'Suppose not.'

Richie had a suggestion. 'Why doesn't one of us go out tomorrow and buy some different food of our own?'

I looked at Tam. 'What do you think of that idea?'

'Ant got any money.'

'What, nothing?'

'Nope.'

'How much have you got, Rich?'

'About a fiver.'

'Non-starter then, isn't it?'

'Yep.'

This meant, of course, that I was going to have to start

pestering Donald for some wages. Otherwise I'd end up lending Tam and Richie money, and I didn't want to go through all that again. For the time being it looked like the canteen or nothing. And we couldn't complain really. The food was good and there was plenty of tea. A little later we were sitting at our usual table when we received another visit from David Hall.

'Finished?' he said.

'Yes, thanks,' I replied.

'Want some more?'

'Er . . . no. Thanks anyway.'

'You'll be taking an early bath then, will you?'

'Well, we'll probably have a stroll down the pub later,' I said. 'Got a phone call to make.'

'And you'll be straight back?'

'Bit later, yeah.'

'I see.' He thrust his hand into his pocket and produced a bunch of silver tags indented with the words HALL BROS. 'Fix these to the fence when it's complete, can you?'

He placed them on the table in front of me.

'Actually,' I said, 'we don't normally put things like that on our fences. Normally.'

'We'd prefer it if you did,' he said.

I glanced at Tam and Richie. They were both looking with interest into their mugs of tea.

'OK, then,' I said, putting the tags in my pocket.

After David Hall had gone, Tam said, 'You didn't ask about a key.'

'No,' I said. 'Forgot.'

As we sat silently draining our mugs, Bryan Hall emptied a

pan of water over the griddle, so that it steamed and hissed. Then he began scrubbing, and paused only to glance at us when we got up to leave.

The walk to the pub wasn't so bad that night, now we knew how many bends there were to go round. It was still a long way though, and I resolved to ask John Hall for a key the following day. When we finally got to the Mason's Arms, Tam and Richie went and got the drinks in while I gave Donald a ring.

'How's it going?' he began.

'OK,' I replied. 'We've got the posts in for the first section, and we'll get the wires on tomorrow.'

'Good. Then you can connect the electricity.'

'Well, we were going to leave that until all the fences were up.'

'You're supposed to be connecting it up as you go along, section by section.'

This was news to me.

'Does it make any difference?' I asked.

'I'm afraid so,' said Donald. 'Sounds to me as if you're putting it off.'

'Not really.'

'We want to keep Mr Hall happy, don't we?'

'Spose.'

'So get it connected section by section please.'

'OK.'

'By the way,' he continued, 'your uniforms are now ready. I'll see to it that they're delivered in due course.'

'Oh . . . right. Er, any chance of some wages?'

'What for?'

'Well, we need money for food and things.'

'It was arranged with Mr Hall that you would be allowed use of his canteen three times a day.'

'I know.'

'Therefore you don't need any money.'

'But we only ever get pies and sausages.'

There was a pause.

'Don't you like Mr Hall's sausages then?'

'Yes, but . . .' At this moment the pips started going. 'That's my last coin.'

'Alright,' said Donald. 'Keep in touch.'

With that the phone went dead. I took a deep breath, crossed the green to the Mason's Arms, and went inside. Behind the bar the publican was busy applying paint to the wingtips of his plane. He gave me a bit of a welcome and said that my 'pals' had already got me a beer. Tam and Richie were sitting at the same table as the night before, in the same chairs. When I sat down they told me quietly that the landlord had been asking all sorts of questions about fencing.

'What sort of questions?' I asked.

'The usual ones,' said Tam. 'Why do they ask questions all the time?'

'Maybe he's interested,' I suggested.

'I don't go round asking people about their jobs do I?'

'No.'

'All I want is a fucking pint.'

'That's all you're getting. Donald says we can't have any wages.'

I looked at Tam and Richie's faces and wondered if Donald realized the consequences of his actions. By not sending any

wages he was more or less pulling the plug on those two. I
knew from my time with them that they could only work in
the day if they had beer to look forward to at night. Donald
didn't seem to understand this, and as usual it was me who
would have to keep them going. It was me who would have
to sub them until he decided to pay us. And, of course, it would
be me who had to deal with the Hall Brothers.

In the event, our next encounter with them wasn't until the
following afternoon when we'd got most of the wires fixed on
and tightened. Richie suddenly spotted John Hall approaching
from the direction of the factory and we all doubly busied
ourselves with our respective tasks.

'He won't find anything wrong with this,' said Tam. 'It's dead
straight.'

Mr Hall seemed to be in expansive mood.

'Yes, this'll do it,' he said, as he joined us. 'This is what will
keep them under control.' He stood looking through the wires
at the adjoining land, his hands thrust deep in the pockets of
his white coat.

'We committed no end of good deeds!' he declared. 'Yet still
we lost the school dinners! Always the authorities laying down
some new requirement, one thing after another! This time it
seems we must provide more living space. Very well! If that's
the way they want it, we'll go on building fences for ever if
necessary! We'll build pens and compounds and enclosures!
And we'll make sure we never lose them again!'

While Mr Hall was speaking Tam, Richie and I stood awkwardly nearby. I wasn't sure if he was addressing us or just
making some general point. Obviously the school dinners
meant more to him than we'd realized. After a few moments

in deep thought he glanced at us and then began to examine the fence again.

'You'll be connecting the electricity next, I gather.'

'Yes,' I said. 'Should be doing that tomorrow.'

'That's good. The sooner it's done the better.' Mr Hall gave his new fence another look, and then returned the way he'd come.

'I'll be glad when we get back on a normal job,' said Tam.

I couldn't agree more, but we had to get this one done first, so as soon as John Hall had gone I got Tam and Richie going again fixing the barbed wire at the top of the fence. This turned out to be a real struggle. It was hard enough working with barb at normal height, but we were having to do it at the top of a seven-foot fence, and there were four strands as well. We got in all sorts of tangles and it was dusk before we finally got the last wire on. Exhausted, we trudged back towards the factory yard in the mounting gloom, with nothing to look forward to more than steak and kidney pie. As we approached the caravan we noticed that the light was on.

'For fuck sake,' I said. 'Now what?'

We opened the door and looked inside. Morag Paterson was sitting on the end of Tam's bed.

16

'Morag, what are you doing here?' said Tam, as she rose to greet us.

'Just paying you a visit,' she replied. 'See how my boys are keeping.'

She was wearing some kind of uniform. It consisted of little more than a simple overall, but the design was such that all the fastenings were concealed. Around the waist she wore a broad belt that served no obvious purpose other than to emphasize the cut of the fabric, which lay more or less perfectly over every contour of her body.

The three of us stood there gawping at her for a few moments before Tam managed to say, 'Well, it's great to see you. Your outfit looks very . . . tight.'

She smiled.

'It just needed a tuck here and a tuck there. You know. Lift and separate.'

'Er . . . like a cup of tea or something?' I asked.

'I'd better give you these first.' A box had been placed on the other bunk, and under the glare of the strip light Morag now began to remove the packaging.

'I've brought your new uniforms,' she said. 'Special delivery.'

'What, from the company?' said Tam.

'Of course.'

'I didn't know you'd joined.'

'Oh, Donald's recruiting all the time. I'm his latest. We've been working very closely together.'

'Have you?'

'Very closely indeed.'

The uniforms had been neatly pressed and folded. They were only overalls really, but they all bore an emblem depicting a sort of half-open portcullis.

'What's this?' I asked.

'The new company insignia,' replied Morag.

'And when are we supposed to wear these?'

'All the time.'

'Not at night, though, surely?'

'While you're here you represent the company. Therefore you should wear your uniform at all times.'

'Therefore?'

'Correct. Now I must go and pay my respects to Mr Hall. After all, I am his guest.'

Morag ran a hand through her hair and slipped out of the caravan into the night. As soon as she'd gone Tam clapped his hands. 'Waap!' he cried. 'You two'll have to sleep in the truck tonight! Ya haa!'

'We're still going to the pub though, aren't we?' said Richie.

'Fucking right!' said Tam, looking at me. 'Alright for a sub?'

'OK,' I said.

'Right,' he said. 'We'll get changed now and as soon as she comes back we can go out.'

Morag's arrival had certainly revived Tam's spirits. I hadn't seen him so enthusiastic for quite a while, although it struck me that he was taking certain things for granted. Very soon kettles were being boiled and hair was being washed as we all 'got ready'. Then we sat down and waited for Morag to come back.

'We forgot to go to the canteen,' I said, after a while. 'It'll be closed now.'

'That's alright,' said Tam. 'We'll get something later.'

'We're going to look like cunts in those outfits,' remarked Richie.

'Well, Morag looked good in hers.'

'She'd look good in anything,' said Tam. 'What's keeping her anyway?'

An hour had passed since Morag left us, which seemed a bit of a long time.

'We've got to see Mr Hall about a key,' I said. 'Why don't we go now?'

'Go on then,' said Tam.

'All of us,' I said.

'Why?'

''Cos I'm not going on my own.'

Tam tutted. 'C'mon then.'

When we got round to the offices they were all in darkness, but there was the usual level of activity in the factory, so we went in through the side door. Once inside we could hear the sound of refrigeration equipment rumbling, and sausage machines doing their work. There were men here and there attending to various production processes. In the centre of the factory floor was a small square office with a frosted glass panel in the door, bearing the words FOREMAN. Behind it we could see two white shapes beneath a single light-bulb. I knocked and one of the shapes came and opened the door. It was David Hall.

'Aha, the truants return,' he said, holding the door open for us to enter.

Inside, John Hall was sitting behind a large desk, examining some papers. Without looking up, he indicated three wooden chairs in front of him. We sat down, side by side, as David Hall went out and closed the door.

'Now then,' said John Hall. 'What can I do for you?'

'Well,' I said. 'We were wondering if we could have a key for the front gate.'

'A key?'

'Yes.'

'Why's that?'

'So we can go out at nights.'

'Nothing was said about any key.'

'No . . . but we wondered if we could have one anyway, that's all.'

Mr Hall looked up. 'Nothing was said about any key,' he repeated. 'You should try studying the small print. There's definitely nothing about any key. Not one word. And if you don't mind my saying so you seem to be treating this place as some sort of holiday camp where you can do what you please. You're always going off somewhere or other. You remind me of herds of wildebeest constantly roaming round in search of water. It's not as though we haven't done our best to accommodate you. Bent over backwards we have, yet all you do is complain about our pies and sausages. You're never satisfied with what's laid on. It so happens that my brother Bryan prepared something special this evening by way of a change. You'd have known that if you'd had the courtesy to turn up in the canteen at the appointed hour. Now you've gone and upset him and he won't get over it for days. Taken it most personally he has. And you walk in here and ask for a key. Bit of a liberty I'd call it.'

'So we can't have one then?' I asked.

'I'm afraid not,' replied Mr Hall.

A moment passed.

'Where's Morag?' said Tam.

'The girl? She's gone.'

'Gone?'

'Oh yes. We couldn't allow a woman like that to remain on the premises for very long. The men would have found it too disturbing.'

'But she can't have gone.'

'Come, come,' said Mr Hall. 'Do you think the whole world revolves around your every whim and fancy?'

'No.'

'Well, then. We all have our disappointments, you know. How do you think I feel about losing the school dinners?'

'That's different.'

'No, it isn't different. It's the same. Disappointment is disappointment. You should know all about that. You've left a trail of very disappointed people behind you.'

Mr Hall sat silently regarding us across his desk. The only sound was the endless churning of the sausage machines, somewhere in the depths of the factory. My chair had begun to feel very uncomfortable.

'What people?' I asked.

'Well,' he said. 'Let's start with Mr McCrindle.'

*

in memory of Shaun Scapens